PRAISE FOR The Laments

"[A] charming first novel about a memorably eccentric family . . . an enjoyable, inviting book . . . [T]he Laments roam all over the globe, experiencing their share of quirky epiphanies and freakish accidents . . . [and each] new stop allows Mr. Hagen the opportunity to show off his ingratiating powers of description. . . . Mr. Hagen has shaped an affectionate family portrait in which the characters come vividly to life, no matter how adrift they may be. . . . Each of them sees new opportunity eternally on the horizon in ways that have the potential to make this a story of crushing disappointment. But Mr. Hagen somehow endows it with brightness and finds a universality here, too. Laments travel, but in essence they are no more rootless than non-Laments everywhere." — Janet Maslin, *The New York Times*

"Part travelogue, part melodrama and part tall tale, *The Laments* is the playful and heartfelt story of a family—and a world—that can't sit still." —*Los Angeles Times Book Review*

"Hagen's understanding of the mix of love, banality, humor, and sadness that are the features of family life is deep and nearly flawless." —*Kirkus Reviews* (starred review)

"There is an admirable and enviable range and ambition in *The Laments*, and something lucidly democratic in the novel's insistence that a wandering life grants perspectives and perceptions that stay-at-homes can't achieve. . . . Certainly, the appearance of George Hagen on the literary scene is a gain for readers everywhere." —*The New York Times Book Review*

"Like the family in Jonathan Franzen's *The Corrections*, the Laments secretly believe that they can correct the errors of their parents' lives." —*The Wall Street Journal*

"George Hagen is here to break your heart. . . . A tribute to the whole catastrophe of life and how we search for laughter after pain. . . . *The Laments* has the emotional pull of one of John Irving's mammoth books." —*The Orlando Sentinel*

"Ambitious, heartbreaking, [and] darkly funny." —*The Atlanta Journal-Constitution*

"*The Laments* is a fine novel about family, migration, identity and the struggle to find it and hold on to it. It is also hugely entertaining and very, very funny." —Roddy Doyle, author of *Paddy Clarke Ha Ha Ha*

"The hype over *The Laments* is deserved—even without its qualification as a first novel, it is a well-put-together story and a really good read." —*The Sunday Oregonian*

"A vital international journey through the vicissitudes of family life. This story, centering on the timeless themes of a child swapped at birth, is immensely readable, funny, and touching—a complete joy." —Elizabeth Strout, author of *Amy and Isabelle*

"Hagen's strong writing offers a significant understanding of contemporary family relationships." —*Library Journal*

"George Hagen's highly entertaining debut novel features an irresistibly headstrong family, a global sweep, and not only a sense of loss and displacement that's perfectly in tune with the world we live in but also a full measure of resilient humanity." —Gary Shteyngart, author of *The Russian Debutante's Handbook*

"A remarkably accomplished debut novel." —*The Indianapolis Star*

The Laments

The
Laments

A NOVEL

George Hagen

RANDOM HOUSE TRADE PAPERBACKS

NEW YORK

2005 Random House Trade Paperback Edition

Published in the United States by
Random House Trade Paperbacks, an imprint
of The Random House Publishing Group,
a division of Random House, Inc., New York.

RANDOM HOUSE TRADE PAPERBACKS and colophon are
registered trademarks of Random House, Inc.

Originally published in hardcover in the
United States by Random House, an imprint
of The Random House Publishing Group,
a division of Random House, Inc., in 2004.

LIBRARY OF CONGRESS CATALOGING-IN-PUBLICATION DATA
Hagen, George.
The Laments : a novel / by George Hagen.
p. cm.
ISBN 0-8129-7218-X
1. Infants switched at birth—Fiction.
2. Identity (Psychology)—Fiction. 3. Moving,
Household—Fiction. 4. Adopted children—
Fiction. I. Title.

PS3608.A36L36 2004
813'.6—dc22   2003066882

Printed in the United States of America

www.atrandom.com

1 2 3 4 5 6 7 8 9

For Terri, my love

God setteth the solitary in families.

—PSALMS

Africa

Unnamed

Perhaps the Lament baby knew that his parents couldn't name him. Moments after birth he displayed a cryptic smile, an ear-to-ear gape at the fuss displayed over his hospital crib as relatives argued over his Christian name. His mother, Julia Lament, particularly felt the burden. A child's name is his portal to the world. It had to be *right*.

"If people were named at the end of their lives, we wouldn't have mistakes like selfish children named Charity, and timid ones named Leo!" she declared.

Julia's namesake was a monstrous chieftain of a great-grandfather named Julius, a surly copper magnate of Johannesburg, South Africa, married three times, arrested for slowly poisoning his last wife through nightly glasses of milk dosed with arsenic. Even after his incarceration, the Clare family insisted on naming their children after him in a desperate attempt to win his favor and thereby keep the copper mines in the family. Hence: four Julias, two Juliuses, a couple of Julians, several Juliannas, and a particularly nasty lapdog named Ju Ju.

Spitefully, Uncle Julius left his fortune to a nurse in the prison hospital. Her name was Ida Wicks, and she was neither compassionate nor attentive; in fact, she belittled her patients' maladies in contrast to her own, which included poor circulation, migraines, lumbago, shingles, bunions, and tinnitus. Nevertheless, Uncle Julius appreciated seeing a woman every morning during his last days on earth, and Nurse Wicks survived her ills long enough to spend his money—a task that kept her cold heart beating a few hours beyond her one hundredth birthday.

Howard Lament, loving husband to Julia and father to the name-less baby, felt a sense of urgency about giving the child a name, even if it was the wrong one. An efficient man, with a broad forehead, a waxen droop of a nose, and a swath of copper hair that curled into a question mark between his temples, Howard abhorred indecision.

"I'll give him *my* name—that'll do," he said. "After all, it's tradition!"

Julia had never been a strong voice for tradition. She had learned a thing or two from Uncle Julius, not to mention having been brought up in the dusty tradition of the girls' boarding school.

"Tradition." She sniffed. "What has tradition ever done for any-body?"

"Oh," sighed her husband, "darling, please don't go on about that school again."

Abbey Gate School for Girls was a Gothic eyesore of immense tim-bers, roofed with gray slate and thick, bulbous chimneys. The absurdly slender windows seemed designed primarily for defense, a hint of the architect's conviction that modern girls needed to be protected from all manner of assault. Guided by sparse incandescent lighting down dark-paneled corridors, the girls walked in single file with silent foot-steps. Learning at Abbey Gate was a regrettable chore requiring swift, accurate replies and a minimum of opinion.

Julia, helplessly opinionated and impulsive, did not fit in. Her raven-blue hair was a tangled mesh that fought the comb and brush, and, when braided, never hung properly like the other girls'. Though her peers took notes with unquestioning faith, Julia granted no teacher that privilege. Not a lesson passed in which her hand didn't rise in challenge, flicking her braid back and forth like a cat's subver-sive tail.

Julia's nemesis was the head of classics at Abbey Gate. Mrs. Urquhart had the face of a spinster—a myopic squint, thin, ungenerous lips, and copious facial hair. Nevertheless, her husband could be found sleeping at all the important school functions. He was a taxidermist with thickly whorled spectacles and a waist that began at his armpits.

Mrs. Urquhart taught Shakespeare as a series of morality lessons— chiefly about the institution of marriage. "*Girills,*" she screeched in her Glaswegian burr, "*girills,* Lady Macbeth drove her husband to a bloodthirsty end, proving, *once again,* that the criticisms of a wife are best kept to herself lest her husband take them to heart and slaughter his way to the throne. . . ."

In a flash, the hand of Miss Julia Clare would shoot up, entwined by the recalcitrant braid, intent on an urgent and passionate rebuttal. The scholarly badger, who hated contradiction and despised the Socratic method, would cast a blind eye to the twitching braid until her pupil's gasps became too insistent to ignore.

"What *is* it, Miss Clare?"

"Perhaps, Mrs. Urquhart, Lady Macbeth was simply *fed up* with listening to her husband complain about his station in life!"

"I cannae hear yuh, Miss Clare, speak louder next time." Mrs. Urquhart smiled, as if that settled the matter.

"Consider Macbeth, Mrs. Urquhart," the girl persisted. "No backbone, no confidence, believing a gaggle of old biddies stirring a cauldron. I mean, what a *dope of a Scotsman!*"

A hush of delight spread across the classroom as the girls watched their mentoress blanch; not one day passed that she didn't wear the official green-and-black tartan of the Urquharts (didn't she play the bagpipes for the school as a special treat on Robert Burns's birthday?). Her great badgerly whiskers rose in outrage; she removed her misty tortoiseshell glasses and drew up her massive Caledonian breast.

"'Ere yuh *presuming* to divine Shakespeare's truh intention, four hundred years after his death, Miss Clare?"

Even as she trembled before this woman, there was in Julia Clare a stubborn refusal to be intimidated by anyone. Softly, she replied, "No more than you are, Mrs. Urquhart."

Now the gnarled, nicotine-stained fingers of her teacher, clutching a yellowed and crusty handkerchief, stabbed the air in the direction of the door.

"Get *oot* of mah class!"

"With pleasure, Mrs. Urquhart."

Julia Clare took the familiar route to the Office of the Head-mistress, sitting in penitence on a hard oaken bench in the foyer— punishment far worse, in fact, than any time spent *with* the head-mistress. Mrs. Grace Bunsen, a woman unrelated to the inventor of the famous burner yet possessed of a bright flame of hair (the color of Red Leicester cheese, curiously similar to the hair of Julia's future hus-band), by virtue of her mercy reinforced Julia's belief that a Christian name is a window into one's character.

Said Grace, "Julia, *when* will you realize that some opinions, how-ever inspired, are best kept to yourself?"

"Forgive me, Mrs. Bunsen, but *every* word out of Mrs. Urquhart's mouth is insulting to women!"

With a dignified frown, Grace Bunsen would ask for the particu-lars—which produced considerable mirth when she conveyed them to the faculty. Julia was unaware of her fame in the teachers' lounge; its shabby armchairs and unemptied ashtrays were the hub for Julia sto-ries while Mrs. Urquhart nursed one of her pungent Malayan cigars beneath a cedar tree on the school grounds, spitting tobacco-stained saliva at the squirrels.

"*BUT WHAT SHALL WE NAME OUR SON?*" asked Howard as Julia stared at the ceiling from her hospital bed.

"I'm busy thinking," replied Julia, though she was really thinking of Beatrice. Parenthood has, as one of its side effects, the quality of re-casting all childhood experience.

IT WAS MRS. URQUHART'S BUTCHERY of Beatrice in *Much Ado About Nothing* that finally dissolved Julia's veil of respect. Beatrice was Julia's favorite character, sharp-spoken, skeptical of love, but, when stoked, possessed of a fiery passion; most of all Julia loved Beatrice's tongue, for she was a character armed with quick and witty retorts, a woman who *always* knew what to say.

It wasn't as though Mrs. Bunsen hadn't warned Julia ahead of time.

"Julia, you're certainly entitled to disagree with her, but do try to express it without insulting her heritage."

"She provokes me!"

"She's your teacher, Julia. Further arguments could lead to your expulsion."

The last thing Julia wanted was to disturb the volatile relationship between her parents. Her father, Adam Clare, a bureaucrat at the Electricity Supply Commission in Johannesburg, had never made enough money to please his wife, and couldn't wait for the weekends to go hunting or fishing. Her mother, aptly named Rose, was strikingly beautiful, prickly to the touch, a woman who had criticism for everyone, especially her daughter. The only thing worse than the disharmony at home was the prospect of being sent home to be the source of it.

In the next month, Julia behaved herself while Mrs. Urquhart blamed Desdemona for Othello's bad end and Juliet for tempting Romeo. Julia, to her credit, resisted the thrashing Mrs. Urquhart gave her beloved Beatrice until almost the very end. She remembered the warnings of her headmistress, and perhaps in the disapproval of Mrs. Urquhart she heard a more primal voice, the voice of Rose, who found her daughter's presence so unsatisfactory that she had bundled her off to boarding school at the age of seven. The classics teacher observed her young foe's reticence—hands buried under her knees, mouth zipped shut—so when it seemed clear that her gadfly wouldn't sting, she ended her lecture with this final remark: "You'll notice how often Beatrice seeks the last word in any scene—clearly an *insecure* and *weak* young woman."

A weak woman? Beatrice?

The girls turned for the volley. Julia wiped the beads of sweat along her upper lip—another quality her mother disliked. "She's assuredly *your* child, Adam. See how she sweats from the most masculine parts of her body!"

Mrs. Urquhart folded her arms—gauntlet dropped. Waiting. Julia bit her lip so hard she could feel the blood on her tongue; her mind was fixed on Mrs. Bunsen's warning. Still, the faces of the girls were trained on her while the hirsute harpy gloated in triumph.

Julia then, without realizing it, fixed one eye on the puckered face of her teacher and raised a skeptical eyebrow.

"Madam, if what you say about Shakespeare reflects life, then all men are the dupes of women, and all women are the mistresses of their destruction. What would *Mr. Urquhart* say to *that*, I wonder?"

Heads were lowered to desks, as if to avoid the return fire from this verbal torpedo.

Mrs. Urquhart squinted, regarding the mock innocence of her assailant with a bobbing craw.

"Miss Clare—you'll *nae* sit in my class *e'er* again!" she sputtered.

JULIA WAS FOUND BY HER FATHER at the train station, in her uniform, a blue-and-gray tartan, a wide straw hat, and white kneesocks. Perched on a large trunk, she cradled her dog-eared copy of *Lambs' Tales from Shakespeare*.

"Well, missy," he said. "What a mess we're in now."

He was a striking man, tall, with blue-black hair cropped short, thick eyebrows, and strong cheekbones. She liked to imagine a more savage version of him slaughtering Hadrian's legions in the heather.

"I'm so sorry, Papa," she replied.

He deflected her apology with a soft shrug.

"How's Mummy? Tell me all the news. Do I look taller?"

Her father hesitated.

"Yes, missy, I think you might be as tall as your mother."

"You must measure us together. Where is she?"

Adam Clare dug into his jacket pockets, nervously looking for his pipe, then, sighing, he dropped his shoulders and looked at Julia with an abashed smile.

"The thing is, missy, your mother and I are divorced."

The sun broke through the fever trees, and Julia tried to shield the harsh light from her eyes with both hands.

"What?" she said, hoping she had misheard, and yet knowing she hadn't.

"Our marriage is over."

"When?"

"Oh, last Christmas, actually." Her father swallowed. "We were going to tell you this next summer, I suppose, but . . . well, here you are."

Here she was. A loose end to the marriage. An attached string somebody had forgotten to clip.

"What will I do?" she asked.

"Well, luckily they've accepted you at Saint Mary's." He smiled. "You'll continue your studies, grow up, and have a wonderful life."

Julia was sure that Beatrice would have summoned the right riposte, but she couldn't imagine what it was. By the time her outrage found words, her father was busy negotiating with a porter for the shipment of her trunk to the new school. Then he offered her an ice cream and Julia heard herself thanking him for the treat through hot tears.

"IT JUST DOESN'T SEEM RIGHT to name a child after oneself," Julia told Howard as she looked at her new baby boy, "when he may not feel kindly toward you later in life."

"What could he possibly have against me? I'm certainly not going to make *my* father's mistakes." Howard laughed.

Julia didn't answer. She recalled her parents making only one mistake—marrying each other.

Though the Lament baby's eyes were closed, the power of his smile was astounding. If ever a child possessed a confident spirit, this one excelled in that regard. No parent could doubt that this baby, in spite of his lack of a name, was destined for a happy life.

Dr. Underberg's Compromise

As the crow flies, Southern Rhodesia lay six hundred and thirty miles north of Johannesburg. It was a different country, a British colony where a young, educated white South African might find new opportunities. In 1954, fresh from Cape University, Julia Clare found a position teaching art and English in a primary school while she pursued her painting career. Howard Lament was offered an engineering position at the Water Works in Ludlow, a township thirty miles south of Salisbury.

It was in Ludlow that they met and fell in love. And their lives might have been no more remarkable than those of any other happy couple had it not been for Dr. Samuel Underberg.

The man responsible for changing their lives was only recently appointed head of the obstetrics ward at Salisbury's Mercy Hospital. Underberg was an exceptional doctor, a man who had logged twenty years and thirty thousand miles delivering African babies and running a postnatal clinic from the back of his mud-spattered Land Rover. His face was ruddy, his shiny head fringed by gray wisps, his body small and wiry, and his gestures emphatic. He punctuated his radical ideas with jerking elbows and splayed fingers. But the trustees of Mercy Hospital passed him over three times because of his wrinkled tweed suit, the tightly gnarled tie he slipped over his head every morning, and the muddy boots beneath his trouser cuffs.

Instead, Mercy Hospital hired a daunting succession of well-attired directors: Dr. Gladstone left for a better-paying position in Nairobi; Dr. Macy defied his contract and took an early retirement; and the last one died before anyone managed to remember his name. With some exasperation, the board of trustees sought a doctor who was young, healthy, and neither upwardly mobile nor financially demanding. One look at Dr. Underberg's Land Rover confirmed the latter of these issues, while one look at the doctor confirmed the former.

Samuel Underberg firmly believed that African mothers could teach the Western world a few things about child rearing.

"First," he declared to his interns, "this notion of taking a child that has been nestled in his mother's womb for nine months and *stuffing* him in a tin pram for the *next* nine months is absurd.

"Absurd!" he repeated, with the index fingers of both hands pointing upward, "to deprive a child of his mother's warmth, her heartbeat, and, *even worse*, her milk. African women carry their children slung on their backs—skin to skin, heart to heart—all day long, and these babies are blissfully content." He gestured casually at a white couple (for this was a *white* hospital) leaving with their newborn in a pram with enormous wheels and a hood. "While *these* people wonder why their children are so bloody miserable all the time!"

"But, Doctor," said a pimply young man in a spotless white coat, "surely you don't expect white mothers to sling *their* babies over their backs like natives? It's hardly civilized . . ."

"Civilized?" snapped the doctor. "A word used to justify everything from bottle-feeding to the atom bomb!"

"You don't approve of bottle-feeding?" whispered another scandalized student.

"In Africa," replied the doctor, "the lack of sterile water makes bottle-feeding a baby *killer*. If bottles, nipples, and formula had arrived two thousand years ago, we'd all be dead of dysentery. No human race left!"

The ruddy philosopher slid to a halt—his rubber soles scuffing the shiny white linoleum—whereupon he dismissed the students and swept into Julia Lament's room.

"NO NAME YET?" he asked as he squeezed the Lament baby's toes.

"Sorry." Julia smiled.

"My dear Julia, I've a favor to ask," said the doctor, who sensed in her failure to name her baby a healthy resistance to convention that suited his newest objective.

"Yes?" she said, both flattered and made anxious by his informality.

"It's an unusual one, but quite serious," he added, frowning to make his point.

"Tell me."

"I have a patient who delivered a two-and-a-half-pound premature infant last night. The child is in an incubator. I wondered if you might be willing to let her hold little . . . little . . . *Lament* here, so that she gets used to touching a baby."

"Touching?" repeated Julia with reluctance.

"The problem is rejection," explained the doctor, "a sense of distance, a feeling that the baby is not really hers."

"Just touch him?" she said with skepticism.

"Actually," said the doctor with a fixed smile, "I meant nurse him, too."

"Nurse *my* baby?"

"Imagine, Julia," said the doctor, holding an imaginary bundle before her, "you have carried your baby for so many months, and then, for thirty days, you can't touch him. He's in an incubator, fighting for his life. Consider the sense of loss. Consider, perhaps, feeling that you don't *have* a baby anymore. Consider sitting in a ward like this with lots of other women holding their newborns while you sit alone. Imagine your breasts full of milk with no baby to take them. You may think my request unorthodox, but I assure you it's quite a common practice."

"In Europe, you mean?"

"No," said Dr. Underberg. "Among African women."

"African women?" she replied uncertainly.

Prepared for the inevitable reaction, the doctor continued, "Not that thousands of years of experience producing happy and healthy infants should make a difference to you"—he sighed—"but this small act of generosity could help a mother who, I fear, is in danger of losing that precious bond with her child."

"Yes," replied Julia cautiously. "What a shame that would be."

"I thought I saw the rebel in you, Julia," said Dr. Underberg, slapping his knees. "The first day we met, I knew you were different. You'll show the establishment a little gumption!"

As the doctor sailed down the hall, Julia's resolve hung in the balance. It had been five years since Mrs. Urquhart's assault on Beatrice. Was Julia still a rebel? She looked down at her darling boy. He let out a peep, and his eyes opened briefly. Then, perhaps it was only in her imagination, but he seemed to tip his head with a small, rallying nod.

A HEAVYSET WOMAN lay in a nearby maternity room with her eyes squeezed shut. There was no baby beside her. She was a mother yet not a mother.

"Mary?" said a voice.

It was her imagination calling. Nobody cared about her. Not the nurses. Not the doctors. Not Walter. Not even God.

"Mary, open your eyes."

I will not.

Perhaps she could just shut out the world this way. Perhaps if she didn't look, listen, or speak she could vanish of her own accord.

"I have someone for you to meet."

She relaxed her eyes enough to see Dr. Underberg place a wee bundle in her lap.

Mary's lower lip trembled at the small face beaming at her. Nevertheless, she gritted her uneven teeth.

"This. Isn't. My. Baby."

"No, but he's very hungry. Perhaps you could feed him as a *favor*."

Mary shook her head, closing her eyes again. "I don't have any milk."

"Will you try? Please?"

She loosened her nightie but shook her head. It wouldn't work. She felt empty of will. Of milk. Of life.

Suddenly the little thing reached out with two tiny grappling palms, and with a snort and a gasp, it climbed toward her left breast, eyes shut, face weaving left and right until it corked its open mouth with her nipple.

Stupefied at the urchin's determination, she watched him begin to suck vigorously from her breast.

"Bloody hell," she whispered.

Dr. Underberg nodded vigorously. "A bit like a homing pigeon, isn't he?"

The baby paused, raising his wrinkled head. The two of them stared at each other like strangers at a social, puzzled at being thrown together. The baby went back to work on her breast, but now he was watching her. Mary felt unable to turn away; between the action in her breast and the baby's hypnotic glance, she was slipping into a pleasantly placid state; then she remembered the doctor standing nearby.

"Why's he staring at me?" she asked.

"Babies do that. He adores you."

"Me?" She looked back at the infant. His eyes regarded her with such clarity, such lack of doubt, that she felt herself falling into his power; together, they were merging. His eyelids closed, and Mary's thoughts drifted, forgetting the empty beds around her, forgetting about the nurses, the doctors, her lost love, and even God's abandonment—everything except the strange new bond she felt with this contented infant.

"WHO *IS* THIS WOMAN?" Howard Lament was pacing the hospital room. "And why does she have *our* baby?"

"African women do this all the time, darling," said Julia matter-of-factly.

"Julia, African women walk around without a stitch; it wouldn't justify your doing the same thing. And, besides, you might have asked my opinion!"

"We're rebels, darling." His wife smiled. "I knew you'd understand."

This gave Howard pause. Standing in his blazer and white pants, he rather liked the rebel idea. He wasn't going to be like his father, living in the same house his whole life; no, he and Julia were going to see the world like the other Laments. There was the Lament who sailed with Cook to the South Pacific; and Great-grandfather Frederick Lament, who arrived in South Africa in 1899 and started the first bicycle shop in Grahamstown. Howard's two older sisters had followed their husbands to Australia; and his cousin Neville always sent postcards from his trips to Patagonia and Nepal. To be a Lament was to travel. Yes, he liked the rebel idea quite a lot.

"HE'S ALL TWITCHES AND STRUGGLING LIKE," said Mary to Dr. Underberg. "I call him Jack because he's always climbing up the hill"—she giggled—"but once he gets to the top, wild horses couldn't tear him away from that pail of water!"

Dr. Underberg noted that the baby *did* seem different with Mary Boyd than with Julia Lament. The infant's movements were more strident, there was more grabbing and pulling, perhaps because Mary was a larger woman and her physical terrain was a challenge to navigate, or perhaps because this provoked more attention from Mary. The doctor made a note to himself to investigate this issue more fully in a paper. In the meantime, it was clear to him that the exchange had restored Mary's desire to live.

"You'll see your own little one after lunch today," he said.

Mary looked up, puzzled.

"*Your* baby, Mary. He's gained four ounces," the doctor reminded her.

"Oh"—Mary blinked—"then you think he'll live?"

The doctor frowned. "Of *course* he'll live! There was never any doubt. Look," he decided, "after you're finished we'll pay him a visit."

THIS WAS MARY'S SECOND VIEWING of her son, and she was disheartened. The neonate was dwarfed by his incubator; hair ran up his tiny spine; he resembled a little bush baby with his enormous eyes and minuscule hands. Like the membrane of an onion, his skin was transparent, exposing the desperate tangle of blood vessels that kept him alive. To her dispirited eye, he was more hatchling than human.

"All premature infants look this way," the doctor assured her. "But in just a few weeks he'll be a bouncing baby. This fellow, Mary, will look just like little . . . *Jack.*" He opened one of the circular holes on the side of the incubator. "Go ahead, give him a stroke."

"A stroke? Like a dog?"

Dr. Underberg looked at her in disbelief.

"He *needs* your touch, Mary. He needs a reason to live, and your warmth will give him that."

Mary patted the tiny creature with her index finger. She noticed its fragile rib cage rise and fall, and winced that her body had produced a mite so ill equipped for life.

MARY BOYD'S ESTRANGED HUSBAND, Walter Boyd, was listening to the BBC's shortwave broadcast of cricket. Australia was about to beat England. Walter could recite the test match scores for the past fifteen years. Though he could never remember the players, he found numbers comforting—phone numbers, account numbers, his last six electric bills: he recited them to calm himself. When the phone rang suddenly, he counted five rings before answering.

"Thought you might want to know that I've just had your baby," said a familiar voice on the other end.

Startled, Walter dropped the weather statistics from his edition of the *Sunday Mail.* He buckled forward, clutching the phone—using the stern voice he reserved for strangers.

"Who is this?"

"Mary. I'm in Salisbury."

"Mary?"

"Yes. Mary. Your wife."

The phone line went dead, but Walter kept it to his ear, expecting somehow to get a full explanation from the telephone company. When none came, he counted the stripes on the cuff of his shirt while the cricket match turned to white noise and the conversation replayed in his brain.

I've just had your baby.

"HOW LONG ARE YOU STAYING IN THE HOSPITAL?" asked Julia's mother, Rose D'Usseau, formerly Rose Clare, formerly Rose Frank, formerly Rose Willoughby. It wasn't that she was hard to live with—she just grew bored with her husbands easily. An elegant, delicate woman with a proud manner, she made a wonderful first impression; men fell for her left and right. Once married, she dressed them, changed their haircuts, reformed their habits, enrolled them in the right clubs, redirected their careers. Her work done, she mentally dusted off her hands and looked for a new challenge.

"Till the morning," replied Julia.

"Thank heaven," sighed Rose, regarding the drab hospital room with disapproval. If she didn't renovate men, she might have set her talents to historic buildings.

"And the poor thing still has no name?" she continued, eyeing the sleeping bundle in Julia's lap.

"He's not a *thing*, Mother," replied Julia. "He's a boy."

"He's a thing until he has the *dignity* of a name," said Rose. "And who is this doctor? He needs a new suit, a haircut, and a *proper* pair of shoes!"

Julia turned to Howard for support; deflecting her mother's verbal assaults required more energy than she could muster.

"Dr. Underberg is the head of obstetrics, Rose," explained Howard.

"He has quite a few things to teach the medical establishment in this country."

"Really, Howard? How marvelous." Rose brightened. Howard always had this effect on her. Julia found her mother's awe of Howard disquieting—and rather predatory.

There was a squeak at the doorway as Nurse Pritchard, the matron of the ward, prepared to announce the end of visiting hours. But the striking resemblance between Rose and Julia gave her pause; she simply tapped her watch and continued on her rounds.

"What about his name?" continued Rose. "Do you need suggestions? I always thought Harold would be a fine . . ."

Julia shot Howard another desperate glance.

"We've *got* names," Howard interjected, "just none that we agree on." Almost immediately he realized his faux pas as Julia closed her eyes in anticipation of Rose's next charge.

"Julia"—Rose smiled in reproach—"can't you *defer* to your husband for a change?"

"Why?" snapped Julia. "*You* never did."

"You're tired, dear," Rose said. "You always snap when you're tired."

"I want to go home," whispered Julia as she rested her head against Howard's shoulder.

"Imagine," Howard said, his face shining at the wonder of his little son. "We'll go home tomorrow—a family!"

WALTER BOYD WAS NOT a spontaneous man; he and Mary might have worked at Eldridges for years—he in Accounting, she in Jewelry and Lingerie—before he made a pass. Mary was impulsive and forward, however; she sat on his desk, folded her legs beside his liverwurst sandwich, compelling him to introduce himself if only to retrieve his lunch. The following spring, when she announced that she was pregnant, Walter took a full day to express his surprise.

"Really?" he said the next morning with a dim smile. "Are you *really* pregnant, Mary?"

"Bloody hell, Walter," she replied. "I've been *chucking up* every morning for three days!"

Though Walter was grave and humorless, Mary liked his intellect and earnest nature. He lacked deceit, and he didn't make her feel stupid, as some men did. With melancholy eyes and a sweet, affectionate nature, he was as stable as a continent. Walter moved an inch a year.

Only an accidental pregnancy could have provoked Walter to propose marriage, but he did the right thing, as Mary had hoped; he even gave her a ring with a sapphire setting. But then that little cloud appeared, the cloud that seemed to follow Mary everywhere. When Mary miscarried, she wailed; she wanted to beat the walls at the cruelty of life. She needed to be held, to be cradled, but Walter just shook his head and rolled the lint from his pocket linings.

"Bloody hell, Walter," she said. "Sometimes I don't think you love me at all!"

When he looked back at her with those sorrowful eyes it made her furious. She slapped him. How dare *he* be the suffering one?

"One two three, one two three," counted Walter softly, staring at the second hand on his wristwatch.

"It was *my* baby!" she roared.

"One two three, one two three," murmured Walter. "My baby too, one two three, my baby too." But Mary didn't hear him. The only way Walter knew to get through his grief was to count. Until, one day, Mary woke up to find him gone, and it appeared that Walter *was* capable of a decisive act.

WALTER BRUSHED THE BLUE JACARANDA BLOSSOMS from the roof of his black Volvo and climbed in. A gardener was clipping the trunk of a date palm on a nearby lawn. After sitting behind the wheel for a few moments, Walter gave him a brief nod. In this quiet white neighborhood in Lusaka, it might seem odd for a man to be sitting in a hot car counting his fingers.

Walter added the weeks since they had slept together, then broke them down into days, and hours. Numbers didn't lie; they might well have produced a baby—though it must have been born prematurely.

He estimated 420 miles to Salisbury from Lusaka. If he drove without stopping, he could do it in seven hours. All he needed was the resolve.

MARY'S BREASTS WERE ALWAYS throbbing by the time her little Jack arrived. The minute she heard his cry, her nipples would start dripping with milk, and by the time the little urchin was in her lap, her nightie would be drenched in two big splotches.

"I can do this by myself," she said to the nurse who had brought the baby in, eyeing her haughtily as the woman's shoes squeaked away on the linoleum.

"Oh, Jackie, you little troublemaker. Mother thought you'd never come. Here I am, like two balloons! Mother thought she was going to burst!"

She had been thinking all day about her baby. It seemed to her that fate had matched her up with this child. Certainly the baby she bore was meant for someone else and little Jackie was for her. Perhaps the mother of little Jackie would be better suited to the creature inside the incubator.

"Want to run away with me, Jackie boy?" she whispered. "I think we were made for each other. What do *you* think?"

When Dr. Underberg appeared a few minutes later, Mary smiled.

"Well, look at you!" he declared. "You're *glowing*, Mary."

"Oh, go on!" Mary giggled.

"What a change," said Dr. Underberg.

"*This* baby is the best medicine," she gushed.

The doctor's expression changed.

"Yes . . . fortunately, by the time he leaves tomorrow, you'll have your very own fellow to nurse."

"Tomorrow?" she replied.

"Yes," said Dr. Underberg. "His mother's ready to go home."

After a moment's hesitation, Mary broke into an anxious smile. "I'd like to thank her. Do you think I could? I'd *so* like to thank her," she repeated.

"Thank her?" said Dr. Underberg cautiously. "Well, it's rather unusual, but I see no reason why not."

"Which room?" asked Mary. "I'll just pop in by myself."

JULIA WATCHED A DUMPY FIGURE edge along the perimeter of the room, footstep by footstep. She had a disheveled mop of mouse-brown hair, flushed cheeks, and a loopy smile.

"I just wanted to see the baby's mother," Mary said with a nervous laugh.

"How's *your* baby?" asked Julia.

"Fine," said Mary with a wilted smile. "But little Jackie's a wonder. I *so* love him."

Julia stiffened, but nodded politely. Mary covered her mouth like a schoolgirl.

"It'll be nice to go home. I'm sure you'll feel that way, too," said Julia.

Mary nodded, and swallowed. "I wonder," she began, "if perhaps I could nurse him one last time before you go?"

Julia was about to say no, but she checked herself. "I'll speak to the doctor," she said, sensing that the woman might not take her answer well. Mary rose to leave, then reached for Julia's hand in farewell. Julia noticed the raw fingertips and the woman's trembling lips.

"Room 303," sang Mary softly as she tiptoed out.

TWO HOURS LATER, the sun was simmering on the horizon; Walter parked his car under a solitary euphorbia tree. A drop of poisonous sap dribbled down the window. He slept as a herd of giraffe crossed the road with stilted poise; their legs merged into the glittering tarmac while their heads ducked gracefully beneath the telegraph wires.

He dreamt he and Mary were in a garden of paradise. Enormous white birds with elegantly curved beaks were crying through the trees as the couple walked along a weaving path with topiary flamingos on either side.

"I'm pregnant," Mary said, and this much of the dream seemed true to his memory. She *had* told him this in a garden somewhere.

"How?" said Walter.

"Screwing three times a day'll do it," she replied with a girlish smirk. That was Mary, all right: thirty-six and rude as a tart.

"What'll we do?" he asked, though he knew the answer. He would marry her, because that would be doing the decent thing.

"But do you love me?"

"I think so. I hope so. Why wouldn't I?" he asked.

She gave a small cry and embraced him; suddenly they were walking, man and wife, through a park in the Cape. Walter wore a straw hat and a jacket and tie. Mary held her sapphire ring up to the sun, casting rays on the stern bronze face of the Boer hero who stood, cornered by four fountains, in a goldfish pond. The pavement was scorching. Mary removed her sandals and paddled into the pool; water cascaded around her, soaking her white linen dress until it stuck to her skin. She giggled in the spray—adopted a pose and spat water from her mouth, held up her sodden tresses and pranced across the pool like a duchess, a ridiculous figure, drenched, her wet belly glistening.

Walter stood by the pond, as rigid as the Boer statue.

"Come here, Walter. Forget yourself and jump in!" Mary shouted.

He watched her, torn between his composure and the naughty glee of his pregnant wife. Then he kicked off his shoes, deciding she was his antidote, the cure to his torpid nature; he tossed his hat and jacket into the air and clambered into the pool. Mary was his liberator, and he thanked fate and embraced her.

The elderly bench sitters winced at this shocking abuse of a public garden. Even the bronze Boer had to suffer this foolishness, with Walter's straw hat perched rakishly on his head. Tears of laughter rolled down Walter's cheeks as Mary blew raspberries at a frowning matron.

He was freed from himself and in love with Mary. God bless her silliness and her vulgar language.

"Walter!" cried Mary suddenly.

Walter turned and saw Mary's dress turn red between her legs.

Her scream was deafening. He opened his eyes.

A marabou was screeching at him through the windshield. Walter jerked in his seat and started the Volvo's engine. The bird, unimpressed, raised its enormous wings in a languid shrug and hopped lazily to the ground. Walter had hunted many times for impala and zebra, and he knew that the minute an animal was down, the marabous and vultures would be first on the scene.

As the Volvo shuddered forward he wondered if the marabou had sensed the blood in his dream.

MARY BOYD TOSSED IN HER SLEEP. She regretted calling Walter; Walter didn't care about her anymore. She'd offered him all her love and he had rejected her. The last time they'd made love she'd suspected that he was really just saying good-bye.

"Well, I don't need you now!" she said out loud. "I've got little Jackie!"

Meanwhile, Walter was driving around the grounds of the hospital in the early morning light, wondering how to find his wife and baby. A sign read, VISITORS ADMITTED 9:00 TO 3:00. He counted the minutes, converted them to seconds, and decided to take a stroll around the rhododendrons to make the time pass.

JULIA WAS IN A LIGHT SLEEP at six A.M. She was used to the sound of the nurses squeaking in their plimsolls past her room; it was a surprise to see a nurse enter the room silently.

"What is it?" she asked.

"Just changing the nappy, dear," whispered the nurse as she picked up the bundle beside her.

Julia listened to the nurse's footsteps and thought about her rather loopy smile. Where had she seen it before?

MARY'S BREASTS ACHED. It had been over twelve hours since she had nursed; the white uniform she had taken from a linen closet grew damp around her nipples the very moment she thought about nursing. As she approached the reception desk, she lowered the large canvas bag casually to her side, praying that little Jackie would be quiet.

The night attendant rose to unlock the door for her. He noticed the two large wet spots on her chest, and averted his eyes as she walked out.

THE FRAGRANT ARCH OF PINK ROSES that greeted visitors to Mercy Hospital was glorious; Julia loved roses, and had paused to breathe them in whenever she came for her appointments with Dr. Underberg. Mary, however, appreciated them only for the concealment they offered. She walked quickly along the length of the whitewashed building with its terra-cotta shingles. An enormous purple rhododendron bush gave her cover as she paused to catch her breath. Her heart was beating furiously. Oh God, what had she done? She checked the baby: his gaze was confident; he beamed at her. Such a happy fellow; she was obviously doing the right thing. But which way to go? How could she hitch a ride with little Jackie in a bag?

"Mary?" called a familiar voice from among the rhododendron blossoms.

"Walter!" she gasped.

He replied with an abashed grin. "Surprised you, didn't I? Didn't think I'd come, did you? Well, here I am, Mary. Here I am!"

He was about to take her in his arms when a small whimper came from inside the bag at Mary's side.

"This is Jackie, Walter. Our baby," she said. "Say hello to your daddy, Jackie."

Walter blinked. Tears clouded his eyes, and he struggled to find words to express this joy while Mary peppered him with questions and demands. Where was the car? Could they leave now? Let Mummy nurse the baby. Walter was overcome, and eager to be Mary's hero again. In a few minutes they were on the road, Mercy Hospital was receding, and a bundle of happiness was smiling at him from Mary's lap.

"WHAT KIND OF A BLOODY HOSPITAL IS THIS?" roared Howard, who had never roared before, but felt *somebody* should be roaring under the circumstances. "How could someone bloody *walk out* with our baby?"

"This is most unfortunate. No mother has ever taken someone else's baby before," Dr. Underberg confessed.

"But steps should have been taken!" said Howard.

"How, sir, do you prepare for something that's never happened?" The doctor was sputtering.

"Shouldn't we be thinking instead about *where* this woman might have taken him?" cried Julia.

"An orderly spotted her in a car leaving the parking lot," said Dr. Underberg. "The police will certainly track her down."

"They could be fifty miles away!" shouted Howard. "And what if it's a ransom sort of thing?"

"Darling, I don't think this is about ransom," Julia said quietly. "I think she *wanted* our baby."

This grim assumption provoked Howard to direct his fury back toward Underberg. "It's *your* fault!" he cried. "If Julia hadn't been duped by your silly ideas . . ."

"I beg your pardon, sir"—the doctor bristled—"but I had only the best intentions."

AS THE VOLVO CROSSED a broad plain, Walter's giddy joy began to fade. He resisted as long as he could, dearly wanting this precious feeling to last, but Mary's house slippers, her disheveled hair, the damp linen uniform, and the shopping bag posed an increasingly upsetting series of questions.

"Had enough, then, Jackie?" cooed Mary. The baby turned away from her breast and gazed at Walter with a sudden grin. Walter couldn't drive and think, so he brought the Volvo to a halt.

"Something wrong with the car?" asked Mary.

"Car's fine." Walter calculated their distance from the hospital.

Mary gazed into the mirror and drummed her fingers. "Then what are we stopping for?"

Walter shrugged. He stepped out and shielded his eyes from the morning sun. The road melted into sky; a few dead trees pierced the flat plain.

"Where were you *going*, Mary?"

"What?"

"When I found you."

"I was taking the baby for a walk."

Walter paused at her window, gazing at her uniform again.

"Mary, tell me the truth."

"All right, Walter. But I'm hot, and so's little Jackie. Start the car and I'll explain."

Walter watched Mary glance in the rearview mirror again. He sighed and got back in the car. But once they were moving, Mary said nothing, and he remembered the old Mary: impulsive, stubborn, and melodramatic.

"All my life, Walter," she said, "I've had a little black cloud following me." Mary wiped a tear from her cheek. "When little Jackie arrived, it disappeared. He's so beautiful, and happy, and loving."

The baby smiled at him, and Walter's head began to throb.

"I don't know if I fancy Jackie for a name," he replied. "How about a nice biblical name? Matthew? Or Paul?"

She stared ahead.

"It's Jackie, Walter. That's final."

"Look here," he said, "I am the father; it's my decision too, isn't it?"

"Not exactly," she said softly.

Walter squinted, his eyes salty with sweat. It was an infernal morning sun. Mary's cheeks were crimson as she glared at him.

"'Not exactly'? What's *that* mean, Mary?"

She bit her lip and nudged the baby to nurse a little more, but the heat was too much; he was lapsing into sleep again.

"I drove four hundred twenty-eight miles to see my baby. *My baby*."

Mary frowned, hugging the baby closer to her breast. She was remembering Walter's defects, his rigidity and lack of humor. What a mistake it had been to get in his car. On the other hand, what choice did she have? She needed him on her side; she needed his sympathy.

"So, Mary," he said. "Whose baby is this?"

"Our baby's in the hospital," she bleated. "Oh, you should see it—it's an awful little thing, barely alive, barely *human;* the doctor asked me to look after little Jackie and he took to me like my very own."

She couldn't look at him now. Didn't want to see his expression. But she reached out, her trembling fingers skating down his stiff cheek.

"I didn't think I could tell you that," she added, her tone brightening. "Surprised myself. But the thing is," she said as her voice gained strength, "we're going to be very happy together."

Walter let out a whimper.

Oh, God, bless little Jackie. And God bless Walter, prayed Mary to herself. *We're going to be so very happy.*

Ahead, Walter spotted a wide enough shoulder to turn the car around. When he downshifted, Mary looked at him with a start.

"Walter? What are you doing?"

"Going to get my baby," he said.

"*This* is our baby, Walter. We're going to be happy with little Jackie, I *swear* we are!"

"My baby's in the hospital." His eyes fixed her accusingly. *"You left him there."*

"Walter, please, we can't go back, if you have any mercy . . . please!"

But the air rushing past the windows drowned out her plea. Walter was as solid and implacable as Mount Sinai. His foot hardened against the accelerator pedal and the engine began to shake. *He* was the black cloud following her, thought Mary. She'd offered him a new start and he'd ruined it with his self-righteous attitude. *Bloody hell!* She shouted her pleas, but he kept his eyes to the road and his knuckles on the wheel. So, with the baby nestled in one arm, Mary struck out at his face with her left fist. He took the blow without a flinch.

"Stop here, Walter. I'll get out now," she said. *"Stop the car!"*

He laughed in disbelief. "You're bloody crazy. Leave you here? You're out of your mind! That baby's got to go back to his parents!"

She hit Walter's nose with the heel of her hand, and he let out a groan. Blood rolled down his chin to his shirt, but he stared ahead. The engine was whining now; the speedometer must have been above eighty when she grabbed the wheel in a fit of despair.

The car seemed to do a graceful somersault into the bush, the rich, paprika-red earth rising in clouds as the machine spun over and over and over.

DR. UNDERBERG PRESSED HIS NOSE to the glass of the incubator. "Look at him," he said.

He was sitting in the darkness of the nursery that evening, staring at the little urchin. Ironically, it had made a dramatic advance; now three pounds, with pencil-thin arms and legs, a faint whorl of hair, and sad-lidded eyes, he hardly seemed equipped for life, but *something* had propelled him this far. The night matron, Mrs. Pritchard, stood in silhouette at the door, clipboard in hand, waiting for an answer to her question.

"Astonishing!" the doctor murmured. "Abandoned, orphaned, no relatives, and yet he holds on to life. Such tenacity deserves reward."

"It's God's will," said the matron, crossing herself.

This provoked a sniff from the doctor. Of the hundreds of babies he'd delivered in the white hospital, and the scores of black babies who had died during his service in the mobile clinic, he'd concluded that God's will was nothing if not a fickle thing.

"Would you like me to call the foster home?" she asked for the second time.

The doctor bristled. "The foster home? *There's* a magnificent institution! Child rearing by bureaucrats and matrons! I can't think of anything worse."

A wry line appeared in Nurse Pritchard's cheek as she registered the sting of his rather personal remark. Nevertheless, she hugged her clipboard like a shield and pressed on.

"Plenty of orphaned children find secure homes, Doctor."

"Secure homes?" retorted Dr. Underberg. "No doubt they produce secure orphans and secure foster children, Mrs. Pritchard, but surely our mission should be to find this child a *happy* home!" He rose from the incubator and walked to the door. "Don't sign a single form for that child until I return!"

With that he tore off his white coat and spun through the door, leaving Nurse Pritchard alone with the incubator waif.

Moments later the doctor's cherubic face reappeared.

"And for your information, I myself was a foster child!"

Now Nurse Pritchard peered at the little urchin. His chapped lips parted slightly to take a breath of air, and hung open in such an expression of grief as to make her sigh. His features were the embodiment of hopelessness in an indifferent world. Still, Mrs. Pritchard decided, at least he was alive. She crossed herself again, thinking of the other poor baby, who had perished in the car.

THE CHALLENGE OF HARD TIMES and suffering can unite a couple, forge their love, and sustain their passion. But Howard and Julia Lament were not so equipped for the death of their Little One. Though they felt united in despair, they chose to suffer in solitude. They told no relatives, and left Mercy Hospital bearing no swaddled bundle, no balloons, no arms laden with the fripperies of babyhood.

Their drive home was spent in shocked silence. Howard entered the house first and discreetly closed the door to the nursery he'd prepared, with its crib, its white lace bumper, the tiny crocheted blanket, and the welcoming audience of teddy bears lined up along the dresser.

They made cups of tea for consolation, but left them untouched. The constant ringing of the telephone was ignored; Julia simply hadn't the composure to speak to anyone. The only cure for their misery was to forget, but how could they ever look at each other without thinking of their child? So each wandered from room to room, trying to avoid the other wretched soul pacing around.

It seemed that Julia's body was no more capable than her soul of forgetting her baby; for as her breasts ached, full of milk, unable to nourish him, she was haunted by his emphatic smiles. She became the very figure she had pitied before, a woman with no child to nurse. Closing her eyes, fingers resting on her soft belly, she doubted that she would ever muster the will to conceive again.

Howard recalled the expressions of his wife and child greeting him in the hospital room just a few days before—his wife's pride and that small, blessed face, wrapped tightly in a cotton cocoon. He'd never felt so solid as he had holding that baby in his arms; he would have done anything for him. But now he was adrift again. The exquisite adventure of a new family, that truly wondrous trinity, was denied him.

UNABLE TO REACH THEM by phone, Dr. Underberg drove over to the Laments' flat on Barabus Lane in Ludlow. It was important for him to speak to them as quickly as possible, to catch them before they had accepted their loss.

"I feel terribly responsible for what has happened," he began.

"Well, it's a bit late . . ." said Howard, but he felt the pressure of Julia's hand on his shoulder urging him to let the doctor speak.

"Improbably, this unfortunate woman became attached to the wrong child. I've seen mothers abandon children, but never has a patient taken a child in place of her own! Imagine *his* predicament!" The doctor paused, waiting for what he hoped would be a spark of compassion.

"The poor thing," murmured Julia. "How is he doing?"

The doctor was hoping for just such a question. "As a matter of fact, Julia," he began, "this boy has made astonishing progress! He's gained weight, has good color, breathes well. I think he's rather special. A *survivor*, you might say!"

But this caused Julia's tears to well up, and she left the room. Howard lingered, torn between going to her aid and exacting some other retribution on a man he now considered an insensitive quack.

Unnerved by Howard's glare, the doctor continued: "Howard, I cannot help but feel that there is some order to things. Fate has a hand in this."

"Fate? What on *earth* are you talking about?" muttered Howard.

"A fine couple, ideal parents, who have lost a baby, on the one hand," said the doctor, "and an orphan, abandoned by his parents, who insists on surviving."

"Yes." Howard forgot his anger for a moment. "I suppose the poor fellow doesn't have much to look forward to, does he?"

Dr. Underberg leaned forward with a light in his eyes. "Not in an institution, perhaps. But what if this child were to be raised by parents like you—young, spirited, *rebels*!"

"Rebels?" Howard's jaw went slack. "If you ever use that word around me again, Doctor, I'll—"

Underberg raised his hands to plead his point. "Look, Howard, we must accept that life deals tragedy and opportunity in equal measures. Only the brave and generous of heart prevail, and only the timid walk away from life's second chances. Howard, I *implore* you to consider this boy's future." Moved by his own words, Underberg wiped his eyes with his tie, rose from his chair, and bade Howard a good evening.

THE FOLLOWING MORNING, Julia and Howard returned to Mercy Hospital and left with their new son. His name: Will Howard Lament. "Will," because only a child with a will of astonishing fortitude could have survived such a sad beginning.

In order to avoid weeks of delay and paperwork, Underberg arranged for the records to state that this was the natural-born son of the Laments, and as far as most were concerned, the matter ended there.

When Rose demanded to see her grandson for a second time, Julia refused, citing a cold first, then a host of other excuses. In time, Julia resolved never to reveal her son's true identity to her mother (or to the rest of the world), for two reasons. First, she felt compelled to protect this child with all her heart; and second, she wanted to punish Rose for denying her the news of the most devastating fact of her childhood—her parents' divorce.

In subsequent weeks, the baby gained weight, and it was expected that any other differences could be explained by the dramatic change every baby goes through in its first months. Several members of the family struggled to reconcile the child's fair appearance with the mother's black thunderhead of hair and the father's coppery curls, but most would declare the child's features a genetic compromise.

Except for Rose. "His coloring looks different," she observed.

"A little case of jaundice," Howard assured her.

"And he's smaller than he was," she continued.

"It's the clothing," countered Howard.

"If I didn't know better, I'd say he was adopted," said Rose.

"Mother, what an awful thing to say!"

"Darling," replied Rose, "if everybody said *nice* things all the time, truth would be in frightfully short supply. Now, about this name, Will. I much prefer Harold. . . ."

"His name is settled, Mother," said Julia.

"I see." Rose sniffed.

As for Dr. Underberg, he would carry the secret of the boy's parentage to his grave, which, unfortunately, he attained only a month later, when he was on holiday.

His wispy halo of hair was no shelter from the sun, so Dr. Underberg wore a kaffiyeh as he ambled along the steep dunes of Port Jeremiah. As sixteen-year-old Tom Price tore across the sand on his Triumph 3TZ, his face broke into a grin at the chance to scare the hell out of an Arab. He raced the motorcycle up a dune, but misjudged the drop on the other side and barely kept his balance when he landed. Then he noticed the kaffiyeh flapping in ribbons around his front wheel. A small, ruddy man lay in the tracks of the cycle, thirty feet back.

After throwing up the three bottles of beer that had launched him on this folly, the boy staggered over to the body. "Are you hurt?" he asked.

"I'm perfectly fine," came the reply, though Underberg made no effort to right himself.

"I'd better get a doctor," said the boy, preparing to climb back on his bike.

"I *am* a doctor!" came the reply.

The boy, stricken to learn that his victim was white *and* a member of the medical establishment, realized that something terrible had happened, and that he was responsible.

"Would you mind straightening out my legs? I believe they're twisted."

"Your legs are fine," said the boy.

"Fine? Are you insane?" came the muffled reply.

But Dr. Underberg must have recognized in the boy's tone the truth; for at the same moment, the boy gained the sobriety to realize that the doctor's back must have been broken.

"Oh God," he cried. "I'll go back to town and get an ambulance!"

"Nonsense, pick me up!"

The youth hesitated, but the doctor was insistent, so he reached under the man's shoulders and knees and lifted him as tenderly as he'd always imagined he would carry his first love. Tears rolled down the boy's cheeks.

"I'm so, so sorry, sir," moaned the boy.

"Stop that immediately!" snapped the doctor. "This is no time to cry! Now, I wish to see the sunset!"

Following the doctor's instructions, young Tom carried Underberg's limp body over another dune on the peninsula until a molten sun became visible over the Indian Ocean. Digging a mound of sand around the doctor, the boy scrambled to position him for the best view of the horizon, moving his legs and anchoring them in the sand as if he were a manikin.

"What should I do now?" asked the boy.

"Be quiet and enjoy the sunset!" snapped the doctor. Then he addressed the Almighty: "And since it's my last, it had better be a *bloody good one*!"

The sunset was as rare as it was glorious: a mackerel sky of coral-pink wedges, their tips edged in brilliant amber, advanced across the heavens, followed by a proscenium arch of purple and indigo flourishes, with golden beams soaring into the firmament like a ladder of angels. As Dr. Underberg uttered groans of satisfaction between his last urgent breaths, he was interrupted by the sound of weeping.

"I'm sorry," the boy sobbed. "I'm so sorry, sir."

For a brief moment, the doctor quite forgot his own crisis. He realized that this piteous young creature would spend the rest of his life saddled with the burden of his death. It didn't seem fair. So he asked the boy his name, and the boy replied.

"Well, don't worry, Tom," said Underberg firmly. "A doctor knows that accidents happen. And a sunset like this inspires one to forgive. . . ."

"Forgive?" echoed the boy.

"Forgive and forget," sighed the doctor as his eyes closed.

SINCE DR. UNDERBERG had been an orphan, there was no family to hold a memorial service; that duty was left to the hospital director, who appealed to Nurse Pritchard for details on the deceased.

"Details?" replied the matron.

"His habits, his eccentricities, a funny story, perhaps?"

"He was the finest doctor I have ever known, sir." Nurse Pritchard frowned. "And I don't see how 'funny stories' would be appropriate at a funeral!"

"Good Lord, woman, all I'm asking for are a few anecdotes, lovable flaws!" cried the director.

"He had no flaws to speak of," replied the loyal Mrs. Pritchard. "He often spoke to God," she added, neglecting to mention that it was usually a torrent of abuse.

"Ah." The director smiled, pleased at obtaining something he could work with.

Those present at the memorial service would hear Samuel Underberg described as a pious man "whose faith runneth over." This remark should have been enough to provoke Dr. Underberg's spirit to haunt the hospital corridors with peals of laughter, but apparently the man was at peace.

Nurse Pritchard harbored only one persistent regret, which concerned the manner in which the doctor had administered the adoption of the Lament baby, and the record of the child's true identity.

The Importance of Valves

It has been said that a child in his first six months is a blob, a helpless creature, capable of only rudimentary wails for food, affection, or a clean bottom. This was not the case with Will Lament.

Julia had no doubt that this child somehow *knew* he had lost his first parents, and was determined not to lose the second pair. He greeted her and Howard every morning with a cock's crow of approval, clutched them with a fierce grip all day, and surrendered himself to sleep only with pathetic cries that broke her heart. Howard took a less sentimental view.

"Why can't he just be happy, like the other one?"

The expression that answered this question was of such deep sadness that Howard would never dare compare the babies again.

"He just wants to be with us," she replied finally.

"Why won't he let us bloody sleep?"

"He misses us in the dark."

It was as if the child were nourished not by milk but by his parents' presence. The baby loved nothing more than to sleep with them; and any attempt to separate him from this arrangement was met with howls.

Woe to the babysitter who came between this child and his parents. Screams lasting two hours were common; the urchin would expend his lungs to the utmost before collapsing in a fit of despairing hiccups.

"This baby will not be *sat*!" declared one elderly babysitter, who admitted to switching off her hearing aid to survive the aria of woe before Julia and Howard returned.

The boy would greet his parents with sobs of gratitude and relief. He forgave them instantly, his bloated, tearstained face emitting coos and sighs, as if nothing had happened. It seemed to Julia that Will was invested not just in their presence but in their union. His tiny arms would reach for both of them, clutching her dress and Howard's belt loop to pull them together, three for one. At the first note of parental disharmony, a word of sarcasm between them, the child would wail. And when relatives with harsh voices arrived uninvited, smelling of Borkum Riff or lavender toilet water, the baby became doubly fitful, conveniently offering an excuse to cut the visit short.

Though Howard came to appreciate his son's intense devotion as much as Julia did, the baby's presence in the middle of their bed was, in Howard's opinion, a crisis. He was damned if the child was ever going to be in the same room when they made love.

"We'll tiptoe to the couch," said Julia, flanking the baby with pillows to simulate parental bodies as they slipped away, only to be interrupted by an outburst of infant hiccups minutes later.

By the end of Will's first year, when he was up and standing, and quite capable of making his way into the living room in the middle of the night, Howard and Julia decided it was time to find a bigger house.

It would be the first reason they moved—not that Ludlow wasn't a fine town, but Howard wanted to travel to new territories. He wanted the thrill of starting afresh, he wanted to live up to the Lament tradition, and, most of all, he believed that satisfaction lay on the road ahead. This conviction would become the true test of his wife's loyalty and his son's devotion.

· · ·

HOWARD WAS AN ENGINEER, a specialist in the conveyance of liquids through valves of every shape and size.

"It's not like being a spy or an actor, but it can be just as exciting," he would explain at parties.

Exciting, if you happen to be fascinated by the way a quantity of anything passes through passages that diminish or expand in size, riveting, if you love stopcocks and ball valves. Mesmerizing, if, as Howard did, you spent your childhood racing out in a rainstorm to catch the water running down the side of the road, blocking it with dams, rerouting it, speeding and slowing its flow with rocks and pebbles, and sending out an armada of leaves to brave its treacherous rapids and falls. He spent more time in his bathtub than either of his older sisters, and typically emerged, prunelike, clutching an odd assortment of homemade waterwheels and rubber tubes. As a teenager, he decorated his room with pictures of deltas and alluvial fans.

By the time he reached adulthood, however, Howard had realized that most people didn't share his fascination, and on more than one occasion he had no sooner explained his profession than the listener walked away. He took to reducing his specialty to one word: valves.

"Valves," said Mrs. Gill, the dean's vapid wife, at his graduation from Cape University. "Then you must like to ride bicycles. Aren't there valves in bicycle tires?"

"Yes, but . . ." said Howard.

"Or do you prefer motorcar tires?" said Mrs. Gill, her mind suddenly taking flight at the potential of the word.

"Actually, I work with—"

"Perhaps the Michelin people could use you; don't they make tires? And I love their guide. I once spent a *glorious* fortnight eating my way through Brittany!"

Though Howard was a shy man, and chose, in the future, not to discuss his vocation with people who hadn't a clue, he knew the world was his oyster. Liquids were everywhere, and valves were essential.

Howard met Julia while working for the Ludlow Water Works. He was pursuing his master's degree and the job was a temporary position, which allowed him, in exchange for doing an efficiency analysis for the township, to conduct research on water conveyance. It was Howard's dream to design a purification system as magnificent as the Roman aqueducts. A system in which water passed through a complex series of enlarging and diminishing valves using only gravity as a propellant. With a little brilliance and pluck, he would save the millions of gallons of water wasted through evaporation and sloppy mechanical design, and build a system that could irrigate the Sahara!

ON FRIDAY AFTERNOONS, as the sun set over the Water Works, Howard would perch outside his office and survey the splendid jungle of pipes, priding himself on knowing where every pipe went, and what it did, and one day he'd show that Mrs. Gill that there was much more to Howard Lament than bicycle tires.

"You're in my way," said a voice one Friday afternoon.

She was silhouetted against the sun, with a tangle of black hair, paintbrush gritted between her teeth, standing before an easel.

"Oh! Sorry," he apologized, ducking first, then attempting to step backward to see what she was painting.

"Don't look," she said. "I can't stand being judged when I'm not finished!"

"I wouldn't judge it."

"You say that, but you *would*," she said, raising one eyebrow sharply. "People are always judging."

The young woman must have been about his age, or a little younger. Pretty, with shiny cheekbones as round as apples, a smallish freckled nose, and that hair, raven-black, tied back and secured with several paintbrushes, geisha style. She wore slacks and a man's large blue shirt, smudged with oil paint in various yellows and oranges.

The conversation abated. She was busily wiping away sections of the canvas with a cloth and reapplying a few carefully chosen lines. Howard stood still, fascinated by her yet frozen in place for fear that she'd accuse him of judging her if he advanced, and not wanting to obstruct her view of the Water Works in his retreat.

"Do you paint for a living?" he asked.

She cocked a suspicious glance at him.

"Why? Does it matter whether I'm a professional?"

"I'm curious," he replied, deciding that she was remarkably pretty.

"I've sold five paintings of sunsets," she said. "I suppose that makes me a professional, or a lucky amateur. Take your pick."

"Really?" he replied, and was about to ask if she had any more sunsets to sell, not that he could afford them—he was an impoverished graduate student—but it would be a good excuse to see her again.

"I'm sick to death of sunsets," she continued. "Such a cliché! It's much harder to make *noon* interesting. Or an overcast day with no sunlight at all! Only the old masters can do that. A sunset is a cheat. That's why I'm here at the Water Works."

"Ah," he said, impressed on the one hand, and wanting to sound as if her last comment were a logical step from the previous one.

He had already decided that he liked this girl. Liked her frank manner, her expressive face, her unruly hair, and her practical use of paintbrushes as a hair ornament. Worried that he might say the wrong thing, he said nothing, and she said nothing, and the painting continued. After a while he liked the fact that he could say nothing without feeling uncomfortable, and that she could say nothing and not look uncomfortable; he was just thinking that this could be a brilliant sort of . . . friendship when she asked the question he dreaded.

"What sort of work do you do?"

"Do you mean where do I work? Or what is my career?"

"Well, I *assume* you work here," she said.

"Yes," he stuttered. "I work here at the Water Works."

"Then . . . what sort of work do you do?"

Howard frowned. Of course he didn't want to say "valves," because if he said "valves" she'd send him away, which would be better than disappointing him with some comment about bicycles, because he couldn't possibly marry a woman who wasn't interested in his work. Marry? Had he just thought *marry*? But if he didn't say "valves," he'd have to come up with something else as a career, which would, if they became friends, be exposed eventually as a lie. And it wasn't good to begin lying to the love of your life. *Love of your life?* What on earth was he thinking?

She paused in the middle of a brushstroke, amused by his hesitation.

"Don't you know what sort of work you do?"

"Of course I do." He swallowed. "I'm an engineer, I work with valves."

"Well," she said, "now there's a conversation stopper!"

He felt his stomach pitch. Christ. He should have lied, at least until they'd become better friends. Now he tumbled into a downward spiral of regret and decided it was time to go home, back to the shabby little room he shared with an oarsman on the boating team. Oarsman! Why hadn't he said he was an oarsman? He loosened his tie and turned to go, but desire compelled him to steal a last glance at her.

With delicately tapered fingers, she was squeezing burnt umber onto her palette. Then she scraped paint from the canvas onto a knife and added the excess paint to the front of her shirt. She pulled back a strand of that dizzy black hair and accidentally gave it a streak. What a beauty, he thought. And what an opportunity lost. Thanks to those confounded *valves*!

"Well"—he nodded, accepting this defeat—"good-bye!"

She looked up at him with surprise. "You can't go! Not until I've finished. You're in the picture now."

But even this didn't raise Howard's hopes, much.

"You might as well tell me a bit about valves! It can't possibly be as boring as it sounds."

"Perhaps it is," he mumbled.

"I doubt it," she said, with an evasive smile, shifting her gaze to her canvas. "Because you don't *look* the boring type."

"The boring type?"

She thought for a moment.

"Oh, like an athlete obsessed with his record, a rugby player or an oarsman."

Dutch Oil

"What Dutch Oil needs," said Gordon Snifter, "is young men with ideas! Unique young men! And you, Howard Lament, fit the mold!"

What young man doesn't want to be told that a crusty old corporation needs his vigor and inspiration? Especially a young man who has grown up seeing that familiar green-and-white windmill emblem on the road—"Look, Mummy, a wim mill!" Gordon Snifter had come all the way to Ludlow to recruit Howard. After a long chat, a few drinks, and a signature on the dotted line, Gordon Snifter would move on, never to be seen again. Meanwhile, Dutch Oil would move Howard and his little family to its refineries on the island of Bahrain in the Persian Gulf, where he would prove his mettle designing more efficient valves for the oil derricks that were pulling millions of gallons of viscous black liquid out of the sand.

Snifter's offer confirmed Julia's belief that Howard was a very bright young man, and what wife wouldn't want to join her husband in a foreign land and absorb a new culture? Besides, with their son so portable, this was the best time to move. As for the painting, after little success with the Water Works, Julia decided that some new terrain might free her creative spirit. It certainly had done wonders for Gauguin!

Her mother wrote to protest:

The Persian Gulf? Beware of the Arabs! Remember, they toppled the Spanish! And their cousins are the Turks; how can we forget what they did to the Greeks!

I am sorry, but I will not set foot east of the Mediterranean. Their toilets are an abomination! How can you expect me to visit you there? Really, my dear, sometimes I have to wonder if you are purposefully trying to keep my grandson as far away from me as possible!

"So, the toilets are keeping her from visiting us here?" asked Howard.

"Nothing is keeping her from visiting but her own prejudices," Julia declared.

Julia prided herself on being as open-minded as her mother was not, so when they had settled into a flat, she was disappointed to find that instead of being a lone foreigner on an island of Arabs, she was a member of a whole community of her own pink and pale brethren. And instead of living in a medina with labyrinthine passageways, she was in a complex populated by people from Manchester and Birmingham.

"What's wrong with being from Manchester and Birmingham?" asked Howard.

"Nothing. But I'd rather meet the English in their natural habitat. I was hoping to see Arabia."

"Of course you'll see Arabia!" said Mrs. McCross of East Birmingham. "The pool at the Club is lined with the most exquisite Moroccan tile," she explained. Mrs. McCross was a buxom woman, married to one of the Dutch Oil directors; she pinched Julia above her elbow as she steered her about the Club, where the English could find tea and watercress sandwiches. "And we'll find you a good nanny for little Willy."

"It's not Willy, it's Will," Julia replied.

"After William the Conqueror, I suppose," said Mrs. McCross. "A Frenchman," she added, in case Julia had forgotten.

AT THE TENDER AGE OF TWO, Will was mastering the subtleties of his mother's expressions—the barbed, skeptical eyebrow she reserved for Mrs. McCross; the furrowed smile of guilty gratitude she directed at Uda, his elderly nanny; and the many expressions she reserved for him: the adoring smile that greeted him on sun-splashed mornings; the firm, plucky wink she gave him when they ventured into the noisy chaos of the medina; and, of course, the indulgent smile that melted away his tantrums.

But there was one visage that puzzled him—it appeared when she stared at him in contemplative moments, that searching glance, her eyes fixed on some point beyond him with a look of undeniable melancholy. Once he actually turned, expecting to see the object of her yearning, but saw no one.

JULIA TRIED TO CONCEAL this despondent state from her son. If Will took a midday nap, she would make herself a cup of mint tea and listen to the Salat al-Zuhr sung over the rooftops by a wizened mullah in a pink tower. Then she would think about the Little One for a few quiet minutes. Mrs. McCross had a knack for ringing her at such times.

"Julia, dear! It's Mrs. McCross. Come shopping with me. I know where we can find some lovely Fortnum and Mason Earl Grey, better than that ghastly peppermint tea, which, between you and me, raises havoc with my plumbing! What time shall I pick you up?"

Julia soon learned to ignore the telephone's midday ring.

Sometimes, when Uda was available, she would set off on a solitary mission to evade her melancholy by exploring the Grand Bazaar with its rug sellers and spice merchants. She found withered old men seated before mounds of salt, cumin, paprika, and turmeric, and smiling merchants who invited her into their plush, muffled enclaves to display any rug she desired—Kilim, Tabriz, Sarouk, Ferreghan, Serapi, Bokhara, and more—and to enjoy tea served from silver urns. There were stalls full of glass jars, powder to enhance your fertility or your lover's virility, and poisons for your worst enemy. Goat meat sizzled on portable grills, smoke spiraled into the latticework overhead in blue trails.

Once, when a group of children swarmed around her with palms extended, and Julia was about to reach into her purse, a sharp voice from behind caused them to flee. She glanced back and saw a man in a white suit. He smiled, extending one hand from his heart in greeting, and she thought of Clark Gable with an unusually dark suntan.

"Pleased to escort you, madam?" he said.

"I'm quite fine, thank you." Julia blushed, doing a quick about-face.

"The medina is like a maze," warned the gentleman. Julia glanced back at him, wondering whether this was friendly advice or a threat. He had a thin mustache and clean-shaven cheeks; his hair might have been lifted from one of Gable's glossies back when he filmed *It Happened One Night.*

"I have a map, thank you," she replied, and, with her heart beating quickly, took the first left turn. But she led herself into a dead end where an old man and a boy sat hammering brass nails onto ornamental chests while a cat lay wheezing in the dust. Consulting the map, she turned right through the muddy courtyard of a tannery, where the foul chemical smell made her swoon; she staggered hurriedly through the only escape, a narrow alley. Still, she saw that white suit in her peripheral vision. Whether by fear or fact, it refused to depart from the corner of her eye.

She started talking to herself—"Now, *listen,* Julia, two rights and a left should bring us out here," as if common sense would stifle her panic. Down another alley, she noticed a little girl with crossed eyes, wailing, and then three old women with sagging faces who passed a single cup of tea among themselves. Frantic, Julia thought of what Howard would say: "Follow the flow of the water, go downhill, and trace your way back along the river." She took this path and eventually found herself at the noisy entrance of the medina.

Here, the sunlight was intense, and the bustle of people and live-stock was joyous. She saw no sign of the white suit, yet she felt his presence. She had paused to catch her breath when a high-pitched voice interrupted her flight.

"Fancy meeting you here, Julia dear! I was just picking up my tea!"

Mrs. McCross pinched her elbow particularly hard, and before Julia could refuse, she was propelled through the crowd by the woman's enormous bosom.

"A white woman can't be too careful here, dear. We're ever so much better off together. So glad I bumped into you!"

Julia wondered why she could spurn a dashingly handsome Arab and yet be helpless against bloody Mrs. McCross.

"And what brings you here alone?" she asked.

"Just some shopping," said Julia.

"Splendid. I'll join you."

Julia tried to bore the woman by spending an indulgent hour in a pottery shop, but Mrs. McCross removed a small brown leather Bible from her purse and read until Julia accepted the merchant's deal for a vase. Then she lectured Julia on the bargaining ritual, and admonished the merchant until he lowered his price.

"Remember, dear," she said, "we mustn't allow the locals to take advantage of us."

"Why not?" replied Julia. "We divvied up their land after the Ottomans, we're stealing their oil, and we slaughtered them during the Crusades."

"Don't confuse politics with commerce, dear. We're not responsible for the Ottomans, the oil companies, or King Richard, though he was a *very* good king!"

Suddenly Julia saw an opportunity to get through to Mrs. McCross.

"Isn't it Christian to be fair?"

Mrs. McCross's breast heaved in indignation. "Fair? My dear, that vase was worth precisely what you paid for it!"

"Yes, but I'd pay ten times that in London."

"But we're not *in* London, dear," replied Mrs. McCross with a triumphant smile. "No use being generous with these people, they won't treat you any differently. Rob you blind, they will. Mark my words!"

THOUGH ROSE WAS thousands of miles away, Mrs. McCross echoed her sentiments with shrill precision. And then there were the messages typed in single-spaced airmail letters:

> *Remember my warnings about the Arabs. And let's not forget Omar Sharif—isn't he from the Middle East? Such a beautiful man, especially in* Lawrence of Arabia, *but a compulsive gambler according to those silly magazines (which I never read).*
>
> *By the way, had a wonderful stay in Geneva overlooking the quai du Mont-Blanc; the Swiss run a hotel to gratify the guest, while the British run a hotel to spite him. There was an American couple there who drove Alfred and me to tears with their mangled French.*

"Alfred?" said Howard, reading over her shoulder.

"Her new husband," explained Julia.

"What happened to the old one?"

"Dismissed, I imagine."

> *How is my grandson? I do hope to see him soon. It occurred to me that his small size might have something to do with the part of our family that is Irish, the ones who never ate but could drink anybody under the table. Do send me a picture!*
>
> *How is your delightful husband? Feed him lavishly at home or he'll stray! Lust is everywhere in the East!*

"Why does she never use Will's name?" Howard wondered. "It's always 'my grandson' this and 'my grandson' that."

"Because she considers it a French name, and the French killed Harold in 1066. My mother," Julia continued, "has never forgiven the

Norman Conquest. The only Frenchman she approves of is one wearing an apron and offering a menu."

"Well," said Howard, patting his stomach, "you'd better feed me lavishly now or I'll stray."

Julia laughed, then struck an anxious note.

"Howard? Have you ever seen an Arabian woman who filled you with desire?"

"Not a one, darling," he replied, glancing at her shyly. "How about you?"

"A man? Of course not," she replied, blushing as she suppressed the image of the white-suited man.

If Julia had described her marriage, she might well have compared it to a medina: though some of its passages were unexplored, its walls were cemented in trust. Ironically, the beauty that breached these walls first wasn't Arabian at all. Rose managed to predict it, in her own inimitable way.

> *I hear there are a lot of Americans in the oil business. Beware! Not only do they have bad manners, and drink like sailors, but they have no memory for history!*

"Ah," said Howard, "people who won't be upset by Will's name, then? Where can we meet some?"

Trixie Howitzer

Christmas in the Persian Gulf was an oddity practiced with fierce determination by the English. Though it was ninety-nine degrees in the shade, the windows of the Club were frosted with fake snow and a few hardy fools even wore woolen sweaters. Mrs. McCross knitted her own; it featured a grinning Saint Nick, but she'd missed a line or two, so the poor fellow had a depraved leer instead. Moments after Julia appeared at the company party, a note of apology arrived from Howard's office—he was too busy to leave, and would have to meet her at home. She took a brief tally and realized that she was the only wife present without a husband; it seemed to render her invisible to all (even to Mrs. McCross, which wasn't such a bad thing). With faint envy, Julia watched the other couples arrive and merge with their national brethren: the Brits picked at the traditional Christmas suet pudding; the Americans crowded the bar, drinking eggnog and liquored punch; and the Indian executives—Hindu, and therefore unable to eat or drink anything served at this event—lingered with pained smiles, revolted by the suet, repelled by the alcohol, but bound out of politeness to remain.

Julia noticed another figure standing alone, a brunette wearing a clingy electric-pink dress that displayed her long neck, formidable cleavage, and defiant smile. Her hair was teased to approximate a tidal wave. Matisse couldn't have produced a paler, more arch composition for a face—chalky skin, rich red lips, Kabuki eyebrows. But there was nothing invisible about the woman in the pink dress. She was watched by all—by the wives with their pursed, aching smiles, and by their husbands, whose eyes rolled with carnal yearning. There was no mistaking it: she was a goddess.

Julia introduced herself. "How do you do? I'm Julia Lament!"

"Trixie," came the reply in a low, whiskey rasp. "Howitzer."

Almost immediately, Julia was offered a glass of champagne by a waiter, and a platter of hors d'oeuvres hovered within reach for the first time. "What a wonderful dress," said Julia, in gratitude for Trixie's magnetic effect on the staff.

"Thanks," Trixie growled. "The way people are looking at me, I feel naked."

Noting the wishful expressions of some of the executives, Julia guessed Trixie's comment wasn't far from the truth. "Well," Julia replied, "it's nice not to be the only one here without a husband."

Trixie nodded. "I thought I'd just pop in for a bourbon, but there's nothing but champagne and punch." As if to console herself, Trixie downed her champagne in stiff gulps, as if it *were* a bourbon.

Trixie was married to an American executive, Chip Howitzer, who had been running Dutch Oil's holdings in Houston, Texas, until recently. She had a son about Will's age. When Julia proposed a lunch to get to know each other, Trixie consented, but only after warning Julia that she rarely got up that early; indeed, some days she *never* got up. This reinforced Julia's hunch that Trixie was not only a rebel but quite possibly the very sort of mistress of destruction that Mrs. Urquhart found wandering rampant through the plays of Mr. William Shakespeare.

BY THREE, WILL HAD BECOME a gentle and observant child. His possessive fits and tantrums had faded, though he rarely smiled and never laughed. When Julia left to meet her new American friend, he didn't whimper, but waved good-bye from the balcony of their apartment in the arms of Uda, who was determined to prove her worth to Julia by completing Will's toilet training. Twenty minutes couldn't pass without the woman pulling down his pants and sticking him on the plastic potty; he could only conclude that she needed his urine for some urgent purpose. Since Uda frequently augmented her own kitchen with items from Julia's cupboards, Will supposed that the amber liquid in the vinegar bottle she slipped in her bag one afternoon contained his pee. When she left with other vessels—wine bottles, olive oil—he made the same assumption.

Julia and Trixie met for a late tea at the Manhattan Club, an old restaurant of ornate plasterwork and aged green tile, American only in name. Chicken and goat meat sizzled on a blackened grill, but they did serve alcohol for the desperate Westerners. Julia had tea; Trixie kept her dark glasses on, ordered a double scotch, and asked only one question.

"What *are* you?"

"What *am* I?" repeated Julia.

"English? Australian? Your accent . . ."

"Oh—South African," explained Julia. "I grew up there, and moved to Southern Rhodesia to teach and paint. My family's English and Irish. Of course, I've never been to England, though I'd love to go. But all my ancestors hail from there, and we think of England as the mother country."

It all came out in a tumble. Something in Trixie's manner inspired Julia to talk, to spill out stories about her school days and family, until, finally, Trixie raised her sunglasses to reveal a swollen and purple eye the size and luster of a ripe plum. Julia's mouth dropped in surprise. Yet Trixie seemed to relish its impact, leading Julia to wonder what awful thing she had done to her opponent to earn it.

Trixie smirked. "What's the matter, haven't you ever seen a shiner before?"

"Not like that," gulped Julia.

"Well, if you're gonna get one, it might as well be enormous,"

Trixie declared casually, as if black eyes were like diamonds, or cars, or ranches.

"Well, I hope it was an accident," Julia replied.

Trixie replaced her sunglasses and dismissed the matter by ordering her second scotch. Just then, a group of Dutch Oil's English wives, led by Mrs. McCross, entered and took a distant table. "Oh God," said Trixie, "here come the redcoats."

"Well, hello, Julia dear!" chirped Mrs. McCross, who approached.

"Have you met Trixie Howitzer, Mrs. McCross?"

Mrs. McCross's features drew together like a string purse at the sight of Julia's companion. She assumed the most feral of smiles, her front teeth bared. "I have. How are you, dear?" she inquired.

"Never better," said Trixie in the manner of a cat that had eaten a mouse's young. With unusual speed, Mrs. McCross excused herself and retreated to her table.

"I was naughty," Trixie explained. "She invited us to dinner a year ago, and I just got damn tired of listening to her talk. So I put my hand on her husband's knee." Trixie demonstrated by caressing the top of Julia's tea glass. "That shut her up."

Julia laughed, eliciting pinched stares from Mrs. McCross's group.

That evening, Julia told Howard about the incident, as well as Trixie's black eye and her blunt manner.

"She sounds awful," remarked Howard.

"No, darling, she's absolutely fascinating," Julia replied. "You'll see. I've invited the Howitzers over for dinner this weekend!"

ON SATURDAY WILL GREW CONCERNED that the urine in his potty was not being removed by Uda, so he took the liberty of pouring it into the carafe of olive oil to be served to the Laments' guests that evening.

Chip Howitzer was a bullnecked fellow of forty-five with no jawline and a perfectly flat blond buzz cut bordered by fiercely dark and bushy eyebrows. By contrast, his son, Wayne, was pasty-faced, with small resentful eyes and a petulant rose of a mouth; he wore a red bandanna around his neck, and a leather vest. In one hand he held a plastic rifle.

"Ride 'em, cowboy." Trixie laughed. "Isn't he cute? I can't resist dressing him up."

No sooner had the boys been left alone than Wayne kneecapped Will with the butt of his rifle. It wasn't until Will reciprocated with a wooden polo mallet that the boys established a truce and proceeded to play in opposing corners of the bedroom.

In the living room, after his first glass of bourbon, Chip made a frank confession. "I like you, Howard, and I don't usually like foreigners." Howard hadn't said much more than a hello at this point, but Chip insisted, "We're gonna be friends."

"We haven't been invited anywhere since that dreadful dinner with the McCrosses," explained Trixie with a wink at Julia.

"It's hard to make friends, isn't it?" agreed Howard affably. After watching Chip survey the armchairs, pick the most comfortable one, put up his feet, and close his eyes, Howard wondered if Chip was going to make up for three friendless years by spending the night there.

"You know, Howard," said Chip, his eyes still closed, "back in the States we have an Irish Catholic in the Senate. Some people think he'll be our next president. Imagine that!" He sighed. "There was a time when an Irishman was treated like a Negro in the States."

"Imagine that, yes," echoed Howard, catching Julia's sharp glance. They had an unspoken agreement: they might indulge the opinions of guests, but they never tolerated bigotry.

"Now, you South Africans still have a good grip on the race situation." Chip grinned.

Trixie leaned over and slapped Chip's arm. "My husband, the bigot," she said with the expression of a wife whose husband arrives with a cold and proceeds to sneeze on the hosts. Judging from Chip's muted reaction, Julia guessed that slapping was common in their house. They obviously weren't called the Howitzers for nothing.

"I haven't said anything wrong, have I?" murmured Chip, winking at Howard as if they were long-lost Masonic brothers.

"Actually," said Julia, "we're both against apartheid and the things that go with it—racism, paternalism; that's partly why we left."

"Oh, it's pretty barbaric here, wouldn't you say?" Chip said.

"But it's not one race being barbaric to another," Howard replied.

"What's the difference? A guy can get his arm cut off for stealing a loaf of bread."

"And husbands can beat their wives for no reason at all," replied Julia, deciding that Chip was something of a brute.

Chip caught her glance and took another belt of his bourbon for support, while Trixie, amused that Julia had spooked her husband, adjusted her dark glasses and smiled.

Suddenly Chip turned to Howard. "Did you know that Trixie and I have a *mixed marriage*?"

"Really?" replied Howard.

"Sure. I'm a Polack and she's a plantation princess."

"I *never* lived on a plantation," snapped Trixie.

"Well, you were from down south, a regular green-eyed Florida beauty, riding bareback on the beach," Chip mused. "I had to buy that horse to get her to marry me," he told Howard.

"I miss that damn horse," Trixie said wistfully. She noticed her husband sniffing the carafe of olive oil. Chip poured a small quantity of the emerald liquid onto a wedge of bread, and savored it. Meanwhile, Julia noticed that Howard was staring at Trixie much as the English husbands had at the Christmas party, and she felt a pang of disappointment in him.

"Say," said Chip. "I love this bread!"

Trixie took the crust from his hand and tasted it.

"It's not the bread, honey, it's the olive oil. It's fabulous! Tangy!"

The Laments sent the Howitzers home with the olive oil, and they made emphatic promises to get together again soon, though Howard tolerated Chip's drunken farewell hug with reluctance.

"DO YOU THINK SHE'S PRETTY?" asked Julia.

They were in bed, with the lights out, for the postmortem. It was a cool night; the bedroom windows were open, and a faint voice chanted the Salat al-Maghrib over the city rooftops as the last red tinge faded on the horizon.

"Not really," Howard replied. When Julia didn't respond, he sensed his mistake. "Well," he stammered, "perhaps she's pretty in an American sort of way."

"Just say what you mean, Howard," said Julia in a faint voice, and Howard realized his blunder. It was a mistake to lie about Trixie Howitzer; her beauty was obvious. So he tried to make up for it as well as he could.

"Darling, I mean she seems gorgeous, but she'd probably scare the life out of anyone who saw her without her makeup. . . . You've never needed makeup to look pretty."

"You're just saying that."

"No," he insisted. "I mean it, honestly."

Julia's hand sought his under the sheets, and they reconciled. Nevertheless, Howard blamed the Howitzers for making the Laments feel vulnerable and, worse, plain.

JULIA, HOWEVER, WAS DELIGHTED to have found a more amusing friend than Mrs. McCross. A few days later, she invited Trixie to go shopping with her in the medina.

"I'm not the dusty, rustic type, Julia. Couldn't we find a museum or something?"

"But this is Arabia!" Julia said, spurred by Trixie's timidity to show off her own adventurous spirit. Thus, Julia led her dubious companion into the bustling heart of the old city, through hawkers, merchants, and clamoring children, until several handsome young men with eager smiles offered their services as guides. Suddenly Trixie's interest perked up.

"Julia, don't we need to hire one of these gorgeous young men?"

"Not really," Julia assured her. "I know *all* the sights."

"I'm sure you do," Trixie replied, "but why can't we bring one along with us anyway?"

"Because he'll spend the afternoon steering us to his uncle, who happens to sell rugs," explained Julia. "And the minute we get there, *he'll* disappear and his uncle won't let us leave until we've had tea and bought something we don't really want!"

Through the labyrinth they went, Trixie wobbling in her high heels while repeating an ardent wish for a bourbon. At one point they passed the Manhattan Club but did not dare go in for fear of encountering the English wives.

Julia steered Trixie farther into the medina until they found another little café. Elderly men, bearded and skullcapped, whispered at a corner table. The women pierced this sanctuary with their wide hats and exposed faces and relaxed at a table, until the old men stopped talking and stared at them.

"They don't want us here," murmured Trixie.

"Tough luck," replied Julia. "Our money's good."

Two of the elderly men started yammering and gesticulating to the man behind the counter. "Let's go," said Trixie.

"Because we're women?" asked Julia.

"Because I want a bourbon," Trixie replied.

By this time the owner had quieted the men; slinging a napkin over his shoulder, he made his way to their table and uttered a few words in Arabic.

"Sorry," said Julia. *"Parlez-vous français?"* But the owner only repeated his Arabic more harshly. The women were preparing to leave when a voice interrupted.

"Madam, so nice to see you again!" It was the man with the white suit. He turned and tipped his hat to Trixie, and took it upon himself to speak a few placating words to the owner. "He says women are not welcome without a male escort"—the gentleman grinned—"but I have solved the problem, as you can see."

Julia felt the most awful blush come over her face. "Actually, we were just leaving."

"*I'm* not leaving yet," remarked Trixie, drinking down the sight of this man with obvious pleasure.

"You wanted a bourbon," Julia reminded her.

Trixie smiled. "I'm not thirsty anymore."

The gentleman wasted no time introducing himself. His name was Mubarez; he was a Saudi businessman, dealing in professional kitchenware. Julia ignored the business card he offered her, but Trixie claimed it for her own.

"Madam," he said to Julia, "forgive me if I offended you when we last met."

"Julia," said Trixie, intrigued, "what on *earth* could Mr. Mubarez have done to offend you?"

"Nothing at all," Julia replied. But the gentleman was clearly smitten with her. When he repeatedly offered to take her sightseeing, Trixie turned petulant:

"Really, Mr. Mubarez, you make a girl feel like an ugly duckling," she said.

"On the contrary, madam . . ." apologized Mubarez.

"Can you tell fortunes?" she asked, extending a pale arm across the table. Thus challenged, Mubarez took her palm and wove her a silly story about fame, riches, and happiness.

"Now *her*," said Trixie, nodding mischievously at Julia.

"I don't want my fortune told," Julia protested, but Trixie insisted, and persuaded her to rest her hand in Mr. Mubarez's. The minute their fingers touched, Julia felt her heart quicken. Mubarez also seemed at a loss for words. With an apology, he released her hand.

Trixie looked fascinated and slightly envious of their exchange. "Well?" she said impatiently. "What's *her* future?"

The man looked abashed. "My imagination appears to have failed me," he replied.

"It's quite all right, Mr. Mubarez," said Julia.

Trixie seized this moment to pepper Mr. Mubarez with questions about his life, steering his eyes back to her when they strayed to Julia. Mubarez spoke of his youth, when he sold the fish he caught to the British submarine crews in the Gulf; of how his father sent him to a school for bankers' children in Jidda; and of how his trade had expanded from tin pots and pans to the stainless-steel equipment sold to restaurants and hotels.

When it was time to go, the women refused his offer of an escort. Julia's last glimpse of Mr. Mubarez was of his elegant suit, a solitary figure nursing a glass of mint tea.

Trixie and Julia walked back through the medina, sharing the giddy satisfaction of an adventure concluded. "What a dreamboat," said Trixie. Then she gave Julia a vexed glance. "I've never had to work so hard to get a man to look at me."

Julia smiled at the compliment, and then shame swept over her face. "Oh God, was I flirting?"

"Not exactly," said Trixie. "*I* was doing the flirting, not that it did me any good."

Julia whispered a confession. "He made me tremble."

Trixie laughed. "You made him tremble too, honey!" Then she noticed Julia's blush. "Oh, for godsakes, don't tell me you're one of those married women who won't even let herself *think* of another man!"

Julia reproached her friend. "Trixie, I adore Howard. No other man has ever interested me in the least."

Trixie laughed. "Sure! But there's nothing wrong with feeling your heart skip a beat, is there? Just for fun." She linked her arm with Julia's. "Honey, both of us know that Howard has nothing to worry about."

"HOW WAS YOUR DAY?" asked Howard that evening.

"Fine," Julia replied tersely. She was trying to coax Will to eat a few more bites of chicken, but he scampered across the tiled floor, leaving her crimson-faced in front of her husband.

"Anything wrong?" he asked.

"No, we just wandered through the medina."

Howard gave his wife a sober glance. "You know, I hear Trixie's a bit of a flirt. She has something of a reputation in the company. Poor Chip." Howard shrugged. "Not that he's any saint, but his wife's obviously a handful."

"I don't like Chip," Julia said.

"Well, so much for the Howitzers," sighed Howard, as if they were in accord, and the Americans had been put to rest.

SHE AND HOWARD HAD NEVER DISAGREED about friends before; it was uncertain territory in their marriage. Since Trixie did not call Julia, that might well have been the end of the Howitzers, if Mrs. McCross hadn't phoned Julia one evening.

"Julia, how are you? How's little Willy? Are you free for lunch to-morrow?"

"Sorry," said Julia, tossing several excuses into the explanation, but Mrs. McCross wouldn't be put off.

"I've been meaning to have a word with you, actually, about your *friend*. I think I speak for a number of concerned souls in saying that your American friend is not of our flock. . . ."

"Our flock?" repeated Julia.

After Mrs. McCross hung up, Julia realized that she wasn't of the flock, either. Furthermore, her time with Trixie had been the most exciting thing to happen to her in Bahrain.

IN DEFIANCE OF HOWARD'S JUDGMENT on the Howitzers, Julia invited Trixie to go to the beach with the boys. She revealed her plans on the day of the outing.

Howard looked dismayed. "But I thought we didn't like them." It was an artful challenge, a matter not of the Howitzers' character but of Julia's loyalty. But she had prepared a reply:

"I was thinking of Will, darling. Wayne is the only boy his age. Wouldn't it be nice for Will to have a friend?"

Howard had to agree.

Will and Wayne took to each other this time. They echoed each other's demands for cheese, or apple slices; and when sated, they trotted across the sand stark naked and set about building a castle. This task was periodically interrupted as the three-year-olds traded the rude words they knew. Will offered a few toilet expressions, but Wayne had a stunning supply of epithets; when he got to "bastard" and "son of a bitch," Trixie sprang up and whispered something in his ear. The boys quickly returned to their construction effort.

"He's not yours, is he?" said Trixie, watching Will.

"What?" said Julia.

"He's not your son. He's adopted."

Astonished at Trixie's percipience, Julia waited until the boys ran out of earshot before replying. "Yes, he is adopted."

"Wayne's adopted," Trixie continued. "Chip and I tried for years. After two stillbirths, I figured that something was wrong in here." She rested her hand on her belly.

"I'm so sorry," said Julia.

When Trixie said nothing, Julia wondered if her friend's hard edge had to do with these losses.

"When I first saw Will at your house," said Trixie, "I knew we had something special in common."

Julia barely had time to discuss this bond with her friend before the boys let out shrieks of alarm.

An oncoming wave crashed near their castle with a hollow roar, and the surf breached its walls, tearing down the tower they had draped with seaweed and fortified with mussel shells. Will looked to Wayne with tearful dismay, but his companion merely giggled and threw himself onto the ruins, leaving the perfect indent of his bare bottom in the sand. This provoked Will's first real laugh—a high, cascading gurgle of joy—so surprising to Julia that she bolted upright.

"What's wrong?" asked Trixie.

"He's never laughed before," cried Julia.

Soon, both boys were leaving impressions of their bottoms all over the beach, and howling in delight.

That evening, as Julia told Howard about the day, Howard realized just how strong Julia's attachment to Trixie had become. Soon the women were spending every day together. What most astonished Julia were the similarities in their teenage years: Trixie's parents divorced at about the same time and sent her to a rigid girls' academy. Yet both of them sought escape in romance—for Julia, it was the idealized sort, in Shakespeare; for Trixie, it was a succession of flawed men.

THEY TOOK THE BOYS to the ornamental gardens of the guest palace in Manama. The three-year-olds chased each other around the palms as Trixie made a confession.

"I've already told Wayne that he's adopted."

"Good heavens, Trixie, why would you do that? How could he possibly understand? A child needs certainty at this age; if he knows he's lost his parents once, he might worry that he'll lose you!"

"He needs to know the truth," Trixie replied. "There is enough lying in my life, Julia. I'm not going to lie to my son."

Julia said sharply, "Do you mean you lie to Chip?"

Trixie paused. "Yes—Chip prefers it that way. So I don't tell him he bores me. And I don't tell him that Wayne is the only thing keeping us together." She hesitated, dabbing the shadow of her black eye. "Actually, I *did* once tell him that, but he seems to have gotten over it. Let's face it: marriage is a compromise."

"A compromise?" Julia frowned. "I think of it more as a bond, an alliance. Howard and I love each other. We share a trust, and we share an adventure."

"Well, honey, you're a helluva lucky woman," Trixie replied.

Julia might have related Trixie's compliment to Howard if he had ever shown a hint of respect for Trixie, but the company gossip had hardened his opinion of her. For months he resisted any suggestion of a gathering between the families. Then, one evening, Chip appeared at the door to make a personal appeal; Wayne's fourth birthday was coming up, and they wanted to host a small dinner. This time Howard accepted—he couldn't deny Will's happy kinship with Wayne.

AS DUTCH OIL'S MIDDLE EAST MARKETING MANAGER, Chip Howitzer was entitled to a spacious pink villa with a dazzling view of the old city. At sunset, the dusty orange minarets turned golden and the city seemed magically suspended just beyond the windows.

But when the Laments arrived, the air had a chill to it. Chip opened the door, dabbing his nose with a bloody tissue.

"Good God, what happened?" asked Howard.

"I'll tell you later. Can I get you a bourbon? That's all I have—bourbon."

Trixie appeared behind her husband. "Chip never met a bourbon he didn't like."

"And you never met a *man* you didn't like!" Chip shouted in reply.

Julia quickly steered Will to Wayne's room, with Trixie following. They found Wayne wearing a pressed sailor suit and white patent-leather shoes; he looked pretty miserable, too. "Can I take it off now?" he asked.

"But you're the birthday boy," insisted Trixie, with a strained smile. Nevertheless, Wayne kicked off his shoes, and urged Will to join him in destroying the wood-block city he had built.

Trixie led Julia back into a spacious living room, where a number of large canvases hung on the walls. Julia recognized several flaccid nudes by an emerging English painter, and some small contemporary sculptures of walking figures.

"Trixie collects that stuff whenever she goes to London or New York," said Chip.

"Art keeps me *happy*!" Trixie shouted back at him.

"Oh, is *that* what keeps you happy?" Chip gestured for Howard to join him in his den, a small alcove with leather chairs and a zebra skin hanging on one wall.

Alone with Julia, Trixie whispered: "Chip found out."

"About what?"

"That dreamboat in the medina, remember? The one who tried to read your palm?"

"Mr. Mubarez?"

Trixie gave Julia the particulars of her affair with Mr. Mubarez, which began with an encounter in a hotel swimming pool. "But then the dope called the house when Chip was home. Chip said he would kill him and me," she said.

Julia gasped. "Well, did you apologize to Chip?"

"Apologize?" Trixie looked startled. "I have never apologized for anything in my life."

As the two women contemplated the ethical chasm between them, Howard came stalking out of Chip's den.

"Julia, where's Will?" he asked sharply.

Julia turned to indicate Wayne's room. Moments later Howard was heading out of the house, with Will squirming in his arms.

As Julia followed, Trixie gave her a tender peck on the cheek, leaving a smudge of lipstick that remained until Julia discovered it in the mirror much later.

Will sensed the tension between his parents, and put up a struggle at bedtime. Howard and Julia bore his demands for water and an extra kiss with unusual patience—anything was preferable to the discussion that lay ahead.

"Julia?" said Howard as he lay in bed, fingers pressed to his temples.

"Yes, darling?" replied Julia.

"What do you know about that man?"

"What man?"

"You know," said Howard, turning to face her in the darkness, "the one she's been sleeping with."

Julia held her breath for a moment. "Nothing, darling," she replied. And waited.

"I *thought* so," said Howard. "Trixie told Chip that the man who called was some fool who had a crush on *you*. I told him it was nonsense. Not only is that woman a slut but she's a liar, too."

It seemed wiser for Julia not to reply. In explaining her own encounters with Mr. Mubarez, she might risk the loss of Howard's trust forever.

Suddenly, Howard sat up in bed. "Julia, this has turned out to be a godawful place. I want to move. Get away from these people."

Julia remained silent. There was no point in defending her friendship with Trixie. But she took her husband's hand to show him that she loved him, and to prove that nothing Trixie said or did could change that. Perhaps things would settle down and Howard's fury would dissipate.

Howard took his wife's gesture as a concession that moving was, indeed, the right thing to do.

THOUGH TRIXIE TRIED TO END her affair with Mr. Mubarez, the poor fellow couldn't accept it. Trixie had pursued him, and he couldn't understand how she had the right to discard him, too. In a desperate attempt to understand his American siren, he bought a copy of *The Postman Always Rings Twice*. It posited a simple solution to his dilemma: murder.

Mr. Mubarez planned his solution using stealth, professional influence, and the resources of the local medina. His plans, however, went horribly awry, and the victim was an innocent bystander.

He had learned that Chip ate lunch at the Royal Oasis Hotel's four-star restaurant every Wednesday; Chip was particularly fond of the chef's carrot soup. Since Mr. Mubarez had supplied the Royal Oasis with all of its pots, pans, and baking trays, it was not unusual for him to pay the kitchen a visit. One Wednesday he brought with him a packet of powder, white in appearance, smelling vaguely of almonds, and slipped the contents into the soup. His plan would have worked perfectly if not for Mrs. McCross. She was served the first bowl and, after the third spoonful, complained of dizziness. A moment later, she pitched over onto the floor like a dead canary and the restaurant was closed.

When Julia brought flowers to Mrs. McCross during her convalescence, she found her in the hospital ward, knitting a sweater picturing Richard the Lionheart, and looking very pale. "Nobody can tell me what happened, but I can't help feeling that *that woman* is involved," complained Mrs. McCross.

After the incident, Howard was more resolved than ever to move, and Julia looked hard for reasons to persuade him to stay.

"What about Will, darling? His only friend is here."

"We'll make new friends wherever we go," Howard assured her. "*Better* friends," he promised.

Copper

"What we need in Rhodesia are smart young men with ideas!" said Seamus Thatcher, the eager recruiter who had flown three thousand miles to visit Howard in the Persian Gulf. It was a familiar line, but Howard was still flattered. The copper-mine company would give him a car and a house, and he would make enough money to save besides. So after a long chat over several drinks, and a handshake with Julia, and a signature on the dotted line, Seamus Thatcher moved on to seek his next recruit, never to be seen again.

"We'll have beautiful rosebushes," said Howard to Julia. "Darling, you'll be able to paint in the garden like Monet at Giverny!"

JULIA SAID HER FAREWELLS to Trixie at the beach so that the boys could have one last time together. Her friend's manner was brusque and skeptical; she hated good-byes.

"Where on earth are you going?" she asked.

"Albo, a copper town in Northern Rhodesia."

"Forgive me if I don't see the appeal," murmured Trixie. "What's in it for you? You'll be bored to death!"

Julia looked wounded by this remark. "I hope to paint again," she said, adding, "I thought you'd be happy for me."

Trixie fumbled for her sunglasses and slipped them on. "You're my best friend. Why should I be happy to see you go?"

The boys danced across the foamy rim of a wave, bumped into each other, and broke up into peals of laughter.

"We'll both write," suggested Julia.

"Horseshit!" Trixie sniffed. "I've never written a letter in my life, and I'm not gonna start now. My boarding school plucked a hair out of your head for every misspelled word, and two for incorrect punctuation. I told those bastards I'd never write again—and I've kept my word." Trixie readjusted her sunglasses. "You know, you're going to get tired of following Howard around."

"I love Howard," Julia replied.

"You know that's not what I meant," said Trixie. "But how long do you expect to last in a mining town?"

"What do you mean?"

"It's no place for a woman with brains."

"Neither is this," replied Julia. "Howard needs a new start."

Trixie shook her head. "America, honey, that's where you belong."

Dabbing at her makeup with a tissue, Trixie drew herself up and called to Wayne. "Come say good-bye, honey!" While the boys hurried over, Trixie placed a gift-wrapped package in Julia's hands.

Wayne blew a raspberry at Will, who replied by thumbing his nose. The women paused, debating whether to press the boys into a formal farewell, but it seemed too wrenching a prospect for either to bear. So they embraced each other, whispered good-bye, and parted on the sands.

"Is Wayne moving with us?" asked Will as he watched the two silhouettes depart.

"No, darling. He's staying here with his mummy."

Julia heard him mutter a small curse. She decided to let it pass this one time.

Later, Julia opened Trixie's present in front of Howard: six shot glasses with the Dutch Oil logo on them, and a set of cocktail stirrers.

"How touching," said Howard. "If she'd thrown in some boxing gloves and a few Band-Aids, we could duplicate their relationship completely!"

Albo

Before the current boom, Albo had not been much more than a bend in the road on a level plain of scrub that lay between two mountains. But world copper prices rose, and those two mountains appeared to be made of that lustrous element; now, in the late 1950s, Albo seemed ideally placed for housing the employees of the mining company. Quickly, the land was bought up and lots were established for the white management with charming street names like Eden Way, Arcadia Boulevard, and Utopia Place. The company also marked out an area for the black workers; these names were more practical: A Street, B Street, C Street. There were other differences. Management had terra-cotta roofs, and plaster walls with small leaded window-panes and heated floors, not to mention a sewer system. The black workers had none of these things, but they did get electric lights. That they were turned off promptly at ten was no cause for complaint; as one mining official noted, these were better houses than the damn lot of them had lived in before.

Howard had been hired to help the company design a water-filtration system to remove other useful minerals from the vast slag heaps left over from the extraction process. This was long before the idea of conservation became popular. Howard's job was to squeeze more money out of the situation.

Rose wrote to protest:

This can't be good for Howard's career! Why are you moving so soon? And why to Northern Rhodesia, of all places? How will I ever see my grandson? You know I don't drive, and I refuse to take that awful train across the falls. Moving is not a good thing for your marriage. Healthy marriages require stability! Consider the Tahitians—marooned on those islands, they don't stray. Their marriages last a lifetime.

Julia answered by sending an out-of-focus picture of Will, one calculated to throw Rose off his lack of a family resemblance. At three, Will had a thatch of fair hair and a round face, but his eyes had a sad cast to them, a hint of his forgotten father, Walter Boyd. Howard's waxen nose and high forehead, and Julia's raven-black tangle and freckled cheeks, were starkly different.

"You're keeping a secret from her, darling," Howard said. "Just the way she kept her divorce from you. Is that what you mean to do?"

"I don't know!" cried Julia. "I just won't be bullied by her!"

"What about him?" Howard nodded toward Will, asleep in the back of their new company car, a cherry-red Hillman with whitewall tires. "We'll have to tell him someday, darling. You know that."

GONE WERE THE MINARETS and the mullahs, gone were the dusty city and the cries of old men hawking their spices. Gone were the ornate plasterwork and geometric tiles, the smoky bazaar and the mystery of women hidden behind veils. Few of these details made sense to a boy of three, but their absence made him aware of the loss of his first friend.

Howard had promised Will lions, gazelles, elephants, and more, but the boy saw nothing but red earth and miles of nondescript road, looping telegraph wires and a vast and seemingly static sky.

"This is Joseph; he is going to be our cook."

The face had deep, dark, shiny cheeks and half-moon eyebrows. He offered his hand in greeting, but Will cowered. The man had a scar on each cheek, a horizontal slash that marred his perfect skin.

"Shake hands, Will," said Julia.

"Why?"

"Because we're all going to be friends."

The roses were tended by a gardener named Abraham, a Bushman with a crinkly face and squinty eyes who smoked a pipe and wore a green banana leaf on his head for shade on particularly hot days. A slow, contemplative worker, he had a brilliant way with roses. The beds along the street side of the house boasted enormous yellow blooms that were the envy of the neighborhood. Buck Quinn, who lived directly across the street, made an unsuccessful attempt to hire Abraham away from the Laments to attend to his own anemic rose beds.

Later, Julia asked Abraham why he turned the offer down.

"Take twice a man's money, he expects twice as big roses!" Abraham laughed.

Julia began painting her roses. But the sun was fierce, and her artistic determination wavered. There was no urgency here, no clock ticking. She dug up her old copy of Shakespeare, and found solace in *Twelfth Night*, where Viola, cast upon the shore of an unfamiliar kingdom, seeks her place among strangers.

During the day, Julia and Will passed their time learning the rituals of the company neighborhood. The children would play in a sprinkler during the hottest hours while the wives shared rumors about the mining company. As their cooks delivered lemonade and the gardeners manicured the flowers, Julia felt an uneasy sense of her own languid corruption. Just as Trixie had warned, she was dying of boredom. But she did not complain.

Howard would arrive home in the evening to an elaborate dinner, and as soon as Will was packed off to bed, they would make love. Howard had no doubt that the move had been a good idea. A month later, Julia announced that she was pregnant.

IN ADDITION TO BEING their nearest neighbor, Buck Quinn was one of Howard's superiors at the mining company. Major Buckley Kentigan Quinn, who had been a British officer in Pakistan during the war, had strong sentiments about Britain and the army; his house was a dumping ground for military surplus equipment: an old jeep, cankered with rust, slumped on the front lawn, and Buck's little boy, Matthew (Will's age), could often be seen running around naked with an empty cartridge belt slung over his shoulder. On alternate Sundays Buck invited the neighbors over for an outdoor meal with his wife, Sandy, a small woman who seemed to do all the cooking while her husband brandished a spatula and held court. Like a king, Buck would declare his politics while his neighbor, Marjorie Pugh, a woman with a long, horsey head and a mouth the size of an olive, agreed with everything he said.

Julia found Marjorie more offensive than Buck. Buck was in his sixties, a spokesman for an older generation entitled to its own stolid opinions. But Marjorie was about Julia's age; she should have known better.

"Hitler," Buck declared, "was a madman, but he could run a campaign!"

"Ooh yes," clucked Marjorie. "A terrible man, but I like his Volkswagens. Such nice little cars!"

"Nice cars?" Julia said. "The man killed millions, and you like his bloody cars?"

"Well," said Marjorie, "they run forever, don't they?"

While the neighbors ate his food, Buck paraded his opinions, as if trying to sniff out the radicals in the group. Julia tried her best to restrain her objections—an echo of her days in Mrs. Urquhart's classroom—for here she wanted desperately to fit in.

"One thing I learned in the war—you can teach these fellows to clean their artillery, build bridges, and wash their pants once a week, but you can't teach leadership! That's why the blacks need us here," Buck said. "They'll never rule themselves without bloody chaos breaking out!"

"Guidance, that's what they need," Marjorie cooed. She elbowed Julia. "Don't you agree?"

"You mean," said Julia, smiling, "as if we're their parents?"

"Exactly," said Buck. "*Somebody* has to tell them what to do!"

"Turn the veal, dear," said Sandy Quinn.

Obediently, Buck flipped the meat, and Julia caught Sandy's glance— a smile of insurrection.

"I've turned the veal," said Buck to his wife.

"Now you can talk, dear," said Sandy.

"Right," said Buck, "what was I saying?"

"But doesn't a good parent know," continued Julia, "when to let the child grow up?"

A boy screamed from across the garden, and all eyes turned to young Matthew Quinn, who, with Will, had advanced to the top of the rusty jeep, pants lowered to his knees in preparation for a pissing contest. The target was a large, sleeping calico cat.

"Go on," whispered Matthew to Will. "Piss on the cat!"

Will was about to oblige him when the calico darted up a tree. He was surprised that neither of his parents acknowledged his transgression. The disapproval on his mother's face was focused entirely on Matthew's father.

Buck chuckled at the boys' attempt. "I was just like that as a boy," he declared.

"He's still like that," murmured Sandy, shooting another glance at Julia.

"Then it can't be hard to imagine the black men you refer to as boys commanding others, just as you did," said Julia.

Buck laughed. "Nonsense!"

"Nonsense!" echoed Marjorie.

"Why is it nonsense, Marjorie?" snapped Julia. She was losing her patience and hungry, too, but wary of eating Buck's food. During this pregnancy, the smell of cooked meat nauseated her.

"Perhaps the blacks will eventually govern each other, but one thing I will never stand for is blacks governing whites. When has a white man *ever* benefited from a black man's wisdom?"

"Let's start with the rose garden," Julia replied. "How many afternoons do I see you begging my gardener for advice!"

At this, the former major of the queen's 6th Regiment of the Pakistan Guard thrust his spatula under his arm and strode over to her.

"I must ask you to leave, madam."

"Why? Because I disagreed with you?"

"Madam, you cannot eat at my table and insult me."

Sandy shook her head sadly. "God knows, Buck's family did enough of that during his childhood, didn't they, dear?"

Buck blinked at this attack from the rear.

"All I know is, one shouldn't bite the hand that feeds one," Marjorie said. "It's just not right."

"I haven't eaten a *thing*!" Julia replied.

"But you're pregnant. You *should* be eating." Marjorie was joined by a chorus of sympathetic sighs from the other women.

This had the combined effect of making Buck regret his ultimatum and casting Julia into guilt about not eating for the sake of her precious cargo.

"Forgive me, Julia," said Buck, giving Howard a respectful nod. "I had forgotten that you are pregnant, and therefore hardly in possession of your faculties."

As Julia considered replying to this, Buck reloaded, and addressed the group.

"I dare anyone to name one modern country where blacks have the vote that hasn't suffered a catastrophic collapse!"

"Here, here," peeped Marjorie, her little pit of a mouth wrinkled with sausage grease.

"There must be some country that's pulled it off," said Howard, with a gentle rallying glance at Julia.

"Not one," asserted Buck.

Julia suddenly remembered Chip Howitzer's remark about that Irish Catholic senator in the United States.

"What about America?" she said.

"America?"

"Yes, Buck. Blacks have the vote, and the walls haven't come crashing down. The trains run on time, the telephone system works better than ours, and they have the highest standard of living in the world. If the Americans can give everybody the same rights, why isn't it possible here?"

It was at this moment that Buck issued an urgent cry for more cold beer from the kitchen, and Julia's words were put to an end by hasty offers of assistance.

Tunnel to China

Julia's pregnancy seemed to be advancing at an unnaturally fast rate. Her doctor concluded that she was carrying twins, and Howard, whose fascination with the natural world knew no bounds, tried to demonstrate the creation of twins to Will by splitting a navel orange down the center. This was upsetting to Will, who was grappling with the prospect of one competitor for his mother's affection, and now had to grapple with two. He said that he hated oranges, and would never eat one again.

But later, when Howard picked up an orange and thrust a pencil through the center to explain the relative positions of Africa and China, Will felt a sudden twinge of compassion for his siblings.

"Don't do that, you'll hurt them!" he cried.

"Who?" replied his father.

"Them." Will pointed at his mother's enormous belly.

"Nonsense," Howard said. "*That* orange, I mean, egg, is inside your mother!"

"Howard, I think you're confusing him," said Julia.

. . .

ONCE A WEEK, ON MONDAYS, Abraham arrived with a headache, and spent the morning cross-legged in the shed, his hands pressed to his temples, moaning. In return for Will's fetching him a soothing cup of tea from the kitchen (so that Abraham's condition wouldn't be observed by Julia), the gardener was willing to answer any question that came into Will's head.

"Abraham," Will began. "How deep do you dig the flower bed?"

"Very deep. Roses like a deep bed."

"Did you ever dig all the way to China?"

Abraham winced. "China! It makes my head ache just to think about it, Master Will!"

From this, Will concluded that such an endeavor required a sound head, and a rose bed was probably a good place to start. He also learned to clutch his head in imitation of the Bushman's hangover. Julia noticed Will gripping his head this way at the dinner table.

"What's the matter, Will?"

"Hangover," Will explained.

"Bloody Abraham," Howard muttered.

Julia became deeply concerned with some of the other habits Will had taken up—sucking on a makeshift pipe made of a stick and a thread bobbin; stowing an old vanilla bottle in his back pocket like a hip flask; and stroking an imaginary beard.

One morning the cook complained that his daughter, Ruth, had nothing to do for the school holidays.

"Joseph," she said, "why don't you bring Ruth over to play with Will?"

And that was how Will met his first sweet love.

RUTH WAS AS GRACEFUL as a crane walking along the riverbank, and she was vain; under one arm she carried the lid of a biscuit tin to admire her reflection. As if this were not enough, she was two years older than Will and thus possessed all of life's important secrets.

"Ruth," Will would ask, "why does your father have marks on his cheeks?"

"His mother and father cut his cheeks to keep away evil spirits."

"Why does that keep away evil spirits?"

"I told you this before, Will"—Ruth would sigh—"evil spirits make their home in a healthy soul. If they see scars on the face, they think the soul is unhealthy, so they leave it alone."

"Why don't you have marks on *your* cheeks?" asked Will.

"Jesus watches over me and my brother, baby Joseph."

"And why is your skin dark?"

"Jesus made it that way," she replied, raising the biscuit tin to admire herself.

Will leaned over and peered at his own reflection beside hers. "And why is my skin different from yours, Ruth?"

Deciding that Will had exceeded his quota today, Ruth arched her long neck and replied:

"Because when Jesus got tired of making beautiful people, he made some ugly ones."

Stung, Will offered no reply, which was, of course, what Ruth wanted.

That Will could accept such an insult without comment was a credit to his love for Ruth. On the other hand, it provoked more questions for his mother.

"Will your babies be black?" he asked Julia.

"No, darling, they'll be just like you."

"Black babies are beautiful," he said.

"Yes." Julia smiled, thinking that this comment would shock her mother out of her shoes.

"Don't you *want* black babies?" Will continued, attempting to reconcile Ruth's widsom with his mother's, for it seemed to him that Julia's desire for more children must have been prompted by some dissatisfaction with him.

"I think white babies are beautiful, too," she said.

Will went back to Ruth and repeated what his mother had said.

"Yes," said Ruth, "but Jesus thinks black babies are *most* beautiful." She picked up her biscuit tin and gave herself a pretty smile.

"Why does he bother to make ugly babies, then?"

"For the same reason that when Baby Jesus got tired of making leopards and gazelles," explained Ruth, "he made a few warthogs and hippos: for a laugh."

"Oh," said Will. "But girl warthogs must think boy warthogs aren't ugly."

Ruth closed her eyes, growing weary of this discussion. When Will feared that he had lost her interest, he tried another tack. "Ruth," he said, "did you know that China's right on the other side of the world? If somebody dug a hole all the way down, that's where—"

"Will," Ruth interrupted with a yawn, "would you do something for me?"

"Of course, Ruth," he replied.

"Dig me a hole."

"Why?"

"I want to see a Chinaman," Ruth replied with an idle smile.

Will was only too happy to accommodate Ruth's wish, but he was troubled by one difficulty: "What if they're sleeping when I get there, Ruth?"

"That's good," said Ruth. "I want to see a Midnight Chinaman."

WILL BEGAN HIS HOLE in the flower bed, where the mulched soil was loose and easy to shovel; in a short time, he had removed two rose-bushes with blooms the size of mangoes. The deep red clay beneath was pungent and cool.

Ruth lay on a hammock, fanning herself with a banana leaf and imagining herself floating down a river, like Cleopatra, waited on by scores of adoring attendants.

"How's this, Ruth?" cried Will.

The brilliant whites of her eyes simmered in the direction of a boy waist-high in a hole.

"Deeper, Will!"

"How far is it to China?" Will asked, but Ruth was already sailing down the Nile.

. . .

THE GNARLED ROOTS of four prize rosebushes lay with their tendrils reaching up to the sky. When Abraham fetched himself a drink of water from the kitchen, he noticed their distressed positions.

"Will!" he cried, pointing with horror. "Your mother's roses!"

"I'm digging a hole to China!"

The distraught gardener rescued the plants and gave them a spot in another flower bed. He'd have spoken more harshly, but he had supplied the shovel for this deed while in the throes of a headache.

"What is it, Abraham?" said Julia when the gardener appeared at the kitchen door rubbing his temples.

"Master Will is digging a hole in the flower bed. I saved the roses, but . . ."

Julia waddled to the side door and called out, not wanting to step into the blazing sun.

"Darling, this digging can't be good for the flowers!"

"It's a hole for Ruth, Mummy. I'm doing it for her."

"A hole for Ruth?"

"I promised I'd make one for her," Will replied.

"A hole? Why?"

Will paused. "I love her."

This first evidence of her son's passion filled Julia with a sweet sense of pleasure.

"That's lovely, darling," she replied. "Try not to make a mess!"

Only when Howard saw the red stain around the bathtub that evening did he realize that his son had been busy in the garden.

"What's up, Will?" he inquired.

"Digging a hole. To China."

"Ah. Long way away, China is," replied Howard.

"How far exactly, Daddy?"

Pleased that his son was showing an interest in geography again, Howard took out an atlas and explained the relative positions of the continents, the depth of the earth's core, and the distance between Albo and Peking.

"So," Howard explained, "when we're having dinner, they're about to wake up for breakfast."

Will was delighted by this fact. Howard decided that Will was a born geographer.

Whether for geography or love, Will tore out of bed the following morning, determined to reach China before nightfall.

WILL'S ACTIVITY IN THE ROSE BED had soon been noted by every child in the neighborhood. As his visitors appeared at the rim of the hole, Will enlisted their cooperation. By nine-thirty, there were four shovels at work, along with a steady stream of yard-high recruits lugging buckets to remove the loose soil.

By lunchtime, several parents had heard of the project and were delighted that the children were busy in *somebody else's bloody garden.*

"Amazing—the Laments willing to sacrifice their flower bed," remarked Sandy Quinn, when little Matthew reported the length and breadth of the project. "Here, darling, take them some sandwiches!"

Another delighted parent eagerly offered up the contents of his garden shed—pickaxes, shovels, and forks.

Fortified, the children expanded their project.

Abraham took the day off. His headache had descended into a toothache.

The object of Will's affection had been enjoying a morning in the hammock between two avocado trees all this time. By early afternoon she had noticed the steady passage of visitors, and her daydreaming ceased. Feeling that she was missing something, she marched over to the edge of the hole, put her hands on her hips, and peered inside skeptically.

A dusty red face at the bottom of the pit gazed up at her.

"This is for you, Ruth," Will said, raising his arms.

A smile played on her lips. She was flattered. This was better than having slaves on the Nile.

"Give me a shovel," she said, sliding down the ladder.

. . .

HOWARD WAS STILL YOUNG ENOUGH to love the trappings of his job—the parking spot at the office, the name tag on his desk, and his engraved business cards. Now, as he rolled his cherry-red Hillman with the smiling chrome grille onto the drive of his beautiful white stucco house, he marveled at how far he'd come.

And this was only the beginning.

His father, in Howard's estimation, had gone nowhere. Ted Lament kept his job as a government requisition clerk for thirty years, and retired with a good pension. Other elderly folk would have taken this opportunity to see the world. But Howard's father spent his retirement commuting from his bed to his armchair. Like a stone in a ditch, mossy and embedded, he lived like this for ten more years. He died of a stroke—taking his wife with him three months later. Howard found fifty-seven cans of tuna in the kitchen cupboard, seventy cans of soup (creamed mushroom), twenty-five cans of baby peas, and sixteen cans of condensed milk. It appeared that his father had become a hermit, hoarding his food so that he could pass weeks without leaving the threshold of his four-cornered world.

Howard wouldn't make the same mistake. He'd already traveled more than his father had his whole life. And he wasn't finished by any means. The copper refinery was merely a stepping-stone to bigger things.

As the Hillman rolled silently up the driveway, Howard savored the quiet tap of the engine, the swish of another car going by, children laughing, the tinkle of a shovel. What an idyllic afternoon. Yes, this was a good life.

"Lament!" called a voice. Buck Quinn waved from across the street, limping from an old shrapnel wound sustained in Pakistan. Once a month Quinn blamed his injury for acting up, took a day off without shaving, and lurched around the neighborhood in his old combat fatigues, looking red-eyed and insane, quite the mad Englishman.

"Mr. Quinn," said Howard. "How are you?"

Quinn frowned. "Children have been busy all damn day. No peace."

"Have they?" said Howard, surprised at the major's uncharacteristic interest in children.

"Damn glad it's not in my garden," said Buck Quinn, taking a moment to scowl at his cigarette.

"Me, too," said Howard, tipping his head respectfully as he disappeared into the house. It was always a trap to get into a conversation with Buck Quinn—the man didn't need a spatula to pontificate.

THE PHONE RANG as Howard removed his shoes and padded across the cool tile, took a beer, and watched the bubbles tumble and rise in the glass. The children seemed louder now. Must be a birthday party.

"That was the Pughs," said Julia, shuffling into the kitchen with one hand caressing her tummy. "They say we've got their children."

"What would we want with their children?" shuddered Howard, giving Julia a kiss and her belly a pat.

"Apparently there's a party in somebody's garden. They claim it's ours," she said.

"Where's Will?" asked Howard.

"Playing with Ruth, I think."

"I'll investigate," said Howard, refreshed by his beer.

The flower bed was a pit as wide as his Hillman was long, and the roses were missing. Gathered around the rim were a number of small creatures covered in red dust, busily passing buckets from hand to hand. Howard blinked. This was his company house. By extension, this was a company garden and a company lawn.

Now there was a company hole, too.

"Look here," he said.

The activity around him didn't stop; nobody looked up.

"Just a minute!" he sputtered.

The little red creatures went about their activity as though he didn't exist.

A chant was spreading through the group.

"China! China! China!"

China? Something rang a bell. *"Will?"* shouted Howard.

"He's down *there*!" answered a voice, for the earthen faces were unrecognizable; a red hand pointed down into the hole.

Howard peered over, but the depth of the hole, and its darkness, made it impossible for him to see anything.

"Will! Come up here this minute!"

Howard looked at the faces sitting around the hole. Who could these urchins be? Then it occurred to him that they were the children of his colleagues at the company.

"What have you done to my flower bed!" cried Howard.

"What flower bed?" said one child.

"The one that's been ruined! You're a menace. The lot of you! Where are your parents?" he asked.

The busy circle of powdery faces offered blank stares. But one little fellow, caked in red clay, offered a shrill reply.

"My daddy said it was all right! He said you worked for him!"

Howard struggled to identify this impudent little savage and finally tagged him as Buck Quinn's son. Another face appeared at the top of the ladder.

It was smeared with red earth, the hair matted and dusty, but there was something familiar about the downturned eyes. "Hello, Dad!"

"Ah, Will," said Howard, momentarily relieved at being able to identify one familiar face. "Now look, Will, this has to stop."

"We're going to China, Dad!"

"Will, this is Mummy's flower bed!"

Titters spread through the group. The hole and the flower bed were opposing realities. They couldn't both exist.

"YOU'RE JUST LETTING THEM DIG?" asked Julia as they watched from a distance. The children around the hole were lifting up buckets of soil and chanting: "Chi-na! Chi-na!"

"If they want to go to China," snapped Howard, who had just opened his second beer, "let them go to bloody China!"

"What about the neighbors?"

"Damn the neighbors. It's their bloody kids who are responsible for tearing up the company garden."

"How can you let them?"

"One of those kids belongs to my boss, *that's* why!"

"What about Will? Where is his common sense?"

"Clearly," Howard said, "he's been brainwashed by these children. What an awful neighborhood." He sighed. "Why did we ever move here?"

A tall African police officer had propped his bicycle up on the garden path and joined the Laments. He removed his khaki pith helmet, dusted it off, and folded his arms to survey the scene.

"Who's responsible for this?" he asked sternly.

"Certainly not me," said Howard.

"Who is the occupant of this house?"

"I am," admitted Howard. "But I——"

"Then you are responsible."

"I'm so glad you're here," said Howard, trying a different tack. "You've arrived just at the right moment."

The officer removed his white gloves carefully, slipped them into his belt, and walked to the edge of the hole so that the shiny tips of his shoes reflected the activity around him. The children looked at him with interest, though they kept chanting and passing buckets.

"Chi-na, Chi-na!" they murmured.

The police officer, much impressed, peered down at the bottom of the hole and made a solemn declaration. "China is a long way away."

"Exactly what I said," replied Howard. "But they wouldn't listen to me!"

The policeman frowned, folding his arms again. "This hole is a menace."

"I know," Howard said. "I work for the copper mine."

"Then you of all people should know how dangerous this is!" fumed the officer. "What if someone fell? What if it caved in? What then? Who would be responsible?"

Howard wilted under the policeman's glare.

"If they dig the hole in the street it is my problem," the officer declared. "But this is your problem."

"Chi-na! Chi-na!" cried the children.

The policeman put on his helmet and gloves and mounted the bicycle.

"Isn't he going to help us?" asked Julia as the officer rode off.

"Bloody civil servants." Howard walked miserably back to the house.

THE AFTERNOON LIGHT SHIFTED abruptly as enormous blue storm clouds approached from the east. The sun was low in the west as the first glittering raindrops struck the soil, sending tiny clouds of dust into the air.

Will paused from digging, and peered up at the circle of sky at the top of the hole.

"It's a monkey's wedding," said Ruth.

"A what?" asked Will.

"When the sun shines and it rains too, it's a monkey's wedding," she explained.

Will felt a delicious shiver of delight as Ruth looked at him. She was covered with red dust, too, which made them members of the same tribe. A rumble of thunder shook the ground, and the chanting grew louder.

"Will," whispered Ruth, "we'll get to China soon!"

He gazed back at her, elated.

Lightning flashed in the distance, and a violent clap of thunder jolted them. Ruth grabbed Will's hand and they both giggled with fear and delight.

Against the advancing storm clouds, a line of red silhouettes danced across the garden. The wind picked up, whipping the red dust into tiny twisters, making the banana trees shake and flail like the long manes of wild stallions; then amber raindrops started pelting the dusty ground like diamonds. In another second, a shroud, black and billowing, engulfed the sun, swallowing light and sound until only the voices of parents could be heard, faint and anxious.

"Ruth! Ruth! Out of the lightning!" cried Joseph from the kitchen. Ruth squeezed Will's hand with a reckless smile and skipped away.

"Hurry, Matthew!" called Buck from the Quinns' house.

Raindrops pelted down fiercely, streaking the red dust from the children's faces. A massive flash of lightning ripped a seam through the sky with an instantaneous roar, and the deluge became a swirling torrent. Stripped of anonymity, the tribe was dissolved, and the children raced home to safety while the crimson earth became a molten stream which grew into a river that crested into a whirlpool at each sewer grating.

When the storm had passed, a clear evening sky remained. The stars glittered overhead, and the smell of ozone lingered—the perfume of cataclysm.

WILL COULDN'T WAIT TO SEE the hole the next day. Julia insisted that Abraham go with him, for fear that it had become a treacherous abyss. What they found, however, was a shallow muddy pit. The storm's torrent had filled the hole with loose clay and the detritus of its assault. By late afternoon, Abraham had repaired the flower bed, and in a week the roses had been replaced. Meanwhile, when the facts of the tunnel's origin were revealed, Ruth received a sound spanking from her father. Julia protested, but Joseph insisted that the clear culprit was Ruth's vanity, and what Sunday school couldn't cure, the palm of his hand would.

Julia and Howard were not so strict. Julia admired Will's romantic streak, and Howard, being a Lament, couldn't blame Will for wanting to go to China.

"After all," he said, "Laments travel! It's what we've always done," he told Julia. "Except, of course, for my father."

· · ·

WILL KEPT DREAMING ABOUT THE HOLE long after it had been filled in, as one does after a task unfulfilled. In one dream, he reached the end of the tunnel; when his fingers parted the earth, he discovered a starlit sky. A face peered into the hole—a slightly amused face with a full, Punchinello jaw, wearing black-and-white silk pajamas with a conical hat. His skin was as blue as a robin's egg, his eyes were small and almond-shaped; embroidered on his silk pajamas were yellow roses. He looked down at Will and laughed, a sound that echoed like a thunderclap.

"What was he?" Ruth asked, when Will explained the dream. "A clown? A ghost?"

"The Midnight Chinaman," said Will. "Don't you remember telling me you wanted to see a Midnight Chinaman?"

"Never!" She frowned, passing her hand vaguely down to her bottom; Joseph's thrashing had apparently adjusted her recollection of the event.

In Will's dreams, however, the Midnight Chinaman began to take on a more awesome and disturbing proportion. In one dream, he opened his mouth to laugh, and Will was sucked into the man's paprika-red throat. In another dream, he lurked by the windowsill when Will had been tucked into bed; he leaped into the room, and when Will tried to cry out, the Midnight Chinaman squeezed his throat so tightly that only a high-pitched whistle escaped.

Africa Divided

Rose was furious. Although she was actually the first to be told by letter from Julia, a chance phone conversation with a cousin had brought her the rumor two days before the missive arrived. Nothing stirred Rose's fury more than being kept in the dark, especially with regard to a matter as important as Julia's pregnancy.

Apparently I am the last to be told that you are expecting! I must assume that you are attempting to injure me by delivering the news in such a shabby way. Although I have not seen my firstborn grandson in four years, an error I blame on your inability to settle down, I cherish my right as Grandmother to see the boy. How can you deny me this?

Furthermore, your letter failed to fully explain when the twins are to be born, what their names will be, nor when I can expect a visit from my grandchildren. What have I done to deserve such appalling treatment?

Spent a horrid two weeks in London, which is even filthier than I remember. Oscar and I endured pubs full of cigarette smoke, and streets choked with petrol fumes. I shall never visit England again!

"We could drive down to Johannesburg for a week," Howard murmured. "And meet Oscar before she divorces him."

"I suppose," said Julia. "But I can't tolerate any of her nasty comments about Will not looking like the family."

"That's inevitable, darling. You can't expect Rose not to be Rose."

"Well, he's getting old enough to understand. I won't see his feelings hurt!"

"Then we should tell her about Will ahead of time."

"But I don't *want* to tell her," Julia protested. "What good will that do? Besides, we don't even have proof. Dr. Underberg's dead, and the papers don't say anything."

"What are you suggesting, then?" asked Howard.

"That we do nothing." Julia threw her fingers into her hair and pulled it back, as if her burden rested at the back of her cortex somewhere (which it probably did).

So it was that the rift between Julia and her mother came to separate half of Africa from itself.

THE INITIAL SIGNS OF LABOR marked Will's first view of his mother in a vulnerable light. To him she had always seemed unstoppable. Though never a graceful woman—she habitually banged the pots, broke glasses, and slammed cupboards as if she were sealing hatches in a submarine—these sounds, for Will, evoked domesticity and a secure home. The bone-jarring jolt of the oven door promised a fluffy banana cake, and the grating clash of copper on cast iron presaged the soothing delight of a mug of hot chocolate.

But when Julia went into labor she became very quiet. Her strained voice, her limp hair, her eyebrows knitted in concentration, worried the boy. He desperately wanted her to whack the cabinets with a poker just to reassure him that she would survive. She saw him to bed that night, but he settled only when she lowered his blinds with a comforting clatter and dropped his drawing pencils and crayons noisily into the crate under his bed. *That* was the mother he knew.

"G'night, darling!" she said.

"G'night, Mummy."

The Midnight Chinaman visited him again that night, arms folded, a mirthful grin on his blue face. When Will asked him what he wanted, the phantom put a finger to his lips and broke into a fearsome laugh that to Will's young ears sounded like wild trumpets.

He awoke to see Howard stubbing his toe on the foot of the bed.

"Ooof!"

"Daddy? You all right?"

"Fine"—Howard groaned—"but your mother has to go to the hospital, so I'm taking you over to the Quinns' while the babies are born."

"I want to be with Mummy," cried Will. But his father ignored these protests, wrapping the boy in a blanket and putting him over his shoulder for the walk across the street.

As Howard noted later, the evening wouldn't have been such a calamity if Sandy Quinn hadn't been visiting her sister in Botswana at the time. Though the Quinns' house seemed like a military surplus graveyard during the day, by night Howard entered a veritable fortress, thanks to the presence of an overweight male Rhodesian Ridgeback named Ajax—a fluke of nature who lacked all a dog's virtues yet possessed a surfeit of its vices: he was disobedient, hostile, flea-bitten, flatulent, mostly deaf, and absent any sense of smell. He barked all night, slept all day, and, because of his sensitive stomach, threw up repeatedly on Sandy Quinn's Turkish Hereke in the hall, for which crime he had been cast out of the house forever.

With his son dozing on his shoulder, Howard heard a menacing growl as he ambled across the Quinns' dark driveway. Pouncing, the hound locked his jaws on Howard's trouser hem.

"Down, Ajax," whispered Howard. "I can't play now." But the animal let Howard drag him, belly on the ground, claws plowing through the gravel.

"Bugger off, Ajax," Howard snarled.

Trying to keep his balance with both arms enveloping Will, Howard rapped on the screen door. There was a sharp pain in his tendon.

"Ajax, you . . . Ouch! Naughty dog!"

Perhaps because there was no response from inside the house, the old Ridgeback became more aggressive. Howard felt another nip at his calf.

"*Quinn!*" he shouted.

The dog's growls intensified, and Howard lunged against the door, shoulder against the button.

"*Quinn! Wake up, for Pete's sake!*"

Suddenly a light switched on, and Buck appeared, his .303 service rifle aimed through the mosquito screen. Ajax scampered away with an eighteen-inch swatch of Howard's left pant leg, shaking the life out of it.

"Put your hands up in the air slowly!"

"Buck, for chrissakes, it's me! Howard Lament!"

"Lament? Good God, man, what are you doing here?"

"Julia has gone into labor, and Sandy offered to look after Will," Howard reminded him.

"Oh, yes. Well, Sandy's in Botswana," Quinn replied, "but of course he can stay here!"

Meanwhile, Ajax, having lost his sense of direction in the darkness, heard Howard's voice and imagined he had found a second interloper. He spun around and lunged. Howard felt a stab of pain in his other calf.

"*Ouch!* Quinn, call off your bloody dog!"

"*Voetsek!*" roared Buck, and repeated the Afrikaans command until the dog dropped into a submissive crouch. Then Buck opened the door frame with the nozzle of his rifle.

Howard hesitated.

"Hurry up, man!" said Quinn.

"I'd be happy to come in if you'd point the gun *away* from my *son*."

Buck grunted, and lowered the weapon.

Howard laid Will down in Matthew's bed, then limped slowly into the kitchen. He reached down to his calf and found blood on his pant leg. Quinn frowned at the small trail of blood on the floor.

"Dammit, Lament," he muttered, "you're bleeding all over my house."

"Well, I wouldn't be if your dog hadn't tried to tear me to pieces!"

"Ajax would never hurt a white man . . ." Buck began, before he realized that the blood on the floor contradicted his point. "Sorry, old chum; here, I've got a first-aid kit."

"Never mind," said Howard impatiently. "I'll see to it later; I really must get Julia to the hospital."

Buck gave Howard a compliant nod. "Well, don't worry about your boy, Lament, he's safe here."

But this promise gave Howard pause. He considered Quinn's dog, and the rifle still in his hand. "Buck, how can you live like this? I could have been killed!"

Buck shrugged this off with an uneasy smile and followed Howard out of the house. "Ten percent of the population is white, old man. One day the other ninety is going to demand majority rule. I'm just keeping my guard up till that day comes."

"Well, if you see violence coming, why don't you just do your family a favor and leave?" Howard said as he limped across the yard.

For a moment, Buck said nothing. He stood in the darkness, shirtless and gray-chested, his jaw flexing and his breath billowing in the night air. "Can't do that, old man. A man's home is his castle, you know!"

THE TWINS WERE UNDERSIZED, though not nearly as small as Will had been at birth. Each one had a swath of black hair and puffy eyes, looking after the rigor of childbirth like a prizefighter after a tough bout in the ring. Will had expected fat, bouncy babies, but these two were scrawny; he felt a sudden surge of concern for his mother and demanded to see her.

"Follow me." Howard limped away, his left foot bandaged to the size and shape of a melon.

A long, diaphanous curtain surrounded Julia's bed. Will's heart turned as he saw what appeared to be the shadow of an angel above his mother's bed. But it was just a nurse folding up a blood pressure gauge.

"Mummy?"

Julia's hair was plastered down, and her lips, usually a brilliant Ektachrome red, were as faded as the bed linen.

"What's happened to you?" he asked.

"I've just had babies, darling," she said softly, confirming Will's fear that the twins, in their bid for life, had almost robbed his mother of hers.

"Are you dying?"

"No, Will, I'm fine. A few more days and I'll be up and about with you." Julia noticed Howard's uneven walk. "Darling, why are you limping?"

"Buck's bloody dog bit me."

"My God, are you all right?"

"I'm fine. But that man is a lunatic. Greeted us at the door with his old army rifle. He's expecting a revolution. We have got to get out of this country before everybody's up in arms."

Julia smiled, as if Howard were talking nonsense.

"Nobody's up in arms, darling. Besides, I've got two babies to raise, and Will. You'd have to find a new job. How could we possibly move now?"

The Devil's Spawn

Howard proposed that the twins be named Julius and Marcus. "Shakespearean names—I thought you'd like that!" he told Julia, who, nevertheless, expressed some skepticism about his choices.

"I don't approve of Julius because it's my great-grandfather's name, and he was an awful man . . ."

"Darling," Howard assured her, "nobody remembers your great-grandfather anymore." Howard wanted to settle the matter quickly, perhaps because he believed that their hesitation in naming the first Lament baby had contributed in some inexplicable way to his loss.

". . . and Caesar *kills* Mark Antony in *Antony and Cleopatra*."

Howard cast his red forelock back in exasperation, gazing at his watch, as though every minute that the twins spent unnamed brought them closer to crisis. "Darling, they're fine names. It's not as though I named them Cain and Abel."

"No, but you picked names out of tragedies. Couldn't you have picked comedies?"

Howard looked incredulous. "Malvolio? Bertram? Bottom? Darling, the names in the tragedies have elegance, gumption, history! We want these lads to have a destiny, don't we?"

As far as Will could tell, the twins' destiny seemed to involve a sacrifice of his own; his doting parents were helplessly distracted by their needs and demands. To his credit, he felt no regret, for he was the first child, and could never lose his place in the family. Yet he knew that he had lost the precious trinity of his babyhood.

Fortunately, Will was now old enough to have a life of his own. The following September, he started school, dressed in a uniform of khaki shorts and white shirt, with a wide-brimmed hat to protect him from the sun. After school, he and Ruth would practice their letters and numbers together. Sometimes Ruth would entertain him by acting out her versions of Old Testament stories; Will's favorite was Ruth's depiction of Delilah, which began with Delilah clipping Samson's long hair and making a wig out of it that made her the strongest woman alive. Ruth would don a mop head and prance around, raising chairs as if they were mountains.

JULIA REMEMBERED LITTLE of the twins' early months, for her time was spent attending to their needs, which were emphatic and unceasing. Their early conquests of the physical world were inspired by camaraderie and competition: Marcus used his brother's head in order to sit up the first time; Julius used his brother's sleeping body as a platform to hurl himself over the crib's side. When Julius made his first independent steps, Marcus thrashed in his sleep for three nights until he could match his brother, step for step.

In their second year, their temperaments diverged, lending credence to Howard's choice of names. Julius was full of grand plans, larcenous impulses, and combative urges. Marcus, on the other hand, was sentimental and sweet, but easily swayed by loyalty and brotherhood; Julius could persuade him to do practically anything. One afternoon Marcus became fascinated by the stinging ants that used to march in long columns around the house looking for dead birds to feed upon. When Abraham came to spray them with pesticide, Marcus burst into tears and wrapped himself around the gardener's leg, wailing hysterically until the poor gardener promised to let the ants live.

"That boy love the animals," he said.

But in spite of their natures, they remained abettors, concealing their plans in expressions that no one save Will, in some circumstances, could divine. When they were three, Abraham caught the twins trying to give one of his prized rosebushes a "haircut." Will saved the rest of the garden by suggesting that the twins behead the Pughs' azaleas instead. Marjorie Pugh was so upset that her little olive-sized mouth puckered shut whenever Julia crossed paths with her.

Of course Julia reproached the boys for their crime; but the twins sensed that in spite of her warnings, she was amused by their sabotage.

One night in the summer of their fourth year, the twins were unable to sleep, so Howard told them the story of the scar on his calf. He turned it into an epic tale of man against beast. Ajax became a hound of supernatural size, and Howard's role became heroic, for, after suffering his injury, he cast the villainous creature into the heavens, denting the stars to produce the constellation Canis Major.

In no time, the story became part of the family lore.

"Daddy," Julius would cry after dinner, "you be yourself and we'll be Ajax!"

"Oof! Not now," Howard would complain as his sons began sinking their teeth into his legs. "Ouch, stop that, Julius. I'm not in the mood!"

As with any legendary battle, it mattered not that the original combatants had made their peace. As far as Julius and Marcus were concerned, vengeance was required. As they went about their games, one subject always came up: how to teach Ajax a lesson. One hot Saturday afternoon, when the house was stilled by a mass of hot, immovable air, and the parents were sleeping and Will lay on the cool terra-cotta floor, drawing with his pencils, the twins concocted a plan that required nothing more than a can of syrup.

They crossed the quiet street and padded toward the Quinn compound; Julius carried the syrup while Marcus held one of Will's drawings—a sketch of a snake, tail in mouth, eating itself into nothingness.

"What if he won't eat his tail?" worried Marcus.

"Ajax will eat anything," Julius promised. "I'd eat anything with syrup on it, wouldn't you?"

"I wouldn't eat my own toes," replied his brother.

"If you were a dog you would," said Julius.

They waved to Sandy Quinn, who was driving Matthew to his piano lesson in town. (Sandy had discovered Matthew masturbating in the jeep one afternoon and decided he needed something else to do with his hands.) As the sun streaked through the lavender jacaranda blossoms, the twins found Buck Quinn sitting on the ground with the gears of his Land Rover's transmission laid on a tarpaulin in the precise order of their disassembly.

"Can a dog eat himself?" asked Marcus.

"Do you see what I'm doing here?" Buck growled.

"What?"

"This took three hours of careful work and concentration," lectured the major.

"You broke your car?" Julius asked.

"No lad, I'm repairing it," said Buck, his eyes glued to the careful assembly before him. "As long as I put everything in *exactly* the way it's arranged here, I shall have saved a fortune on a mechanic."

"Where's Ajax?" asked Julius.

"God knows," muttered Buck as sweat dribbled down the white stubble of his jaw. The twins gave him a wide berth.

They found the legendary hound sprawled a few yards away, legs quivering with dreams of rabbit in tooth, his bloodshot eyes rolled up, tongue hanging out, grunting and oblivious to the two titans. There was a buzz in the air nearby—the chorus of insects on a hot day; a deep, industrial hum emanated from the massive hornets' nest under the eave of Buck's bungalow.

Satisfied that the dog was asleep, Marcus took a flat stick and stirred the golden mixture. Preparing to apply it in dribs to the tail of Howard's four-legged nemesis, he paused, shooting a worried glance at Julius.

Julius, sensing his brother's hesitation, took the stick and proceeded to douse the dog's tail.

"Now if he eats his own tail, we'll see him disappear!" said Julius.

He clasped his hands in excitement, already thinking ahead to the next plan, which was to entice Mr. Quinn to do the same thing.

As the syrup sank into the hair follicles of the Ridgeback's tail, and a few molecules of the mixture entered the atmosphere, the pitch of the hornets' drone changed.

Julius clamped the lid back on the syrup can and waited while his brother poked Ajax out of his rabbit dream. A few striped prospectors descended to investigate, and Ajax flicked his tail at them. Now the cry went out, and within half a minute, a swarm had gathered around Ajax and he let out a belly yelp of surprise.

Marcus and Julius watched with giddy wonder as the game shifted. Instead of eating his tail, the dog was trying to get as far from it as possible. Forgetting his age, Ajax leaped over the rusty jeep, baying and howling, dove beneath the veranda steps, and spun through the billowing washing line, flailing the sheets with streaks of golden syrup plastered with six-legged dive-bombers.

Then the dog tore across Buck's tarp, scattering transmission cogs into chaos, and galloped across the street.

"You bloody . . ." roared Buck, cutting short his cry to duck under the tarpaulin as the swarm approached. When he emerged, there was no sign of the dog or the hornets. Buck staggered over to the twins, who were squatting by the storm drain.

"Where is my dog?"

Marcus and Julius pointed down. Frantic, Buck raised the grating to free the dog.

"Ajax! Ajax!" he shouted. "Come, boy!"

Misery wailed from the bowels of the sewer system.

But first a sudden cloud of hornets burst from the drain. Moments later, a fetid stench hurled the boys backward, as the slime-covered hound leaped up and out—he had found safety from the hornets in a pool of shit.

"Hell's bells!" shouted Buck as a new swarm surrounded Ajax—flies, big bluebottle flies, eager to bury their eggs in this walking shit-pile. The miserable beast now raced back toward the house, with Buck sprinting after him in a desperate attempt to bar the animal's entry.

"Those two are the devil's spawn!" Buck roared at Howard, later. "They can never come on my property again!"

THAT EVENING THE TWINS had a fine time explaining their adventure over dinner. Though Howard took delight in the story, Will sensed his mother's distraction. She had been listening to the radio, and he noticed her wrists braced against the countertop, as though a weight were pressing from above.

"Mummy, what's on the radio?"

Julia wiped the tears from her cheeks and turned from the window. "Nothing, Will."

"Why are you crying?"

"Oh God," she replied, putting her hand to her face, "oh my God."

The twins were still shrieking with laughter. They had come to the point in the story where the dog was covered in poop. But Howard had risen from his chair, and after exchanging a quiet word with Julia, he opened his arms and Julia rested her weight against him.

"What's wrong?" asked Will.

"A man died. Far from here. An American president," said Howard.

Will hadn't seen his mother look this vulnerable since she had given birth. The resignation in her posture was alarming, and he couldn't help asking more questions.

"Who? Who was that?"

"A man named Kennedy," she added, wiping her cheek.

The name was unfamiliar. To Will's young ear it sounded more like "Candy." A man died. Far from here. A man named Candy. It was tragedy even an eight-year-old could understand.

Even in a faraway little town like Albo, people suspended their small talk to discuss the assassination. The Laments noticed that everyone adapted the news to his own philosophy. Buck Quinn, for example, considered America the lawless expanse depicted in the few westerns he'd seen. "No respect for authority. *That's* what's wrong with America," said Buck when he heard the news. "Wouldn't surprise me if it was a black who shot the president."

"Actually, they caught the man and he was as white as you are," Howard replied.

THOUGH KENNEDY'S DEATH would be a seminal event for millions, Buck Quinn considered the election of Northern Rhodesia's first black president, in 1964, to be the defining event of his life. Within a year, Northern Rhodesia had become Zambia, and Quinn began talking about moving to Southern Rhodesia to stop the same thing from happening there.

Shortly after President Kaunda's election, Matthew Quinn came over to play with Will carrying a plastic hand grenade, with two cartridge belts strapped across his shoulders, bandolier style. Will begged to wear them, but Matthew refused.

"Promise to fight for the whites?" asked Matthew.

Will nodded.

"Even if you're the last man standing?"

Julia spotted Will parading around the garden with the belts trailing against his shins. She was horrified, and began to fear that her influence on her son was being subverted every time he ran out to play with the neighbors.

HOWARD WAS PLEASED that Julia was having misgivings about Albo. "*That's* why we have to go to England," Howard said. "The English are a bit more civilized and enlightened. As Shakespeare said . . ." Then he paused with an abashed smile. "What was it he said, darling?"

"'This happy breed of men,'" replied Julia, "'this little world,/ This precious stone set in the silver sea . . .'"

England was an obvious destination for the Laments. Her history was taught in every colonial school, her daily conventions cast across the globe, from boiled egg and toast in the morning to afternoon tea. You might say being British was its own religion, with the queen as its pope, the objects on its altar being the brand names found in every colonial grocery: Tate & Lyle, Marmite, Fortnum & Mason, and Crosse & Blackwell.

THOUGH JULIA CONCEDED that the family should leave Albo, she observed that whenever the Laments moved, they lost something. Howard, for example, always felt a little betrayed by Julia after Trixie's affair. He couldn't understand her affection for such a reckless woman, and Julia couldn't explain it to him. It was more than motherhood and similar childhoods they shared—Julia believed that she and Trixie were after the same elusive goal, and with more time together, they might have found the words for whatever it was. After Albo, Howard and Julia lost all affection for colonial society. And as the Laments packed for England, a few more things were mislaid—a gray stuffed elephant belonging to Marcus, a little magnifying glass Julius used to burn holes in newspapers on sunny days, and Will's lacquered Chinese pencil box. Though Julia promised to replace these items, one intangible thing was lost forever—no matter where he went after Africa, Will would always feel like a foreigner.

They boarded a train driven by steam engine for the almost-three-thousand-mile trip to Port Elizabeth. Will watched the engine's shadow flicker across the rusty shacks, trees, rocks, and pasture, while coal particles bounced against the windows of their sleeper like black hail. The twins endured this ride with limited patience, much screaming, and many bribes; it was only when Howard entertained the boys with stories of England—the slaughter of the Stuarts, and graphic details about the bubonic plague in London—that they were willing to let the miles roll by without complaint. They crossed the Victoria Falls, continuing south through Matabeleland and Bulawayo, past desert and bush dotted by herds of impala, wildebeest, and zebra, then across the border to South Africa, through Pietersburg and Pretoria, to Port Elizabeth, where the Indian Ocean and the Atlantic converged.

And Rose was waiting for them.

The Audience

Her hair was pinned tightly to her head, but Will recognized his mother's wild tresses and the freckles on her cheeks concealed under a powdery sheen. He also saw his mother in Rose's eyes—their direct and combative stare, now fixed expectantly on him. She was quite beautiful, he thought, though she possessed one curious imperfection—a bluish vein on the left side of her face, giving her beauty an icy cast.

"Now, Will, what do you say to your grandmother?"

Will sensed, from this greeting, that he should stand to attention.

"How d'you do?" he replied, on his feet.

This seemed to please her. But her reply was directed at Julia.

"Not a family voice, nor family features. Where *does* this child come from?"

"I'm from Rhodesia," he said. "But I've lived in Southern Rhodesia, Bahrain, and Zambia—and," he added with pride, "tomorrow I'm going to England!"

"Mmm, you've certainly traveled a *lot* for a boy your age," Rose said, glancing reproachfully at his mother.

She smiled at Will.

"Your parents," she continued, "never stop moving."

To Will, this implied the sort of wriggling a mouse or lizard might do. "I like your house," he ventured.

"He's certainly polite," murmured Rose to his mother. "And why didn't you bring the twins?"

"They'd tear your house down," said Will confidently.

"This is a hotel; it would hardly matter to me," said Rose.

"They're only four," said Will. "I'm almost nine."

"So you are," said Rose. "And for that, you get a present."

She led him into the bedroom, a plush bed covered by a white spread with blue blossoms. Everything was white and blue here—including his grandmother. On the dresser he noticed a silver-framed picture of a younger woman with the same icy beauty.

"That's for you," said Rose, directing Will's attention to a parcel on the bed.

"Thank you," he said. From the looks of the thin, rectangular bundle folded in brown paper, it wasn't a toy. By instinct, most children recognize the difference between a playful gift and a responsible one.

"Open it," she said, sensing his hesitation.

The box of ivory writing paper had the watermark of a castle; there were matching envelopes, and a silver fountain pen. Will looked to his mother, who gave him a sympathetic but cautionary glance.

"Thank you, Granny," he said.

"I mean for you to write to me, Will."

"I don't write very well," he said.

"You will improve if you keep at it," she said. "I will expect you to tell me what's what, *wherever* you are in the world. Promise?"

He nodded. "I promise."

God of the Sea

To a child, an ocean liner is confinement aboard a roaring kettledrum: the relentless throb of engines; fences and railings everywhere; first words learned aboard ship—DO NOT ENTER. The *Windsor Castle* seemed too regal a name for this floating prison with its overpainted pipes, hatches, rivets, and shiny brass levers. Most of all, Will feared the elderly folk propped in endless rows on deck, shrouded in blankets, stoic faces in sunglasses, their noses pasted white with lotion.

Once, when he broke into a sprint to get past them, Julia hoisted him up by his shoulders.

"Don't *ever* run on deck," she snapped through cat's-eye sunglasses and scarlet lips. "If you slip and fall here, you'll either give somebody else a broken leg or end up in the *inky black*." Julia was referring to the water, too far down to touch, an undulating expanse cut by the ship's steel prow, leaving an unraveling froth that for two weeks would trail the ship like a scar across the hemispheres.

"I won't ever again," Will pledged.

And she released him. In truth, Julia was more worried about the twins. Will had a certain athletic grace, but his brothers, at four, were clumsy like her, and also reckless. On the first day of their voyage, Julius split his lip on the gangplank railing and Marcus skinned his knee on the steel stairs. Furthermore, she doubted the competence of the ship's doctor. He was the gentleman at the captain's table who gulped down three glasses of sherry before the entrée (and four afterward). The burst capillaries in his cheeks confirmed his habit. This might not have bothered her if he had shown that he could at least hold his wine, but after the crème brûlée was served, he burst into song—a ballad about a one-legged prostitute in Singapore—and slurred the words.

"Will, I'm counting on you to keep the twins safe from the *inky black*."

"Yes, Mummy!" replied Will, embracing this role with all his heart. Perhaps, *perhaps* he could win back the adoring smile of those sun-splashed mornings when he was an only child. For now, Julia was inaccessible, harried, consumed with the challenge of keeping his siblings from misstep and mischief. And on those rare moments when she looked at her eldest, he feared the yearning expression he recognized in her eyes from long before.

So it was that Will made a silent vow to draw his mother's affection back with unceasing loyalty.

THERE WERE BRIDGE GAMES on the *Windsor Castle*, and Will was entrusted with the twins while his parents played with another couple— Mr. and Mrs. Perkins.

"How nice to have children," sighed Mrs. Perkins, a large woman with dimples where her elbows should have been, and small, widely set blue eyes. "I wanted children, but Horace didn't."

Mr. Perkins didn't reply to this. He was balding, with bushy nostril hair and round tortoiseshell glasses. Julia saw that Mr. Perkins was a child in adult guise: he sulked when Mrs. Perkins was diverted by conversations with strangers and caught her attention by tugging at her fingers like a toddler.

"But, darling, by not having children we've been able to spend our money on holidays," said Mr. Perkins, beaming. "Like this one! We're going to America next!"

Mrs. Perkins gave him an impatient glance. "Horace, the Laments have *three* children, and they're on holiday just like us."

"And we'd never have time for bridge," said Mr. Perkins. "We'd have to afford a babysitter, too!"

"*They* don't have a babysitter," replied Mrs. Perkins. "The eldest takes care of the young ones. That's the beauty of it." She sighed, and paused to regret a road not taken.

Howard sensed that Mr. Perkins was beginning to wish for different bridge partners.

AT THIS SAME MOMENT, Will was trying to prove his age and competence against the twins. Howard's shaving mug had been shattered in an experiment in the bathroom. One of Julia's slippers was stuffed down the toilet. Perhaps the twins needed to run around and blow off steam.

"If I let you out into the corridor, promise you won't run or scream?"

"No," said Marcus.

"No," echoed Julius.

"You *must* promise," said Will, "or we'll stay in here all night."

How eagerly they changed their answers. As Will unlocked the cabin door, and shrill cries launched their getaway, he realized Pandora's box was open, and he was compelled to keep them from harm. There were no stars that night, just a fuzzy smear of moon behind a scrim of clouds. Anybody who fell overboard would be lost for good.

On the upper level, the twins hurdled chairs and crashed into the last old gentleman left on deck. As his chair collapsed, the man's jaw fell open, and something rolled out of his mouth, down his chest, and across the deck and clattered past the railing, bouncing into the *inky black*.

Julius blinked. "Sorry."

The gentleman's mouth, blacker and inkier than the sea, hung open as he gazed around the chair.

"By teef! Where are by teef!"

"What?" said Julius. "I can't understand you!"

The gentleman turned to Julius and opened his mouth, pointing at his puckered maw.

"By teef!"

Horrified, the boy ran as far from the old codger's deathly gob as he could get. Moments later, Will chanced upon the old man, bent on all fours, hobbling toward the railing.

"Have you seen two boys, sir?" asked Will.

The old man looked up at Will, his eyes glittering and, touching his gums, gestured to the *inky black*.

"Gone. Gone. Down dere!"

Will gazed over into the darkness, hot tears filling his eyes. The old codger was now spitting into the wind, his arms flailing as if to accompany some ghastly incantation that sealed his brothers' fates. Grief-stricken, Will clutched the railings, his knees bobbing with fear, wondering whether he should take the leap himself rather than confess this tragedy to his parents.

Then he heard a giggle. Peering upward, he saw two beaming faces on the upper deck.

Impelled now by revenge, Will screamed their names out and leaped up the stairs, capturing each sibling by the arm just before he faced the brilliant white uniform of a ship's officer.

"What do you think you're doing?" said the uniform. Above the gold-braided collar was a strong chin, with a thin mustache above the lip, and, farther up, eyes as gray as the limitless horizon on a grim day.

"Nothing, sir," said Will.

"Not running?"

"No, sir. Finding my brothers."

"He was running after us, but he couldn't catch us!" boasted Julius.

Will shot Julius a warning glance and turned back to the officer.

"A big boy like you shouldn't be lying."

"I'm not lying," Will insisted.

"I'm the captain of this ship, and I don't appreciate lying. What's your name, then?"

"Will Lament, sir."

The captain smiled at the twins, offering each a peppermint drop from a little tin before replacing it in his gold-braided pocket.

"Look here, Will Lament, there will be no messing about on my ship. When I see your parents I'm going to speak to them about you."

The blush of injustice rose in Will's cheeks as he marched the twins back to the cabin.

JULIA AND HOWARD RETURNED with severe faces. The captain had spoken to them.

"I wasn't messing about," Will protested.

"You were supposed to stay in the cabin."

"They promised not to run!"

"You talked back to the captain," replied Howard sternly. "We're all very embarrassed."

Will ran to his bed, burying his humiliation in a pillow.

Later, when the children were in bed, Julia approached Howard. "Darling, perhaps the twins deserve some blame, too."

"It's his attitude that bothers me," replied Howard. "If he doesn't have respect for authority, how will he get on with people, darling?"

"Well"—Julia paused, thinking of Mrs. Urquhart—"I know how he feels; I didn't have much respect for authority at his age, either."

"And what good has it done you?"

Julia looked amused. "I don't know, darling. What *harm* has it done me?"

"Be realistic, Julia. *You* don't have to answer to a boss, to prove yourself on a daily basis. He'll have to do that one day."

Julia's smile faded.

WILL WAITED FOR HIS MOTHER to set things right at bedtime. He wanted to hear the slam of the door and the clatter of toys being stowed away. But a different figure came through the cabin doorway, resembling, for a brief moment, the captain.

"We have something to discuss," said his father.

"Why can't Mummy come in?"

"Because I have something important to say. You're becoming a young man, Will, and you need to show responsibility and respect. You can't be rude to the captain of the ship."

"I was just looking after them," Will replied, his voice muffled in the pillow.

Howard stood in the darkness, torn between the desire to embrace his son and the conviction that the boy needed some sort of punishment, if only to toughen him up—hadn't he asked for his mother just a moment before? What if he was picked on by the children at his new school? His mother couldn't get him out of that. Howard resolved to be more forceful with his son.

"No talking back. Go to sleep!" Howard said. Yet he couldn't leave without adding, in a whisper, "Sweet dreams."

Will waited for his father's footsteps to retreat before he began to cry. His sobs were drowned in the throb of the ship's engine, his sorrow unheard, unseen. When sleep overcame him, he dreamt about Ruth. It was an epic dream in which he relived the digging of the hole. There were hundreds of children helping this time, and he and Ruth aged into adults as they dug deeper and deeper. The hole took on the proportions of a cathedral as they neared the center of the earth; indeed, they were married at the altar by Abraham, crowned with a banana leaf, and by the time they neared the other side of the world, Will and Ruth had grown-up children of their own, and grandchildren. When they were close to reaching the far side, there were thousands of red children behind him, cheering as he and Ruth, hand in hand, climbed up to see a starlit night bursting with Chinese fireworks.

In the next cabin, Julia lay awake in the dark, feeling a different brand of indignation. Howard's words echoed in her ears: *You don't have to answer to a boss, to prove yourself on a daily basis.* What was the legitimacy of a job? Wasn't she a fine mother, educated, politically aware? Yet she hadn't held a job or touched a canvas in years. When was there time, when she was chasing after two impulsive toddlers? Had her presence in the adult world vanished into the *inky black*?

MR. AND MRS. PERKINS were seated when the Laments arrived for breakfast. Mrs. Perkins waved them over emphatically, while Mr. Perkins sulked behind his teacup.

"Tell me, Mr. Lament, are you going to the Equator Party?" The glance Mrs. Perkins cast at her husband suggested that this was a matter of contention between them.

"No, I crossed the equator as a teenager," said Howard. "A school trip to Athens," he added.

"Have *you* crossed the equator before, Mrs. Lament?"

"Never," said Julia.

"Then you must! It's glorious, a rite of passage. I've done it before, but Horace hasn't. He should, shouldn't he? Don't you think?"

"Get dunked in the swimming pool by a bunch of fairies in makeup and fish costumes," groused Mr. Perkins. "Bloody ridiculous!"

"Of course it's ridiculous!" Julia said. "That's just the point!"

As his wife began laughing with Julia, Mr. Perkins silently observed that he had no choice but to make a fool of himself—or risk looking like a man without humor. Bleakly, he wondered how many men like himself suffered such humiliations simply to sustain their marriages.

POSEIDON LAY SPRAWLED on the diving board, his body dyed turquoise, his hair a shaggy wig of shells, sequins, and seaweed. He drank from a goblet, spilling a rich, amber broth down his chin, and consulted a long green scroll.

The passengers to be initiated were all dressed in swimsuits, clustered in a group at one end of the pool, surrounded by the flamboyant deck staff: women in glittering emerald-sequined bikinis, and men in skimpy suits, their skin streaked with green dye, looking ravishingly exotic. Howard settled the boys into seats near the pool; Will was quite upset, for he recognized, behind Poseidon's green beard, the cold gray eyes of the ship's captain.

"Call up the first victim!" roared the ocean god.

As luck would have it, Mr. Perkins emerged first from the group of initiates. He wore a baggy pair of black trunks, which emphasized his pale skin and slack body. Will noticed that Mr. Perkins's ankles still bore the indentation of a very tight pair of socks: ridges ran up his pallid shins to a beaded line below his knees.

"Horace Perkins, as ruler of the seas, I welcome you to the Northern Hemisphere," said the steel-eyed Poseidon.

Reaching into a basket, the god produced a herring, its silver belly flashing in the sun, and without warning he plucked out the waistband of Mr. Perkins's trunks and dropped the herring inside. Bawdy laughter grew around the pool, ending, of course, with Mrs. Perkins's mirthful shriek. Will, however, shrank back against his father. He was not amused.

A couple of rude-looking potbellied fellows with seaweed wrapped around their privates stepped forward, grabbed Perkins by his wrists and ankles, and hurled him headfirst into the water. There was a rousing cheer from around the pool, capped again by his wife's uproarious squawk.

Mr. Perkins's disappearance horrified Will. He searched the water's surface for a sign of him. Not even a bubble appeared. There was a worried murmur from the crowd, then, suddenly, bursting from the depths like a cork out of a bottle, Mr. Perkins soared up, one hand clutching his glasses, the other raised in a triumphant salute. Everyone applauded this robust reappearance.

To Will's astonishment, a bevy of mermaids swam out to Mr. Perkins to escort him to the edge of the pool, their eyes made up with thick green eye shadow like Liz Taylor's in *Cleopatra*, their lips painted fluorescent pink, and their buoyant breasts cupped in shiny plastic scallop shells.

After one look at his rescuers, Mr. Perkins decided against leaving the pool. There was more laughter. Mrs. Perkins came down to the poolside to offer her hand. Perhaps Mr. Perkins's eyesight was compromised. He ignored his wife and paddled toward one mermaid, whose breasts were a bit large for the scallop shells. With a ravenous grin, he clamped his arms around the creature, planting his tongue firmly between her hot pink lips.

Without the use of their arms, they sank.

Mrs. Perkins's little blue eyes narrowed to points.

Moments later, the scallop shells floated up to the surface, followed shortly by the mermaid, gasping frantically for breath and faced with a dilemma, because while she needed to paddle with her arms to keep herself above water, her breasts insisted on surfacing as well, and modesty compelled her to use her hands to cover them, which sent her back underwater again. Several fully dressed male spectators, seeming to sympathize, eagerly dove into the pool to render assistance.

Horrified by the whole exchange, and noting that his mother was Poseidon's next victim, Will tore across the side of the pool to talk her out of submitting to this wretched rite.

"Mummy!" cried Will.

"No running!" roared Poseidon.

"It's all right, Will!" cried Julia.

But Will's feet slipped, he felt the crash of water around him, and the surprised faces of the crowd rippled and vanished as he sank into a silent, blue world, unable to scream or breathe. After a few moments he found himself sitting on the bottom of the pool, rays of light playing on his arms and legs, when, suddenly, a hatch opened near his feet. Will recognized the almond eyes of the Midnight Chinaman, smiling kindly, as if to reassure him that he was safe.

"Will?" said Julia.

He could see his mother in a yellow print dress and pearl earrings. There was a glow about her, and he wondered, briefly, if this was heaven. Closing his eyes, he heard one of the twins talking, and it occurred to him that either everybody had drowned or nobody had. He opened one eye and saw Marcus peering at him.

"Will he live?" asked Marcus anxiously.

"Yes, he'll be fine," Julia whispered.

"Are you sure he's not dead?" said Julius, with disappointment.

"I'm fine," said Will.

Suddenly there was a knock at the cabin door, and Julia turned to answer it. The captain entered, without his wig and sequins, his midriff wrapped in a diaphanous fabric streaked with blue dye.

"How's the patient?" he said.

Julia and Howard turned to Will, who shrank back at the sight of his tormentor. "Will, *answer* the captain," said Howard.

"Fine, thanks," said Will tersely.

"Will . . ." began Howard, and turned to the captain with an apologetic smile. "He's clearly not himself."

"I'm fine," insisted Will.

"Darling, you owe the captain some gratitude," Julia said gently. "He saved you from drowning."

"Swam down to the bottom and carried you up," added Howard. "You owe him your life."

WILL BROKE THE SEAL of Rose's box of watermarked paper and issued the first of many letters to his grandmother. It was sent from Gibraltar:

> *Dear Granny,*
>
> *I almost drowned while Mummy and Daddy played cards. And the captain wears a dress.*
>
> *Love, Will*

On the last week of the cruise, the Laments were invited back for dinner at the captain's table. Will was reluctant to attend, but when he saw his parents getting dressed up, he relented; Howard wore a black suit and tie, Julia a red velvet dress. Will thought they were the most glamorous couple on the ship. The twins considered the dinner an ordeal, refused to eat, and slipped under the table to fight. Howard dragged them out, kicking and crying, for a breath of air on the outside deck. Within moments, Will saw his father running past the dining-room portholes in pursuit of them.

Meanwhile, the captain and Julia shared a conversation for a few moments. With increasing disapproval, Will watched them talk. When Howard sprinted past the doors a second time, Will interrupted their conversation.

"My dad's running on deck," he remarked. "Aren't you going to arrest him?"

LATER, AT BEDTIME, Julia confronted Will about his rudeness, but he was sullen and unresponsive.

"Will, please speak to me," she said in exasperation.

The boy chose this moment to say what was really on his mind. "Why do we always have to move?"

"We don't *always* move, darling."

"Granny says we do."

"Perhaps we move more than other families," conceded Julia. "You know what Daddy says: 'Laments move—it's what we do.' "

Will frowned. "Will I have to look after the twins wherever we go?"

"Of course you will. A family looks after itself," she said. "Especially a traveling family."

He considered this fact for a moment. "How will I *ever* make a friend if I'm always looking after my brothers and moving away?"

"You'll make a very good friend in England, I promise."

But as Will closed his eyes and his breathing settled, Julia told herself that in the future she would make no promises she couldn't keep. As she rose, she noticed that Marcus was still awake.

"When will I die, Mummy?" he asked.

"Oh, you'll live a long life, Marcus, a very long life."

"How long? How old will I be?"

"I can't really say, Marcus."

She recognized Marcus's panicked stare; he hated uncertainty. Perhaps that was why he clung to Julius, who never seemed to have a doubt about anything.

Julia smoothed back his hair and secured his covers. "You'll be a hundred years old, Marcus. People will be traveling in jet packs and having holidays on Jupiter's moons. We'll all have robots serving us tea and washing our dishes."

"A hundred. I like that," said Marcus, turning over and closing his eyes.

Julia stood. Two minutes after making her resolution, she'd broken it. All to get a boy to sleep.

Southampton

It was a grim day when the Laments arrived at Southampton terminal. Rain, cold drafts, and blotchy gray skies greeted the *Windsor Castle*. Will peered at the awkward current of chinless people in damp tweed jackets and raincoats, frowning apologies as they bumped and jostled one another through clouds of cigarette smoke. He cast a wistful glance back at the enormous ship.

Howard looked for a taxicab while the family sat on a chaotic heap of suitcases.

"You'll love England," said Julia to Will, as if sensing his regret, or, perhaps, her own.

As the last passengers came down the gangplank, Will yearned for time to halt, for the travelers to reverse their steps, shed their overcoats, put on their swimsuits, jump back into their deck chairs, back to the bridge tables, back to the quoits and the volleyball courts, and back to the middles of their mystery novels.

"Can we go back?" asked Marcus, echoing Will's sentiment.

"You'll love England," Julia repeated as she urged them toward a waiting taxi. Will noticed that her nose had taken on a shiny redness in the damp cold.

"No, I won't," snapped Julius.

"I won't, either," added Marcus.

Howard slammed the taxi door shut. Will peered through the foggy glass and spotted Mr. Perkins standing on tiptoes to plant a kiss on Mrs. Perkins as a fresh downpour swept over the windshield. And the Laments went forward.

England

You'll Love England

"Oy, mate!" screamed the ruffian in the playground on Will's first day at Avon Heath School. Will had never been called a mate before, so he said nothing. Undeterred, the boy stalked up to Will's ear and shouted the greeting again with a fiercely hot and foul breath.

"Oy, mate, where'd you come from, then?"

"Africa."

When the boy heard this, his feral features dropped with surprise, and a singular paradox struck him.

"Africa? Why aren't you black?"

"Because I'm not," Will replied.

The ruffian switched to a freckled squint. He looked Will over, down to his shins, as if a few inches of black skin between his knees and ankles would explain the contradiction. Ian Rillcock was the same height as Will, wearing the same school uniform—gray shorts, white shirt, blue-and-gold tie. A runny egg stain on the blazer almost concealed the school emblem.

The ruffian's black shoes were worn into holes at the toes; his knees

were scabbed. His teeth were small, yellow, and as pointed as matchsticks.

"I can beatchu up, y'know!" the boy snarled, raising one scabby fist
with black fingernails.

"Why?"

"Watcha mean, why? Gimme any lip'n I'll beatchu up!"

They were interrupted by the Bell Boy, an older classman who
sprinted across the schoolyard ringing a hand bell to mark the beginning of class. The ruffian forgot Will and joined the small mob pursuing the Bell Boy. Will watched the older classman lead his assailants
directly into the path of an elderly teacher. With a chorus of apologies,
the mob did an about-face and tore into the building.

"You'd better introduce yourself," said his teacher, Mr. Brogh, a
mountain of a man with an alarmingly small head, gray-framed
glasses, and a wattle neck that would have made a pelican envious.

"I'm Will Lament."

"And I can beatchu up!" shouted a voice from the back of the room.

"Who said that?" barked Mr. Brogh. When no one owned up, the
class was given lines: *I will not speak out of turn.* "Written one hundred
times," murmured Mr. Brogh in a malevolent singsong.

Will raised his hand.

"Yes, Lament?"

"Do *I* have to write lines, sir?"

"No exceptions, Mr. Lament," sang Mr. Brogh. "No exceptions."

"But I didn't—"

"Until someone owns up, *everybody* writes lines, Mr. Lament. Is
that understood?"

Justice in Mr. Brogh's classroom was severe. As Will discovered a
week later in history, it was also arbitrary.

"The best way to remember Henry VIII's wives," said Mr. Brogh,
"is by reciting the following: 'Divorced, beheaded, died; divorced, beheaded, survived'!"

A nervous titter came from Raymond Tugwood, in the front row.
Then a blackboard eraser came flying from the back. It missed Will by
an inch and smacked Tugwood, leaving a white smudge on the back of

his head that remained for the rest of the day. Will glanced back, and noted Rillcock's gloating squint.

"Who spoke? And who threw that?" demanded Mr. Brogh.

"I spoke, sir," said Tugwood, giggling. Now Mr. Brogh narrowed his eyes at the back row, but Rillcock's head was nowhere to be seen.

"So *Mr. Nobody* threw it, eh?" Mr. Brogh said. "I'll have no speaking out of turn in my class." He looked at Tugwood. "You think beheading is funny?"

"No, sir." Tugwood nervously twirled a lock of hair at his temple.

"Perhaps you'd like a demonstration."

Raymond Tugwood glanced at the yardstick in Mr. Brogh's hand and uttered another nervous giggle.

"Who wants to behead young Mr. Tugwood?" barked Mr. Brogh. "How about Mr. Rillcock?"

"Wif pleasure, sir!"

"There's a good lad," Mr. Brogh sang, his massive wattle throbbing over his necktie.

Directed to stand, Tugwood began twirling his hair with feverish intensity.

"Step forward, Tugwood."

Tugwood kneeled on the floor, poised over a makeshift chopping block fashioned from two volumes of the *Encyclopaedia Britannica*. The eager ruffian stepped forward and raised the yardstick over Tugwood's neck. Mr. Brogh fastened a black scarf over Tugwood's eyes.

"Traditionally, the victim's eyes were covered," murmured Mr. Brogh. "Ready, Rillcock?"

The rest of the class watched bleakly as Rillcock dug his matchstick teeth into his lower lip, delighted at the prospect of delivering further torment to Tugwood.

"When I say 'three,' Rillcock shall execute Tugwood in much the same way that Anne Boleyn was beheaded on Tower Hill in 1536. Understood?"

"Right, sir," said the ruffian.

"One."

Will noticed Raymond Tugwood's finger twirling his shoelaces now, round and round. Though his eyes were concealed, the boy's mouth hung open in dread, his fingers bone white at the nails.

"Two."

Rillcock raised the yardstick a little higher, and Will was suddenly reminded of a ghost story Howard had told him, in which the victim was frightened to death by nothing more than a pinprick.

Tugwood's pants turned dark in the crotch; a puddle widened around his knees.

"Three."

But before Rillcock could bring the yardstick down, the teacher seized a third volume of the *Encyclopaedia Britannica* from the bookshelf and swatted Rillcock on the side of the head with everything from Corpuscle to Dynasticism. The force of the volume sent Rillcock flying across the room.

"*That's* what you get for throwing things and not owning up to it, Sonny Jim!"

A quivering heap on the floor, Rillcock let out a woeful sob and proceeded to vomit his breakfast in the corner—in Will's fascinated estimation: boiled egg, bacon, toast, and a few peas and carrots.

The children stared like the audience of some grotesque circus in which two acts had simultaneously failed; their grim faces turned with disbelief from Rillcock's vomitous breakfast in one corner of the room to the puddle of Tugwood's piss in the other.

The next morning, Tugwood's mother showed up in the playground. A wiry woman with a scarf tightly bound around her face, she clutched Raymond by the hand and shook her fist at the children, spit flying from a hole between her teeth.

"You leave my boy alone, you little buggers!" she cried in a thick brogue, while Raymond twirled his finger around the lock of hair at his temple.

Rillcock's punishment seemed only to drive him into repetition. In the bog—the boys' toilet—famous for its long trough painted with shiny black tar, he sang the same song over and over in the stall.

Oy c'n beatchu up, Oy can, Oy can!
Oy c'n beatchu up, Oy can!

Nevertheless, Rillcock had piqued Will's curiosity about his own heritage. Will brought it up while touring the new supermarket on High Street with Julia.

"Mummy, why aren't we black if we're from Africa?"

This brought on a pained glance from his mother, who could see that his question was the mere tip of an iceberg.

"Well, darling, most people *originally* from Africa are black. But you, being descended from Irish who colonized Africa in the turn of the century, are a *white* African."

"So I'm Irish?"

"Well, darling, you're not *exactly* Irish. Our ancestors were known as *planters*—English who were *planted* in Northern Ireland in order to establish a British presence in the area. The Irish would most definitely consider us British."

"Then I'm British!"

"Well, not exactly, darling, because that was a long, long time ago; the British would consider you a colonial."

"A colonial?"

"Yes, somebody from one of the colonies."

"Then what *am* I, Mummy?"

"Well, you're from Southern Rhodesia."

"So that's what I am."

"And what am *I*, Mum?" asked Marcus.

"You're a bugger," said Julius, who had heard Mrs. Tugwood's diatribe in the playground.

"That's enough, Julius!" snapped his mother.

At that moment, Will happened to spot a familiar face in the frozen-food section: the ruffian, poised like a cat, teeth together, hair on edge.

"Oy, mate! I can—" But the boy was interrupted by a fierce woman with a vast head of curlers whose thunderous voice made the fish sticks tremble on their shelves.

"Ian! So 'elp me I'll belt you round the ear 'ole if you don't catch up this minute!"

Chastened, the ruffian mimed the rest of his warning, and hurried after his mother, who was heaving cases of baked beans into her shopping cart.

"Friend of yours, Will?" asked Julia.

"No. Enemy," he replied.

"Didn't he call you 'mate'?"

Will sighed at the paradox. "'Mate' means friend *or* enemy here, Mum."

Next afternoon Rillcock followed Will home, dancing behind him, fists boxing the air, but whenever Will whirled around, the ruffian leaped clear of him.

When Will turned in to his front garden, Rillcock stopped at the fence post, calling after him in triumph.

"Now I know where you *live*, mate! I'm gonna get all me friends, and—"

"And do *what*?" cried Will with exasperation. "Throw up on me?"

"YOU MAY HAVE TO FIGHT HIM," said Howard when the matter reached the dinner table. The twins had finished their food and were running around the table while Howard, Julia, and Will tried to talk. Eventually, Marcus tripped, Julius landing on top of him.

"I can't believe we're talking about English boys!" said Julia. "Who are these little savages?"

"Just boys," explained Howard, watching Julius sink his teeth into Marcus's calf. Marcus let out a scream.

"He won't leave you alone until you fight him, Will," said Howard.

"Fighting is no solution," Julia snapped as she wrenched the twins apart and clamped her feet around Julius's waist so that she could wash off Marcus's bite wound.

"Look," Howard said, "this boy obviously wants to establish a pecking order. If Will does nothing, this brat will torment him all year."

"You mean I *have* to fight?" said Will.

"Yes, you do," said Howard.

"No, you don't!" countered Julia.

Howard blinked at Julia. "If he doesn't, he could become a pariah, an outcast."

"You're behaving as though we're still in Africa," Julia said. "This isn't some backward wilderness!"

"It has nothing to do with being *backward*," replied Howard. "Boys are simply man in his most primitive stage: tribal, savage, and violent."

"I should have had girls," Julia said.

"I wish we'd never moved," Will said.

"Cheer up," Howard told his son. "All you have to do is bash this boy's lights out."

Convinced that Will needed to adapt, to toughen up, to be more English, Howard proposed boxing lessons in the backyard. With the twins cheering them on, Howard taught Will to feint, to guard his face, and to punch. Julia watched from a distance, arms folded and lips pursed, until her anger came to a boil.

"And what about the twins? Are *they* going to have to bash some-one's lights out, too?"

"The twins are different," snapped Howard. "God help the little bugger who tries to bother *them*!"

At that moment, Will lowered his fists and his father clipped him, sending him flying backward against the door of the old coal shed.

"Gotta keep your guard up, Will! Up you get!" Though the boy staggered to his feet, he avoided his father's glance and tore into the house. Julia heard footsteps, and the slam of Will's door.

"See what I mean?" said Howard. "Soft."

Julia looked up at Will's window. "Howard, I don't think he likes being told he's different."

"What do you mean?"

"He looks at himself in the mirror. Marcus's hair is getting like mine. Julius has your face. I think Will feels like the odd man out."

"Well, once he can fight, he'll fit in just fine."

Julia gave Howard a lingering glance. "And how are you fitting in, Howard?" she asked. "At work, I mean. You haven't said a word about it."

"Fine," he replied. "Absolutely fine, darling."

TWO MONTHS PREVIOUS to their arrival in Southampton, Howard had flown to England in search of a job. Nigel Barr, the man who had recruited him, lacked the enthusiasm of Gordon Snifter or Seamus Thatcher. Mr. Barr didn't travel; he merely sat in the headquarters of Pan-Europa and interviewed applicants every twenty minutes.

"*Another* South African," he said with a yawn, punching a small brass-and-wood chess clock to begin the interview. "Lament, eh? I was in a college production of *The Laments of Father Jeremiah*. Ever heard of it?"

Howard shook his head—a critical mistake, because Mr. Barr insisted on relating the plot, as well as his brief dramatic career. "I was the youngest Captain Hook in history. When I was fifteen, my voice ripened into a baritone, you see, and that made me *indispensable* in pantomime!" Soon Mr. Barr's baritone was interrupted by the ding of the chess clock, followed by a rap at the door from the next candidate. Howard made a desperate plea as Mr. Barr escorted him out.

"I can be very flexible about salary," he said.

"Duly noted!" boomed Barr.

There were interviews at seven other companies, but no job offers. Howard feared the same South African Mr. Barr had alluded to was preceding him at each company to which he applied. So when a letter came from Pan-Europa offering a position in a branch office in Denham, Howard wasted no time accepting and booked the family's tickets to England.

The offer wasn't generous by English standards. It was a little more than he had made in Albo, but in Albo his house and car were free and he could afford a cook and a gardener. In England, only the rich could afford a staff.

Pan-Europa delivered oil and natural gas to cities all over Europe. It was a massive conglomerate, a household name, just like Dutch Oil. The logo was everywhere, on trucks and gas tanks and on ads in the tube stations, but Howard felt little pride this time around. The field office in Denham was essentially a bunker with stacks of file cabinets and blank walls, except for a stuffed perch mounted on a plaque, high above his desk; on rainy days the fish appeared to smile—in recollection of better days, perhaps. That was Howard's guess, at any rate. He would do no designing for Pan-Europa; they had plenty of smart young men to do that. Howard was dispatched to check on complaints from Pan-Europa clients. He examined pipe fittings, assessed faulty valves, and arranged for repairs by qualified Pan-Europa engineers. From a row of twenty three-ring binders full of names of engineers from Düsseldorf to Edinburgh, Howard would select the right man for the job and issue precise instructions.

When clients complained to him about shoddy equipment, he was supposed to be unflappably polite. Poor Howard Lament. This was not a job for a bright young man with ideas; this was a job for a bureaucrat. What had happened to his plan to irrigate the Sahara? What about his design for an artificial heart? How had he—a rebel, a bright young man—managed to derail his career?

He had spared his sons the dubious honor of being privileged whites in an impoverished African nation (and the risk that they might follow their peers to another repressive white supremacist regime). He had given up an affluent life for a semidetached house in Avon Heath with a clear view of his neighbor shaving every morning, plus a secondhand Morris 1100 that refused to start in the rain—which seemed to fall nine days out of ten. Worst of all, there was a feeling in the pit of his stomach that his soul was trapped.

Only the fact that he had a loving wife and three healthy boys could comfort Howard. And perhaps the fact that at thirty-five he was still a relatively young man. Things would surely improve.

God Help Rillcock

On Fridays there was a service held in the mornings in the school canteen. While everybody sang "Jerusalem," Will tried to imagine what kind of Jerusalem would fit amid the dreary council houses on Ratcliffe Street, with their postage-stamp front lawns and battered TV antennas. He recalled climbing a cedar tree in his back garden the previous day, surveying the rows and rows of semidetached houses, like sliced bread, separate yet jammed together so closely that the knife's incision seemed purely theoretical. No wonder the British spread out across the globe—they wanted to get out of these rotten little buildings with their narrow staircases and lilac floral wallpaper and rattling plumbing.

Mr. Brogh read from the Old Testament while cooks banged pots and released unforgivable odors from the school kitchen. The Friday menu was a particular assault to the senses: frozen fish cakes, glutinous gravy, flavorless peas, and, for dessert, scoops of brilliant purple blancmange—a substance with the texture of whipped petroleum jelly, sickeningly sweet, whose color would be all the rage on Carnaby Street in just a few years.

After Mr. Brogh's reading, it was Tugwood's turn to read a passage from the New Testament.

"He that is without sin among you, let him first cast a stone at her," read Tugwood. As if on cue, a milk carton flew across the room, smacking Tugwood on the back of the head. Mr. Brogh smiled coldly, his gaze fixed on the back row. There was no doubt that he would make the offender pay.

Will had been all set to fight Rillcock, but the sermon gave him pause. Wasn't he, in effect, casting the first stone? What had the ruffian actually done to him but deliver a few threats? How would he get into the kingdom of heaven if he bashed Rillcock's lights out? As he pondered this issue, a fierce rictus caught his eye from the corner of the room.

"*Oy c'n beatchu up,*" it mouthed.

There was nothing in the passage about Jesus having to put up with some feral squirt on the way home from his lessons. Will tried to imagine Jesus kicking the crap out of such a kid. No, Jesus would have appealed to his father for advice. And what would God have said? "Turn the other cheek"? What if the little swine kept up the attacks? What would it have taken for God to say, "Bash thine enemy's lights out, my son"?

On the way out of the service, Will saw Rillcock elbow Raymond Tugwood, who let out a squeal. Mr. Brogh promptly grabbed both boys by the ears and dragged them across the playground, their feet helplessly dancing on tiptoes.

The following Wednesday, Julia needed to get the car serviced in town and arranged for Will to walk the twins home from school. Usually the twins tore off when Will showed up, but this time they were waiting meekly by their schoolroom, conspiracy in their faces.

"What's wrong?" said Will.

"Nuffink. Nuffink's wrong," said Marcus. The twins had dropped their Rhodesian accents for the local Cockney variation. Curiously, Marcus kept one hand pressed to his cheek.

"Nuffink's wrong wif 'im," added Julius.

Marcus nodded. "Nuffink."

Will pulled Marcus's hand from his cheek, revealing a bluish crescent just below his right eye.

"What's that, then?"

"Nuffink."

Will turned to Julius accusingly. "Did you punch him in the face?"

"No," replied Julius, adding with a sidelong glance, "and it wasn't Rillcock, neither."

"What?" said Will.

The twins shared a look.

"Oh, nuffink," said Julius.

"You're sure it wasn't Rillcock?" asked Will.

"Yes, 'cos I promised Rillcock not to say so," said Marcus earnestly.

A BLOCK AHEAD, Will saw Rillcock jabbing his fists and dancing, as he described his conquest of Marcus to two mates. Will recognized them as Digley, a popular boy with a mop of blond hair that fringed his eyebrows, and Ayers, a lean fellow with a sneer, whose trousers were always an inch or two short of his gangly ankles.

Will felt a flash of hesitation; the last thing he wanted was a group fight. If they ganged up on him he'd be the one pissing on the floor for the rest of the year. But he glanced at Marcus's black eye and felt a new surge of outrage. His father was wrong. The twins did need his protection; thus, his conscience was soothed, his blood was up, and God help Rillcock.

"Whatchu want, then?" said Rillcock.

"You hit my brother."

"Who, me?" Rillcock blinked.

Will turned to the twins. "Marcus, is *this* the one who *didn't* hit you?"

Marcus paused to unravel the question; it was getting so complicated. "Um, yes."

"Hold on, that means I *didn't*," said Rillcock.

"He told you to say he didn't hit you, right?"

"Yeah," said Marcus.

"You idiot!" said Rillcock. "What I told you to say was—"

"Right," said Will, and before he knew what was happening, his fist flew at Rillcock, who sank to his knees so quickly that Will wasn't even sure he'd touched him. Then Rillcock began to writhe, and his lips turned scarlet.

Will looked with horror at his victim. The scream at the base of Rillcock's throat was still waiting to escape, like a teakettle preparing to whistle.

"Think he needs a doctor?"

"No, he's fine. He *always* does this," Digley said.

Ayers winked at Will. "The best part is when he screams. Play football?"

"Yes," said Will.

Rillcock's bottled scream finally escaped, and echoed against the houses. *"Ahaah, ahaah, ahaaaaah!"* he cried. "I'm telling me mum!"

"Your mum will wipe the floor with you when she hears you beat up a little one," Digley retorted.

The ruffian cowered, as if afraid his big-headed mother was going to materialize out of thin air. Will took his brothers by their hands and headed in the direction of home, but Ayers called after him.

"Lament! See you at the game in the morning!"

ON THE WALK HOME, Will sensed a change in his brothers. They stole envious glances at him, and at his swollen left hand.

"Will really bashed his lights out," said Marcus.

"Blood everywhere," cooed Julius.

"Will could bash anybody's lights out, I bet," said Marcus.

Will said nothing. His heart was still thumping; a giddy, victorious sensation rose into his temples. And even though his limbs were still trembling, he felt brave. He knew he had the twins to thank for his courage.

Julia took stock of their injuries when she arrived home. "Well?" she asked. "What happened?"

"Nuffink," said Julius.

"What's that bruise on your face, Marcus?" she said.

Marcus adopted an expression of noble suffering. "It's nuffink, Mummy. Rillcock didn't do it and Will didn't beat him up!"

Julia was silent for a moment. Finally, she fixed Will with a surly eye. "Well, you don't have to look so proud of yourself."

Stunned, Will replied indignantly, "But Dad told me—"

"That's enough, Will. Off to your room."

Will felt his stomach roll. Didn't he deserve praise? Hadn't he protected his brothers? Since his father was away on business, Will chose the only remaining outlet for his frustration: he wrote to his grandmother.

Dear Granny,

We like England even if Mummy has to cook and garden by herself. She says it is a more civilized country, though the toilet makes noises at night and a boy punched Marcus. They want us to be as good as Jesus here, and then go to heaven. Since I have punched the boy back who punched Marcus, I suspect I will not go to heaven. Mummy says this is nonsense, and says many people go to heaven who do awful things like the Crusaders who killed lots of people, and soldiers in the last war.

Love,
Will

A most unusual boy, thought Rose. Even through the eyes of a nine-year-old, she was gratified to have some insight into the life of her daughter. It struck her that Julia had no shortage of strong opinions, a quality Rose believed her daughter had inherited from her, and which Rose regarded as a defect.

The First Holiday

"**W**e're going to see a bit of history," Howard explained to the twins.

"Will there be anything to eat?" asked Julius.

"It's something truly marvelous, a two-thousand-year-old fortress built without stone!"

"I hope the food's not as old as that," Marcus griped.

It was an economical holiday: a motoring trip to one of England's great sights. Maiden Castle was a hill fort that dominated the countryside near Dorset. A plain of grass was all that was left, protected by rows of deep concentric ditches visible most clearly by airplane. It had finally been conquered by the Roman Vespasian in A.D. 43. The thirty-eight tribesmen protecting the fort were buried in their battle gear by the Romans as a gesture of respect. Howard loved these facts and did his best to convey his enthusiasm to the boys on the way there.

The twins were unimpressed. It wasn't until one of them jabbed the other with his elbow that they began a backseat vendetta that made the trip interesting, and forced Howard to pull the car over and rearrange the seating so that Will was between them. Will invented a game that involved naming a food for every letter of the alphabet. After sausages and tarts, however, there was an impasse because nobody could come up with a food that began with "u," and the boys fell asleep from mental exhaustion.

IT WAS DURING THIS LULL that Julia made another attempt to find out about Howard's job.

"How's work, darling?"

"Oh—fine," said Howard.

"Really?"

Howard felt her skeptical gaze.

"Well, it's not perfect," he admitted. "But what job is?"

"What's wrong with it?"

Howard said nothing. There was a fork up ahead, and a similar choice in his brain. He veered to the left and flicked on the windshield wipers as a fresh downpour pitted the glass.

"Tell me, Howard."

Howard could have complained about the money, but the trouble wasn't just that—it was about his derailed aspirations. If he admitted that the job was a big step down, that he'd made a horrible miscalculation, what would Julia think of him—the man who'd once planned to irrigate the Sahara?

"Well, it's the money," he said.

"Yes, I quite agree," said Julia. "You're not paid what you're worth."

"Money doesn't go as far in England as it did in Africa."

"I know," said Julia. "We *were* very well off, weren't we, darling?"

"Yes." Howard swallowed. Julia gave his hand a comforting squeeze.

There was a silence as Howard steered through a roundabout and continued west. The houses were falling away behind them now. The castle plain lay ahead, broad and green, and the clouds were churning overhead as Julia and Howard contemplated their good fortune gone by.

"Darling?" said Julia. "Why don't you ask for a raise?"

"I can't yet; I haven't been there long enough."

"But you're doing a wonderful job, aren't you?"

"Of course, but one doesn't ask so soon."

Julia frowned at being reminded that she knew little of such things. Howard had a boss. He knew.

The sun appeared as they got out of the car. The boys tore ahead, leaping and rolling down the steep embankments, then charging up the adjacent incline until their war cries were shrill with exhaustion. Eventually, they reached the level grassy center of the site, the figure eight of windswept field, surrounded by widening channels. Without walls or towers, it was a naked fortress. Julia leaned against Howard, her arm folded tightly in his as a breeze swept up her hair and snapped at his trouser hems. For a few moments, they contemplated this humble plateau in their alliance—the friendship Julia had lost in following her husband; the shabby job Howard had taken to support his wife and family. No one had warned them about these sacrifices. In spite of this imperfect union, however, Julia and Howard still believed that they shared the same course, and followed the same stars.

While the twins simulated a bloody clash between Briton and centurion, Will lay on his back, trying to imagine himself living in a settlement here, a thousand years ago, when people stayed in place, before there were cars and ocean liners.

Hitler's Ghost

Will scored a few goals during the morning football games. This brought him the favor of Digley, who invited Will over to his home, a council house he shared with his mother and older sister. The lawn was tiny but immaculate: a perfect square of green, surrounded by a well-clipped hedge.

Up the narrow stairs, Will peered into the doorways—there seemed to be a different floral wallpaper and cat in each room.

"My dad was in Egypt during the war. It was *bloody hell*," explained Digley. "He climbed the Pyramids. Died of pneumonia after I was born. But he left his uniform. Has a big hole in it where he was stabbed with a bayonet!"

Digley showed him the uniform. His father must have been a giant; it was a big green thing, woolen and coarse (and covered with cat hair). Will poked his finger through the bayonet hole and felt a deep, morbid shiver. Digley's bedroom was strung up with model airplanes. A fat tabby gazed at them from Digley's bed.

"That's Goebbels," said Digley. Turning to the air display, he added, "And this is the Battle of Britain."

Digley could identify every plane in the German Luftwaffe, from Messerschmitts to Fokkers, and all the British planes, too. Digley's mother was a nurse; his sister was a supermarket cashier. At teatime, Digley rummaged through the fridge, while Will tripped over the milk saucers that seemed to be placed in every corner.

"Bloody hell," said Digley. "Nuffink to eat!"

They shared a plate of chilled baked beans.

"This is probably how they ate in the war. But better than a belly full of lead, eh?" Digley grinned.

"WERE YOU A SOLDIER IN WORLD WAR TWO, DAD?" asked Will later, at dinner.

"No—I was too young," said Howard.

"Didn't you even have a uniform?"

"Not even a uniform. I was only fifteen when the war ended."

Will's disappointment lingered into bedtime.

"You're lucky to have such a young father," said Julia when she found Will brooding under his covers.

"I didn't *say* there was anything *wrong* with it," he shot back.

"Of course you didn't," said Julia. "But let me remind you that war is a terrible thing! We left Africa because of the possibility of war. In war, lots of people die or lose legs and arms. You should be happy to have a father in one piece!"

Though Will loved his father, he thought one small bayonet wound wouldn't be so bad.

"Bloody hell," he muttered.

"First fighting, then swearing like a sailor," complained Julia. "I don't think your new friend is a very good influence." Julia had other complaints about England—the odor of roast beef, the awful knocking sound when she turned on the water, the twins' constantly runny noses, the lack of sun, the surfeit of rain, and the queen's obnoxious corgis.

"Even Buck Quinn's Ajax was preferable to those revolting little creatures with their stunted bodies!" she exclaimed.

. . .

SADDLED WITH THE BURDEN of a young father who had no experience in World War II, Will compensated by becoming an expert on the Battle of Britain. He memorized every plane in the Luftwaffe, and every major air battle. He built his own plastic aircraft models and hung them all over his bedroom. He pored through comics bursting with salty army characters who dismissed the Jerries and Japs with a few well-placed kicks and punches, destroying the Axis with plucky camaraderie. In the comics Hitler was a bumbling stooge surrounded by foolish yes-men with silly accents and ridiculous salutes. Hitler's life story could be found in a dozen books in the school library; Will knew Hitler's hat and shoe size.

"Some people think he's alive and living in Argentina," said Digley.

"I think he's dead," said Will. "Swallowed a suicide pill."

"My dad and Hitler wear the same size trousers," said Ayers. "If he *is* alive, I'm going to go after him when I'm bigger, steal his pants for my dad, and blow him to smithereens."

"He'll be dead of old age by then," said Digley.

"Then I'll have to kill his family, and his pets," replied Ayers.

"Not his cats," warned Digley. "Cats are innocent creatures."

Digley and Ayers took Will across the wheat fields on the outskirts of the village to climb around the crumbly concrete platforms where the anti-aircraft guns were placed to shoot down German planes. It was almost twenty years since V-E Day, and World War II was still everywhere.

One morning, Julia beckoned to Will to watch the television. "Never forget this," she whispered. "This is history."

On a screen the size of a tea saucer, Will watched the fuzzy images of a horse-drawn carriage on its solemn procession through London. Winston Churchill's funeral was being covered by the BBC. Will was old enough to fear death, and the dark carriage with its black horses became lodged in his nightmares. The Midnight Chinaman seized the reins, and when he cracked his whip, the horses' eyes glowed and steam billowed from their nostrils.

. . .

THE WAR PRESENTED WILL with some puzzling moral questions.

"Dad, why did Hitler want to fight Britain?"

"He was collecting countries," explained Howard.

"What's wrong with that?"

"It's greedy," said Julia.

"Was it greedy for England to collect Ireland, Scotland, and Wales?"

"Yes!" snapped Julia. "It's an awful thing!"

"Then why did you say that we'd love England?" asked Will.

Howard frowned. "What's that got to do with Hitler trying to rule the world?"

"Well, what about England ruling India, Canada, Australia, and all the African countries?"

"Look at the time." Howard yawned. "Off to bed."

Later, Julia complained about the conversation.

"What's this obsession with Hitler?" she said. "Can't he find something more *positive* to think about?"

"Well, you have to admit, the damage is everywhere. Will's school was bombed; have you noticed that his classroom is actually a Quonset hut?"

The woman at the sweet shop entertained Will with stories of the blackouts, when whole towns would strike out their lights to prevent the German bombers from spotting targets from the air.

"Can't everybody get over the war?" asked Julia one morning when the twins started making machine-gun sounds at each other in the garden.

"Not until something bigger comes along," Howard said. He was drumming his fingers to the song on the radio—the Beatles, singing "All My Loving."

WILL INVITED DIGLEY TO HIS HOUSE. Julia roasted a chicken. Digley told Will that Julia had a nice smell and looked like a movie star, like Natalie Wood.

"Well," remarked Julia later, "perhaps he's not such a bad fellow after all."

Will met Digley's sister the next time he visited Digley's house. Elaine Digley wore cat's-eye glasses and served warm baked beans on toast for dinner. Her hair was teased up into a beehive, her fingernails were an inch long, and Will couldn't take his eyes off her.

"I like your cats," he said.

Elaine smiled. "You're a charmer," she said. Then her false upper eyelashes got tangled with her false lower ones and she disappeared into the bathroom to fix them.

"She's got fake everything," whispered Digley. "Even her tits. Stuffed with tissue. Everything but her bottom. That's real enough. She sat on Goebbels, broke his leg."

After dinner they waited outside for Julia to pick Will up. Digley hunted for cigarette butts in the street, lit one, and offered Will a hit.

The taste was foul, but the wickedness of the act appealed to Will.

"I can summon the spirits," declared Digley as he studied the smoke curling from the stub. "Good ones and evil ones. The spirit world is everywhere."

"Who have you summoned?" asked Will.

"My dad, of course," replied Digley. "All the time. Told me he met Churchill and Hitler. Had tea with Genghis Khan and his naked harem . . . ugly as hell, all of them, my dad said, all with bottoms as big as my sister's."

Will wondered if the Midnight Chinaman was a spirit, too, and if his nightmares were actually attempts by this specter to sabotage the family. He remembered the Midnight Chinaman beckoning from the bottom of the ocean liner's swimming pool, and shuddered.

In the distance, he saw the old gray Morris approach with Julia at the wheel.

"You'd better toss that," said Will. "There's my mum."

Digley flicked the cigarette away and winked.

"You're a good man, Lament."

Will smiled. For a moment, he felt as though he actually belonged. No longer the foreigner, he had a place beside Digley, his mate.

Will's Second Love

Sally Byrd sat in the front row, directly in front of Mr. Brogh, who had taken such a liking to Will's class that he was accompanying them into their next year. When she smiled, Sally's mouth turned down rudely, and her eyes hinted rebellion beneath a moptop haircut. Only Sally could turn an agonizing history lesson into an uprising. And the astonishing thing was that Mr. Brogh didn't seem to realize it. He'd be pacing the aisles, droning on, while, across an unreasonably large clock face, the minute hand seemed to die a slow death.

"And Oliver Cromwell's men were known as the——"

"Roundheads," Sally would say, a *split second* before he said it. She loved history.

"The Roundheads, yes, and he was a——"

"Puritan," interrupted Sally, again a beat ahead of him.

Mr. Brogh blinked. "Have I covered this already?"

"Oh, yes, sir." Sally smiled, sparing the class an hour's worth of agonizing facts and dates. Sally could do no wrong. Perhaps Mr. Brogh preferred girls, or simply preferred Sally, but she made good use of his biases—and he was a man with many of them.

If Brogh was in a bad mood, he would pick on the foreign-looking students. "What's your name?" he asked a new boy with a brown face in the front row.

"Paulo, sir."

"You're not *English*, are you?" Mr. Brogh said, as if the boy had sneaked into the school by nefarious means.

"I live here, sir," said Paulo. "I was born in Malta, which was under British rule until last year, sir."

Mr. Brogh sniffed, as if the boy's presence had plunged the nation another inch or two below sea level.

"Wouldn't that make him English, sir?" asked Sally Byrd.

"Not a *native* Englishman."

"Member of the British Empire, *at least*, sir."

"What's left of it," Mr. Brogh muttered.

"The sun never sets on the British Empire," said Sally with a peppy smile. "Rule Britannia, sir!"

Mr. Brogh, overcome by instinctive nationalism, blinked painfully. "Of course, of course." Then his eyes settled on Will.

"You're from Africa, aren't you, Lament?"

"Yes, sir."

"Why'd you come here?"

"My father got a job here, sir."

Mr. Brogh sniffed again. Britannia was sinking further. "No jobs in Africa? Had to come all the way up here and displace an Englishman, eh?"

"Lots of Englishmen went to Africa to displace the Africans, sir," said Sally, giving Will an indulgent glance.

"Ah, but they offered their talent and ingenuity. They built bridges and systems of law, they——"

"Perhaps they could use *you* in Africa, sir," remarked Sally, smiling.

"I DON'T LOVE HER," Will told his mother when she inquired about this Sally girl he was always chattering about.

"Julia, he's too young for that," said Howard later that night, when they were alone.

"But he's always been romantically inclined." Julia was remembering Ruth and the tunnel to China, which now seemed so long ago.

Howard thought of Ruth, too, and reminded himself to lock up the shovels before Will invited friends over.

In spite of Brogh, Will looked forward to school. Thinking of Sally made him smile. There were no carnal thoughts; he simply liked her laugh. And her wit. And her intelligence. And her taste—Sally liked Mars Bars, but only the top half.

So Will bought her one and sliced it in two layers with his penknife. He took the bottom part, she the top with the caramel. Sally wasn't allowed sweets (her father, Benjamin Byrd, was a dentist), so they'd scarf the Mars Bar by the school football field.

It might have gone on much longer if not for Digley.

That autumn, Digley was the conker king. Conkers was a game in which the boys drilled holes through the strongest chestnut they could find and strung it on a shoelace; then championships would be held in the playground. One boy let his conker hang while the other swung at it with his in an attempt to smash it to pieces. Then they'd switch places. The duels took place all October. Shattered conkers littered the playground; the building superintendent cursed as he swept up the remains every morning. Digley had been the season victor for two years. Rillcock had been disqualified the year before, when it was revealed that he baked his conker until it was rock hard. That year, Digley chose his championship conker from the chestnut tree in Will's back garden. Soon everybody wanted to pick conkers from Will's tree. But this season, when Digley called, it wasn't about conkers at all.

"LAMENT? WANT TO COME OVER?"

"Not today, Digley. Sally's over here."

Nobody ever turned down Digley. He was the conker king.

"Sally Byrd?"

"Yes."

"She's ya girlfriend, then?"

"No."

"Then she's not?"

"Not really," Will replied bashfully.

"Not that I care. Just asking," said Digley, hanging up. Digley, it seemed, didn't care if Will played with a girl. Girls weren't important; they didn't even play conkers.

Will felt a prick of shame after this conversation. Sally watched him put down the telephone.

"Who was that?"

"Digley."

"Oh," she groaned. "He's awful."

This surprised Will. The conker king? Awful? Everybody admired Digley. All the girls sighed over Digley as he walked by, and he knew it. If Digley wanted your chips or your Mars Bar, you gave it to him. Doing so was an honor. Digley was a charmer, all right. He got away with murder. Sally was the first to say it.

"Yes," said Will, "he is awful, isn't he?"

When she laughed, it was a rude little snort. Another thing he liked about her.

WILL SAW DIGLEY a week later in the bog. He had pissed a good five inches past Magnus Hobb's famous initials—a chalk "MH" about six feet above the urine trough. Now Digley was conker king *and* master of the bog.

"She's only a girl, isn't she?" said Digley.

"Yes," agreed Will.

"What do you do with her?"

"Talk. Play games. Have a laugh."

"Can't be as much fun as with a bloke."

"I suppose." Will shrugged. "Well, *you* know. You have a sister."

Digley cringed. "I never played with me sister. Her bum's too big and she's always having to run to the loo to fix her eyelashes."

"Well, think of playing with your sister: that's me and Sally," said Will.

Digley rolled his eyes. "You're a daft one."

Sally turned up in Will's dreams. Once, he soared through the boughs of a massive oak tree with tendril branches and Sally Byrd soared with him. Once he dug his way to China; when he broke through, Sally appeared, a blanket of stars behind her. As Will took her hand, the Midnight Chinaman galloped toward them atop his funeral carriage, a look of fury on his blue face, the fire-snorting steeds stamping their hooves. Will reached for Sally, but her arm snapped off like a piece of porcelain; he fell back through the tunnel, feeling her fingers turn cold and hard.

JUST TO PROVE the dream wrong, Will held Sally's hand when they walked home together one day. She smiled at him, her grip tight, as if she'd never let him go. But when they came in sight of a house with a brass shingle that read DR. BENJAMIN BYRD, DENTIST, Sally shook his hand loose with a cheery nod.

"See you tomorrow, Lament," she said.

He hesitated.

"Can I see your house?"

"No, Lament," she said. "I have a violin lesson today."

Will walked home wishing he'd feigned a toothache. She might have invited him in for a quick dental exam.

They walked home together every day, even in the rain. Their chatter was breathless; they told jokes and interrupted the punch lines to share silly thoughts and scandalous stories about classmates. Time seemed to race by when they were together—Will decided this was the surest sign that he was in love. One afternoon he arrived home two hours late.

"Where've you been?" squawked Digley over the phone.

"With Sally."

"Why?"

"I don't know," said Will defiantly. "Talking."

"About what?"

"Nothing," said Will. How could he possibly explain his affection for Sally? He'd told her all of his secrets: Sally knew all about Ruth and the Midnight Chinaman and even about how awful the twins could be—something Will could never tell his mother.

"IT'S A NASTY COLD," Julia said the next morning, pulling the covers so tightly around him that he couldn't move.

"Why can't *we* be sick?" screamed the twins when they saw Will with the thermometer in his mouth.

"I'm fine, really," Will croaked.

"Nonsense," his mother said.

"I've got a fever, too," cried Marcus.

"I've got blackwater fever!" insisted Julius.

Will faded in and out of consciousness. Meanwhile, the twins were told to be silent and banned from stamping up the stairs. The next day he slept, barely aware of the passing hours until he woke to see the reflections of a wintry sunset streaming across his wall. When his fever lifted, another day had passed.

WILL'S EAGERNESS TO GET BACK to school was tempered by a fear that somehow things had changed in his absence. Traveling does this; one day out of the routine and one prepares for the possibility that the physical world has been reorganized. Nevertheless, he passed the wrought-iron school gates and observed that they were still an over-painted and chipped forest green; the same rusty arc on the pavement marked their daily path. The acrid stench from the boys' bog was familiar, and the Quonset hut classrooms hadn't changed position. The ghastly odor of institutional gravy still emanated from the canteen, and the air-raid shelter that had resisted Hitler's bombs had survived his absence, too. Relieved, Will practiced his smile for his first sight of Sally. Digley waved to him from the distant end of the playground.

Will waved back and looked for Sally standing with the girls, but there was no sign of her. Perhaps she had been sick too. But as he scanned the faces, he felt an uneasy twinge of recognition.

He turned back to Digley. The conker king was holding a girl's hand.

"YOU WERE RIGHT," said Digley, "it's not the same as playing with a boy. Girls are sweet."

"Yes," said Will.

They were in the bog. Magnus Hobb's mark had been removed, and Digley, standing on the porcelain rim of the trough, was chalking his initials up on the wall—the new master of the bog.

"No hard feelings about Sally, right?"

Will attempted a smile, but his mouth seemed to resist.

"I mean," said Digley, "you said she wasn't your girlfriend. If you hadn't said that, I wouldn't have asked her to be mine."

"But I didn't know you liked her."

"Well, after everything you said about her, I couldn't help myself."

Then Digley smiled gratefully at Will, as if he'd found another championship conker in Will's yard.

The Second Holiday

Pan-Europa had a poor year. There were problems in the Middle East causing supply difficulties, and a company tanker had spilled its guts off the coast of Brittany, ruining scores of beaches and killing thousands of birds. The cost to the company would be enormous. Howard was told not to expect a raise. He explained this to Julia, relieved, in a way, to be able to point to the pictures of oil-soaked birds in the newspapers. It wasn't his fault they couldn't afford a proper holiday.

"Well, we have to do something for the children," said Julia.

"Of course," said Howard, nodding. "I have a plan."

He proposed a beach trip to the south coast of England.

The Morris 1100 was ten years old; between its squeaks, its rattles, and its smell mingling with the odor of picnic food in the hamper, the Laments were sharply aware of the economy of their trip. The twins squabbled for hours, then dozed off, while a crackling radio issued a succession of increasingly frightening storm warnings. Julia tried to put a positive aspect on the trip by thinking of their last one, but she couldn't resist asking Howard about his work again.

Howard's jaw stiffened. "Work is absolutely fine," he replied in a measured tone that struck Julia as both condescending and hostile.

"Howard, sometimes I feel as though you think I'm incapable of understanding your world."

"Of course not," he replied without elaborating, which only proved Julia's point.

"Then tell me something, Howard. Anything will do, since I know absolutely *nothing*."

"It's just an office job," he protested. "There's nothing to tell."

Howard tightened his grip on the wheel, but what leaped out of his mouth was beyond his control.

"All right," he said. "It's *horrible*. I hate the job. I'm bored to death. I wish we'd never left Rhodesia. It wasn't a perfect world, especially from a political point of view, but we were happy there, as a family."

Julia stared straight ahead for an interminable period and Howard instantly regretted his confession. Then she glanced back at the children to make sure they were still asleep.

Julia replied softly. "Howard, we were both worried about the children, remember? We both wanted to leave."

"So we did. And this is the price of a good conscience, isn't it?" said Howard. "A cut-rate holiday and a dead-end job in bloody Denham."

Julia looked at him.

"Are you saying you want to go back?"

"No, of course not. I . . . I just regret my, I mean *our* decision."

With his eyes facing forward, Howard realized he had never admitted to such unhappiness and doubt. He had always prided himself on being positive, on coping. He resolved to be stronger in the future.

Startled awake by the horn of a passing car, Julius and Marcus opened their eyes. Their faces were beginning to look more distinct. Julius was getting his father's high forehead, and the reddish tinge to his hair was more pronounced. Marcus's hair had darkened and turned curly over the last year, and he had developed Julia's freckles. They found something to argue about almost as soon as they woke up.

"I know what Jesus looks like," Marcus declared suddenly. "Long hair, beard, blue eyes."

"Nonsense," retorted Julius, who loved a bluff.

"What does he look like, then?"

"You're right about the beard, but he has curly black hair and weak eyes, glasses probably," said Julius. "Looks like Rolf Harris, on the telly."

"What, the Australian fella who paints?"

"Swear to God," said Julius. "Spitting image of Rolf Harris. Look in any church. Beard, curly hair, black glasses."

"I never saw a Jesus with glasses!" said Marcus.

"Keeps 'em in his pocket. Look closer next time."

Marcus nudged Will awake.

"Does Jesus look like Rolf Harris?"

"I dunno—he lived two thousand years ago."

"He *does,*" Julius insisted, winking at Will. "Jesus came from Australia."

"Get off. There are no kangaroos in the Bible."

"There's one. In the Book of Job. Job trips over a kangaroo."

"Mummy, did Job trip over a kangaroo?"

"Not now, Marcus—I'm talking to Daddy," replied Julia, though, they were not, in fact, talking anymore.

Until the twins' argument, Will had been dreaming of Sally. She had turned to face him across the classroom with that rude smile, but now it made him feel unbearably sad. When he woke, he was relieved to see the thin blue line of the sea ahead. To forget Sally, he imagined a sandy shore—swarthy men throwing beach balls to each other, children with windswept hair and careless smiles running through the water hand in hand with their parents. Oh, harmony. He had some faint memory of a sandy beach. He thought of sand castles, and sea foam, and laughter.

Howard tried to rest his hand on Julia's; he wanted to make up before they got out of the car. He wanted to retract his admission, because even if it was true, he admired Julia's strong conscience and, ultimately, he thought he could live with his regret. But the opportunity to say this had been missed now that the boys were awake.

In the last fifteen minutes, the car descended abruptly through

Sodham, a steep, cobblestoned wedge of a town. They rolled past hotels, restaurants, and souvenir shops; the air turned thick, moist, and
pungent with fish-and-chips smells and the salty damp; the twins
reached a fever pitch of excitement, peering past their parents to get a
desperate view of the sea ahead.

"I see it!"

"No, ya don't, I do!"

Then all of a sudden Julia's fury seized her. "Why did you wait this
long to tell me you hated your job? Why didn't you tell me *ages* ago?
Why can't you ever tell me what's going on, Howard? What are you
afraid of?"

"I'm not afraid of anything!" Howard shouted. "Instead of attack-
ing me, why don't *you* get a bloody job? Then you'd understand what
it's like."

Suddenly Marcus burst into sobs. Julia now felt her fury rise in defense of the children.

"That's quite enough, Howard!"

The sharp words spoken up front, along with a precipitous descent
to sea level that had the Morris creaking and jiggling violently, put
everyone in a panic that the car was about to burst apart, and the family with it. At last, Howard pulled the emergency brake, signaling the
end of the journey and, the children hoped, the end of the argument.

Waves pounded the surf just ahead of them. The family staggered
out. Will breathed in the sea air and cast a cautious glance at his parents, wondering if they could ever be persuaded to sit together for the
return journey.

"What's that awful smell?" Julia was gasping.

Will peered into the back of the car. The food hamper had tipped
over; sardine sandwiches, pieces of ham, boiled eggs, and cubes of
warm Swiss cheese were smeared into the fuzzy lining of the trunk,
their smells tainted by those of oil, transmission fluid, and the rubber
pungency of the spare tire.

"It's the food. Bloody car's going to stink forever," Howard muttered.

"What about our lunch?" Julia climbed out. "Is it edible?"

"Have a look yourself," snapped Howard.

Julia circled the car and examined the damage.

"Christ," she said.

"Mummy, did you know Christ looks like Rolf Harris?"

"*Quiet!*" said Julia.

Howard started picking lint off the sandwiches and carefully shaved the oily parts off the boiled eggs with his penknife. Observing this, Julia closed her eyes with revulsion.

"Howard, this won't do."

"What's wrong?" said Howard, casually popping a half-mashed boiled egg (stained with a big oily fingerprint) into his mouth. "It's fine." He grinned.

"It didn't look like that when I packed it," replied Julia.

"It's not a pretty sight in your stomach, either."

"We'll eat at a restaurant."

"At seaside prices? Not likely!"

Julia looked at Howard in disbelief.

Meanwhile, the twins had a revelation about the shoreline; their faces froze in stricken dismay.

"Where's the sand?" asked Julius.

"There's no sand!" wailed Marcus.

The beach, that glorious winding ribbon along the water, was in fact as hostile to the local visitors as it had been to the Romans twenty centuries ago. The shore was a bed of stones.

Will looked at the beckoning sea, still strangely unreachable, and noted the absence of swarthy men, sand, and smiling children; there was only a bearded man in striped pajamas, who was shouting at the seagulls and waving a full roll of what appeared to be toilet paper in his left hand.

"How can we play 'ere?" screamed Marcus.

"You mean 'here,'" Julia said.

"'Ow can we play with no sand, Mummy?" moaned Julius.

Julia looked to Howard, her eyes like cold steel.

"Couldn't you find us a sandy beach?"

"Bloody hell," exclaimed Howard. "A beach is a beach!"

"Picking up language from the *children*, are we?" whispered Julia. "Look, it's hardly a beach if they can't walk on it, and this is hardly a meal if it tastes like the floor of the car."

Howard turned to the flinty shore. The man in his pajamas had stepped up to a prominent rock, and now stretched out his arms in a blissful embrace of the view.

"Look how content that man is!" Howard protested.

"The hell with that man—this is not what we promised. Howard, you must find us a *sandy* beach."

"So that the children will have sand in their food, too? Is *that* what you want, darling? If that's what you want, I'm happy to oblige. I just think we could be quite happy here. What do you think, lads?"

The twins' complaints faded abruptly. "Hey, Mum!" said Julius. "That geezer's *pooping* in the sea!"

All eyes turned to the man on the rock. The bottom half of his striped pajamas had fallen to his ankles; he dropped to a squat in silhouette, and appeared to be shitting into the surf, wiping his ass with toilet paper from the roll under his arm.

Will saw the chasm between his parents instantaneously vanish. All it took was a lunatic with his pants off.

"Right," declared Howard. "I'll find another beach."

A cold breeze picked up, and Julia tied back her hair under a scarf and began rubbing lotion into Marcus's shoulders.

"But there's no sun," protested Marcus, gazing up at the grim clouds while his skin turned to gooseflesh.

"Not a word," Julia warned, replacing Marcus with Julius. Thunder cracked overhead.

Smeared with suntan lotion they didn't need, the twins tore across the rocks. But the lunar landscape had them hopping in pain within a few yards of the water.

Howard ambled back from the car, folding his map with a satisfied snap. "Good news—I've found a sandy beach."

"How far?" asked Julia, detecting some fracture in his confident smile.

"Only sixty miles, darling."

· · ·

PASSING MOTORISTS WOULD HAVE ADMIRED the rugged family deter-
minedly eating its lunch on the inhospitable shoreline of Sodham as
rain pattered down in an overture for the black storm approaching
from the west. Only on closer inspection would anyone have noticed
that the two adults faced in opposite directions.

Out of the Rut

Julia had started painting in the evenings. The living-room walls were adorned with her efforts. There was an impressionistic landscape of Maiden Castle, with the grassy furrows crosshatched in windy currents, and a view of their semidetached house in Avon Heath, the battered Morris parked in front of the garage. She was at work on a coffeehouse scene. The details were Arabian: ornate plasterwork on the walls, geometric tile on the floor, a featureless man in a white suit at a table, nursing a glass of mint tea.

This was no idle pastime. Julia was driven by a sense of purpose. The holiday in Sodham had left her feeling ashamed of her own passivity. Poor Howard, she had thought. If he couldn't get out of his rut, it was up to her to make a contribution. He was absolutely right—she needed a job. Now that all three boys were in school, there was no justification for all the spare time she had.

Howard sat in his armchair reading a biography of the American inventor Charles Goodyear. He was at the exciting part, when Goodyear vulcanizes rubber, but he put the book down because he had something important to say.

"Look here, Julia. You know, after that awful holiday, I started thinking."

Julia looked at him, relief on her face.

"So have I, darling."

"I had no right to say what I said."

"Neither did I, Howard. I feel very ashamed—"

"No, darling," interrupted her husband, "you shouldn't. In fact, as luck would have it, I might actually have a new job soon. I've been talking to somebody."

"Somebody?"

"Yes. Somebody I met. An American businessman."

Julia lowered her brush, rattling it in a jar of turpentine while surprise played on her face.

"An American? When were you going to tell me?"

"I *am* telling you . . . Well, I wouldn't have told you until it was pretty definite," Howard explained.

"Honestly, Howard," said Julia, "getting information from you is like pulling nails out of a bull's bum!"

Howard averted his eyes. Julia had given up trying to improve her children's language and had started adopting it.

"Well, it's an American company. And these Americans seem interested in taking me on as a design engineer. Americans are like that," he added. "They like innovation, while the English . . . half their plumbing is left over from the Romans!"

"Well, Howard," Julia replied, "it happens that I've applied for a job, too."

THERE WAS A POSITION AVAILABLE at the boys' school for an art teacher. Julia had prepared her résumé and culled some of her newest paintings, and that very morning had attended a meeting with the headmaster, Mr. Henley. A tactless man, Henley judged her paintings as if he were in a holiday gift shop.

"I like this one, don't like that. *That's* not bad."

Finally he looked up at her and knitted his brows. "I see no recent employment, Mrs. Lament."

"I've been raising children," Julia replied. "Three boys. They're all your students, as a matter of fact."

Mr. Henley offered a paternal smile. "So why the sudden urge to work, Mrs. Lament?"

Julia felt her anger appear as a blush. "Well," she stammered, "to take the burden off my husband a bit, and to keep occupied."

Mr. Henley smiled thinly. "I merely meant, Mrs. Lament, that you have three children to raise. I would think that your hands are *full*."

The headmaster promised to be in touch.

A WEEK LATER, Howard waited for the children to be tucked in before expressing his concerns to Julia.

"Darling, I've been thinking about this job idea of yours, and you know I support you wholeheartedly . . ."

"Of course I know that, Howard."

"But what if one of the children falls sick? What about the housework? And supposing we have to move? What then, what about our mobility?"

"Darling, I would never want to hinder our mobility," she began. "But surely if I was making a contribution to our livelihood you would take that into account before suggesting we pick up and leave."

There was a pause before Howard nodded. Julia sensed that he hadn't considered this possibility before. Nevertheless, she believed, and hoped, that he would be reasonable about it.

"Of course, Julia," he said finally. "We make these decisions together."

"Oh, darling, I'm so glad you said that," cried Julia, and they embraced. She had feared that Howard was so comfortable with leading the family from country to country that her opinion had become superfluous. Now she was reminded of his decency, and the strength of their marriage. Trixie and Chip could never have come to such an understanding.

"Howard," she said, "the truth is that I didn't get the job."

Howard shrugged, with a relieved smile. "Well, that's all right," he confessed. "Nothing's definite about the American job, either."

Bonfire

When the leaves fell down in Avon Heath, it was common practice to dispose of them with a bonfire. Howard zestfully explained to his sons that "bonfire" was a contraction of "bone fire," meaning a cleansing rite of burning bodies during the plagues. The twins were both very impressed with this fact. Julius made an effigy to burn in the fire, a stuffed figure sewn together from his outgrown clothes that he named Mr. Henley; this in retribution for the six hard raps on the knuckles delivered by the headmaster when Julius threw blancmange across the school canteen.

Marcus, on the other hand, was fascinated by the embers in the center of the fire—those glowing chunks of wood, blackened on the outside, golden red within. He pictured a miniature world of citizens who went about their lives in this wondrous furnace. Fire was beautiful to Marcus, and he drew himself so close to the embers that Howard had to caution him repeatedly to watch out lest he burn his Wellingtons. Will felt a consequent pang of anxiety when Howard left him in charge. By now, the flames leaped over the twins' heads. Julius found a long stick to prod the headmaster with, and added a few incantations in Pig Latin to speed the flames. When he lunged at the figure with his spear, he sent a cascade of sparks into the twilight. Will paused to marvel at the glittering updraft until he noticed a second fire a few feet away.

"Marcus?" Will cried out. Marcus was nowhere to be seen. Will advanced cautiously toward the small fire and his stomach did a slow turn.

The fire had arms and legs. Its hands were beating at the flames.

Will grabbed an arm and dragged his brother across the ground, rolling him over and over, until the flames were smothered. Marcus's jackets and pants were badly burned, and his face stank of burning hair, but aside from the patches where his eyebrows used to be, and a few singed spots on his scalp, he seemed all right.

"Why didn't you shout!" cried Will, panting, as he hoisted his brother up.

Marcus had a dazed stare. He smiled, looking back at the big bonfire.

"If you can live in a fire, it means you are immortal."

"Well, you're *not*," said Will. "You'd be a cooked sausage! God, you smell awful!"

Will led his brothers home, brushing the cinders from their clothing and hair in fearful anticipation of his mother's reaction.

But Julia directed her fury at the victim.

"Oh, Marcus," she cried, "have you no sense at all?" She proceeded to give the boy a vigorous scrubbing, which seemed, to Will, a vain attempt at washing the stupidity out of his brother.

Will was surprised to see Julius appear at his door just after bedtime, his long face streaked with tears.

"What's wrong?"

"Marcus almost died," murmured his brother. "I was so busy with Mr. Henley that I didn't see him set on fire."

"He's all right," Will said.

"I know," sobbed Julius. "But who would I play with if he was gone?"

Will walked Julius back to the twins' bedroom. Marcus was already asleep, snoring with his mouth open. Julius was still sobbing as Will tucked him into bed, and fell quiet only after Will found him a miniature King Kong figure to clutch in one hand. Will kneeled by his brother's bed until the boy's eyes closed.

But a hollow ache throbbed in Will's chest as he considered Julius's question—*Who would I play with if he was gone?*—for clearly his presence was of no consolation to Julius; and this reminded him of his position in the family, the solitary son between two couples.

MARCUS'S RESCUE PROMPTED WILL to volunteer as Bell Boy for the month of January. It was a task for the courageous—running around the school's perimeter jingling a bell to mark the change of class, tagged by a mob of boys who apparently believed that if there were no bell, school would consist of six hours in the playground. So pursued, Will employed speed, agility, and, when all else failed, the bell itself, wielded as a blunt instrument, to make his rounds. On the third day he evaded the mob by taking a detour through the air-raid shelter.

That was where he found Sally, huddled in the shadows, nursing the butt of a cigarette. Her smile was wary.

"Hello, Lament," she said.

He watched the mob scream past and disappear around a corner.

"Are we still enemies, then?" she continued. "You've been looking *through* me for almost a year."

"Well," Will replied, "Digley asked you to be his girlfriend and you said yes."

"He said you didn't fancy me anymore," said Sally.

Will denied this. "I came back from being sick and you were holding hands."

"I tried to talk to you at the gate every day, but you walked past me." Sally took a last miserable draw from her cigarette.

Will raised his bell. "I'd better finish."

Sally gave him an urgent glance. "Anyway, Digley's not my boy-friend anymore."

"Really?" he replied.

She nodded.

They walked back to the classroom together. The mob dropped back when it saw the Bell Boy escorted by a girl.

England Isn't What It Used to Be

Will wrote to his grandmother. All he meant to describe was his rescue of Marcus and the family's relief. It was a letter that sent tremors across the globe.

Dear Granny,
Marcus almost burned to a crisp when he caught fire. I rescued
him and Mummy told him that she'd kill him if he ever went
near flames again. Julius stabbed and burned his headmaster to
death, but it was a dummy. Daddy hates his job and thinks
England isn't what it used to be.

Weeks later, Julia received a reply:

Dear me, what has become of England? Judging from the violent
and self-destructive tendencies of the twins, I advise you to send
them to an institution capable of dealing with such juvenile issues.
As for Howard's unhappiness, Julia, I urge you to remember your
wedding vows. I would also suggest that you bring the children
back to Africa, where they can enjoy a normal childhood!

Howard insisted on taking the family on yet another motoring trip to see exactly what England *used to be*. They drove about thirty-five miles down the old Roman road that lay between London and Chichester to the South Downs. A wooden barn housed several preserved mosaic floors and some gold and pottery.

Will was fascinated by the mosaic of a Roman nobleman seated on a marble dais, flanked by two hunting dogs. It reminded him of their old neighbor Buck Quinn.

The twins, however, were in revolt; Marcus felt like a freak with his singed eyebrows, and brooded in the car until Julius enticed him to join him on the floor of the museum, where they stamped their heels, shaking the jewelry cabinets, until Howard threatened them with a meal of soap flakes.

"Will!" barked Howard. "Will you *please* take your brothers outside?"

Grudgingly, Will left the mosaic and led his brothers into the sunshine. On the hillock, the twins escaped from his grip and tore off, leaving sleek wet trails through the wild barley. Since they could come to no harm here, Will found a patch of wall to sit on, and rested his arms on his knees.

"Do you know where you're sitting?" said a man's voice.

Will noticed only the tweed jacket and leather elbow patches of his visitor.

"No, sir," he replied.

"That was the bedroom of a Roman governor. I was plowing this field, precisely where you are, with nothing but barley in every direction . . ."

He waved at the stalks standing still like golden ranks of soldiers in the faint morning mist as the twins returned, whining like dive-bombers through the barley.

". . . when I hit something hard. Thought it was a rock, but when I got off the tractor and checked the blades, I found a sword and a small golden ring."

He held up his hand to display a ring with a stone etched with a small male figure wielding a sword.

"Mars, the god of war," said Will.

The farmer gave a delighted nod. "Well done, boy." He took Will a few paces farther. "Where you're standing now is where the owner of this house, fifteen hundred years ago, would receive visitors. He owned all the land he could see from this spot in all directions."

"He took all this land from the English?" asked Will.

The farmer laughed. "*English?* There were no *English*, just a group of savage tribes, each more bloodthirsty than the last. The Romans brought them a system of roads, plumbing, a system of government, a code of law. Without the Romans, we'd all still be running about with spears and painted faces.

"Here—try it on," said the farmer, offering the ring. The stone was a deep pink with a heavy gold girdle around it. "Remember this"—the farmer winked—"you've worn something priceless on your finger!" The farmer slipped the ring back on and walked away to greet another group of sightseers.

On the trip home, Will considered priceless things. He remembered the bayonet hole in Digley's father's uniform, and Sally's smile in the air-raid shelter.

His parents were talking in the front seat—awed remarks about the treasures on display.

"Why do you *like* the Romans?" asked Will.

"They were a great civilization," said Julia.

"Are *we* a great civilization?"

"That'll be for somebody else to decide," said Howard.

His parents started talking about other things, and Will stared out the window. He thought of the Roman nobleman in the mosaic who resembled Buck Quinn, and the ring with the tiny figure of Mars, and his mother telling him to remember Churchill's funeral. The England his parents had so much affection for was clearly not the one they lived in but a world hinted at through artifacts. For the first time, he wondered whether his parents were pursuing something imaginary in their travels.

Farewell Again

"Lament? Y'know what my favorite record is?" Sally Byrd whispered this question during geometry class.

"What?" said Will.

"'Bits and Pieces,'" whispered Sally.

"What?" said Will again.

"'Bits and Pieces,' by the Dave Clark Five. You could come over to my house and hear it," said Sally.

There was a now-or-never mood in class these days. The year was coming to an end; primary school would soon be over. They'd all taken the eleven-plus exam, which demarcated everybody's future pretty clearly: the ones who passed would go to a college preparatory school; the others would go to trade school.

"Where the ditchdiggers and plumbers go," Howard joked. "Don't worry, Will. You'll pass."

The letter from the examiners was addressed to Julia, who glanced at the first line and gave him a tight smile.

"Sorry, darling, you didn't make it."

At dinner, Howard appeared stunned. He read the letter several times, then pronounced it irrelevant.

"But I don't want to dig ditches for a living," complained Will.

"You'll never dig ditches," said Howard. "You're smarter than any of them."

"Why didn't I pass, then?"

"Probably because you're a foreigner. This exam's for English children, and you didn't have the background. Don't worry, you can take the exam again. They let you keep taking it until you pass."

Will looked around the classroom the next morning with a new-found sense of estrangement. He wasn't the only one: Digley had passed the test, but Ayers hadn't; Raymond Tugwood had passed, but Sally Byrd hadn't; and Rillcock had passed, to everyone's amazement. The little heathen danced past their desks, pausing to gloat over Will.

"Don't worry, you can fix my washing machine in a few years, eh, Lament?"

"Has your family ever *used* a washing machine?" snapped Will.

In those last few weeks of school, mates were split apart, futures hurled in opposite directions. And, of course, those destined for the same lot made alliances.

Will and Sally drew close again. He was invited to her house one afternoon; they passed from Dr. Byrd's modern dental office, with its chrome chairs and fittings, to the Byrds' cozy living room, the walls papered with blue lilies and hung with an assortment of decorative plates marking the queen's coronation, her marriage, and the births of the royal offspring. They ate buttered toast smeared with Marmite in the kitchen, and proceeded upstairs to Sally's bedroom.

"I share it with my sister," she explained.

Sally and her sister were collectors, too; the beds had frilly lace covers with piles of stuffed animals. Glossy photos and pictures clipped from magazines were taped to the wallpaper like a pop mosaic: the Beatles, Elvis, Lulu, Cliff Richard and the Shadows, Cilla Black, Engelbert Humperdinck, Gerry and the Pacemakers, and the Rolling Stones. Iridescent black 45s, foot-high stacks of them, were on the floor, with others spilled across the bed. Pasted to the door were news-paper pictures of TV variety-show hosts like Val Doonican and Rolf Harris, movie stars like Anita Ekberg and Brigitte Bardot, and comedy teams like the *Carry On* casts and the Goons.

The record player was white and plastic, with a red arm. It wasn't anything like the sober gray box at home, which Howard declared could play only Beethoven, Haydn, and the odd Gregorian chant. Sally's record player was an instrument of fun and wickedness. It played Peter Sellers doing Twit Conway and Flanders & Swann singing a love song between hippos. It played "Puppet on a String," "Those Were the Days," "Telstar," and "The Green, Green Grass of Home." And, most important to Sally, it played "Bits and Pieces."

The sound was scratchy but loud.

"Do you like it?" asked Sally.

Will's mouth hung open as he stared at the line of lipsticks on the dresser, the stockings hanging over the chair, the rows of heels below the bed, and the purple boa draped over her headboard.

"Oh, yes," he said.

This room was another country, a shrine to teenage girlhood, and he was on his knees.

"Where's your sister?"

"God knows," said Sally. She started nodding her head to the music, her Beatle hair shaking in all directions just the way theirs did on TV. The music ended, and Sally stacked a few more 45s on the turntable.

"My sister *loves* 'Bits and Pieces.' Don't you think it's groovy?"

"Groovy. Oh, yes," said Will. "What else does your sister like?"

"She likes the wet look," said Sally, pointing to a fire-engine-red PVC skirt draped on a chair. It was a shiny piece of nothing. Will wondered if one could fall in love with somebody's sister without ever seeing her.

"Where is your sister?"

"She's never home," explained Sally. "Boys, y'know."

A deep voice seemed to speak from the carpet.

"Sally?"

"Yeah, Dad?" cried Sally, looking at the red shag rug.

"Can't hear meself work, Sally!" said the deep voice. "Turn it down, love."

Sally lowered the volume; they lay on the floor with their heads together, near the record-player speaker. Her hair smelled of coconut shampoo. They listened to "Bits and Pieces" half a dozen times, then to Cliff Richard, Lulu, Dusty, and "Bits and Pieces" six times again for good measure.

When it got dark, Will explained that he had to go. Sally walked him downstairs. At the door she held on to his sleeve and glanced back to make sure they were unseen.

"Bye," said Will.

"Hold on," she said, and gave him a moist kiss on the lips. Will looked shaken.

"It's all right, Lament," Sally said. "My sister kisses *all* the boys good-bye."

Will changed his mind. It was Sally he was in love with. Her lips tasted like coconut, too.

NOBODY SEEMED PERTURBED by his late arrival. His parents were in the kitchen, talking in a low murmur. The twins were out near the garage. Julius was attaching a Ping-Pong ball to the tail of the neighbor's cat.

"What did I miss?" Will asked.

"Nuffink," said Marcus.

Julius released the unhappy creature, which tore off into the darkness with the ball clicking and clacking all over the street.

"That's cruel," said Will.

"I *told* you it was cruel," complained Marcus to Julius.

"We're moving to America," Julius said.

"What?" said Will.

"Dad's got a job there."

"And Mummy's got a job, too," Marcus said, "but it's here." He paused. "They're fighting."

Mr. Henley, apparently inspired by Julia's attempt to augment the household income, hired his *own* wife for the art teacher's position. Two months later, he urged her to withdraw from the job—Mrs. Henley was a good art teacher, but she hadn't been keeping up with the housework and the ironing, and Mr. Henley abhorred an unpressed shirt. Julia was offered the position. Meanwhile, Howard's American company had made him an offer.

"I don't want to go to America!" Will declared.

"You see," said Julia to Howard. "It's not just me."

"Surely you don't want to go to ditchdigging school, Will," Howard joked.

"You said I could take the test again!" Will replied.

"Will," said Howard, "*everybody* wants to go to America!"

But Will was already up the stairs, his door slammed shut.

"Have they got lots of cats in America?" asked Julius.

"Of course they've got cats!" Howard said.

"I'll go where Julius goes," said Marcus.

Julia sat back, her arms folded, her mouth firmly set.

"You'll love America, darling," Howard insisted. "It's the most progressive society around. And the taxes are lower."

"We'd be starting all over," Julia replied. *"Again."*

"I'll make *twice* what I make here!"

"What about school for Will? And what about my job offer?"

"Darling, every American child can go to college. It's a matter of money, not aptitude. And I'll be paid a fortune, which is why *you'll* never need to work in America!" This was clearly the wrong thing to say. Another door slammed, and Howard found himself alone with the twins.

IT TOOK ROSE'S LETTER to unite the family:

America? What a crass and vulgar place. What have the Americans given the world? Soft drinks and Doris Day! Isn't it bad enough that we have to hear them mangle the English language in their films? Must you submit your children to such a fate? They'll be outcasts, reviled by their kin, and they'll have those awful accents. Americans are as crass as Russians, almost as crude as Italians, and as snobbish as the French. For the sake of the children, don't do it!

Julia told Howard that she would go to America, but with conditions.

"First: I might well take a job, whether we need the income or not," she said.

"But you won't . . ." began Howard.

"Not just to make money, Howard, but for my own sense of worth."

"Well, of course, darling," replied Howard.

"And *my* pride should be as important to *you* as yours is to me, don't you agree?"

"Absolutely."

"Second: I won't be led around the country. I'm getting older, Howard. I want to settle down; so do the boys."

Howard eagerly accepted Julia's conditions; there was no doubt in his mind that the next place would be the final stop. America would supply everything that England lacked. In America, people became millionaires because of their inventiveness. Assuredly, Howard would find his destiny there.

UNLIKE THE TWINS, Will had strong misgivings about leaving. He knew that all his routines would change, and the faces of his friends and neighbors would never be seen again. This time he wanted to savor his farewells. Sally was out sick on his last day of school, so he visited her house to say good-bye.

A tall girl with Sally's eyes but with a more petulant mouth answered the door. Will tried to imagine this girl in a wet-look skirt, but the sneer on her face stifled his imagination. He asked for Sally.

"Sally? She's out." The girl gave him a rude glance just like her sister. "What d'you want, then?"

"To say good-bye."

"Come back later," she replied.

"I can't. I'm leaving for America," he said.

"America?" She cocked her head in interest.

Will noted that Fiona Byrd had a good four inches on Sally, and she wore peach lipstick and her fuzzy peach sweater displayed small, pointed breasts.

"You're that Lament boy, aren't you?" she said, and swept her hair over her shoulder as though his destination warranted some adjustment in her appearance.

Will nodded.

"Elvis is in America, y'know."

Will said he knew this. Fiona played with the little gold chain hanging from her neck with one long, pink fingernail and finally asked a favor.

"Will you give him a message for me if you see him?"

"Who? Elvis? What's the message?"

The fingernail gestured for him to approach. Will complied. Then Sally's sister put her lips up to his and Will felt her tongue slip into his mouth. It was over in a blink, and she shot him a sideways smile.

"Think you can remember that?"

Will swallowed. She'd been sucking on a lemon lozenge. Normally he didn't fancy lemon, but this was different. The fingernail waved good-bye, and Will felt his pants tighten strangely.

IT STARTED TO RAIN as he walked home: a soft English patter. Will realized that everything he did today would be for the last time. As he nodded a farewell to the corner where he had fought Rillcock, tiny droplets of rain formed on his sweater, like glitter. He would miss this sweet, gentle rain. Not like an African rain at all, with its bombastic thunder and torrential streams cutting chasms in the earth. He wondered what an American rain would be like. Will stuck his tongue out, savoring the last lemony vestige of Fiona's kiss. He passed a row of council houses, and the recreation field nearby. Two figures were kicking a ball around. They were Digley and Ayers.

"I'm leaving tomorrow," Will said.

"Say hello to Elvis!" said Ayers.

"Say hello to Marilyn Monroe!" shouted Digley.

"She's dead," said Ayers.

"Is not," said Digley.

"Idiot," said Ayers.

"Ditchdigger," replied Digley.

America

Citizen of the World

Their spirits were high, perhaps because Howard was never happier than when he came to a new land; like Adam finding a new Eden, Howard was ready to start afresh. They bounced along a six-lane highway in a shiny sapphire-blue Buick with a black roof and two-tone blue vinyl interior. When the twins weren't arguing over the Sonomatic AM/FM radio, they were gazing at the enormous greetings flashed in neon from Howard Johnson, Holiday Inn, Burger King, and that delightful elderly gentleman offering fried chicken from Kentucky. Everything they saw from their windows looked friendly, exciting, and new.

Julia took silent stock of the family's passage. They had their health, the house had been sold, the mortgage was paid off, the slate was clean. And yet she worried what it would cost them. Experience told her that there was always something lost.

She reflected on Albo, the material comfort they had abandoned; on Buck Quinn's affluent white society and its resentment of black rule. The minute they arrived in England, they faced the paradox of being white Africans—reminders of Britain's colonial glory but a burden to its struggling modern economy.

The huge screen of a drive-in theater loomed over the highway. Rows of speaker poles stood in the empty lot. 2001: A SPACE ODYSSEY, read the marquee. The twins peered with fascination.

"What's an odyssey?"

"A journey. Like ours. But longer."

"We'll go to a drive-in," Howard promised the boys. "*That's* something you won't find in England!"

Julia sighed to herself; as if Howard needed to remind them of England's shortcomings. A mere glance under its skirts had revealed a hostile shoreline, squalid plumbing, and children as tribal as their ancestors. It offered her gifted husband a miserable job, and refused to give her son more than a tradesman's education. *Good riddance to the sceptered isle,* she thought.

HOWARD'S NEW OFFICES were in one of many newly built research parks on the edge of Route 1—one of New Jersey's arterial highways— a cluttered four-lane strip divided by concrete, with incessant traffic lights, fast-food outlets, and automotive franchises. A passing sign pointed to Princeton. The university buildings poked through the trees to the west, school of F. Scott Fitzgerald in his youth and Einstein in his old age. On either side, country roads branched off into woodlands, which were hastily being razed to situate housing developments for the growing workforce. The cachet of Princeton guaranteed that every developer name his tract after it; hence Academy Manor, College Fields, even Einstein Cottages.

The Laments had found a house in University Hills, a development that was actually flat. The house was a sprawling split-level with eight white pillars and a false brick façade, a winding driveway, two-car garage, central air, and baseboard heating. Every other house in the development was identical, except for its mailbox. Americans appeared to enjoy individuality only in this respect—the boxes were painted to resemble turkeys, eagles, ducks, trains, barns, or cartoon creatures.

Howard loved the jet-stream shower and the toilet that flushed without a chorus of knocking pipes; Julia liked the dishwasher, the sprayer nozzle in the sink, and the vast refrigerator. Instead of three channels there were seven, some running all night long; the twins learned to talk like Americans in a matter of weeks. Their new diet depended on infusions of Bazooka gum, Twinkies, and Big Macs. And they rejoiced at these new things, for America was strange and wonderful and they were free to roam as never before and utterly consumed with their own company.

Will, however, was grieving.

Every night he dreamt of a tunnel with Sally at the other end beckoning to him. Behind her lay a faint rainbow and his conker tree. In his dreams, he heard a soft rainfall that smelled of lemon lozenges. As he climbed through this tunnel, he noticed familiar sights embedded in the earthen walls: the Midnight Chinaman's jubilant and wicked smile, Ruth clutching her tin vanity box, Buck Quinn riding a chariot drawn by his howling Ridgeback; the *Windsor Castle*'s captain borne across the waves on mermaids with breasts cupped in bright plastic scallop shells; Ayers dancing in Hitler's trousers, and Digley summoning spirits with Goebbels the cat on his shoulder. Before Will's lips reached Sally's, however, his dream was always interrupted by his alarm clock, and the jarring fanfare of the AM radio station with its unfamiliar accents.

He was back to square one: a foreigner again.

"What are you so upset about?" asked his mother.

"I hate moving."

"But you're a Lament. The Laments have always traveled. All of them except your grandfather, that is."

"Perhaps I'm more like *him*."

"Impossible," said Julia.

"Why?"

Julia hesitated, knowing she had to protect him from the truth. "Because he just sat in his armchair all day."

Will frowned. "Why?"

"Daddy said he had a weak heart."

"Who am *I* like? I don't look like you or Daddy or the twins. Who *am* I like?"

"Darling, it's not important who you look like," said Julia, embracing her son.

"But you look like *your* mother," came the distressed reply.

"Darling, you're terribly special; you're a very lucky person, a traveler, an explorer, a citizen of the world! You're a Lament, do you understand?"

Will was puzzled by his mother's answer because, though it was emphatic, it lacked consolation. To be a Lament was to be a perpetual stranger.

Where Is Chapman Fay?

On his first day at work, Howard was told that the man who had invited him to America could not be found.

"You mean he's late?"

"Not exactly," explained his secretary. "He's missing at sea."

CHAPMAN FAY WAS the visionary leader of Fay/Bernhardt, a company that built specialized devices for NASA, the military, and medicine. What were these devices? Future technologies, explained the company literature. By all accounts, Chapman Fay was a genius. A high school graduate at fifteen, he earned a doctorate in chemical engineering at twenty. By twenty-five, he had amassed three more doctorates, in Chinese mythology, quantum physics, and pre-Columbian art. At the age of thirty-two he was running a think tank for Ethical Utopians in Napa Valley, by thirty-eight he had plans to build a rocket ship to carry them to Mars. Fay/Bernhardt was founded to build this ship, but after shortfalls in funding, Chapman Fay changed his goal. He decided it was better to save the world before leaving it, and he proceeded to invent a few devices that were designed to do just that.

Pan-Europa had been interested in one of Chapman Fay's inventions, a chemical that forced spilled oil to congeal into an iridescent goop on the surface of water so that it could be extracted easily. The procedure was called the Rapi-Flux system; at Howard's recommendation, Pan-Europa bought the gear from Fay/Bernhardt for its rescue tankers. Howard supervised the testing of the system in a saltwater tank near Southampton with a team of beefy merchant marines with bullnecks, their faces flushed from a life of hard drinking and rough North Sea weather. Halfway through the test, a slight man with brilliant blue eyes and a shock of white hair bound in a ponytail entered the facility, dressed in an avocado Nehru jacket. The marines may have sniggered about his outfit and his hair, but the moment he issued orders, they responded without hesitation.

After the exercise, Chapman took everybody to lunch at a local pub. It was there, over a pint of Watney's, that Howard told him about his plans for the Sahara, and the artificial heart he'd been thinking about ever since his father died. As he rose to leave, Chapman pumped Howard's hand and, instead of saying good-bye, offered him a job.

"You're a man of ideas," said Chapman Fay. "Come work for me in America."

"WHAT DO YOU MEAN HE'S MISSING AT SEA?"

"His yacht lost radio contact about five days ago. Don't worry, Mr. Fay is a genius. He'll show up," said the secretary.

Howard was assigned a room twice the size of his Denham office. It was paneled in mahogany, with one glass wall that offered a view of a Japanese garden of weeping cherries, a pool of koi, and a stately blue heron. He spent the first two days putting tabs on his binders and filling out the forms needed for his medical coverage and retirement fund. On the third day, he began to fret.

Fay/Bernhardt occupied a large building carefully designed for privacy and singular focus; it was impossible to see anyone else working. People went about their business without a lot of talk in the corridors. Perhaps, conceded Howard, this is the atmosphere of a place where brilliant ideas are hatched, but it was isolating, too. There was no one to talk to until one day he ran into Chapman's partner, Dick Bernhardt, a ruddy fellow with laughing eyes, who wore a Moroccan djellaba in the office.

"What should I be doing until Chapman returns?" asked Howard.

"Relax," said Dick. "If Chapman hired you, there must have been a reason. Chapman will take care of you, don't you worry. Have you tried our cafeteria? The chef comes from a restaurant in Brittany, four stars in the Michelin Guide."

"HOW IS THE NEW JOB?" asked Julia.

"The cafeteria is extraordinary," Howard replied. "And you should see my office."

"But the work?" she asked. "How is your work?"

"Not bad," said Howard, thinking it premature to admit his dilemma. He was being paid more than he had ever earned in his life. For doing nothing.

The Himmels

Julia looked forward to the start of school in a few weeks, when the boys would be out of the house and she could look for work. Until then, she spent her time getting organized—buying clothes for the boys; lamps, blinds, and bedside tables for the extra bedrooms in their enormous new house. One morning she was greeted at the door by a woman with an eager smile and a basket of chocolate chip cookies.

"Hi! I'm Abby Gallagher," she said, gesturing toward her house. "Number Thirty-three, with the pear tree and the beautiful green lawn."

Julia followed Abby's glance and found herself instantly envious of the woman's casual pride. She remembered her roses in Albo, and it seemed possible that she and Abby already had something in common.

"It *is* a beautiful lawn," agreed Julia.

When Julia invited her in, Abby inspected the kitchen appliances while explaining that she had two sons about Will's age. Then she ran her fingers over the parquet floor in the dining room.

"Walnut," she sighed. "We wanted walnut; they gave *us* pine. Where are you from? You sound English!"

"No, I'm from South Africa," Julia replied. Then, in a breathless ramble, she ticked off the other countries she'd lived in and the difficulties of starting up in a new culture, and topped it off with an earnest wish to see all of America because it was a culture that had assimilated its races the way, she feared, South Africa never would.

Abby looked confused. "South Africa." She blinked. "You don't *look* African."

Julia silently admonished herself for talking too much; it had been many weeks since she had chatted with anyone other than family and salespeople.

"I'm Irish," said Abby.

"Really?" said Julia. "Which part of Ireland are you from?"

"Cork," Abby replied, "but that was three generations ago."

"Ah." Julia smiled. "So, you're just a *little* bit Irish."

Abby paused. "I celebrate Saint Patrick's Day, if that's what you mean. That makes me as Irish as anybody, doesn't it?"

"Actually," said Julia, "my family lived in Ireland a few generations ago, but I wouldn't dare call myself Irish."

What was left of Abby's smile vanished.

With a desperate sense that she had blundered, Julia attempted to rescue the conversation. "But I *love* Irish literature," she added. "Who are your favorites?"

Abby blinked again. "I'm actually late for a tennis game," she said, and rose from her seat. Julia thanked her for the cookies, aware that she had made a mistake, without knowing precisely what it was. But Abby's parting comment rankled.

"Y'know," Abby said, nodding at the blue house next door, "you'd like the Himmels—they're foreigners, too."

"THEY'RE FOREIGNERS, TOO," repeated Julia as she cut her veal into ribbons that evening.

"But she *did* bring you cookies," said Howard, thinking that women judged one another far more harshly than men did.

"Perhaps," Julia said, "but I don't understand why an American would call herself Irish when she hasn't been to Ireland, doesn't read Irish authors, and probably couldn't even find Ireland on the map!"

Howard was amused by Julia's outrage. "Clearly, darling, you know more about the Irish than any Irishman, but isn't the point to make *friends*?"

When Madge Finch brought over a fudge cake the next day, Julia was appreciative and cautious. Madge cocked her ear at Julia's accent.

"Are you English?"

"No, South African."

Madge confessed that she was Scottish—adding that her favorite game was golf, and did Julia know that golf originated in Scotland?

"No, really?" she said, even as she remembered Mrs. Urquhart listing every great Scottish invention, engineer, writer, and poet.

"My favorite Scotsman is Rod McKuen," confessed Madge.

Julia imagined Mrs. Urquhart tossing in her grave.

"You really ought to meet the Himmels," said Madge. "They're from Germany."

JULIA VENTED HER FRUSTRATION to Will as the twins watched a *Gilligan's Island* rerun on television.

"I just don't understand why people cling to these nationalities when they're so obviously American!"

"Perhaps we'd like the Himmels," he suggested.

Julia frowned. "After what the Luftwaffe did to London, I can't quite imagine bringing them a basket of cookies!"

Will raised his eyebrows. "But you're the one who said it was time for the English to forget about the war, Mum."

This provoked an abashed glance from his mother.

"You're quite right, darling," she replied, adding skeptically, "I'm sure the Himmels are very *nice* Germans."

THE HIMMELS WERE NOT as gregarious as some of the other neighbors. Though their house lay beside the Laments', they didn't appear at the door with gifts or questions about the parquet floor. The Himmel house glowed at night, but not a Himmel was to be seen entering or leaving during the day. Julia understood from the mailman that there were two Himmel daughters, one Will's age, one a year older.

"Why does everyone keep saying we should meet them; we don't know the people on the *other* side of our house, either," said Julius.

"Perhaps I'll go over and say hello one of these days," Howard said.

"That would be a first," remarked Julia.

ABBY GALLAGHER'S HUSBAND, Patrick, greeted Howard with a wave one morning. He ran a production line that made radios for Ford motorcars. But Abby hadn't told the whole truth about their children; while they had two sons, Mickey and Kent, twelve and thirteen (who were never seen without their hockey sticks), there was a third son, Lionel, nineteen, an acid freak who had dropped out of Rutgers and spent his time roaming the neighborhood wearing cherry-tinted glasses and communing with the fire hydrants.

Three doors down were the Finches, from Texas, blessed with a freckled son and daughter, Wally, thirteen, and Tess, eleven. Frank Finch was a public relations man for AmGas, with a bone-cracking handshake; Madge, besides playing golf, liked Louis Prima records and always wore something plaid at their weekend barbecues.

The Imperatores had a large family of lazy-eyed children; the eldest boy, Vinnie, was also about Will's age, and had confronted him shortly after the moving truck departed. Though Vinnie didn't resemble Rillcock, Will detected a similar note in the boy's manner.

"My house is twice as big as yours," he declared, though their houses were identical, right down to the holly bushes on either side of the front door.

Before Will could respond, Wally Finch came over to argue that everything was bigger in Texas. This provoked Will to ask whether the toilets were bigger. Wally nodded, so Will suggested that a Texan's backside must be larger, too, or else he would fall in. This friendship lasted no longer than the one with Vinnie.

The only neighbor without a wife or family was Rusty Torino, a former TV star who now owned a retail carpet business in Trenton. As an adorable towheaded youngster, Rusty had costarred with Tiny, a Yorkshire terrier who rescued him in every episode from kidnappers, burglars, and various other villains with English accents and white spats. The ensuing years had not been kind to Rusty; at thirty, he was a stocky fellow, with abundant chest hair and a blond pompadour that was dark at the roots. Each day he plodded out to retrieve his newspaper dressed only in a black silk bathrobe, clutching a terrier identical to his original costar.

"I think he's, y'know, *funny,*" explained Abby Gallagher.

Julia concluded that in Abby's world there were two kinds of funny people, foreigners and homosexuals.

"But I do feel sorry for him," sighed Abby on Rusty Torino's behalf. "Nothing to look forward to but eternal damnation."

MEANWHILE, THE HIMMELS had continued to inspire Will's curiosity. To him, their foreignness implied a potential kinship. Their two-car garage housed two old Mercedes. One white 1959 two-door sedan with rusted wheel rims, and one powder-blue four-door coupe. Once he spotted the father, wearing a homburg, rolling out in the white car at 6:45 A.M. The garage door closed with a well-oiled hum. The next day Will set his alarm to 6:44, and a minute later the door went up; Mr. Himmel was always on time. At around ten or eleven the second car would emerge, mother in front, hair whipped into a big blond meringue, cigarette in the hand dangling from the window. The girls' heads were usually visible in the back, always as far apart as possible. When they returned, the blue Mercedes drove into the garage, and the door rolled shut behind them. Did these girls never play? Were they prisoners? Did they yearn to escape?

Abby Gallagher's theory was that the Himmels had inherited wealth from one of the German weapons manufacturers during the war, and while they lived a modest existence, their fortune gathered interest in a Geneva bank. "Why else would they get so uptight whenever anyone mentions World War Two?" she asked.

Three weeks before school began, Will took up a position behind a tree, armed with binoculars and a red apple for sustenance. It was a cool day with an impulsive breeze. Fast-moving clouds swept by the sun, bringing the Himmel house in and out of shade while the cicadas droned.

Finally, that faint metallic hum announced the emergence of Mrs. Himmel's car. Smoke curled from the cigarette in her window hand, but just one silhouette was visible in the backseat.

Where was the other Himmel daughter?

Will thought he spotted a movement behind the lace curtains on the second floor. He trained his binoculars on them for fifteen minutes before giving up. Was she watching him watch her? he wondered.

At noon, frustrated, he tossed the uneaten apple onto the Himmel lawn and wandered inside for lunch.

HE FOUND THE TWINS watching TV. Julius loved the reruns of *Star Trek* and *Bonanza*; the pyromaniac in him loved the way the Bonanza ranch curled up in flames at the beginning of each episode. Marcus adored the commercials. His favorite was a soft-drink ad of a blond girl singing on a hilltop. She was beautiful and sweet, and he watched television simply to see this girl again and again.

"I want a Coke," Marcus said to Julia at lunch.

Julia disapproved of soft drinks, not just because they were loaded with caffeine and sugar but because of the shady American merchandising that went with them. Ask for a Coke in an English restaurant and you'd get a can of it, probably lukewarm, but a can nevertheless; ask for the same thing in America and you'd get a glass of ice with a dribbling of syrup at the bottom.

"Wish again," she snapped. "It'll destroy your teeth and ruin your life."

"How could it ruin my life?" asked Marcus, thinking of the pretty blond girl in the commercial. Her smile would surely make his life perfect.

"The answer is no," Julia declared.

After lunch, Will found the apple thrown back on his lawn with a bite taken out of it. He glanced at the Himmel house and detected a fluttering of the lace curtains in the upstairs window. After taking a fresh bite from the apple, he tossed it back onto the Himmels' lawn.

The next morning, Will found the apple back on his side of the yard. There were three bites in it now. Clearly, it was a reply, but what was its meaning? Will took a fourth bite from the apple, but no sooner had he tossed it back than he noticed Vinnie Imperatore squinting at him from across the street. The boy's huge overbite looked like a smile until he approached; then it became a territorial sneer.

"What'ja do *that* for?"

Will glanced at the lace curtains and sensed that Vinnie had followed his gaze.

"They don't *ever* come out," Vinnie said.

"Why not?"

Vinnie shrugged. "Foreigners," he explained, and squinted at Will. "What the hell you wearin'?"

In spite of the American clothes Julia had bought him, Will preferred his Avon Heath school uniform. It made him feel closer to Sally somehow. In a few weeks, when school started, he would switch to jeans and shirts.

"Goin' to church today?" asked Vinnie.

"I don't go to church."

Vinnie sneered again. "You don't go to church? Then you're goin' straight to hell. Are ya Catholic?"

"Catholic? No," said Will.

"Then it don't matter—you're goin' to hell no matter what."

Vinnie was Catholic. He explained that all Catholics were oppressed by non-Catholics.

"That's why the non-Catholics are goin' to hell. Yessir. Burn in flames a mile high." He then named all the families in University Hills who would burn in hell for *not* being Catholic.

"What about the Himmels?" asked Will. "Are *they* Catholic?"

Vinnie paused and peered up at the lace curtains.

"No, they ain't Catholic, but they ain't gonna burn in hell."

"Why not?"

"They're just not! Well, the parents might, and Marina might, but Astrid won't."

"Why not?"

"Never mind," said Vinnie, marching away. Then he cast one last warning over his shoulder. "If I were you, I'd see about convertin'!"

Will's notepaper had been lost on the trip to America, but he couldn't shake the habit of keeping his grandmother informed, and sent her a long letter that included a few choice quotes from Vinnie Imperatore.

I was just sitting down to the Thursday luncheon at my club—a particularly delicious vichyssoise concocted by our Belgian chef—when I opened my grandson's most recent letter.

Imagine my shock and surprise when it turned out to be a rather emphatic expression of his concern that I might suffer the flames of hell for eternity if I did not convert to Catholicism as soon as possible!

Well, it quite put me off the soup, not to mention the roasted lamb and walnut salad that followed! What has become of my grandson?

I can't imagine anybody in our family succumbing to such religious extremism except under incredible duress. Of course, I remind myself that America is first and foremost a country of religious fanatics. What else but lunatic theology could compel anyone to brave the Atlantic to start a new life in a wilderness with nothing to show for itself but the tomato and the turkey?

The Garden Party

It was a beautiful Sunday in early September when the Finches held their end-of-summer barbecue party. Frank Finch liked to echo the picnics of his childhood in the Houston suburbs, with checkered tablecloths, a beer keg, and a big, black oil-barrel-shaped barbecue rig with three kinds of sauces, stainless-steel carving knives, and enough smoke to simulate a midsized brushfire.

Mrs. Urquhart had taught Julia that Shakespeare liked to use storms for his pivotal moments, but Julia would note that disaster struck the Laments in docile weather. It was their fifth week in America. A crisp breeze sent the silver birches whispering; Rusty Torino's maple had turned early, the fringes of its lower leaves ignited in amber and yellow tips. The boys were impatient for school to begin, and Julia hoped the garden party might be the perfect ice-breaking opportunity; perhaps she could finally meet an American friend like Trixie.

Frank Finch wasn't a talker like Buck Quinn, but he reminded Howard of the man as he hacked and wheezed in the smoke, checking and rechecking his glorious tenderloins and brushing sauce over the Cornish hens huddled in one corner of the grill.

"Beautiful sight, man," said Lionel Gallagher, peering over his cherry-colored shades.

"Yes, that's Black Angus beef, son."

"I meant the smoke."

Frank glanced in the direction of Lionel's parents, who had brought deck chairs and were bathing in the sun's last rays, sipping tall glasses of rum and Coke.

"Lionel," murmured Frank, "do me one favor?"

"Sure, man."

"Keep your clothes on at my party. Will you do that for me? I don't want a scene like last Christmas, d'you understand? Not in front of the kids."

"Last Christmas?" murmured Lionel; he had forgotten the day when the Finches and the Imperatores came caroling to the Gallaghers' house. Lionel had opened the door, naked from head to toe and clutching a three-foot bong. This caused a stampede among the carolers, and the collapse of the second verse of "Good King Wenceslas."

As Lionel fondled the curly stubble on his chin, Frank entertained a brief impulse to clip it off with his stainless-steel cleaver. Sensing Frank's hostility, Lionel retreated to the porch, put his hands together in prayer, bowed eastward, and assumed the lotus position. Meanwhile, the Laments were greeted by Cosmo Imperatore, husky-voiced, with a thick neck and a habit of blinking furiously when he spoke.

"Nixon's gonna win this war," he told Howard. "Makes me crazy seeing these hippies make fun of the president. Just once I'd like to see some freaks in Vietnam getting killed by the communists, just so they could understand what we're fighting for!"

"War is over if you want it!" Lionel sang in a falsetto, from the porch.

"Thank you, Lionel!" growled Frank through the billowing smoke; his three chins glistened with sweat. In his leather apron, tongs in hand, Julia thought he looked like Vulcan at his forge.

"Have you met all the neighbors?" asked Frank.

"Most of them, except for the Himmels," Julia replied. "We haven't met any black families yet. Do any live here in University Hills?"

Frank smiled as if Julia had just arrived from a distant planet. "Oh, no. Not around here. I guess they like to be around their own kind."

"Their own kind?" said Julia incredulously. "I thought America was quite integrated."

"It is," said Frank. "Why, there are Italians, Germans, Irish here! I think we even have a Jewish family down the street."

Rusty Torino plunked a half-empty bottle of Chivas on the beverage table and sank into a deck chair, clutching his terrier. He wore a billowing Hawaiian shirt over his expansive gut, white boating shoes, and mirrored sunglasses even though the sun was barely an ember through the cluster of birch trees on the horizon.

"Well, the movie star's here," said Frank. "You want a burger, Rusty?"

"I can't eat a thing," said Rusty, while his terrier peered miserably at the Cornish hens, whose size and physique roughly approximated his own. Frank stuffed a beef morsel into Tiny's mouth. The Yorkie scarfed it down and immediately threw up on Rusty's shoes. This did not stop Frank from introducing Julia and Howard to Rusty. "You must have heard of Rusty Torino; he was on a famous TV show."

"Sorry, we've just arrived in America," said Julia with an apologetic smile.

Looking slightly disappointed, Rusty glanced from Julia to Howard. "You're English," he noted.

"No, actually we're—"

"Always had English villains on my show," continued Rusty wistfully. "Something about that accent made them sound evil, y'know."

THE FINCHES' TIRE SWING was the main attraction for the kids. Wally Finch asserted his dominion by commandeering the tire from the more helpless tots and swinging, upside down by his knees, across the driveway and over Frank's barbecue setup. He landed just short of the beverage table with rippling haunches and a fearsome grunt. Though Wally

was overweight and clumsy, he commanded respect the way a bull elephant seal governs the beach, by mass and bluster. When greeted by the
crafty smiles of the Lament twins, he sensed a threat to his primacy.

"Can I do that?" asked Julius.

"Nope," said Wally. "My party, my swing, my turn."

"I'll have the next turn," Julius said, undaunted.

"And me!" cried Marcus.

"When I *say*," said Wally.

Wally dragged the swing back to the porch roof, followed by the
twins, and again soared over the party. When he landed, he lost control
of the tire for a moment, and Julius was waiting to grab it. Wally
marched up to Julius, butting him with his chest.

"Did I *say* you could have that?"

"You let it go," said Julius, handing the swing to Marcus. Wally
lunged at Marcus, who handed the swing over to Julius, leaving Wally
sputtering.

"Let him have a turn," said Will.

Wally spun around to face Will, which freed the twins to scramble
up onto the porch roof. Muttering a silent curse, Wally marched over
to the chip and pretzel table.

Mickey and Kent Gallagher were clambering up Madge's latticework as Julius took flight above them. They flailed at him with their
hockey sticks until Frank Finch threatened to take them away. Vinnie
Imperatore's little brothers and sisters tore after Julius as he landed,
but he evaded them in an effort to get the rope back to Marcus for his
turn.

Hearing Lionel Gallagher begin chanting *om*s from the porch,
Will observed that Lionel bore no resemblance to his parents or brothers. For a moment, Will worried that this disaffected lunatic was his
own fate staring back at him.

Then the evening light changed hue. Perhaps it was the smoke
from Frank's fire as it lifted its cloaky haze to reveal the approach of
two figures; Will recognized them merely by their profiles.

The first figure, a tall, gangly man with a large head and enormous hands that swung by his side, was followed by a diminutive woman with a vast swirl of blond hair. She wore a Bavarian peasant blouse with puffed sleeves, and a neat blue skirt and blue pumps. Halfway across the street, the couple stopped, and the father turned to his house, beckoning with a sweep of his arm.

"Astrid! *Komm mit!*"

A figure emerged and danced across the grass to catch up with her parents. Though her face and figure might have been judged plain by themselves, there was a sweetness in her manner and open smile; it was enhanced by her hair, not merely blond but golden, catching in its tresses the last glimmer of the sun.

Rusty put the terrier down in order to fully appraise this vision; Frank Finch wiped the sweat from his chin; Cosmo Imperatore put down his cigar, and even the women regarded Astrid Himmel with the awe reserved for a wonder of nature. Suddenly it became clear to Will that Astrid was the Himmels' carefully kept secret.

As everybody greeted her, Max and Maria Himmel beamed with pride at their daughter's social glory. Even the infant Imperatores swarmed toward Astrid.

Then a moan came from the porch.

"Astrid! Astrid, I love you!"

It was Lionel. He had wrenched off his shirt, dropped his pants and underwear, and stood writhing with yearning, revealing a half-erect penis and imploring arms.

Vinnie's mother made the sign of the cross as Frank Finch bounded over and wrapped his barbecue apron around Lionel, hoisted him over his shoulder fireman style, and carried him through the trees while the acid freak wailed.

"I'll always love you, Astrid!"

For a moment, Max Himmel seemed genuinely amused by the spectacle, but a private remark from his wife quickly turned his expression into somber disapproval.

In the midst of this fuss, Abby and Patrick Gallagher sipped their drinks, apparently content to pretend that Lionel was no relation to them.

"Teenagers are such free spirits these days," sighed Madge. "Frank would never have been seen without socks at that age."

Cosmo lowered his cigar and shrugged. "Thank God for clothes, that's all I can say."

Julia and Madge were both diverted by Cosmo's white T-shirt, rotund belly, and the lavender plaid Bermuda shorts that emphasized his pale, knobbly knees and hairless legs. This ensemble was completed with black socks and sandals. The women met each other's glance and burst into laughter. It was the kind of moment Julia had hoped for at this party.

Max Himmel greeted Howard with a vigorous handshake, but Howard was puzzled by his neighbor's tone, which veered sharply between amusement and outrage.

"Here we are, Howard, 1969, and I look at the television, and this show, *Hogan's Heroes,* very funny, you understand, but it makes every German a *buffoon.* But every Japanese is *inscrutable* and *wise.* Was it not the same war?"

"Hmm, perhaps Americans feel remorse for dropping the bomb on Hiroshima?" suggested Howard.

Max narrowed his eyes. "Yes, but what about Dresden? The Allies firebombed Dresden, a city of innocents just like Hiroshima. Yes, the Jews died in the millions, I know this, but did no innocent Germans die?"

Howard conceded that some had.

With a wry smile, Max beckoned Howard closer. "America, my friend, is like a big cocktail party," he whispered.

"A cocktail party? What do you mean?" asked Howard.

"I mean it looks easy to fit in—just smile, wave, have another drink—but we are all so different!" Max's smile faded as he looked around the garden party. "And always the pressure to fit in! People tell me to change cars," he said. "Buy a Ford! A Chevy! Get rid of the Mercedes—don't be so *German.*" Max rolled his eyes. "Even my wife wants a Ford. She says, 'Think of the girls, *act* like an American.'"

Then Maria summoned him with a tilt of her head, and Max excused himself with a defeated shrug, following her to the buffet table.

. . .

ASTRID SMILED AT THE LITTLE CHILDREN who were clustered around her like moths drawn to a lamp. Beyond them, Vinnie, the Gallagher boys, and Wally gathered in a group, all obviously smitten.

Will knew instantly why he wasn't inside this gathering. He thought of Digley's games in the playground. He'd been in the group; he'd been outside the group; and, frankly, the view was better from the outside. But one thing perplexed him: he couldn't picture Astrid taking bites out of his apple. There was no hint of rebellion in her pretty face.

Then Will noticed an unfamiliar girl skirting the party; she had Max Himmel's wide forehead, stormy gray eyes, and a pall of dark hair pulled back by a tortoiseshell barrette. The sleeves of her sweater tapered past her hands, and she wore wool stockings in spite of the warmth of the evening.

"Ah, Marina, finally!" said her father.

Will could see how, in some bizarre exchange of genes, Astrid's beauty was a combination of all the conventional features of her parents, while Marina had inherited what remained—her mother's vulnerable mouth, her father's long stride, and the unsettled look in his eyes. Hers was an uneasy kind of beauty. Now Will recognized the girl who had bitten into his apple: she watched the boys fawning over her pretty sister with silent scrutiny, just as she must have watched him from her window.

The boys quickly turned their ardor into a contest: Vinnie eagerly offered Astrid the potato salad, the Gallagher boys each grabbed one of four variations of cold pasta, and Wally Finch presented her with the meat platter. Astrid gushed at her devotees while Marina circled like a stray cat.

She came to a stop behind Will's shoulder, making it impossible for him to look directly at her.

"You're a spy," she murmured.

"What?" said Will.

"Watching my house. I saw you," she whispered, lowering her chin behind his ear. "You're a spy."

"You bit the apple, didn't you?" he replied.

Marina cast him a mischievous glance. "Why don't you offer my sister the chips?"

"Why should I?" he replied.

"Don't you like her? *Everybody* loves Astrid." There was a hint of derision in her voice, but Will wasn't sure whether it was directed at him or her sister. "You should see her tap-dance and play the piano," she continued. "And she's on the honor roll. She sings in the choir, front row, every Sunday."

ALL THIS TIME Marcus had been sitting on the roof of the Finches' house with the rope in his hand. A joyous epiphany had struck him. Astrid Himmel was the living embodiment of his dream girl—her face, her hair, her figure. All the elements of his favorite commercial had come together.

"Marcus! I bet you can't swing from your legs," Julius challenged.

Marcus didn't reply. His eyes were fixed on Astrid, who was laughing at something Vinnie had said.

"Hey, Marcus!" repeated Julius.

Astrid looked up as Julius repeated his dare. Marcus blushed as he felt her bright gaze.

"Bet you can't swing over everybody, just by your legs!"

"Of course I can!" Marcus replied.

With the golden girl's attention now fixed on him; Marcus dusted off his hands and mounted the swing.

HAVING RETURNED from the Gallaghers' house, where he had dumped Lionel after a stern lecture on public behavior, Frank loaded up a serving platter with the last few T-bones. He was debating taking the two large steak knives into the kitchen to be cleaned when Madge suggested that he have a bite before the meat disappeared. He propped the two knives in the rack so that the blades would face down. But one knife wouldn't go in all the way. It was the long knife, a twelve-inch stainless steel from Sheffield. About six inches of the blade sat just above the rack, exposed. Frank looked around, concluded that it would be safely out of reach of the little kids, and went off to have his T-bone.

"MARCUS, GET ON WITH IT, or let me do it," complained Julius as he shot Astrid a cocky grin. Both twins were aware of the girl's attention now, and each wanted the spotlight.

"I'm going. Don't rush me," said Marcus, turning anxiously for some signal from Astrid. She raised her hand to shield her eyes from the sun, and smiled.

Hanging from his knees, Marcus swung across the driveway. His path took him directly over the barbecue grill and he continued on his way, toward the soft earth for his landing, but he didn't let go. Perhaps it was because he knew that he would fall on his face, and he didn't want Astrid to see this, or perhaps he simply misjudged when to release his legs. He saw Astrid watching him, her mouth open with surprise. Savoring every second of her attention, Marcus let the rope swing him back.

At this moment, Frank Finch realized that Marcus's hands were reaching out for a way to stop his fall, and that he was heading for the grill.

"Stop!" cried Frank.

Marcus released his legs and flew over the heads of the children, over the Imperatores, the Gallaghers, and the Finches. He imagined that his hand had merely bumped the grill, because the rig clattered as he made his landing on the grass, a giddy smile on his face.

People would talk later about the accident with awe, as if, in spite of what happened, Marcus's first few seconds aloft had been glorious. Indeed, as he flew, it was a remarkable sight, even to Astrid; but the smile on Marcus's lips and the eagerness in his eyes as he soared overhead would haunt her for years.

Aftermath

Will blamed himself. He should have been watching. Perhaps he could have persuaded Marcus not to hang by his feet, or caught him in midair, or pushed the enormous barbecue rig out of the way, and perhaps Marcus wouldn't have landed on his hands, and his right hand wouldn't have been sheared off by the stainless-steel carving knife that Frank Finch had propped up between the bars of the grill a moment before.

Julius saw his brother's wrist bleeding before anyone else did; he grabbed Frank Finch's fresh apron and wrapped it, tying the apron strings around it tightly, for a tourniquet; it was something he had learned on TV, which discounted Julia's attempt to blame television and the Coca-Cola Company for what happened—though she tried. Julius blamed himself for teasing Marcus, and wept all night until a surgeon at the hospital told him that his tourniquet had probably saved Marcus from bleeding to death.

Astrid was sobbing as the Himmels led her away; Mrs. Himmel covered her daughter's eyes with her hand, to shield her from the awful sight. Marina lingered behind her parents, torn between their commands and her morbid curiosity. She was the last person to see the severed hand cooking on the grill before Frank Finch secretly buried it in his backyard. This would weigh on Frank's conscience for a week, until, unable to sleep, he went out one night with a shovel, only to find that a dog had dug it up. Rusty Torino found his terrier playing with something resembling a shriveled gardening glove. He tossed it into Cosmo's yard, where it was discovered a week later by Cosmo's wife. Deemed an object of no significance, it was thrown in the trash.

MARCUS WOULD BE THE FIRST to accept his new condition; it would take everyone else forever. That's the way it is with children. They get up and carry on.

Not so for Julia; she had brought America a healthy boy and, in return, America had deformed him. There was no consolation, even in sleep. In one dream she found herself searching through an enormous department store, going aisle to aisle, opening box after box, believing that she was getting closer and closer to finding Marcus's missing hand. When she finally reached the top floor and opened the last box, she found not a hand but her lost baby, grinning that ear-to-ear smile from long ago.

Howard gave Julia comfort when she cried; but his own sorrow was expressed in a desperate smile that always seemed moments shy of collapse. This expression settled permanently over his face.

Marcus's prosthetic hand was a flesh-colored plastic device with two hooks that could pinch together. He operated it by clenching the muscles in his forearm. Over time, with mounting facility, he managed to do everything from flipping quarters to opening soda bottles. Julius began to envy him, and said he wanted his own prosthetic hand, which elicited dark stares from his parents.

Julia put off looking for a job while Marcus recuperated. During the first weeks of school, which he missed, Julia coached him with his brother's homework.

"Will I be stupid when I go to school?" he worried.

"You'll be smarter," replied Howard, "because your mother is teaching you."

Julia became most disappointed in the neighbors, who kept their distance from the Laments over these weeks. Nobody called, or offered a sympathetic word, until Rusty Torino showed up at the door one afternoon.

"Just thinking of you folks," he said. Rusty was dressed in his most somber outfit, a black Hawaiian shirt with tastefully small golden palm trees. He produced a box of chocolates for Marcus, and white irises for Julia.

"How thoughtful of you," said Julia, shooting a fierce glance at the houses behind him. "You're the only one, you know!"

"The only one?"

"To express any bloody concern! Honestly, the people around here are unspeakably callous."

"Maybe they're just shocked," suggested Rusty. "What happened to you guys is any family's worst nightmare."

"Unforgivable," Julia continued. "It's television that's to blame! Everybody's too used to changing channels when they see something upsetting!"

Rusty looked bewildered by Julia's fury. "Well, I can't speak for them, I just . . ."

Suddenly Julia felt remorse for lashing out at Rusty. "Of *course* you can't—please forgive me," she cried. "And do tell me, how's . . . that little dog of yours?"

"Fine," Rusty sighed. "Thanks for asking."

As the man retreated, Julia decided to ring Madge.

"Thought you might be wondering how we're doing," she began, her rage barely concealed.

"Julia, how . . . *is* everybody?" asked Madge with obvious discomfort.

"Thank you for asking," Julia said. "Everybody's all right except Marcus, of course. He's learning to write with the other hand."

"Oh my," said Madge. "We're just devastated. Frank will *never* have another barbecue. And poor Wally will *never* . . . I mean, it happened in his *own backyard*."

"Poor Wally?"

"Devastated. He'll never eat meat again," explained Madge.

"You have my sympathy." Julia slammed down the phone.

WORD GOT AROUND that Marcus had been given a claw to replace his hand, and there always seemed to be one or two children near the house, angling for a sideshow glimpse. Marcus, at Julius's urging, stuck a ghastly rubber eyeball to one of his eyelids and, waving a twisted garden fork with his prosthesis, ran out with a bloodcurdling cry to execute Julius in the front yard. Julius dribbled ketchup from his lips, wailing for Christ and the Virgin Mary before assuming rigor mortis, his eyeballs frozen on his audience (he then repeated this performance three times for newcomers).

This time the Laments received *lots* of phone calls for traumatizing the neighbors' children.

"Perhaps they shouldn't *be* outside. Perhaps the little darlings should have been watching *television* instead!" Julia replied.

AS DR. UNDERBERG HAD ONCE TOLD HOWARD, life deals tragedy and opportunity in equal measures. It was because of the garden party that Will finally met Marina Himmel, and though she was nothing like Sally Byrd, she was just what he needed. When she whispered over his shoulder, Will got goose bumps. Perhaps it was her voice, with its familiarity, its intimate murmur: *You're a spy*. She spoke the truth. He *was* a spy. She knew him in this secret way, for she was an outsider too.

But there was a complication.

When Marcus fell from the Finches' tire, Will felt an awful sense of guilt. If not for Marina, and her slate-colored eyes and delicate mouth, he might have saved his brother. But the more shame he felt, the more he thought about her. These two emotions, guilt and infatuation, were thus entwined. And the more guilt there was, the more desire.

Desire for what? Even if he was a romantic, he was only thirteen. A kiss was his precipice. Any further arousal would have been sweet death for him.

Miss Bayonard

When he knocked at the classroom door, a jolt of Eau de Fleurs pinched his nostrils. The classroom was foggy with the stuff, enough to overwhelm the musty odor of old textbooks. By the time Will came to his senses, he was seated, eyes fixed on the vertex of his teacher's thighs and the hemline of her apricot minidress as she walked back to her desk.

"Class, this is Will Lament. Will is from England. I'm sure we can all learn a lot from him," said his new math teacher, Francine Bayonard.

When she smiled at Will, his pulse throbbed like a Harley. Her auburn hair was parted down the center; twenty times an hour she cleared a stray hair with a long, lacquered fingernail. When she enunciated "multiplicative inverses," her frosted lips beckoned to him. And it didn't help that it was a steamy room. He became feverish as Miss Bayonard multiplied fractions. Then Marina turned up in the seat behind him.

"I'm watching you, Lament," she murmured.

With Marina whispering her taunts behind his ear and Miss Bayonard stirring his loins, Will was in torment.

"Are you all right, Will?" asked the teacher.

"Hmm?"

"I know this must be a lot to absorb—a new country, new class-mates."

"Yes, Miss Bayonard," he gasped. "It's a lot."

At the end of the day, Miss Bayonard took him aside to suggest that he stay after school for a few weeks to catch up on his math.

"With you?" he choked.

"Yes. With me."

TWO MONTHS HAD PASSED since Howard had reported to work, and Chapman Fay was still absent. There had been a radio report from In-donesia, but the details were sketchy. His boat needed repairs. He wired for money. Apparently he planned to continue around the world before returning to Fay/Bernhardt. It would be another month or two.

"Howard, your job is safe," promised Dick Bernhardt, who had grown a goatee since Howard last saw him. "Consider this time an opportunity to build up your portfolio of ideas! When Chapman gets back, you'll be ready."

With that in mind, Howard laid out his theories for irrigating the southern Sahara. He then put together a design for a mechanical heart with a series of valves that required the tiniest power source. He had been toying with this idea ever since the death of his father, when hearts were irreplaceable. Howard found an engineer in the basement of Fay/Bernhardt to build a plastic mock-up for him; it was a wondrous-looking device, made of translucent plastic and stainless steel. But Dick Bernhardt refused to examine it.

"Look, I run the company, I don't deal with new projects. Just wait for Chapman to get back."

Howard was beginning to worry that Chapman Fay was a phan-tom, a taunting illusion encouraging his youthful idealism. He made an extra effort during dinner to keep the conversation off the subject of his work.

"So what's your teacher like?" he asked Will.

"Fine," replied Will, using a tone that made Julia think of Howard's miserable replies to her questions about Pan-Europa. She might have pursued the matter if she hadn't also been worrying about Marcus, who was trying to serve himself peas with his prosthetic hand. Every time he spilled, she would flinch, desperately wanting to help though she'd been cautioned by the doctor not to fuss too much over him. Dinnertime was exhausting; between the cooking, Marcus's half-baked attempts to feed himself, and Julius's jealousy, she felt unappreciated and spent.

"Whoops!" Marcus cast a spoonful of peas across the table at Julius.

"That was on *purpose*!" shouted Julius. "He's shooting at me on purpose! *He's shooting at me on purpose!*"

"Julius, stop!" warned Julia, glaring at Marcus.

"I'm innocent," Marcus insisted, with a beatific smile.

"What's the teacher's name?" continued Howard.

"Bayonard. Miss Bayonard," answered Will.

"Is she nice?" Julia asked.

Will paused, and nodded, thinking of Miss Bayonard climbing into her little gray Karmann Ghia. She had to hike up her minidress a few inches and wriggle sideways into the low bucket seat. This took considerable effort, her feet kicking at the curb for leverage, a glimpse of her peach underwear, the car rocking excitedly on its wheels. Some boys enjoyed watching a backhoe dig a trench in the street; Will would happily have watched Miss Bayonard squeeze into her sports car for an eternity.

But his reverie was interrupted by another storm of peas flying across the dinner table.

"It's the claw—I can't control it!" exclaimed Marcus.

"Marcus, that's enough!" Howard warned him.

"How come *he* gets away with stuff I can't get away with?" Julius complained, shaking the peas out of his shirt collar.

"Because I'm pitiful," Marcus gloated.

"Eat your food," said Howard.

"Hey!" roared Julius, as Marcus steered his prosthetic hand toward Julius's crotch, clenching it firmly on a bulge.

"Can't control it"—Marcus smiled helplessly—"it's got a mind of its own."

"Can't we just have dinner like a normal family?" shouted Howard as the doorbell rang.

JULIA FOUND A STRANGER at the door—a young woman, her hair in a bun, with a spark of warmth in her eyes, holding a wad of flyers and a clipboard.

"Hi, I'm Martha. I'm collecting for battered women."

"Sorry. I'm not . . ." began Julia.

"Oh, you have nothing to be sorry for," replied Martha brightly, "unless you're a battered woman yourself, in which case you should be feeling *very* sorry for yourself!"

"I certainly am *not* a battered woman," replied Julia, smoothing her blouse and thinking that she did feel sorry for herself, which made her sorrier still.

Martha caught a glimpse of Marcus and Julius trying to bite each other's shins beneath the dining room table.

"Not battered, just frayed around the edges, perhaps?"

"Perhaps," admitted Julia. She looked at the eager face in the doorway, wondering whether her visitor was demented, naive, or perhaps, by some generous act of God, a kindred spirit, just when she needed one.

Martha explained that she was fund-raising for a group called the Women's Congress, which helped battered women find accommodations when they were trying to escape from an unhealthy relationship, and that she also belonged to a group of women who met once a week to talk about women's issues.

"I'm not furious enough to be a women's libber," Julia replied.

"Neither are we," said Martha with amusement. "We talk, debate, and encourage each other. Why don't you drop in one time?" Martha gave Julia her phone number, and walked down the drive, casting Julia a last, gentle smile. "We meet on Thursdays," she added.

"You were gone a long time," said Howard when Julia found him emerging from the bathroom, where the twins were having their bath.

"Trouble with the boys?" she asked.

"Darling, I can certainly handle them for a few minutes." Howard laughed. "After all, you cope with them all afternoon!" At that moment, Julia heard the sound of a colossal wave of water striking the bathroom floor.

"Of course you can," said Julia, watching the circle of wet carpeting expand beneath Howard's feet. "Actually, Howard, I was wondering how you'd feel about my taking a night off once a week to join a women's group. Just to talk?"

"Good idea," Howard insisted, not realizing that his Thursday evenings would never be the same again.

MARTHA WAS A POTTER; her small clapboard house was adorned with delicate vases and splashy paintings by her five-year-old son, Lennon. She had met her husband, Jake, on a commune in Penobscot Bay.

All the women in Martha's group welcomed Julia in turn. Phyllis Minetti, compact and tightly strung, explained that she was childless. "But my husband is a successful cosmetic surgeon in New York and my life is complete," she added with a tidy smile.

This provoked a smirk from Avé Brown, a big woman with a top-knot, and eyeliner like the early Supremes. Avé, the mother of four boys, was a high school dropout. "Tell her about your degrees, Phyllis!" she said.

"I don't like to brag, Avé," replied Phyllis.

Avé whispered to Julia, "Watch her, she's going to work it into the conversation anyway."

The last woman in the group was Frieda Grecco; she had a timid, pretty face framed by ringlets of glossy black hair and large black-rimmed glasses. She said nothing, but laughed at the exchanges between Avé and Phyllis to the point of tears. Julia noticed that when Frieda pulled her ringlets back behind one ear, she revealed a bruise by her temple. It made Julia think of Trixie's black eye. But when Frieda sensed Julia's scrutiny, she hastily pulled her hair down.

The stereo played Mozart, Aretha Franklin, and Dave Brubeck. Wine and cheese were served, as well as marijuana in a bong Avé had borrowed from her teenage son. At the end of the evening, Julia felt relaxed and in good company, and nobody had mentioned even once that she was a foreigner.

"Julia, will you come back next Thursday?" asked Martha as she saw Julia to the door.

"I wouldn't miss it," Julia answered. It had been a long time since she had been in the company of friends.

IT WASN'T EASY getting the hang of converting decimals when Miss Bayonard was wearing shiny thigh-high black boots.

"Will, you're not concentrating."

"Sorry, Miss Bayonard."

When they got to absolute values, she wore a herringbone jacket and miniskirt with black stiletto heels. Will loved the dimples in her knees. He hobbled to the blackboard with his hands in his pockets, trying to conceal his arousal.

And it wasn't any easier at night. His dreams had changed. Instead of the Midnight Chinaman, Miss Bayonard appeared, offering to discuss powers of ten, wrapped in nothing but a black feather boa.

"I think Will's having wet dreams," said Julia to Howard after Will had left for school.

"Already?"

"He *is* almost fourteen," she replied.

"He seems anxious these days," Howard remarked. "I'm not sure whether this tutoring is helping. Whenever I ask about it, he turns red in the face!"

"Let's invite her for dinner," Julia suggested.

. . .

IN THE WEEK PRECEDING Miss Bayonard's visit, Will felt a torrent of panic. For his teacher, a figure of erotic fantasy, to set foot in his house was the collision of two separate worlds.

He was thinking about this during a study session in the library when Marina noticed him. "What's wrong with you?" she said. "You look like you're about to throw up."

"Nothing's wrong," Will sputtered.

"How's your brother doing?"

"Fine," said Will, adding, "I think he's finally over your sister."

"What do you mean by that?" replied Marina.

"He was looking at her when he had the accident. He thought she was the Coca-Cola girl. That silly hair."

"Her hair?" repeated Marina, looking upset.

Will nodded. "Her hair is what did it."

Then Marina slapped him. It was a quick, sharp blow that made his eyes brim with tears. But, to his astonishment, he noticed tears rolling down her cheeks, too.

"Why'd you do that?" His face began to throb.

"Shut up about my sister's hair!" she cried, and walked away.

Will felt Marina's slap on his cheek for the rest of the day. There was nothing visible in the mirror, but his humiliation lingered. On his way home from school, she followed him, eventually catching up.

"I didn't mean to hit you so hard," she said.

Will kept walking.

"I thought you were blaming my sister for what happened, which wasn't fair to her."

For four blocks, Marina continued by his side, though she didn't say another word.

"What *is* it?" he finally asked.

"About eight years ago, my sister lost her hair. She wears a wig."

"I don't believe you," he replied.

"It's true. When we came to America, I was five, and she was four, and her hair was beautiful, and it hung down to her shoulders. We couldn't go anywhere without people talking about it. Then, a few weeks after we arrived here, it began falling out. Every morning she woke up with less of it. So my mom bought her this beautiful wig. And she's worn it ever since."

"What's wrong with her?"

"There's a name for it, but I've forgotten. The doctors say her hair might come back, or it might be gone forever." She gave him a warning glance. "It's a secret," she said. "Do you understand?"

Will nodded, and Marina headed toward her house. At her door, she paused and looked at him before disappearing inside. He sensed that he'd been told more than a secret. Marina had given up a burden.

When he walked up the driveway, Will noticed Marcus sitting on the steps, cracking acorns with his prosthesis.

"What were you talking to her about?" asked his brother.

"Nothing," Will replied. How could he tell his brother that he had lost his hand for a girl who was a complete illusion?

THREE DAYS LATER Marina appeared on the lawn as Will carried out a bag of trash from the kitchen.

"Did you tell anyone what I said?"

"Yes. Everyone," he replied. "I told the whole world that your sister was as bald as a coconut."

She stared at him, unamused.

"I'd kill you," she murmured.

Marina told Will how ignored she had felt as her parents became obsessed with Astrid's problem. As the first child, she had been demoted in affection. Will sympathized with this; he told her about the twins' misbehavior, the story of the Ridgeback, the cat with a Ping-Pong ball attached to its tail, the escapades on the *Windsor Castle*. As elder siblings, Will and Marina became allied. It was like having another Sally Byrd. No, it was better than that, Will decided, because Marina knew what it was like to be a foreigner.

"You won't tell anyone what I really think, will you?" he asked.

"And you won't tell anyone what *I* really think, will you?" she answered.

ON THE NIGHT of Miss Bayonard's visit, Will fussed over his appearance in the mirror. He was almost as tall as Howard; his dark-blond hair fell to his shoulders, and his eyes had retained their melancholy cast. He searched for some family resemblance, the way he always did, and found none, then made one last attempt to tame his hair with the blow-dryer.

"Trying to look nice for Teacher?" asked Julius, watching from the bathroom doorway.

"Go away," said Will.

"It won't work, Will," said Marcus sympathetically. "Your hair looks like an exploded banana peel."

The doorbell rang.

"I'll get it," said Marcus with wicked delight, but Will beat him to it.

A New Jersey state trooper stood at the door. Black pants with a blue stripe, massive gun hanging at his hip, blue hat with shiny black visor, cuffs on the back of his belt, and a nameplate: SCHNEIDER, B.

"Hi, I'm Franny Bayonard's husband," explained the trooper.

"Come in, come in!" said Julia while Will stood in shock, his hand glued to the doorknob.

"She's on her way; we came from opposite sides of town."

"Will!" said his mother. "Please keep Mr. Schneider company while I bring out something to snack on!"

Will sat down with the cop in the living room. What do you say to your teacher's husband, especially when he turns out to be a trooper? Was Miss Bayonard even old enough to have a husband? Luckily, Marcus showed up. He blinked at Trooper Schneider and grinned.

"My brother's been working on his hair for hours because his teacher is coming," explained Marcus.

"That so?" said Trooper Schneider.

Will calculated the seconds it would take to pull the trooper's service revolver out and . . . but reason prevailed.

Marcus bounced in his chair, eyes on the ceiling, trying to think of something else to say; then he grinned. "I've got no hand, wanna see?"

"Well . . ." began Trooper Schneider.

"Look," said Marcus excitedly, pulling off his prosthesis.

Julia set a beer down for the trooper, then noticed Marcus waving his stub at the man.

"Marcus," she cried, "for godsakes, go watch television!"

Trooper Schneider smiled nervously at Will, and dabbed at his forehead with a napkin. Will noticed that the man's sideburns went down to his jawline.

"How do you like class, Will?" said the trooper.

"I love her—it—I mean, I love *it*," said Will. He tried to think of a question to get off the subject. *How do you like shooting people,* perhaps?

When the doorbell rang again, the twins raced to answer it. Soon Miss Bayonard came up the stairs and smiled at Will. She looked different. Her glasses were missing; their absence made her eyes seem beady.

"Hi, Will." She blinked.

"Hi, Miss Bayonard," said Will.

"Honeybunch," murmured Schneider, "where are your glasses?"

"Oh, Bernie?" She squinted. "Is that *you*?"

For Will, what was most irritating about the meal was the way his parents seemed to share so many of their private aspirations with her.

"When did you decide to be a teacher?" asked Howard.

"Oh," Miss Bayonard said, "when I was halfway through college, I just *knew*."

Julia nodded. "I felt the same way."

"Do you still teach?"

"No, I stopped with my first pregnancy, but I plan to work again," said Julia, glancing briefly at Howard.

Miss Bayonard linked hands with Trooper Schneider, and there was a brief pause as the adults looked for something new to say. To Will's horror, their eyes seemed to converge on him.

"Will's a wonderful boy," said Miss Bayonard, beaming.

"And how is he doing?" asked Howard.

Will felt himself blush. Now he was merely an object in the discussion. Miss Bayonard said something nice about his progress and assured his parents that the tutoring was just to introduce math concepts that weren't covered in the British system until later.

Will watched Miss Bayonard eat chicken wings with her fingers, getting her long pink nails greasy and her lipstick smudged. During dessert, a strand of her hair fell into her ice cream bowl; she pulled it free, but it hardened. For the rest of the evening it stuck stiffly out of her head until Trooper Schneider set it right.

Will began to wonder what he'd ever found sexy about her. He wandered away to watch TV with the twins. It was a show about an impossibly happy family of six boys and girls.

"Will, come say good-bye!" called Julia later.

Will observed that Miss Bayonard looked rather squat next to his mother. And her eyes had wrinkles, like the doughy creases around mattress buttons.

"Well," his mother said at bedtime, "she seems nice enough. And she thinks you're clever. But we knew that, of course."

"That's nice." Will brooded, for Miss Bayonard's approval had lost its appeal. Strangely, he found himself thinking lustfully about Marina. She had something he'd never considered important before: youth.

Lost at Sea

TIMES-TELEGRAPH-DISPATCH

MELBOURNE, AUSTRALIA, APRIL 18, 1970: The partially decomposed body of an American businessman was discovered by coastal authorities aboard a yacht floating in the Coral Sea, 20 miles east of Brisbane this morning. Sails in tatters, its fuel tank empty, the "Inspiration," as it was named, had travelled some 1500 miles since its last radio transmission. Dental records have confirmed that the body was that of industrialist Chapman Fay, president of Fay/Bernhardt, a company based in Princeton, New Jersey.

Mr. Fay was a renowned inventor and ecologist, but he was best known for his attempts in 1967 to build a spaceship intended to colonize Mars. The spaceship venture, ridiculed by critics as a Noah's ark fantasy, was abandoned for lack of funding, and Mr. Fay turned his efforts to improving the environment.

The deceased had no survivors. His remains have been stored

cryogenically, and the majority of his estate has been left to a foundation established for paranormal research.

When Howard stopped going to work, the boys assumed he was sick. He rose late, and padded around in his pajamas. Julia told neighbors that Howard had been offered a paid leave of absence. This much was true, except that it was permanent.

American History

Though Will's grades were high, he was horribly bored and drew caricatures of his teachers in the margins of his notebooks. The history teacher, as thin as a wraith, had gray mutton chops and a righteous air. Mr. Wallace claimed to have eaten squirrel regularly for dinner during his childhood in the Depression. Will drew him eating a dozen of the creatures at a gulp. When Mr. Wallace taught the American Revolution, Will perked up, unaware that the British, heroes for the last six years of his schooling, were about to become villains. When Mr. Wallace asked for an explanation of the events of 1776, Will's hand shot up. But another boy in the front row, Ernest Woodbine, caught his attention.

"Yes, Ernest?"

"The British were imperialists, Mr. Wallace . . ."

Ernest spoke only to Mr. Wallace. This was probably why he was dismissed as a teacher's pet by his classmates. He was frequently afflicted with nosebleeds and often found his bootlaces tied together when he stood up from his desk. Will nicknamed him Scabby because his eyelashes were perpetually crusty from pinkeye, and depicted him in his notebooks as a naked cretin licking Mr. Wallace's boots.

"They oppressed the colonists with taxes and precip . . ." Scabby paused. "Precipitated a conflict."

The other kids also hated his big words. But this was Scabby's lucky day. He might have been a bootlicker, but he wasn't a foreigner.

"Just a minute!" said Will.

"And, sir," Scabby continued, "they forced the colonists to stage uprisings that led to the Revolution."

"Yes, Will?" said Mr. Wallace.

"Forced them? They wouldn't pay taxes," Will argued. "Was the British army supposed to serve the colonies for nothing?"

"Unfair taxes, sir," corrected the bootlicker.

"Taxes that paid for the soldiers who kept the peace," argued Will.

"An oppressive army of redcoats, Mr. Wallace," added Scabby. "Americans wanted freedom, justice, liberty—"

"Freedom? They *were* free!" argued Will. "They just didn't want to pay taxes!"

Suddenly blood began pouring from Scabby's nostrils. Quickly, he reached for the massive box of tissues inside his desk, clamped a wad to his nose, and, with a dramatic gulp, attempted to speak.

"Mr. Wallace? I don't believe my ears. Is he calling the Founding Fathers cheapskates?"

Until now, a bluebottle fly had distracted most of the students with its drone as it looped around the fluorescent lights. But all seats creaked forward at Scabby's cry. You could almost hear a fife and drum start up in the room. Mr. Wallace cast a troubled glance at Will.

"I don't think we need to insult the Founding Fathers, son," he said.

"I wasn't insulting anyone. All I said was that it was about money!"

"It was about liberty," blubbered Scabby through a wad of crimson-clotted tissue.

"Go back to England!" shouted a wise guy in the back row.

A girl in the second row stopped braiding her hair to glare at Will. "I think it's disrespectful to call our Founders cheapskates!"

"I think he should apologize!" said another.

Will shrank before a sea of unfriendly faces.

"But I didn't say *cheapskate*. . . ."

"Let's move on," said the teacher.

"Why can't I disagree, Mr. Wallace?"

"That's enough, Will," he replied.

During the soccer game in gym, Will felt a thud on his back and was hurled forward onto his chest, the wind knocked out of him. Above him stood three smiling figures.

"Sorry, limey," said one.

In the afternoon, he found a note on his desk that said GO BACK TO INGLAND. He stuffed the note in his pocket.

During assembly, he was hit by a spitball, and recognized the malevolent stare, two rows back: Scabby Woodbine, patriot nose-bleeder.

THOUGH JULIA AND HOWARD ENJOYED each other's company at home for the first week, Howard refused to discuss the future. Julia couldn't help but assign blame. She felt Howard had been betrayed by charlatans, and since there was no one to call (Fay/Bernhardt's offices were closed and emptied), she lost her temper with Howard.

"So much for the bloody American dream!" she cried. "Chapman Fay took care of that. It's as though we came here for nothing!"

"Well," said Howard, "it wasn't his fault. He sailed into bad weather."

"And what have *we* sailed into?" Julia was despairing. "Perhaps *that's* our problem as well; it's not bad weather, it's our own expectations! We must have been mad to come to America!"

"We were miserable in England," Howard murmured.

"Look at us now, Howard!" Julia went on. "I'd settle for miserable. Poor Marcus, he'd have been better off in England." She sighed. "The poor boy is a dreamer, just like *you*!"

"I'm sorry, darling," Howard whispered.

Immediately, Julia felt ashamed of herself. How could she blame Howard for being a dreamer? It was one of his most admirable qualities. So she bumped around the room, adjusting the salt and pepper shakers, realigning the glasses, until she could compose herself.

"How long can we last, Howard?"

"They're giving me regular severance checks. We'll be fine for five or six months."

GO BACK TO ENGLIND said the second note Will found on his desk. He showed it to Mr. Wallace, who addressed the class the following day.

"Class, yesterday a member of our class expressed an opinion, and we should have shown him respect. After all, in America we all have the right of free speech, which means the right to say what we think without fear of reprisal."

Later, Scabby Woodbine would clarify the matter when they were both pissing into urinals.

"You're a traitor, Lament. A lousy traitor. This is America, and you're a guest here. Don't forget that."

Will could hear Scabby's pee hitting the porcelain with all the force of a fire hose; he wondered how Woodbine would have done against Digley in the bog.

"I'm not a traitor, I'm from England. I'll defend England anytime I want!" Will replied.

Ernest Woodbine's attack on the porcelain stopped. He looked at Will.

"I respect your loyalty, Lament. But you're still a limey," he replied. "And if our nations ever oppose each other in combat, I swear I'll rip your heart out with my bare hands."

Scabby Woodbine's bare hands gave his penis a vigorous shake, and he marched out of the bathroom, his combat boots squeaking on the wet floor.

MEMORIAL DAY WAS ONE of only three days a year on which the Finches lowered their Texan flag from its little pole on the garage and replaced it with the Stars and Stripes. Rusty Torino, the Imperatores, and the Gallaghers hung bunting from their porches. Once a dozen neighbors did anything in University Hills, it became mandatory.

"Where's your flag?" asked Madge Finch when she saw Julia in the supermarket. It was the first thing she'd said to Julia since their awful phone conversation after Marcus's accident.

"My flag?" Julia blinked.

"You don't want to be the only house on the block without a flag!"

Even the Himmels posted a little flag on their mailbox. This inspired Julia to retrieve a scarf from her closet, which she tacked to the front door.

It was a four-foot-square Union Jack. "*There's* a bloody flag for them," she murmured.

An hour later, Will reported that he'd noticed a few cars slowing down when they passed the house.

Then there was a knock at the door.

"I couldn't help noticing your flag," said Rusty Torino. Though the skies had been overcast for weeks, his tan was still deep, and he wore a Hawaiian shirt with lots of little bald eagles clutching little Old Glories in their talons.

"I came over to offer this," said Rusty, producing a little hankie-sized flag, "just in case you guys couldn't find one over at the hardware store."

Julia gave Rusty a withering smile. "I take it you want me to replace my flag with this?"

"Just so people don't get the wrong idea. We're a community here."

"Well, of course we are," replied Julia. "But Memorial Day recognizes the soldiers who gave their lives in the wars, and lots of British soldiers died, too."

"I realize that, Julia." Rusty put his hand on his heart in a gesture of sympathy. "But that's *not* what the flag thing is about."

"No?" bristled Julia. "What *is* the flag thing about?"

"Look, Julia," said Rusty softly, "*nobody's* the same in this neighborhood. That's obvious. The Gallaghers do their Irish thing, the Imperatores are proud of their religion, and then there's Frank with his Texas flag, and me . . . with no kids, no wife, no girlfriend, and a little dog." He paused, looking her directly in the eye. "Look, I *know* what people say about me. But the point I'm trying to make is that the flag is just a way to remind everybody once in a while that we all share the same principles. Doesn't that make sense?"

"Yes, I see what you mean, Rusty. But I won't put up a flag just because everybody else does it. Besides, Memorial Day is an occasion to remember the dead, not gratify the living."

"Julia," warned Rusty, "you're going to upset *everybody*."

Julia accepted this warning, but her smile was firm. "I'm sorry, Rusty," she said softly. "But whenever I try to please everybody, I just end up disappointing *myself*."

ALL AFTERNOON, THE LAMENTS HEARD honks of outrage from passing cars. Though Julia and Howard seemed united in their resistance, Will cringed at every blast from the street. To a boy who thought of nothing but trying to *fit in*, his parents' attitude bordered on insanity.

"Do you want them to hate us?" he asked Julia.

"Hate us? Of course not. I just want to broaden their perspective a bit. No reason for every house to be a carbon copy of the next, even if the developer planned it that way."

"But at this rate I'll never make friends!"

Julia looked remorseful for a moment. "You shouldn't worry so much about pleasing people, Will. It's important for . . ."

Marcus drummed the windowpane with his prosthesis. "There's a kid out there staring at us!"

"He's muttering things," added Julius.

"Oh, Jesus," Will groaned, "that's Scabby Woodbine!"

"A friend of yours?" asked Julia.

"No. He hates me."

"Why?"

"Because he thinks I called the Founding Fathers cheapskates, because he's a lunatic!"

Julia joined them at the window. Scabby, in black boots and a T-shirt bearing the slogan MY COUNTRY RIGHT OR WRONG!, was wheeling his orange chopper bicycle in circles, with his crusty eyes fixed on the offending Union Jack.

"He keeps his boots very well polished," observed Julia. "When was the last time you polished your shoes?"

"Mum," Will barked, "I wear *sneakers* . . ."

But before Will had finished his sentence, his mother strode out of the house.

"Oh God." Will clutched his temples. "What's she *doing*?"

A moment later, Julia was leading a bewildered Scabby into the house. "You *must* have lunch with us," she said.

"Why?" protested Scabby.

"I want you to be friends with my son," replied Julia. "Please have lunch with us."

"I can't!"

"Mum?" said Will. "He doesn't *want* to!" He glanced at Scabby, surprised to be defending him.

"But you must, Scabby, you *must*!" declared Julia, propelling him up the split-level stairs to the dining room, where Howard was seated, the twins still at their lookout posts by the window. "That's Howard, you know Will, and that's Julius and Marcus!"

Scabby was momentarily distracted by Marcus, saluting with his prosthesis; his pink eyes surveyed the hands of the other Laments in case this was a family trait.

Julius grinned. "Hi, Scabby."

"My name isn't Scabby, it's Ernest!" said the boy with indignation.

"Ernest? Well that's a *wonderful* name," said Julia. "How on earth did you get that awful nickname?"

"I didn't know I *had* it!" he sputtered.

"I see," said Julia, casting a critical eye at Will. "And are you *really* enemies with my son, Ernest?"

"No, ma'am," gulped Scabby.

"He attacked me in class!" Will retorted.

"I *disagreed* with you," said Ernest. "This is the United States of America. I have a right to my opinion."

"Of *course* you do!" said Julia, extending Scabby an unnecessary amount of compassion by Will's account.

"I don't believe this!" cried Will.

"That's enough, Will," Julia said. "I think we're all hungry. Let's wash up, boys."

During lunch, Scabby Woodbine answered Julia's questions with the giddy delight of a boy who was rarely allowed to speak in his own house. Will, in protest, ate nothing. When Julia noticed Scabby's pinkeye, she insisted on treating him with the silver iodide solution that the doctor had prescribed for Julius a few weeks before. In spite of the hostility of her children, she was determined to put her patient to rights, for here was a child with a problem she could actually cure.

As for Will, it was one thing to sense the competition of a vanished sibling, another to be eclipsed in affection by the twins, but her attention to Scabby was raw betrayal. He stamped out of the house in protest, and hid in an overgrown clump of ferns in the backyard, a bitter sense of injustice gnawing at his insides.

"I LIKE YOUR FLAG," said a voice.

Marina's eyes rose from behind a spray of yucca petals in the Himmels' yard. She sat against a tree with a half-eaten apple in one hand.

"Oh," said Will. "Yeah, my mum put it up."

"She's cool."

"Or mad."

Marina shrugged. "My dad wouldn't *dare* put up a German flag. I suggested it; after all, plenty of Germans died in the war. He said nobody *cares* how many Germans died."

Will's eyes settled on the apple in her hand. Normally he loathed Granny Smiths; they were too tart for his taste. But now he regretted refusing to eat lunch, and eyed the fruit with yearning.

She followed his glance.

"Hungry?"

"Yes."

She held it toward him. He reached. She pulled back slightly, pleased at her own deception.

"*Boy*, are you hungry," she marveled, casting a cautious glance at the dark shapes of her parents on their screened-in porch.

"Come," she said, leading him to the end of the yard, where the ferns sprang wild and abundant. They were fiddleheads, their immature tips whorled like the scrolls of violins. Primordial ferns. He and Marina sat in the thick of them.

"Here," she purred, taking a bite from the apple and offering it to him.

Will bit into the apple; then she took a bite. They took turns this way, until Will noticed her mischievous smile and a trickle of moist pulp clinging to her lip. He leaned forward, and licked it off. Her mouth was Granny Smith sour. Somebody called from the house, but Will wasn't listening.

Tic-Tac Night

Scabby's mother, Pattie Woodbine, worked at the Dandy Doug bacon factory in Trenton. She sent two pounds of bacon over with Scabby the next Saturday as a gesture of thanks to Julia for curing his pinkeye.

Scabby began dropping by every weekend; Julia listened to him with a tolerant ear, which was more than Pattie had ever done.

"His eye's cured; why does he have to keep coming over?" Will asked Julia.

"Because I don't think Scabby's mother pays him enough attention," Julia replied.

"What about your own children?" shouted Will, storming out of the door just as Scabby walked in.

HOWARD BEGAN LOOKING for work. Several mornings a week he dressed in his dark gray pin-striped suit and took off in the car for meetings in the city. He would return six hours later with a smile bordering on despair.

"Awful people, couldn't stand them!" he'd say.

Howard had promised himself not to fall for a man like Chapman Fay again. And he had no patience for the Gordon Snifters or the Seamus Thatchers of the world, either.

"Howard, do you honestly *want* a job?" asked Julia one evening.

"Of course, darling, but I want the *right* one this time," Howard assured her.

WILL HAD SCABBY TO THANK for his first encounter with Marina among the fiddlehead ferns; lust propelled their subsequent rendezvous. Along the railroad tracks behind University Hills they'd wander, until they found themselves far from home, where the birch woods opened out into corn and alfalfa fields, a horizon broken only by telegraph poles and the idle swoop of a hawk. They would tightrope in tandem along the rails, fingertips touching across the ties, until one of the endless cargo trains rattled near, then would dive into an embankment and kiss for as long as it took for the cars to pass, their tongues hunting and probing. Marina let Will put his hands on her small, fig-shaped breasts, but whenever his fingers slid down to her tights, she pinched him sharply in the ribs.

IT WAS ON THE ADVICE of Frieda Grecco, the quiet woman in Julia's Thursday group, that Julia took a preparatory course for the New Jersey real estate exam.

"If my husband can do it, you *definitely* can," said Frieda. Her husband sold commercial property in Trenton. Business hadn't been good for twenty-five years, but he scraped along, selling factory space and storefront property in West Trenton to a seemingly endless parade of hopeful entrepreneurs.

"Take the course *with* me, Frieda," said Julia.

"Oh no, I'm a cook. Besides, Stevie would *kill* me!" whispered Frieda. "He's *very* competitive."

Steve Grecco had once threatened a butcher because he gave Frieda a discount on sweet sausage. It amused Julia just to imagine Howard doing such a thing.

When the course was over, Howard drove Julia to the real estate exam. "I'm sure you'll do extremely well," he said.

"I hope so," said Julia. "It's been a long time since I've taken any sort of test."

"Nonsense, darling. There is nothing you can't do," said Howard as she climbed out of the car. He shot her his rallying smile, the one that reminded her of Buck Quinn's barbecue, when the subject of America first came up. America, where blacks had equal rights and the trains ran on time, except that there were no blacks in University Hills, and everybody preferred to drive.

JULIA PASSED WITH HIGH MARKS; the family celebrated with a roasted chicken and a toast to her success. Then she asked Howard to help her prepare a résumé.

He looked surprised. "You mean you're actually going to look for a job?"

"Well, of course," she replied. "Otherwise, why take the exam?"

"I thought you did it for the challenge. It's just a matter of time before I get another position, darling."

"Now look, Howard," said Julia, "remember our agreement? I gave up a job to come to America. You even said—"

"Of *course* I did, darling," he said hastily. "You should go ahead and seize the opportunity!" Then he fell silent.

Julia was surprised. She had expected one of her husband's over-confident assurances, but he seemed to lack the energy for this. His face resumed the vulnerable cast it had worn since Marcus's accident.

That night, Howard lay awake thinking that he'd give Julia one day to realize what a bore it was to go to a job. One day. She'd see. Then they'd be in the same boat. Disgusted. Disgusted with the whole system. Then he gasped, realizing the degree of disenchantment he felt.

He didn't want a job. Not here. He needed to begin again, somewhere else.

"GOT ANY SOAP, MUM?" said Marcus.

"Soap?" Julia said. "One of my sons wants soap?"

"Two or three bars, if you have them," replied Julius.

"It's Tic-Tac Night," explained Marcus.

"What's that? Oh, let me guess—a night when all the filthier children in the neighborhood decide to give their parents heart attacks by washing themselves spotless?"

"No, it's Mischief Night," said Julius. "You play tricks on your neighbors. Soap up their windows, throw toilet paper on the trees."

"Well," said Julia, "I'm delighted that my children won't be doing nasty things like that."

A chorus of groans answered her.

"Because my children aren't *savage heathens*," she concluded.

Shortly after dinner, Will was caught slipping casually out the door.

"Just a minute! Where are *you* going?" asked his mother.

"Nowhere," said Will.

"Well, where did the *soap* go that was in the bathroom?"

"I dunno," said Will.

"Where are the twins?"

Will shrugged helplessly. All he wanted to do was meet Marina in the ferns.

"I want you at home," snapped Julia.

"But, Mum . . ."

"Don't argue. I'm going to look for the twins before they get arrested. Stay here with your father."

"Where is he?"

"In the basement fixing a leak. Why don't you see if you can help him?"

The door slammed, and Will heard footsteps so sharp they might have punctured the concrete path outside. There was a strong wind that night; the withered maple in the front yard was lashing one of the pillars. When the phone rang, Will hoped it was Marina.

"Hello?"

There was a pause. "Your mom there?"

"No, Scabby, she's not," replied Will testily.

"I gotta talk to her."

"Can't it wait until Saturday?"

"Look, I'm calling because *they're going to get your house tonight*," said Scabby.

"Who?"

"You know. Ever since your mom put up that flag, they've been planning this."

"You little creep," said Will. "It was probably all *your* idea!" He slammed down the phone.

The phone rang again.

"It wasn't me," insisted Scabby. "I swear! That's why I'm calling to warn you. They're going to—"

"All right," Will snapped, and he hung up before the impulse to thank Scabby for his trouble struck him.

IN THE DIM WATTAGE of the basement, he found his father on hands and knees, grunting as he scrubbed at the floor with a steel brush. The odd thing was that Howard was wearing his business suit.

"Dad?"

"A sinking foundation, cracked floor, mold—this damn house was built by a thief," Howard muttered. His ginger hair was splayed over his temples, his tie hung to the floor, his expression was rigid, the lines in his high forehead exaggerated by his effort. Will had never seen Howard quite so angry over something so odd. Still, he explained Scabby's warning call.

"Attack our house? That's ridiculous," said Howard.

"It *is* Mischief Night, Dad."

"Ow!" shouted Howard, scraping his knuckles on the cinder block.

Cursing, he threw the wire brush across the floor and sat with his legs out in front of him, like a toddler exhausted by a temper fit. Will re-examined his father's attire—the pin-striped suit and black leather shoes. The suit was stained with rusty smudges and the shoes were scuffed. These were his father's best clothes.

"Are you all right, Dad?"

"No," his father replied. "I cut my bloody hand. Hurts like hell," he added.

"Why don't you come upstairs?" suggested Will gently.

Howard drew his knees up to his chest and clutched his temples. "Your mother wants to get a job, Will. She's going to find out that it's no picnic. And I'm speaking from experience. Lots of experience."

Will spoke to his father slowly and clearly. "Dad, somebody's about to attack our house!"

Then the doorbell rang. Sucking at his bleeding knuckles, Howard began to curse again.

Will walked back upstairs, alone.

When he opened the door, he saw five figures standing in the front yard, dressed in dark blue hooded sweatshirts, wearing identical masks. He faced five Nixons; five receding hairlines; five ski-jump noses.

"Trick or treat!"

"What do you want?" replied Will.

"Trick or treat!" they repeated.

Will made out more Nixons in the dark—some holding white bars of soap and rolls of toilet paper and cans of shaving cream. He felt his knee bobbing; fear always announced itself in his extremities.

"Halloween's tomorrow!" Will shouted. "Go away!"

The figures laughed, and some jeers erupted on the periphery. The Nixons stepped forward en masse, their plastic faces shiny beneath the amber streetlight.

"It's a free country," replied one Nixon.

"If you don't like it, go back to England!" shouted another.

Now both of Will's knees were bobbing uncontrollably. More than twenty Nixons had converged on the curb. A particularly aggressive Nixon threw a roll of toilet paper over Will's head. He watched the roll bounce on the roof and unravel, down the incline, tripping on the gutter, dropping to the lawn, where, seized by a restless breeze, it wrapped itself around Will's legs.

"Stop it!" Will shouted, as the emboldened group began throwing more rolls at the roof.

A dark figure ran behind him and disappeared around the side of the house. Will stood paralyzed on the lawn, unable to retreat or charge. How could he defend his house with his father huddled in the basement, his mother roaming the neighborhood, and the twins on their own rampage?

Another roll of toilet paper missed the roof and landed at Will's feet. He picked it up and hurled it at the closest Nixon, hitting him square in the face.

There was a muffled groan.

"Goddammit, Lament!" said a voice that sounded like Vinnie Imperatore.

Another Nixon had been tossing a baseball from one hand to the other; it seemed to grow into a hot coal as he palmed it back and forth until, finally, he wound up and lobbed it at Marcus's window, shattering the glass.

"I'm calling the police!" Will shouted.

This seemed to give the Nixons pause; then somebody in the back laughed.

"Go ahead, call 'em!"

Will tried to summon up enough fury to replace his terror, but he could only hear the brassy laugh of the Midnight Chinaman. This attack had a sick logic: the Laments were strangers, they'd flown their own flag and challenged the Founding Fathers. Then it disgusted him that he was in sympathy with his tormentors.

Suddenly a jet of water shot across the grass, blasting a Nixon mask off Wally Finch's jowly face, and he stood, sputtering, drenched from head to foot.

Will turned to see a man squatting by the house, wearing a suit, a tie flapping over his shoulder. Howard aimed the hose at the next marauder and proceeded to douse one Nixon after another.

Unable to breathe through the ski-jump nose holes, they pulled off their masks—first the Gallagher boys, then Vinnie—and retreated hastily into the darkness as the torrent pursued them.

"Little buggers," murmured Howard as he turned off the water.

Will stared after the fleeting figures. "I hate being different."

Howard might have reacted defensively, for this was a fairly potent condemnation of their travels. Instead he replied, "But you *are* different! You are a Lament, and Laments go their own way. A Lament would never act like *that*."

He nodded in the direction of their tormentors.

"A mindless mob of hooligans. You'd think a country full of refugees from persecution would know better than to act that way."

With that, Howard pulled his tie loose, stuffed it in the pocket of his ruined suit, and stamped back into the house. Will hesitated, struck by his father's metamorphosis from the troubled soul scrubbing the basement floor to the hero on the lawn. He took a last breath of the cool evening air and hoped the madness of the evening was over.

JULIA CAUGHT THE TWINS outside their school soaping obscenities onto their classroom windows. Not fully content with this, they began composing limericks about their teachers—there once was a teacher named Decker, who limped from the weight of his pecker—and proudly signing their names after them.

"You silly fools!" cried Julia, hurriedly rubbing out their signatures.

"But they're funny!" argued Marcus.

"Then write them on paper, like normal poets!" she grunted as she hauled them home.

HALLOWEEN NIGHT WAS A MUTED AFFAIR. Most children avoided the Laments' house, for the garden-hose story had spread like wildfire. Nevertheless, the twins were determined to collect candy from every house in the neighborhood. Marcus dressed as a pirate with an eye patch and a beard; Howard fashioned a gnarled hook for his prosthesis.

"I've got the only *real* hook!" declared Marcus.

At the last minute, Julius decided not to be a pirate.

"Why not?" asked Marcus.

"We can't be the same anymore," replied Julius with a forlorn look. Though the twins hadn't resembled each other after toddlerhood, they had felt like physical equals until the accident. Now Julius couldn't challenge his brother to climb or to swing from a rope anymore. The accident had changed that. He was angered by the probing eyes of strangers and by the inordinate share of sympathy and morbid curiosity Marcus received.

"Why don't you be Julius Caesar?" suggested his mother.

Julius didn't take to the idea until Howard suggested he dress as the *assassinated* Julius Caesar. This delighted him; he ventured forth with six kitchen knives sticking through the folds of his toga into a board strapped to his chest.

Nobody recognized the twins until they saw Marcus's hook. Abby Gallagher threw up when he appeared at her door. This made the whole evening worthwhile.

Everything Will Be All Right

The Laments' second winter in America began with a stunning November blizzard that issued flakes the size of pennies, and, by morning, rendered University Hills as placid and pretty as a pastry-shop window. It was more snow than the boys had ever seen in their lives.

The twins raced out in their pajamas and built snowmen until their bare feet and hands were glowing. The car wouldn't turn over. School was canceled. When the mail finally arrived at four in the afternoon, there were two important letters, one addressed to Julia, the other to Howard.

"Darling," said Howard at bedtime, "I have wonderful news!"

"Oh good. So do I, darling!" replied Julia. "You first."

"Well," said Howard, "I've decided that Australia is the place for us."

Julia paused. "Australia?"

"Yes. The climate is glorious. Everybody speaks English, and there are lots of job possibilities."

"Howard," replied Julia, "do you *have* a job offer in hand?"

"Well, not yet. But I'm sure——"

Julia held up her letter. "Well, I do have an offer. A position at a real estate office."

Howard sighed. "Darling, that's marvelous news, but this envelope contains my last check. We simply can't afford the mortgage on this house. That's a fact."

"Then we'll just have to find a house we *can* afford, Howard, because I'm not going to Australia."

With that, Julia gave Howard one of the more tepid kisses of their marriage, and turned over. And neither of them slept very well.

LOVE IS ALL YOU NEED. Love is in the air. Love makes the world go round. Love is a many-splendored thing. The songs on AM radio sang only to Will and every song was about Marina. They walked to school together, they walked home together. They slipped notes to each other in class. They signaled each other from their bedroom windows at night. The glue that bound them was teenage contempt for an adult world full of pretense and hypocrisy. Their love was sweet and infinite. On Valentine's Day they wouldn't be corrupted by candy and corny sentiment; those were for phonies and show-offs. Marina and Will carved their initials high up on an ancient birch tree, where the mark would remain for a hundred years.

WHEN THE ANNOUNCEMENT was made at breakfast, the boys realized that the balance of power between their parents had shifted. Julia explained their plans, and this time the light of new adventure was in *her* eyes. Howard spent a considerable amount of time buttering his toast.

"Are we broke?" asked Julius. "I don't want to be broke."

"Nonsense," replied Julia. "We're just moving to a more affordable house."

"Where?" asked Will.

Julia expected Howard to answer this question, but Howard's attention was focused on removing every trace of butter from his knife.

"Darling?" she prompted him.

Howard blinked, and asked for the question again. "Queenstown," he finally explained. "It's not far from here, farther out in the countryside; you'll go to a new school."

"Well, I don't want to move," announced Will, hoping that he saw some leverage in Howard's hesitation.

"Did Daddy get a new job?" asked Julius.

Julia turned to Howard, who eventually replied. "No, Julius. But Mummy's got a job."

The twins picked up on Howard's ambivalence.

"Is it a *good* job, Mummy?"

"Of *course* it is," Julia replied.

Marcus was most worried that he and Julius might be separated, but Julia assured him that they would be together, which left them with Will's protestations.

"I won't go. I'm staying here!" he declared.

I'M LOSING YOU. Breaking up is hard to do. I fall to pieces. Only you. Curiously, the songs on the AM radio addressed his heartbreak, too. Now every song seemed to be about losing Marina. He wept on the way to school, and on the way home. They shared solemn glances across the classroom, knowing exactly what sadness each felt for the other. Nobody understood their pain. It was awful and exquisite and unlike anything that had happened in the universe before.

"I won't be too far away," said Will.

"Miles and miles."

"I could call you on the phone."

"It won't be the same."

"I could write letters."

"My parents might not give them to me."

The zeal with which Marina said this prompted Will to wonder if, in some way, she was enjoying this a little more than necessary.

"When I leave, will you forget me?" asked Will.

She paused. "Never."

Marina told Will that there had been changes in her house. Mr. Himmel had traded in one of the Mercedes for a gleaming white Ford Galaxie, and Astrid had been sent to a boarding school in Vermont.

Will observed that Marina was going through changes of her own. She shed her familiar sweater and donned leotards, gray ones that matched her eyes and showed off her breasts. She threw out the barrettes and wore her hair pulled back in a ponytail. Once tentative and catlike, Marina now walked with a confident stride. She was no longer the mischievous girl who whispered behind his shoulder.

"You look beautiful these days."

She smiled, playing with her hair in the dappled sunlight. Then she glanced back at him. "Do you like these?" she asked, fluttering her newly painted fingernails before him.

"No," he said. "I preferred when you bit them to pieces."

She smiled. "You're so strange, Will."

He looked at her with regret. "Yes, and you used to be *just* as strange." When this amused her, he continued bitterly: "You'll find somebody else, the minute I'm gone. . . . But I'll probably find somebody else too."

She searched his eyes, unsure if he meant to be so cruel.

"Probably forget you in a few weeks," he added. "When you move, it's better to forget people, or you'll just be sad for the rest of your life."

Tears welled up in her beautiful gray eyes. In another moment, she was sobbing. He wanted to grab her and apologize, but he resisted: better to leave than be left.

THE TRUCK THAT ARRIVED on moving day was a six-wheeled leviathan that swallowed their possessions and proved that the Laments could vanish from University Hills without a trace. Across the street, the Imperatores watched without comment or farewell. Abby Gallagher made no parting gift; she had not forgiven the twins for their Halloween visit.

"I'm sure the people will be nicer where we're going," said Howard.

"Yes," echoed Julia, "they would have to be."

Julia recognized Howard's attempt to rally the charge. If their alliance had been shaky, the move secured it. It was all part of the Lament tradition. Moving is good. Damn the neighbors. On to better things.

But just as they were getting into the car to leave, Rusty Torino trotted by with his terrier. "We'll miss you folks," said Rusty.

"Actually, I'm sure everyone will be relieved to see us go," declared Julia.

"Not me, ma'am," said Rusty sincerely. "You and the Himmels gave us an *international* flavor."

If only he'd stopped before that line.

"International flavor? So we're a *condiment,* are we?"

"That's not what I—"

"And I suppose we offered a *handicapped* flavor, too!" Julia was helpless against her own sarcasm.

Though Howard was tempted to intercede, to smooth the ruffled feathers, he held back, relishing Julia's desire for a send-off that would make them feel good about leaving.

"Look," Rusty sighed, "what can I say? 'Best of luck'? How's that?"

"I hope you'll give the *next* family an even warmer welcome," concluded Julia.

"Sure!" said Rusty. "I was just going to ask you about them. Are they foreigners, too?"

"No," said Julia acidly. "Americans. From Montgomery, Alabama."

"Southerners!" said Rusty. "Great! Kids?"

"Three."

"Ah, and what's their name?"

"Washington."

Rusty's smile changed just slightly. "Washington? No kidding? Like Booker T.?"

Howard ordered the boys into the car.

"Are they black? They'd be our first black family. Of course, I do hope they'd be comfortable here. Sometimes people can be a little, well, hostile."

He pressed his hand to his heart. "Not me, of course. I'm not a racist, but there are people less tolerant than me. . . ." He squinted at Julia. "*Are* they black?"

"Washington." Julia smiled. "Such a patriotic name. I'm sure *they'll* hang the flag on Memorial Day!"

WILL'S THOUGHTS WERE ELSEWHERE; he was gazing at the blue house, looking for a trace of movement in the window. A sign. A farewell wave. *Something*. With the family waiting in the car, he ran up to the Himmels' door and knocked. But no answer came from inside. *I'm sorry,* Will mouthed to Marina's vacant window. He slumped into the car, slamming his door, head bowed.

"How far is it?" asked Marcus.

"Only twelve miles," replied Julia as Howard started the car.

Only twelve miles, but Will knew an infinite chasm lay between him and Marina. Not only would he probably never see her again, but he had left her hating him. That was the Lament way: burn your bridges and move on.

"I hated that place," said Marcus, peering back at the Finches' yard with its infamous tire swing.

"Me too," agreed Julius.

Julia and Howard said nothing, but in their minds they were re-shuffling their opinions of the neighbors and the sprawling house with its leaky cellar, putting their memories in order, and preparing for that new and improved Somewhere Else.

"What's the new house like?" asked Will.

"It's old, rustic, charming; we'll be very happy," said Julia.

Howard nodded at the boys. "Your mum sounds like a real estate agent already," he remarked.

"Thank you, darling," Julia replied, sensing her husband's barb, but refusing to let it draw blood.

Starting Over

It was an old house, all right. Number 33 Oak Street was a gray Georgian with peeling clapboard, a gable roof, and a small, drooping porch. Its doorways were low, the floors uneven, the cellar an earthen pit. The walls were plastered and stained from leaks and ancient repairs; the kitchen featured an ancient Kelvinator fridge with rounded corners, and a dirty enamel stove. But Julia pointed out its charms—the staircase had a solid oak banister, carved with acorns and oak leaves. The windows were small, with warped glass panes, and the rooms were bright, with stenciled designs on the wainscoting.

And, of course, it was close to the boys' school and to Julia's job.

Roper Realty was perched on Route 99, in the center of Queenstown. A former county jail, it was a one-story building made of granite blocks. Claude Roper, the deceased founder, had bought the building from the county for a song and wooed business with a blend of flattery and self-deprecating humor. The office was cold and damp, and on windy evenings the walls whistled. Claude used to joke that after you visited Roper, any other house would seem like a palace.

The office was full of men attempting second careers: there was a former detective, Mike Brautigan, a sleepy-eyed Brooklynite with a thick accent who told unintelligible stories of his adventures on the force; Emil DeVaux, a former football coach, a balding, forlorn fellow with a handlebar mustache; and Carey Bristol, Roper's manager, an older fellow, big as an ox, his nose a mess of burst capillaries. But Carey was tenderhearted and the first to reach out to Julia.

"When's yer birthday, Julie?" he growled.

"It's *Julia*, and it's none of your business, sir," she replied.

"Look, lady," said Carey, pointing a meaty finger at her, "in this office we celebrate *everybody's* birthday. Even if yer older than Methuselah, you getcher birthday up on Carey Bristol's calendar, got it?"

"June sixteenth," Julia replied grudgingly.

Bristol's eyebrows shot up. "Bloomsday, eh?"

"Yes," said Julia, with surprise.

Carey nodded. "An Irishman should know his writers, and I *am*, and I *do*."

In spite of her co-workers' male chauvinism, their repeated declarations that they'd never let *their* wives work, and the constant questions about Howard (what kind of man sits at home while his wife beats the pavement?), Julia liked her new colleagues. She sensed that in spite of their thickheaded opinions, they were trying to accept her.

"So, what will it take for all these women's libbers to go back home and quit trying to wear the pants in the family, Julia?"

"I couldn't possibly speak for every woman, Emil," replied Julia.

"Then speak for yourself. What will it take for *you* to go back to the washing and the ironing?"

Julia thought for a moment and smiled. "Oh, I suppose hell would have to freeze over. That's all."

Then there was the stir when Mike Brautigan picked up Julia's takeout lunch from the Chinese restaurant on the other side of Route 99.

"How much do I owe you, Mike?" she asked.

Brautigan frowned. "I never let a woman pay me nothin'."

Julia settled her gaze on him, her eyebrows fixed like pikes. "You'd turn the woman down who wanted to buy a house from you, then?"

This brought laughter, but Brautigan stuck to his guns. "When Mike Brautigan treats a woman, her money's no good."

"Well then, I'll have to stop eating," Julia replied.

"Christ, what's your hang-up, Julia?" cried the ex-detective. "Those goddamn feminists have you brainwashed!"

Julia replied softly, "Michael, you have your pride, and I have mine. My money should be as good as yours, shouldn't it?"

Brautigan tossed his head. "Look, I buy Carey lunch all the time!"

"Only when you owe me," muttered Bristol.

Emil DeVaux frowned. "You never buy *me* lunch, Mike."

Julia placed her money in Brautigan's breast pocket. He took the money, rose, stuffed it into the jar marked COFFEE FUND, and returned to his desk. A tense silence followed.

But finally, Bristol got up, squinted at the jar, and slipped his thumbs under his jacket lapels.

"Ladies and gents, this is history in the making," he said. "First time Brautigan donates to the coffee fund. Maybe now we can afford a new pot!"

THE CEMETERY OF the Queenstown Presbyterian Church extended along Oak Street for about three lots. Six thin weather-scarred tablets just beyond the wrought-iron fence identified patriots who had died in the Revolution. These graves always had fresh roses upon them, bestowed (according to a brass plaque) by the Daughters of the American Revolution. Will had never actually seen a Daughter of the American Revolution replacing the roses. But the flowers were always fresh; to make sure, he hurdled the fence one icy November morning to pluck a few petals. When they bruised between his fingertips, he decided that the Daughters were ghosts, wraiths draped in old flags, gossamer hair tied up in buns, doomed to mark the graves of these six American patriots for an eternity. Passing this graveyard was the most unsettling aspect of his journey to his new high school each morning.

In that first year, Julia also passed the graveyard every morning, and she noted one white marble stone featuring the cameo of a woman, Eliza Seward, good wife to John. Eliza had given birth to five children, three of whom didn't live past the age of two; their tiny headstones lay on Eliza's grave, three white tablets poking out of the ground like baby teeth. Julia regarded those little tablets with a pang of guilt. Had she deserted her children by taking on this job? Those three white tablets troubled her. Poor little abandoned souls.

ON THE WAY TO SCHOOL one morning, the twins spied a magazine stuffed between the bars of the wrought-iron cemetery fence. It was a *Playboy*—discarded, no doubt, by some guilty sinner. The boys studied the glossy pictures with slow steps and befuddled awe. At ten, they were too young to be aroused by what they saw, but they recognized the inherent power of these erotic pictures. Marcus wanted to toss the magazine out before they arrived at school, but Julius insisted on tucking it under his shirt, where it remained until he could stash it safely under his mattress. Every few weeks, Julius would secretly consult the magazine, until his dreams began to taunt his dormant libido with naked women absurdly clad in cowboy chaps, medieval armor, construction gear, astride horses, crocodiles, tigers, snakes, motorcycles, and missiles while cuddling power tools as if they were teddy bears.

Marcus's dreams also went through a metamorphosis. But his fantasies were of having two perfect hands. With seamless grace, he swung from tree to tree in a vast jungle. He rowed across a mirror-still lake, his hands wrapped around oars, feeling the tremor of the current in all of his fingertips. He flew like Icarus up to the sun, and when his wings fell apart he dove into the Mediterranean with two perfectly formed hands piercing the azure waters, and down he plunged, into the welcoming arms of a mermaid with hair billowing like a thunderhead.

And then he would wake up.

Without looking at his hands, Marcus would open his eyes and pray that a miracle had occurred overnight. He would rise from bed, walk to the bathroom, and piss in the toilet. Finally, reaching for his penis to give it a shake, he would feel the rounded stub of his arm, and curse his imagination. Always the sentimental twin, Marcus clung to his faith in wishes. He had a drawer full of lucky rabbit feet and a Magic 8-Ball and a genuine gold ingot. None of them worked but he kept collecting, and dreaming.

Marcus had never felt as different from Julius as he did now. While his brother seemed to have a natural ability at school to assert himself, Marcus was timid, afraid of people's reactions to his hand, and he kept his conversations short and his prosthesis hidden in his lap.

ON THE FIRST ANNIVERSARY of their arrival in Queenstown, Howard was a thinner man, with graying temples. His anxious smile had settled into a permanent look of dismay. He slept late and went to bed early. He let his suits be devoured by moths and began wearing the clothes of his early years with Julia, happier times, when he was an ambitious young engineer—khaki slacks, a cricket jersey.

What did he do with his time? He cradled cups of tea, and paced the floorboards of the slumping, gray-clapboard structure with its long narrow porch overlooking Oak Street, the busiest street in town until a shopping center had opened on Route 99. Howard still applied for engineering jobs, but he appeared reluctant and distracted in his interviews. The fact was that his last two jobs had been solitary exercises— he had spent his workdays in the little office in Denham, the mahogany cell at Fay/Bernhardt—and solitude had begun to seem normal, even necessary. With the boys at school and Julia at work, he did exactly what he had done as a working man; he entertained grandiose ideas, but passed the time doing very little. And though Julia made a few sales that first year, they couldn't have survived without their rapidly dwindling savings.

Sometimes Howard sat on the porch and surveyed the storefronts. An elderly barber occasionally waved to him from his shop across the street; one day he was carried out on a stretcher and the barbershop closed, though its empty leather chairs and marble sinks could still be seen through the darkened window. There was a drugstore with a busted neon sign, with wheelchairs, walkers, and crutches featured in its window; and a candy-and-newspaper store with a withered strip of flypaper dangling from the ceiling fan. To Howard's eye, his house was a terminus on a dead-end street. Eliza Seward, good wife to John, might have ended her days in such a house; it was certainly old enough, with its dirt cellar, low doorways, and uneven floorboards. But Julia insisted on its virtues: it was cheap, distinctive, and solid, while the cookie-cutter houses of University Hills were all sinking in their foundations.

JULIA'S THURSDAY MEETINGS tempered her anxiety about Howard, because even if he was in a slump, her marriage sounded so much healthier than those of her friends, all of which were under siege. Phyllis Minetti's husband had revealed that he had a second wife living in San Diego, which explained his frequent flights to the coast and his peculiar habit of addressing Phyllis as Bunny during sex. Avé Brown had found Denny in bed with her mousy sister, a Jesus freak who ended every phone call with "I'm praying for you." In the midst of these revelations, Frieda, who had become Julia's closest friend in the group, remarked that forgiveness was a critical component of a strong marriage.

"Excuse me?" bristled Avé Brown, her topknot quivering with fury. "How dare you come in here talking that crap when your husband rearranges your face every week with his fists!"

Nobody had dared address Frieda's bruises before.

Frieda's hand flew to her cheek. "I—I walked into a door."

"Oh God, Frieda," said Julia. "You have nothing to be ashamed of. If he's beating you, you *must* leave!"

Dawn Snedecker

Will's loneliness, and his accent, put him at a distance from his new classmates at Queenstown High School. He made no new friends, and the drawings in his notebooks became fabulous and bizarre. The margins were filled with sketches of unnatural Boschian creatures, spoons with shapely legs and tails, cups and saucers with mournful eyes and gnarled fingers and feet.

Unlike his parents, Will indulged in reminiscence. The grief of losing Marina was like the lingering ache of a lost tooth. It tantalized, it aroused, and it couldn't be left alone; the wealth of these feelings was better than their absence. He could still feel Marina's open lips in the fiddlehead ferns, the tart-apple taste of her tongue, that burred sweater, and the way she pinched him when his fingers strayed. But one day he forgot the sound of Marina's voice.

Dawn Snedecker was as different from Marina as apples from oranges.

Oh, Dawn. What a sweet, wonderful name. She had moved there from San Rafael, California. She had a gentle smile; she wore peasant blouses, painter's pants, moccasins, and wire-framed glasses. Her hair was a spray of gold, woven into braids that wound about her head like a halo. She always wore a pin on her shirt: FREE THE CHICAGO SEVEN, or BOYCOTT GRAPES. Though she smiled easily in those first days, she didn't talk much. She ate alone and healthfully: a container of yogurt, a banana, and a thermos of orange juice. If only he could muster the courage to speak to her.

After a week, he summoned the nerve during lunch. She was cradling a book.

"Reading something good?" he asked.

She marked her page with her pinkie and blinked at him.

"Oh, yesh," she said.

"What is it called?"

"The Autobiography of Malcom Xsh."

"Ah," he said. "Been meaning to read that."

"It'sh really good."

He nodded. And nodded again. "See you," he said finally, beating a reluctant retreat behind an elm tree so that his heart could slow down. God, she was sweet. And her way of speaking—unique. Will suddenly wished he had a speech impediment. A complementary one, like Elmer Fudd's. *Wabbits are weawwy dewicious! Oh yesch!* Between them, they could screw up the entire language.

During English class she gave him a smile and peered at the little drawings in his notebook.

"You're quite artishtic," she said.

"It's nothing," he said.

"Have you taken art clashesh?"

"No. I just scribble when I'm bored."

Dawn cocked her head, listening to him.

"Tha'sh a foreign acshent. Are you British?"

"Not exactly; I'm from Africa."

"What part?"

"Southern Africa—Rhodesia."

"Oh," said Dawn, narrowing her eyes. "You lived in a shegregated shoshiety?"

"What?"

"A shegregated shoshiety. A white shupremashisht regime."

"I suppose so," said Will. "But I'm not a white supremacist."

Dawn's tone became skeptical. "Did you have a cook or a gardener?"

Will paused. "I was eight."

"You were still benefiting from the shuffering of blacksh!"

Will was startled. Nobody had ever accused him of this before. It was a double shock to hear it from the sweet lips of Dawn Snedecker.

"ARE WE WHITE SUPREMACISTS?"

"What on earth are you talking about?" asked Julia at the laundromat that evening. The new house had no washing machine, so they washed their clothes at a laundromat three blocks away. Julius insisted on picking out his clothes with his teeth while Marcus stacked underwear on his head.

"Julius! Marcus! Stop acting like savages!" she cried.

"A girl at school said I was a white supremacist. So *am* I?" Will asked, rescuing a sheet before Julius dragged it across the dirty linoleum floor.

"Will, do *you* believe that whites are superior?"

"Of course not." Will frowned. "But she said that because we had a cook and a gardener, and we lived in Rhodesia . . ."

"Who said this?"

"Nobody," he assured her. "Nobody important."

"Look," said Julia, "some people actually believe whites are a superior race, and they believe that white domination is justified for that reason. We do not believe that. Therefore, we are not white supremacists."

Will seemed relieved.

"However," continued Julia, "America is a country with a double standard. Its laws may be liberal, but I come across plenty of neighborhoods where people don't want to sell houses to black families. There's a racist in America for every racist South African; they just don't have the law on their side, or the separate toilets."

· · ·

WHEN DAWN NOTICED HIM sitting at the far end of her lunch table, she made her feelings clear.

"I cannot shit at a table with you." The pin on her collar read FREE ANGELA DAVIS.

"What?"

"I won't share my table with a white shupremashisht."

"But I told you, I'm not."

"Yesh you are."

Will had no other friends. There was no one to defend his character.

In the following weeks, Dawn attracted a small circle of disciples who shared her politics. They would sit cross-legged in a circle in the outdoor lunch area, singing Dylan songs and weaving macramé belts.

Once again, Will desperately wanted to belong. It was Calvin Tibbs who answered his wish.

CALVIN TIBBS HAD NO CHIN. His bulbous head diminished as it neared his neck, like a pear perched upside down on a lollipop stick. Calvin sat behind Will and asked questions during Mr. Steuben's German class. His breath was bitter and smoky. His T-shirt smelled of sweat and engine oil, and his utility boots kept a steady drumbeat on the floor. Calvin Tibbs knew where Rhodesia was.

"Rhodesia's near South Africa, right?"

"Right," said Will.

"Your people know how to deal with niggers, don't they?"

"What do you mean?"

"Well, you got the whites-only buses and drinking fountains, just like they had in the South."

Will was bewildered by Calvin's admiration, but he didn't argue with him. Calvin was muscular; he shoved kids aside in the halls. So Will kept silent until he got home.

"Yes," Julia admitted, "there are plenty of bigots in this town, too, darling."

"Why did we come here, then?"

"Because at least America has laws against racism. It's a step in the right direction. America is South Africa's future."

"Is there a place that's America's future," asked Will, "where people just get along?"

Julia smiled faintly. "People have never just gotten along."

Calvin sounded off about niggers every day, and Will observed the complicit smiles of the other white boys. How many more Calvins were there? Will wondered. Did they proliferate like the latex Nixons on Mischief Night? Perhaps South Africa could trade its oppressed blacks for America's bigoted whites; he imagined an impossibly tidy exchange, a load of Calvins on the *Windsor Castle* sailing east to Africa in their oil-stained T-shirts, tapping their utility boots on the railings, sprawled on deck chairs, playing bridge, and having herrings dropped down their pants by the great god Poseidon. At some midpoint they'd spy the blacks on *their* ship, going in the opposite direction. There'd be a pause as each group saw the other; the ships would issue a deafening blast from their horns, and they'd wave good riddance to each other.

In gym, Will was Calvin's fourth pick to play on his baseball team.

"I want *Mr. Rhoh-desia*! Mr. Rhoh-desia is with us!" Calvin said with his idle smirk, and most of the other boys seemed to understand what this meant, though it obviously had nothing to do with baseball.

THAT EVENING WILL CAME HOME to find Howard and Julia grimly inspecting the front of the house.

"Falling apart, see?" said Howard. "A few more years and it'll all collapse into a pile of junk."

"What are you proposing, Howard?" asked Julia. She saw the shabby façade with its cracked wooden eaves and peeling paintwork as charming, part of the house's character.

"The pillars have rotted through because rain is leaking down from the porch roof. The whole thing must be replaced soon, or we'll have a disaster on our hands."

Julia cast a glance at the boys, and chose her words carefully.

"Darling, our finances won't permit a renovation."

But Julius's ears seemed to prick up at this comment; he had remembered his mother's assurance that they weren't broke when they left University Hills.

"I thought you said we had plenty of money!" he cried.

"We do, darling," replied Julia.

"It doesn't require plenty of money," said Howard. "I'll do it myself."

"Darling, you've never repaired a house before."

"All the more reason to do it," said Howard. "I like a challenge."

Julia had noticed Howard's energy diminish over the last year; his zeal to embark on a project like this was encouraging. "You'd need help, darling."

"Behold, three sons!" said Howard, clasping the boys' shoulders. All at once, Howard seemed the one with the energy, while his sons gazed fearfully at the porch.

Julius replied warily. "You mean, carrying things?"

"Hammering, sawing, lifting, and building!" replied Howard. "It'll be fun!"

Persuaded by his enthusiasm, Julia decided this project might help Howard pull himself together; and perhaps her blindness about the house's defects reflected her inattention to family life, now that she was a working mother. For all these reasons, she gave him her blessing.

That weekend, Howard enlisted the boys' help in replacing the four rotting pillars with pine two-by-fours. To Will's eye, the supports looked too unsteady for the enormous porch roof, and his father appeared similarly fragile. Though Howard looked tall and substantial in a suit, in jeans and a red flannel shirt his lack of muscle was obvious.

"Are you sure those beams will hold up the porch, Dad?" Will asked.

"Absolutely." To prove his point, Howard gave one of the supports a confident rap with his hammer. At this, part of the porch ceiling fell away and Julius, standing below it, was showered with black dust.

"That needs to be scraped and painted," said Howard. "I'll add it to the list."

Later, Julia drew Will aside to ask how the renovation was going. Will sensed that she was more concerned about his father than the project. "I'm just afraid that he'll hurt himself," she admitted.

After promising to keep an eye on Howard, Will asked Julia a question that had been worrying him all weekend.

"Mum, how can I play for Calvin's team when he's a bigot?"

"If it bothers you, why don't you join the other team?"

"Then I'll make an enemy out of him, and they'll probably bench me for being a foreigner."

Julia sighed. "As Hamlet said, 'Thus conscience does make cowards of us all.' It's only baseball, darling."

IN THE FIRST GAME, Jed Nissen, first baseman and Calvin's star hitter, slapped his knees with laughter when Will struck out.

"Man, you really suck, Lament!"

"He hardly played the game before," said Calvin. "Keep at it, Mr. Rhoh-desia, you'll get the idea."

"By then, it'll be basketball season," Nissen laughed. He was the only member of the team opposed to having Will join them. He loved baseball. The girls adored him, with his dark eyes, square jaw, and mischievous grin; even Dawn Snedecker's glasses fogged when he smiled at her.

After striking out a second time, Will offered to sit out the game.

"Stick it out!" said Calvin. "You'll get the hang of it. Anyhow, we ain't gonna lose against a bunch of niggers."

The other team was mixed, black kids and white kids. One of them was a boy Will recognized from riding his bike to school. Roy Biddle had deep black skin and almond-shaped eyes. His hair was always cropped incredibly short, with the indent of his jaw visible behind his ears. He'd heckle Will from his porch in the mornings.

"Hey, English," Roy would shout. "Gimme a ride!"

Will would shake his head as he passed by, and Roy would leap from the porch and sprint until he was running alongside Will.

"Gimme a ride, *English*!"

"Sorry," said Will.

"Why not, English?"

"Because I saw you take somebody's bike last week."

"Goddamn English!" Roy would shout, grinning, and he would pump his arms and legs and tear ahead of Will to prove that he didn't actually *need* a ride on anybody's bike. Roy was one hell of a runner. And a pretty good batter, too.

On Will's third turn at bat, he struck out again. He offered, at this point, to withdraw from the team.

"No way. I picked you," said Calvin. "You're on my team, for good!"

To Will, this seemed more of a sentence than a vote of confidence.

When the other side was up at bat, Roy Biddle hit a ball that tore down the foul line at eye level, and struck Calvin's cheek. Stunned, Calvin dabbed his face and held up a bloody finger for his teammates to see.

"Hey, coach, that nigger almost killed me!"

"That's enough, Tibbs!" snapped Coach Lunetta, examining the wound. "Go to the nurse and clean it up. While you're at it, wash out that filthy mouth of yours!"

Refusing to see the nurse, Calvin paraded around the pitcher's mound, making sure the wound was visible to everybody.

"Tibbs! Throw the ball or get off the field!" shouted the coach.

Roy hit the next ball in a steep arc way above center field, where Will was standing. Will reached out with his bare hands. He preferred the English habit of not wearing gloves to catch a ball.

"He's gonna drop it!" sneered Nissen.

Roy threw down his bat and began running, knees and elbows pumping like pistons, the dust rising from his feet in little explosions, advancing toward first base while his eyes shot back and forth between the careening ball and Will's outstretched hands.

"You can't catch *nothin'*, English!" he roared as he sprinted for second base.

Will heard the echo of Roy's voice along with Nissen's scornful remarks, but he made no step, no adjustment in preparation for the ball's arrival. He just stared. For a moment the ball eclipsed the sun, and then hurtled toward him. As his teammates shouted in dismay, Will splayed his fingers and the ball stopped dead in his palm.

"Yes, Rhoh-desia!" shouted Calvin.

"Lucky sumbitch," said Nissen.

"Goddamn English!" moaned Roy as he collided with the second baseman.

Nissen whistled. "If his mouth was open he'da swallowed the damn ball!"

Calvin gave the story his own spin.

"Nigger tries to kill me, so Mr. Rhoh-desia here wipes him out! Doesn't move, just *plucks* that thing out of the sky like a ripe apple. See this cut here? That's a racist attack on my person. I say Roy Biddle got what he had coming thanks to Mr. Rhoh-desia here!"

"Calvin, please don't call me Mr. Rhodesia anymore," said Will.

"Aren't you proud of your background?" replied Calvin.

"No, because it doesn't *mean* what you think," said Will. "I don't hate blacks."

"Well, I'm Irish," replied Calvin. "And my dad said the Irish were the white niggers back when."

In Calvin's society, as far as Will could tell, *somebody* had to be the nigger.

News about the catch spread around school. By the end of the day, everyone was calling Will Mr. Rhodesia. But in English, Dawn Snedecker threw Will a sharp glance.

"I hear you're Calvin Tibbsh'sh besht friend now. I'm not shurprished."

"All I did was catch a ball," he replied.

"You're dishgushting!" she answered.

Will began to feel she was right. He had unwittingly become part of a mob—the very thing his father abhorred.

Poverty

The school baseball season was cut short by three weeks of continuous rain in October. This was a blessed thing as far as Will was concerned, but it was a crisis for the Laments. On Monday, the hot water vanished. On Tuesday, Howard ventured into the basement and found the hot-water heater immersed in a pool of mud. On Wednesday, the plumbers explained that the previous owner always got flooded in rainy weather, and suggested that Howard dig the cellar floor deeper. The boys were enlisted to do the job on Saturday morning, but when Will returned from a trip to the store he found the twins rolling over each other in a mud fight. Whatever progress they had made was destroyed in the scuffle.

That evening it rained again, and so much water collected in the porch roof that the two-by-four supports snapped like matchsticks. The entire structure fell with a monstrous crash.

By noon on Sunday, a building inspector was rapping at the Laments' door. Will couldn't help studying the inspector's face—it was alarmingly familiar.

"You've endangered the safety of everyone on this street, Mr. Lament."

"Nonsense," replied Howard. "I took every precaution. And not a soul has been hurt!" Any authority in Howard's voice was belied by his hair, which pointed up like a thistle.

"Well, Mr. Lament, let's just say you're a lucky man. Now, unfortunately, this being a commercial zone, there's a fine." The inspector took a citation book from his satchel and licked his pencil.

"A commercial zone? What are you talking about?" said Howard.

The inspector wrote in a tight script, pausing to lick his pencil every line or so. "There's a barbershop across the street, a drugstore two doors down, and the laundromat another three blocks east. I believe fines are doubled in a commercial zone."

"But this is a residence and it's my first offense. Can't you be lenient?"

The inspector peered at Howard over his wire-rimmed glasses with an expression appropriate for the worst kind of criminal.

"Lenient? You could have killed somebody's grandma."

"Nonsense!" Howard was incensed. "Do *you* have a granny who could hurdle the rope surrounding my porch, and fall asleep on bare floorboards under a leaking roof during a bloody thunderstorm?"

The building inspector's lips tightened. "My grandmother's passed away, sir. I couldn't say." Again, Will was sure he recognized this fellow from somewhere. "As for the fine, it'll be five hundred dollars."

"Five hundred? Outrageous. What is your name, sir? I will lodge a complaint."

"My name is Ralph Snedecker. And I'll take that check now."

Will shrank back. It all made sense—the wire-rimmed glasses, the righteous disapproval: these must run in the family.

After Howard wrote the check and Mr. Snedecker went on his way, Will felt a crushing sense of shame. The Snedeckers would tell the whole town that the Laments were not only racist but reckless misfits.

"Don't worry, Will. We'll give Mr. Snedecker a run for his money. That check's going to bounce," said Howard.

.   .   .

IT WAS A PARTICULARLY COLD NOVEMBER. The fuel bills were high and Howard locked the thermostat at sixty-five degrees; everybody dressed in layers and wore socks to bed. Julia was sensitive to the cold, and despite her long underwear and two pairs of socks, her nose would run while she slept. One evening in the darkness, when the wind was especially shrill and the third notice had arrived from Mr. Snedecker, Julia voiced her concerns.

"Howard, what are we going to do? The savings account is empty and we've got bills we can't pay."

"Australia," came the groggy reply. "We'll go to Australia."

"Australia?" she replied. "Howard, please, be serious!"

"I'm busy fixing our home, darling. You'll just have to sell more houses at that job of yours."

Julia couldn't miss the edge to his voice. *That job of yours.* His point was simple: if they couldn't travel, their debt was her problem.

Howard's obsession with moving was intensified when he discovered five years' worth of *National Geographic*s stored in a rusty tin trunk in the basement. For the next week he forgot the renovation and pored over the pictures, dreaming of faraway escapes.

As more rain came and the basement flooded again, Howard abandoned the cellar and set his mind to another task; the living room ceiling was sagging.

"But what about the porch?" Julia said.

"Can't afford to fix it just now, darling," explained Howard cheerfully.

"And the basement?"

Howard muttered something about needing dry weather to finish. One evening, he sawed a hole in the ceiling while they were watching television, and a mess of foul-smelling debris landed on the carpet. A dribble of water from the toilet's supply hose had done the damage. The next morning, Howard rented a blowtorch to repair the toilet valve.

"Are you sure you're comfortable doing that?" asked Julia with delicacy, as she prepared to leave for work.

Howard reacted indignantly. "Darling, it's a *valve*. If there's one thing I know about, it's valves!"

When she returned that evening, there was an enormous scorch mark on the bathroom wall and Howard was nowhere to be seen. Julia's heart began a drumbeat as she searched the other rooms, unable to find him or any of the boys. She was about to call the hospital when Howard clambered out of the basement cradling a stack of *National Geographic* maps.

"For God's sake, Howard, what happened in the bathroom?"

"Oh, that!" Howard chuckled. "Had a bit of a fire. Don't worry. A little wallpaper and nobody will ever know."

"Wallpaper? What about the ceiling? And the basement? And the porch?"

Julia stared at her husband as he muttered some excuses; she tried to suppress the awful realization that Howard and the house were locked in some bizarre contest that would culminate in their mutual destruction.

"Darling," she said, forcing herself to change the subject, "there's a Christmas party at the realty office this week. It would be wonderful if you could bring the boys in, combed and brushed, so that everybody can meet them."

Howard nodded, sweeping the cellar cobwebs off his cricket sweater. "Of course," he replied. "Combed and brushed; I suppose that includes me!" he added with a defeated expression.

"Of course, darling," she replied gently. "Everybody is looking forward to meeting you, too."

CAREY BRISTOL ANNOUNCED that there would be presents for everyone at the Christmas party. It had been a good year for Roper Realty, though Julia had sold only two houses.

"We all have tough years," Carey assured her. "Next year will be better."

At five o'clock, Emil DeVaux's four daughters were ushered in by his wife, Dorothy, a dark, fierce little woman who glared at Julia.

"She thinks you're a temptress, just working here to seduce the men," explained Brautigan.

Julia tried to introduce herself, but Dorothy avoided her, so Julia lingered by the door, welcoming visitors while checking her watch in anticipation of Howard's appearance.

Brautigan's daughter, Shelly, a willowy fourteen-year-old with braces, soon arrived. But Carey refused to hand out presents until Julia's children appeared. That wasn't until six-fifteen, over an hour later.

"Sorry, darling," Howard apologized. He wore his yellowed cricket jersey and paint-spattered jeans. The twins wore sweaty P.E. shirts from school; their hair was wild, their noses runny. Howard chuckled at the sight of them. "Couldn't find them anywhere!"

"Howard Lament! We were beginning to think you didn't exist," said Carey Bristol.

"Ah," Howard said, giving Julia a surly nod. "So much for wishful thinking."

Julia blushed deeply. It was the first time in their marriage that Howard had slighted her in public.

"This is Carey Bristol, Mike Brautigan, and Emil DeVaux," she said.

Howard shook hands with them. "You fellows probably know my wife better than I do these days!" he joked. Julia put her hand to one temple in embarrassment.

"You're a lucky man, Howard," said Brautigan.

"Why's that?" Howard replied. "She hasn't sold a house in months."

"Neither have I," replied Brautigan. "But you're married to a fine lady."

Ignoring the compliment, Howard surveyed the office disapprovingly, as if the very walls were responsible for his entrenchment. While Emil DeVaux presented the boys with wrapped boxes, Julia steered Howard away for a quick word.

"What's wrong with you?" she whispered, the lines of her forehead crosshatched with shame.

"What could be wrong?" replied Howard.

"I'm *disgraced*!" said Julia. "How *dare* you speak about me that way!"

When he saw the tears in her eyes, an expression of contrition spread over Howard's face.

"Julia, please forgive me——" he began.

But his apology was interrupted by the twins.

"Mum, look what *we've* got!" cried Marcus. The boys were holding air rifles.

"Jesus Christ," murmured Julia, and she spun around to Emil with all the bottled-up anger she had intended for her husband.

"You gave my children *guns*?"

Emil, for once in the year, actually had a merry smile on his face.

"Yeah." His eyes darted over to the boys. "Why? Do they *have* guns?"

"Emil, I left Africa to get my children *away* from bloody weapons! How dare you?"

Julia took the rifles away from the boys and handed them back to Emil, whose mustache drooped, his brief Christmas cheer shattered.

HOWARD HAD WALLPAPERED the bathroom with the free historical maps that came with the back issues of *National Geographic*. Madagascar lay above the sink. Antarctica could be found just above the toilet-paper dispenser. As Will lay in the tub, he memorized the twists and turns of the Amazon. Marcus became an expert on Virginia geography because the toothbrush holder lay on Chincoteague Island. Howard placed a map of Australia at eye level so that when he shaved, he could memorize the southeast coast; he chanted the towns like a mantra: "Ulladulla," "Gerringong," "Kiama," "Wollongong," "Bulli."

That last week before Christmas, the Laments were unable to summon any yuletide cheer. Julia and Howard lay in bed, back to back, frozen in place and far apart.

"Julia?"

"Oh God, Howard, please don't mention Australia again."

After a pause, Howard nudged closer to her.

"What about New Zealand?"

"Oh, Howard!" cried Julia. "We can't go *anywhere*. I'm paying for groceries with a credit card. We can't even afford to buy the boys presents."

After a silence, Howard looked at her. "You talk to me these days as if I were a fool."

Julia was too angry to apologize. As she lay in bed, she thought of Howard when they had first met at the Water Works. He seemed so brilliant and knowledgeable then, and all at once she felt terribly ashamed of herself.

ON A STARK AND UNGENEROUS Christmas Day, the sunlight was absent, the temperature low, and a biting wind stole the peal of bells that announced the holiday service at Queenstown Presbyterian Church. Julia gave the boys presents from the Presbyterian thrift shop, a barren storefront several windows down from the laundromat. She and Howard had agreed not to exchange gifts, but at the last minute she found him a woolen scarf that reminded her of the style he wore to the Ludlow Water Works on frosty African mornings.

"I thought we weren't exchanging gifts," said Howard.

"Yes," said Julia, "but then I saw this, and I couldn't resist."

Howard blinked. "But I didn't get anything for you because you said *not* to! *You* made the rule."

"It doesn't matter, darling," she said. "I wasn't expecting anything from you."

But, of course, she had been. And because Howard gave her nothing, Julia felt unloved; and because Julia gave him something, Howard felt like a fool, again.

Julius received a sweater. He picked it up as if it were a skinned cat.

"This isn't new!" he cried. "It smells!"

"It's *like* new," insisted Julia. "As good as new."

"But I wanted something *new* for Christmas," he protested. "Are we that broke?"

"Of course not, Julius. We just can't afford *new* things right now," explained his mother.

Julius jammed his teeth together. "I got an *old* bike for my birthday, and an *old* radio last Christmas. *I wanted something new this time*." He turned to Julia. "Mum, you said when we moved that we wouldn't be poor!"

Howard rose to Julia's defense. "Stop complaining—at least you got *something*. There are children on the other side of the world who don't get much more than a banana for Christmas!"

"At least bananas are *new*, Dad," said Julius with contempt. "Nobody gives someone an *old* banana, do they?"

When no one rebuked Julius for speaking to him with such disrespect, Howard went down to the basement to sulk, only to emerge for the family dinner, which was held that evening at a diner on Route 99. The holiday platter included two slices of overcooked turkey, a splash of gravy, a mound of mashed potato, and flaccid green beans. Christmas carols like "Hark! the Herald Angels Sing" and "Silent Night" played on the radio with numbing repetition. The windows had been sprayed with fake snow, even though there was snow on the ground.

New Year's Eve passed without celebration in the Lament house, though they each made a resolution. Julia vowed that she would sell more houses, and that they would never have a Christmas like this again. Howard resolved that he would never again act the handyman. Marcus and Julius swore to be rich when they grew up, and Will's resolution was to defy Calvin, to trade his cowardice for a stronger conscience, and, in doing so, win Dawn's affection.

FRIEDA CAME TO THE final Thursday women's meeting of the year with her arm in a cast.

"I have to be more understanding of Stevie," she confessed. "He doesn't like me working. And my going out on Thursday nights makes him even more frustrated. He gets violent because he's *insecure*."

"Jesus, honey," said Avé. "The man is sick. When are you going to get the point and walk out?"

Frieda refused everyone's offers of help.

Avé grew exasperated. "Frieda, you're not stupid. How many broken arms does he have to give you before you get the message?"

"I think Frieda's very brave," said Julia. "It's much easier to walk away from a man than to cope with his problems. Frieda is a loyal wife, and I respect that." She shared a rallying smile with Frieda until Phyllis spoke.

"Personally, I have no problem with loyalty, but there's a big difference between a husband whose problem is depression and one who breaks your arm for looking at him the wrong way."

The Matron's Files

They gave Mrs. Pritchard a delightful send-off at the hospital in Salisbury: a table full of her favorite deviled ham sandwiches, some rosé, and a little chocolate cake with almond flakes topped with a single candle. Somebody had even thought to make the balloons green, white, and red because she was beginning her retirement with a trip to Italy. The director wanted to smooth things over, because even if they were glad to see her go, she had given Mercy Hospital forty good years.

But whenever people asked what Mrs. Pritchard was going to do with herself, she gave the same bitter reply:

"I have had a rich and fulfilling career; all I want is to stay."

As matron of the obstetrics ward, Mrs. Pritchard had always been a model of order. Thousands of babies had passed through the system, and she had the file cabinets to prove it—banks of them, with alphabetically ordered names, and color-coded labels according to sex (blue and pink) and destination, that is, natural parents, foster care, or adoption (labeled in purple, orange, or turquoise, respectively). Give her a name or date and she could tell you size, weight, all the particulars of the parents, and, if the baby was an orphan, where he went, and to what institution. Any name.

Just about any name.

When she began work at the hospital in Salisbury, she had been a young nurse with a head of rich auburn hair and a complexion as fair as that of any Irish girl raised in County Kerry. Though the lines of her eyes looked more brittle now, she was still a handsome woman—the late Mr. Pritchard had always said so. When she turned sixty-five she had no intention of retiring, but to her dismay, a replacement was hired without her knowledge.

Her successor was a colored woman named Beauty Harrison. Beauty! The audacity of the names Africans chose. Mrs. Pritchard protested in a letter to the director, ten pages long and single-spaced. As she tried to explain, even if Beauty Harrison turned out to be a first-rate matron, many patients and staff wouldn't take easily to a colored superior all of a sudden. Then there was the matter of Mrs. Pritchard's filing system. It couldn't be entrusted to just anyone. Blacks and whites think differently. File differently. The director responded by urging Mrs. Pritchard to begin her retirement a month earlier than planned.

Mrs. Pritchard's second letter to the director clarified her motives in twelve single-spaced pages. She wasn't being racist; she merely judged people by virtue of forty years' professional experience. Furthermore, she judged others by no more exacting a standard than she applied to herself. Indeed, her files included seven devoted to the deadly sins. For every five chocolate bars she ate, she placed one wrapper in the Gluttony file. The Envy file was full of those letters from her sister, who, God knows, had been handed *her* life on a silver platter. Lust had been vacant for a long time, as had Sloth. And Pride? Well, wasn't she entitled to a little pride after devoting her life to mothers and children? As for Greed, she lived modestly, and she reserved her Wrath for inferiors only.

But the director was firm. "It's time to let go, Mrs. Pritchard," he cooed. "It's time to move on with your life."

"This hospital is my life!" she insisted, "and I won't see its standards go down!"

"I'm glad you see it that way," replied the director with a steady glance. "We don't want any mistakes, any names lost, any files misplaced, do we?"

"Of course not," replied Mrs. Pritchard. Then uncertainty clouded her features. Files *had* been misplaced. She couldn't remember the exact details, but the embarrassment she felt over the matter was still palpable. Had it been a month ago? Or just a week? Critical papers, lost. Amazingly, they had turned up in the trunk of her car. What a relief it was to have found them. And then she realized with solemn dismay that her retirement had nothing to do with her age at all; it was her memory that was at fault.

"What will I do now?" she wondered out loud.

"Mrs. Pritchard, aren't there things you've always wanted to do? Places you've wished to go?"

She remembered the walks she had taken with her late husband, Venable Pritchard, a large man advised by his cardiologist to exercise or face an early demise. Each night they strolled through town after dinner while he wheezed and sputtered like a teakettle. As they trudged past the storefronts of the business district, the exhausted Mr. Pritchard would catch his breath near a travel-agency window with its tantalizing posters of foreign vistas.

"Look, Alice!" he said between gasps, pointing to one such vision. "*That's* the Ponte Vecchio! That famous bridge in Florence! The bridge of lovers!

"Oh, Alice," he continued, "there's no more romantic spot in the world! Did you know that five hundred years ago lovers leaped from it hand in hand to guarantee they would spend eternity together!"

His stories became more and more fantastic.

"In 1943, the heroes of the anti-Fascist resistance were caught on the bridge in a cross fire," he gasped, "and shed their blood on the cobblestones, which, to this day, remain a rusty red! Widows and widowers frequently find the ghosts of their loved ones pacing the bridge, trapped in a limbo above the river, unable to cross onto terra firma. Darling," Mr. Pritchard vowed, "I'll take you there if it's the *last* thing I do!"

Alas, his heart was no match for his imagination. The last thing Venable Pritchard did was to die in his sleep beside his wife in Salisbury, Southern Rhodesia.

After the party, Mrs. Pritchard took her personal files home. Under the word *Retirement,* she discovered a number of items filed over the decades. They were all familiar to her—certainly nothing wrong with her memory *now*, thank you very much. There was a list of classics she had planned to read, a floral swatch that she had hoped to reupholster her couch with, a postcard of the Ponte Vecchio sent from Florence, and a slip of paper that said, simply, *Lament.*

Dutch Oil

True to her resolution, Julia sold two houses in February, one right after the other. Carey Bristol insisted on opening a bottle of champagne in the office to celebrate.

"You see? That's the way houses sell," he explained. "Nothing for weeks, then bang, bang, bang."

The first house was a brand-new split-level, bought by a young Canadian couple named Robertson. Julia recognized the young wife's anxious optimism; the husband was beginning his career at an electronics corporation in New Brunswick. The second sale was a modest Cape buried in the Humbertville woods; the buyer was a woman, five years older than Julia and recently divorced, setting up a new life for herself and her three daughters. Coincidentally, her name was Julia, which Julia Lament found both auspicious and unsettling.

Unfortunately, the commissions on these houses were immediately swallowed. The advances she had received from Roper over the past year had to be paid back, and there was the fine from Mr. Snedecker, and the credit card bill. The Laments were in serious debt.

When the cold-water faucet became clogged with rust and Julius was scalded during his morning shower, Howard solved the problem by lowering the temperature of the hot-water heater. With just the hot faucet on, they could have a lukewarm shower. Marcus protested that this wasn't hot enough for him.

"We can't afford a thousand-dollar plumbing repair," explained Howard. "Speak to your mother about selling more houses."

Meanwhile, Howard was convinced that Julia would soon concede the hopelessness of her career and free them to continue their journey to some better place. To prepare for this moment, he phoned Roper's rival and invited the agent over to appraise the gray-clapboard Georgian at 33 Oak Street.

FOR MOST OF THE WINTER a dirty, residual snow that had hardened into ice made it impossible for Will to ride his bike to school. Will loved riding his red Raleigh with its white-rimmed tires. It was a carefree vehicle compared to the fuming, temperamental machines that rattled into the school parking lot. Calvin, for example, drove a battered springtime-yellow '65 Mustang given to him by his brother after a rollover accident.

When March offered a warm breeze and enough sun to do away with the ice, Will pumped up his tires and oiled the chain and the gears. As he passed Roy's low-slung porch, Will recognized a voice.

"Hey, English, gimme a ride!"

True to his resolution to follow his conscience, Will slowed down. An old Rottweiler chained to the lattice released a few emphatic barks before settling into a weary heap.

"Hop on," said Will, sliding forward. In an instant, Roy had leaped off the porch and climbed on, although he looked doubtful that Will's offer was sincere.

"No tricks, English," Roy muttered.

"Don't call me English," said Will.

"Then how about *Mr. Rhodesia*," said Roy.

"I'm Will. Call me Will."

Roy tossed his head. "Call you whatever I want, English!"

"Look, can we clear something up? I don't have anything against you. Just because Calvin thinks I'm a racist doesn't mean it's true."

"Everybody's a racist," said Roy. "Even my uncle."

"Your uncle?"

"Shit, yeah," said Roy. "Calls me a Chinaman on account of my eyes. Probably got some Chinaman blood in me on account of my dad being from Cuba—they got plenty of Chinese down there. Other times he calls me Midnight, on account of my skin being blacker than his. Blacker than all my cousins put together. Y'know what they call this kinda black?" Roy held the back of his hand in front of Will's face.

"What?"

"Urple."

"Urple?"

"Ain't that a nasty-sounding word? Urple. Worse than being a Midnight Chinaman."

"I guess so," Will agreed. He was puzzled by the coincidence of Roy's nickname and the villain of his nightmares, but it seemed wiser to say nothing.

They were approaching the narrowest point on the road to school, the trestle bridge, which was paved with narrow logs. Beneath the bridge lay tracks for the commuter trains to New York and Philadelphia. It was a precarious spot for a cyclist if there were cars passing, because their weight would bend the logs and spring a cyclist off the shoulder, either into oncoming traffic or onto the tracks below. When a motor revved behind them, Will felt Roy twist to see who it was.

"Goddamn!" cried Roy. "It's Calvin!"

"So?"

"Goddamn Calvin always burns rubber when he sees me. Pump those pedals, English!"

Will sped up, but Calvin slowed his yellow Mustang alongside them and rolled down his window. "Hey, Mr. Rhodesia!"

"Hey, Calvin!" said Will.

"Mr. Rhodesia," said Calvin, "are you aware that there's a *nigger* riding on back of your bicycle?"

"I'm giving *Roy* a ride, Calvin."

Calvin raised his eyebrows quizzically; this didn't compute. "How much is he paying you, Mr. Rhodesia?"

"I ain't paying nothing," said Roy with a furious grin.

Yards away from the trestle bridge, Will slowed down, but Calvin kept pace.

"See you at school!" shouted Will.

But Calvin wasn't finished with Roy. "Riding on the white man's back is gonna cost you, boy!" he shouted.

Roy muttered something.

"What'd you say?" Calvin demanded.

"I said how's your brother, Calvin? How's *Hopalong*? Tell him Roy says hi, all right?"

Calvin's face crumpled, and the Mustang swerved; Will felt the front of the bike stop, jammed between tire and curb, and he and Roy went flying.

By the time Will had disentangled himself from the raspberry bushes on the embankment beside the railroad tracks, Calvin and his bicycle were nowhere to be seen. Then he looked around for Roy. There was no sign of him along the road or in the bushes.

"Hey, Roy? Roy!"

A hoarse cackle came from the raspberry bushes a yard or two farther along, and Roy crawled out backward, nursing a cut on his hand.

"You see his face?" cried Roy. " 'Hopalong' works every time!"

"Who's Hopalong?" asked Will.

"A nickname. Calvin's big brother, Otis, broke into the lumberyard and stole a chainsaw about a year ago. My uncle Joe was night watchman, so he chased him. Otis runs for the railroad tracks, thinking he can get across before a train comes. But the railroad ties are wet, see, and Otis *slips*. My uncle sees that boy hopping across the tracks like a jackrabbit and—*wham!*—the train takes his leg off, clean at the knee. So I call him Hopalong Cassidy, see? Makes Calvin crazy!"

Will listened to this story with puzzlement; he saw nothing funny about a brother losing a limb. Roy was still slapping his knees in hysterics as Will came to grips with an even more unsettling fact: his freedom, his escape, and his only joy lay at the bottom of the hill, a crumpled and unsalvageable heap.

CALVIN CAUGHT UP WITH WILL during German class.

"I'm sorry about yer bike," he remarked.

"Jesus, Calvin, you almost killed us."

"Roy's got a big mouth," Calvin said bitterly. "Why'd you give him a ride, anyway?"

"Because I felt like it!" snapped Will.

"Herr Lament," interrupted Mr. Steuben, "*sprechen Sie deutsch, ja?*"

Will hadn't realized he was shouting, but he noticed that his anger seemed to make an impression on Calvin.

"Look, I can help you get a new bike."

"How?" replied Will.

"I work over at Dutch Oil Research. Emptying trash, polishing floors. Three hours a night. They're always looking for people. In a month or two you'd make enough money for a new one. Easy."

THE DUTCH OIL RESEARCH FACILITY was about two miles from Will's house, down a country road bordered by cornfields. Formerly the Blackwell estate, it had poplar trees along the entrance road and a red-brick mansion with a green copper roof and a cupola that overlooked all four hundred acres of the Blackwell property. Dutch Oil had turned the mansion into its executive offices, adding a circle of low brick buildings full of laboratories and engineering shops. The rolling meadow and woodland behind the big house was sold to developers, who quickly built identical ranch houses for the chemists and engineers who worked there. It was exactly the sort of place Howard might have worked, if he'd been able to get past the interview.

The following night, Calvin drove Will to Dutch Oil and introduced him to the maintenance manager. Eddie Calhoun's rapidly receding hair was greased and combed into a flattop; he hummed as he spoke.

"Everybody starts on bathrooms, *hmm*? If you can do that, you'll move on to dumping trash in the labs, polishing tables, *hmm*, replacing water coolers and putting in fluorescent bulbs. If you steal, you're fired. *Hmm*? If you ingest, inhale, or absorb any substance from the labs, you're fired. *Hmm*? You get one break, ten minutes; enough time for one cigarette. You smoke?"

"No," said Will.

"*Hmm!*" said Eddie. "You'll go far."

Eddie instructed Calvin to teach Will how to clean the toilets and sinks the fast way: a fistful of wet powder rubbed fiercely over the porcelain, allowed to dry, then wiped off with a clean paper towel. Calvin also demonstrated the quickest way to mop the floor and a technique of hitting the paper towel dispensers so that they'd open without a key.

"Doesn't that break them?" asked Will.

"Who gives a shit?" scoffed Calvin.

By the time Will had cleaned the bathrooms on three floors, he had an earful of Calvin's views on the sexes.

"Women are pigs. They dump their purses out on the sink and leave used tissues, lipsticks, old Band-Aids. Men don't do that."

"Men leave a little splash of piss under the urinal," observed Will.

"That's just the old guys. It's a matter of bad *aim*."

Calvin explained that his brother had had bad aim ever since his accident.

"You mean when he stole the chainsaw?"

Calvin looked at Will. "Roy's a liar. My brother didn't steal nothin'. Roy's uncle stole the chainsaw and blamed Otis for it."

"Why did he run across the tracks, then?"

Calvin shrugged. "All I know is, my folks sued the railroad and won. That *proves* he was innocent. Otis got a hundred thousand bucks for his leg. Lawyer said if the train had rolled over his balls, it would have been a lot more." Calvin sighed, as if his brother's castration would have been worth it.

After his first week, Will had mastered his job so efficiently that he asked Eddie for more to do.

"What d'ya mean, *more*?" said Eddie.

"I'm getting finished pretty early. Anything else I can do to fill up the time?"

"Yes," said Eddie. "Nothing."

"Nothing?"

"If management finds out you can do twice the work we'll all be working twice as hard, get it?"

Will took care of Building A's bathrooms. Calvin polished the floors. A couple of high school girls, Felice and Roberta, cleaned the offices. The girls took smoking breaks together, wore identical "wedge" haircuts and Day-Glo lipstick.

At the end of the week, Felice accepted a ride home with Calvin. She chatted with Will while Calvin bought soda at a 7-Eleven.

"I like your accent," said Felice. "You're from Africa, right?"

"Right," said Will.

"Tarzan was from Africa," she reminded him.

Will sighed. "Yes."

He was relieved to see Calvin return. But Felice pouted when she saw the big bottle of orange soda under his arm.

"I thought you said we were havin' cocktails!" said Felice.

"We *are*," said Calvin, emptying some of the soda onto the asphalt. Then he produced a shiny tin canister from beneath his seat. Will recognized the bottle from one of the labs.

"Calvin," he said, "this is pure ethyl alcohol. You can't mix it like gin—it'll rot out your guts! Besides, you'll get fired if Eddie—"

"He ain't gonna fire me," said Calvin, smirking. "I got seniority." He opened his glove compartment and the contents, all items from Dutch Oil, spilled out—rubber gloves, tubing, a bottle of ether, paper napkins, conical cups from one of the water coolers.

When Calvin offered a cup to his passengers, Will refused.

"Cocktails in a Dixie cup?" said Felice.

"C'mon, Felice . . ." muttered Calvin. "Use your imagination, for chrissakes!"

"Calvin, don't do it," said Will. "This stuff will eat out your insides!"

Unheeding, Calvin poured some of the mixture for Felice, who took her cup as if it were a urine sample.

"Calvin," she said, "what about my insides, I mean, what *he* said?"

"Your insides are fine!" exclaimed Calvin. To prove it, he tossed the cup's contents down his throat. His Adam's apple rose and fell in one defiant throb. After glancing at Will through the rearview mirror, Calvin closed his eyes with a smile of exultant satisfaction.

"Oooh, I want some of that!" said Felice, but before she could tip her cup, Calvin shuddered, and all at once his arms and legs began moving in spastic jerks.

"Calvin!" cried Will.

Calvin struggled to answer, but his jaw stiffened and his eyes rolled up into his head. The car rocked as the boy's convulsions became wilder and more violent.

"Calvin, honey, are you all right?" sobbed Felice.

"We'll have to get him to a hospital," said Will, trying to climb out of the backseat. But the car was a two-door, and it was impossible for him to get past Calvin.

"Felice, let me out!" he cried, but Felice seemed paralyzed by the sight of Calvin's convulsions.

Then, as if the demon spirit had decided to wrench itself from his body, Calvin slumped forward over the steering wheel. He was still as stone, the cold moon icing his wild hair. Felice, her chest rising and falling in great heaves, uttered a deep wail.

"Oh God, don't let him be dead!" she cried.

Will squeezed her shoulder, and there was a silence as they both considered this desperate wish, and its obvious futility. Then a whistle of air seemed to burst from Calvin's chest, and he hiccuped and began to laugh.

"Oh, you guys," snorted Calvin, "that was beautiful. You would have saved my life. I'm *touched*, man, really touched!"

The Vigilant One

Howard was nursing a solution to the family's problems. His theory was that the sale of the house after two years' accrued equity would yield enough to travel to Australia and set up house again. If there were quibbles about its condition, he would take a lower price and move to Canada—someplace nice like Vancouver, a port city. Julia would never consider an idea like this in theory, but if he could present her with a dollar value for the house, the numbers would surely convince her.

The night before the agent came, Howard tossed and turned. After a few hours he went to the kitchen, where he could pace, thinking about all the good things that could come of moving. Imagine the Pacific Ocean lying just beyond the kitchen window. Imagine a fresh start. The exhilaration of a new town, a new culture, and the relief of leaving this wretched existence behind.

The fellow showed up promptly at ten, just as Howard had planned, when everybody was out of the house. Howard poured on the charm, referring to the house in reverent terms, as if he were its first and only owner. He led the agent hastily past the fallen porch (an easy repair), then quickly through the living room, where the patched ceiling resembled an exploding white tumor. The useless kitchen stove, he promised, would be replaced once a sale was made.

"Who did the ceiling?" asked the agent.

"Actually, that's *my* work," said Howard proudly.

The agent nodded and whistled. He peered into the bathroom and sighed. "You know, I been in this business twenty years and I never saw wallpaper like that."

"I'm thinking of patenting the idea," explained Howard.

The agent squinted.

"*Educational* wallpaper." Howard glowed. "What if you could have the Magna Carta in your library? Or the *Kama Sutra* in your bedroom?"

The agent gave him a worried smile. "You're certainly full of ideas, Mr. Lament."

After surveying the basement, with its muddy watermark and rusted tools, the agent announced that he had seen enough. But he hesitated on the stairwell, pausing to admire a carved acorn on the banister post: the man caressed it as one would touch a wounded animal for which a quick death is the kindest option.

"Well?" said Howard, rubbing his hands. "What's the good news?"

ON THURSDAYS, WHEN JULIA had her group meeting, Howard started taking long walks from which he would return with an odd assortment of items that he stored in the basement: a wrought-iron rocking chair, an oil painting of a dog smoking a pipe, a set of buck's horns mounted on a Dutch oven, a little bedside bureau with seashells glued to its surface, and a plastic bust of Liberace, which he placed on a lime-green toy piano. One Thursday Howard came back with two rusty Yankee Clipper sleds he'd pulled from a large trash heap.

"I'll take you sledding!" Howard said to the twins.

"It's spring, Dad," murmured Julius, without lifting his eyes from the TV. "Won't be any snow for a *year*."

"A simple thank-you would have been sufficient!" Howard snapped.

Since that awful Christmas, Julius and Marcus had come to treat Howard as a tired joke. They snickered at the yellowed cricket jersey and stained khaki pants he wore daily. Except for his Thursday night rambles, Howard ventured out of the house only to buy cases of tuna and canned fruit, just as his father had done before him.

"We eat like we're in prison!" cried Marcus.

"We *are* in prison," muttered Julius.

Late on Thursday evenings, Will kept vigil in the kitchen until his parents came home. Perhaps it was an echo of his infant state, long ago, when he yearned for their return. Or perhaps the family seemed particularly vulnerable on Thursday evenings. Julia looked invigorated when she returned, but her smile was always tempered by the sight of Howard shuffling in from a ramble, hollow-eyed, carrying some old and peculiar object.

"Did you talk about anything interesting with the ladies tonight, Mum?" Will would ask, or, to his father, "What did you find, Dad?"

Though terse in their responses, his parents were appreciative of Will's concern, for he never went to bed until they were safely home.

ON ONE SUCH EVENING, long after his parents had gone to bed and the house had settled, Will thought he smelled something burning.

He examined the oven first, but it hadn't worked for weeks. Then he followed the troubling odor to Marcus's door. The knob, which was worn, wouldn't turn. Will ran to the kitchen for a skewer, and sprang the lock. The door opened to reveal a foot-high stack of comics on fire in one corner of the room. A funnel of white smoke spilled out into the hall. A Navajo blanket covered Marcus's unconscious form.

Will grabbed the blanket and threw it over the comics. Smoke rose through the fibers and subsided. Then Will shook Marcus roughly, but he refused to wake.

"Marcus? Get up! There's a fire!"

His words seemed to have no effect, but then Marcus began coughing so violently that he hacked himself awake.

"Did you fall asleep smoking?"

"Of course not," Marcus replied, glancing at the remains of the cigarette stuck in the pincers of his prosthesis.

Marcus watched as Will wrapped the billowing stack of comics in the blanket, twisted it tight, and tossed it through the window into the rain, which was now drumming the roof like so many impatient fingers.

"My comics!" cried Marcus.

"They're burning, you idiot."

"They're worth a fortune—or they *will* be," Marcus said, explaining his plan to be a comic-book millionaire in adulthood.

Will reminded his brother of the bonfire incident in England, when he'd found Marcus rolling in flames.

"You keep having these accidents," he said.

"Just lucky that way," Marcus grimly replied.

Surveying the bedroom for some clue to his mental state, Will settled on a poster of a Hindu deity with an elephant's head.

"Who's that?" he asked.

"Dad found it in somebody's trash. . . . It's Ganesh, protector of the home," explained Marcus. "His father chopped his head off and replaced it with the head of an elephant. . . . I feel just like him sometimes."

Will looked at his brother's fading smile.

"You weren't trying to kill yourself, were you, Marcus?"

"Kill myself?" Marcus looked incredulous. "No. I'm going to be very rich when I grow up." He glanced at the window. "Maybe not with comic books, but somehow, I will. I'm determined."

Marcus raised his prosthesis and put a fresh cigarette into the pincers, then hesitated, realizing that Will had never seen him smoke before. With a sigh, he flicked the lighter open and lit up. Will noticed the SEMPER FIDELIS engraving on the cover. Marcus wore a green army jacket and collected patches and stripes from the local Army-Navy. Deep in his subconscious, the military clothing and his missing hand went together. One gave dignity to the other.

The rain was drumming harder now. Marcus took a draw and gave Will an anxious glance.

"What are you going to tell them?"

"Nothing," Will replied. "They'll just get worked up and do something crazy."

"They *are* crazy," said Marcus. "You know, sometimes I think Julius and I are adopted."

Will had to smile. "Both of you? Why?"

"Nothing they do makes sense. If they were our real parents, wouldn't their insanity *seem logical* to us?"

"Marcus, you've got Mum's face and hair, you idiot."

"Well, perhaps I'd *rather* be adopted," replied Marcus.

Will offered no reply to this. The idea of being adopted would explain some things, but it scared him, too.

Abroad

Mrs. Pritchard's trip to Rome was awful, the temperature unbearable, the petrol fumes stifling. Near the Fontana di Trevi, dark-eyed women clutching wailing children hemmed her in against a railing until she threw them coins. At St. Peter's she waited forever to get into the Sistine Chapel, and couldn't enjoy the view for the crick in her neck and the swelling in her feet. Everywhere she looked, there were longhaired Americans with peace signs on their shirts. She didn't think much of the Colosseum, either. If only Venable had been alive, he would have spun a story or two about the Caesars or the Borgias, to put her in the traveling spirit.

Amid the columns at the Palatine Hill, Mrs. Pritchard found a bench and caught her breath. She composed a postcard to her sister. "Dear Olivia, can't say enough good things about Rome!" (which was the honest truth). When Mrs. Pritchard had finished, she noticed a stranger sharing the bench: a trim elderly woman a few years older than herself, wearing a black dress with tiny white polka dots.

They exchanged a brief smile and surveyed the poplar trees on a far hill. A breeze blew a candy wrapper past the stranger's black leather pumps.

"What a ghastly mess," sighed Mrs. Pritchard. "Blessed with the ruins of one of the greatest empires on earth, and they can't keep it clean!"

The stranger nodded. "Shocking, and *so* typical of the Italians."

Mrs. Pritchard stole another glance at the woman and felt an eerie sensation that had come upon her several times during the journey when she had misplaced something or forgotten a simple, pertinent fact. Her companion looked familiar, and she worried that they might have crossed paths recently.

It was awful, this forgetfulness. Pride compelled Mrs. Pritchard to remain silent, but she stole another glance at her companion: her hair was white and thick, held in place with a handsome silver clasp at the back. She had probably been beautiful as a younger woman, her face marred only by a faint blue vein running down her left cheek.

"The French are no better, you know," said the woman. "The Seine is *filthy*!"

"I'm not surprised," replied Mrs. Pritchard, comforted by sentiments so similar to her own. That said, the stranger offered her a farewell nod and continued on her way.

Mrs. Pritchard returned to her hotel, slept fitfully that night, ate a hurried breakfast in the morning, and boarded the nine o'clock train to Florence. She found an empty compartment and opened up her copy of *Middlemarch*. A few moments later, a voice greeted her in English.

"Hello again."

It was the woman from the Palatine Hill, carrying a calfskin leather suitcase and a matching bag and settling herself into the compartment. Mrs. Pritchard still couldn't place the woman in her past, but she became seized by the idea that they were *meant* to meet.

Cautiously, each lady then confessed a few facts about herself that proved coincidental: they were both widows, both single, and both traveling to Florence. Mrs. Pritchard learned that her companion was not a Southern Rhodesian but a South African, from Johannesburg. At one point, the woman left to powder her nose, leaving a cardigan on the seat with a little address book poking from one pocket. As the minutes passed, Mrs. Pritchard debated glancing at the book. Surely *curiosity* wasn't a deadly sin? After peering down the corridor for signs of her companion's return, she seized the book and leafed quickly through its worn pages.

The names were written in large curly script with little notes scribbled in the margins: two dentists; several doctors; a podiatrist; a homeopath (marked "quack"); three hairdressers—one marked "cheap," one marked "expensive but worth it"; florists; cleaning ladies ("never avail. Tuesdays"); and a piano tuner ("lock up the scotch!"). Mrs. Pritchard began to feel ashamed of herself as she found names crossed out, with the word "dec." beside them. But then she saw a word that made her regrettable Italian holiday take on a fateful significance.

Lament.

Of course! This was the mother of that unfortunate woman whose child was stolen at Mercy Hospital. Her hair had been deep black at that time, but Mrs. Pritchard remembered the blue vein on her cheek. There was nothing wrong with her memory now. She recalled the late Dr. Underberg's efforts to bring a mother back from the brink, and the tragic result. She remembered trying to decide what color tab to put on the file afterward, since it was an unofficial adoption and no forms had been filed. What a breach of procedure. What a blemish on her record. After Dr. Underberg's death, she had *longed* to confess the matter, but to whom?

When Rose returned to her seat, she sensed that her companion was seized by some dilemma. Or perhaps it was merely the condition of strangers that they are forever searching for a soul with whom to share the truth about themselves.

With this in mind, Rose proposed that they meet for dinner that evening. She knew a wonderful restaurant, and with the wine flowing freely, they might both unload whatever burden they wished.

Shortly before the meal, Rose went for a walk near the Uffizi Gallery. At sunset an amber glow suffused the buildings. Such glorious light! The evening breeze was delightfully cool, and even the traffic sounds were muted and respectful of this magical hour. Rose gazed down at the Arno, winding through the old city like a vein of gold. This was why she came every year. Though her husbands changed, Florence was as constant as the points of the compass.

Rose met her new friend at Resistance, a small restaurant nestled in the crypt of a church near the river. The staff always remembered her, inquiring about her stay and her lodgings. The tables were set in limestone cells with candlelight and red carpeting. Mrs. Pritchard seemed quite moved by its name, and noted that the anti-Fascist resistance had been shot down a short distance away. Then, with alarming speed, the ex-matron polished off her first glass of Chianti.

"Italians have the best food and wine, but they have no sense of moderation," Rose warned her.

"Pity," agreed Mrs. Pritchard. Oblivious to Rose's hint, she topped up her glass.

"What these walls must know," sighed Rose. "Many a secret told, many a plot revealed, Mrs. Pritchard."

"Do call me Alice. We seem to be getting along so well. Your name is . . ."

"Rose Pennington," said her companion.

"Speaking of secrets," Mrs. Pritchard began, "I believe we've actually met before." She explained her former profession, and recounted having seen Rose sixteen years before at her daughter's bedside. "And something has weighed on my conscience ever since."

"I see," Rose said, watching Mrs. Pritchard empty her second glass and pour another, which made her wonder if all Rhodesians drank like fish. "Well, obviously, dear, I'm not a priest; I don't take confessions."

"It's not a confession, exactly."

"Good," said Rose, looking at her watch. "You see, Alice, I'm having a wonderful time this evening and I'd hate to have it spoiled discussing some vulgar matter."

But Mrs. Pritchard, her eyes closed to prevent the room from spinning, was intent on a mission urged upon her by the slip of paper that read "Lament"; if nothing else, she would share this fact with another soul, and thus relieve herself of the only mistake she could remember making during her career at Mercy Hospital.

"Sixteen years ago a little boy was born to a couple named Lament," she began, "and shortly after his birth he was kidnapped by a disturbed mother."

Rose might have been moved to tears (or gratitude) if her pride hadn't interceded. How dare this stranger presume such intimacy? What was her motive in delivering such a revelation? To savor Rose's grief, perhaps? Well, she wouldn't give this woman the satisfaction.

"Several hours later, she, her husband, and the Lament baby were killed in a car accident. Against my advice, the doctor persuaded the child's mother to take the child belonging to the disturbed mother as her own, without a formal adoption procedure."

As she finished her story, Mrs. Pritchard became aware of a lightness in her spirit. She opened her eyes, and was astonished to find herself alone at the table.

Rose's veal piccata lay half eaten, the knife and fork splayed; her bag was missing.

Waiting for the woman to return, Mrs. Pritchard took a matchbook from the table and slipped it into her pocket. After a few minutes, she concluded that Rose was not returning, and a feeling of loneliness pervaded her. She paid the bill (the load off her conscience seemed worth the price), collected her bag, and walked out into the Florentine evening.

Clutching a faded postcard in her hand, Mrs. Pritchard made her way toward the Ponte Vecchio, the bridge of lovers and patriots, determined to see it at sunset, just as her dear husband had described it.

What a heavenly bridge it was! Couples walked past the jewelers' booths while the sun's last gentle rays bathed their faces in a celestial glow. It *was* a place for lovers. She remembered her husband's words: "Heroes of the anti-Fascist resistance shed their blood on the cobblestones, which, to this day, remain a rusty red!" *Oh, Venable,* she thought, *if only you were here.* Do widows and widowers *really* find the ghosts of their loved ones pacing the bridge? Mrs. Alice Pritchard swooned, feeling as though she were not alone anymore. She drew herself up onto a ledge to see the river, with Venable's voice whispering in her ear. "Impassioned lovers leaped from it hand in hand to guarantee they would spend eternity together. . . ." Perhaps it was the Chianti, or her husband's voice, but suddenly she felt possessed by a simple antidote to her loneliness.

THE NEXT MORNING, Rose felt a brooding irritation with her acquaintance of the night before. If her grandson was adopted, what business did that woman have in carrying this information around? It was also infuriating that Julia had kept the secret from her. But it explained so much.

Rose took the tour of the Duomo that went into the ceiling of the cathedral. Single file, the visitors were led into the rafters. She peered through one of the windows overlooking Florence, with its uniform terra-cotta rooftops. Such a beautiful city. Such order. Suddenly she wondered whether Julia bore her some grudge. A spike of guilt struck her, and she found herself gripping the iron handrail.

"Can I help you, ma'am?" asked the American wearing a porkpie hat and sunglasses behind her.

"I'm fine, thank you," she replied. Her knuckles were white as she steadied herself.

Rose then grasped at her unfinished thought—Julia's grudge—and recalled, five years after her divorce, when her daughter was teaching in Ludlow, a call from one of Adam's hunting friends informing her that her ex-husband had committed suicide during a foray in the bush. He had sent his assistant on an errand, and then blown his brains out using a coat-hanger wire attached to his shotgun. There was a note left behind, asking Rose to convey the news of his death to Julia. Rose was overcome not with grief but with anger at her ex-husband. She decided not to call her daughter until she felt capable of expressing gentler sentiments. She waited a week; in that interval, Julia heard the news from Adam's distraught housekeeper. It was a regrettable mistake, and the second time that Rose had failed to tell Julia of a momentous fact.

Rose decided to take a nap when she got back to the hotel. This, however, turned out to be impossible.

A young Italian police officer, flanked by two others, greeted her at the hotel.

"Signora, can you confirm for us that Mrs. Alice Pritchard was your dinner guest last night?"

"Mrs. Pritchard and I dined together. Is something wrong?"

The officer replied with another question.

"May I ask when you last *saw* Mrs. Pritchard?"

A pretty man, she thought. Like her second husband, perhaps even handsomer.

"At dinner. In fact, I left before she did. Would you please explain what this is about?"

"Signora, a woman with Mrs. Pritchard's identification drowned off the Ponte Vecchio last night. In her pocket we found matches from the Resistance restaurant, and the proprietor directed us to you and your hotel."

Fidelity

Because a Christmas party had brought them together, Julia often thought about Trixie as the holiday approached.
She wrote seasonal letters, giving the details of the Laments' travels,
and addressed them to the American Express office, guessing that Trixie
could always be found by way of her credit card. Though she never replied, Julia believed the letters reached her, because they were not returned. So when Trixie suddenly phoned from New York, asking to see
her, Julia was both delighted and anxious. She suspected that something important must have provoked her friend to call after such a
long silence.

Trixie arrived at Roper, still as tall as a Greek marble, with a long
neck and pale skin, her hair—a little darker—combed back and down
to reveal a widow's peak and those formidable cheekbones. Brautigan
would have classified her style as Park Avenue Kabuki—a shorthand
expression for too much money and too much makeup—but it hardly
addressed Trixie's considerable sex appeal.

"Julia should be here in a moment," promised Brautigan. His fingers jingled the change in his pockets. "Looking for a house?" he asked.

"I *have* a house," she replied, gazing skeptically at the listings. "In New York."

"I bet it's a palace," he said, trying to be urbane and charming; then he offered his hand and introduced himself.

"Trixie," she replied, "Trixie Chamberlain," squeezing his fingertips with a cool, precise grip. "When do you expect her?"

"Ten minutes ago." Brautigan grinned. "Have a seat."

Ignoring his invitation, Trixie surveyed the worn metal desks, the threadbare chairs, the fluorescent fixtures, and the obvious clash between the plaid carpet and everything else in the former county jail.

Go ahead, stand, thought Brautigan. *You're better than a goddamn centerfold.* He looked down almost immediately, wishing he'd resisted such a shabby thought.

"New York's a fine city," he said, to fill the silence. "I served on the NYPD for twenty years as a homicide detective."

"Really?" Trixie's interest lit up, and her gaze became intoxicating. Brautigan was about to tell her how he had once avoided death on a tenement fire escape when Julia arrived.

"Trixie!" she cried. "Good heavens, I can't believe it's really you!"

The two women hugged, and Brautigan felt himself become invisible.

"Mike," said Julia, "have you two met?"

"Oh yes," answered Brautigan. "I was about to tell her how—"

"Perhaps another time, Mike," Trixie replied, flattering him with the use of his first name.

JULIA TOOK TRIXIE to the tap room of the Nassau Tavern in Princeton, where Norman Rockwell's mural of Yankee Doodle was displayed. Women had recently protested this all-male bastion, and there were angry articles in the papers, until finally the doors were opened to the opposite sex. Julia noted the irked stares of the ruddy-faced Princetonian bucks at every table—irked, that is, until Trixie stepped into their line of sight.

"Julia," said Trixie as they were seated, "you always seem to find a handsome man in the middle of nowhere. What's his name, Bortigan, Booligan?"

"Mike Brautigan?" Julia replied as those years in Bahrain came back in a flood of images. She remembered the bourbons, the black eyes, the tidal-wave hairdos, Will's first laugh on the beach, and, of course, Mr. Mubarez.

Trixie nodded slyly. "I like his type; the silver hair always gets me. Married?" she asked.

"Recently divorced," said Julia.

"And you and Howard, are you still—"

"Howard and I are fine," replied Julia sharply; though delighted to see her old friend again, she had no desire to discuss any of her troubles at home.

Trixie laughed at Julia's defensiveness, and remembered the old Julia—the wild mane of black hair (now traced with a few gray strands), and the barbed eyebrows, which were as principled and judgmental as ever.

"Julia, it's so wonderful to see you again," admitted Trixie. "I kept the American Express card in Chip's name just for your letters."

"But you never answered?"

Trixie was unapologetic. "Julia, you *know* how I feel about writing."

"What happened to Chip, and how is Wayne?"

Trixie sighed. "There's so much to catch up on. I left Chip about ten years ago. He still sends postcards from one godforsaken place after another. After my second divorce I came to New York and opened a gallery—those paintings Chip used to joke about were worth a fortune. I have a town house in the Village now." She relished this vindication for a moment.

"So who's this Chamberlain you've taken by name?" Julia asked.

"Oh"—Trixie groaned—"that was the second husband, in Chicago. I only kept his name because it was better than being a Howitzer."

Julia was amused. "Howard thought 'Howitzer' suited you fine."

Trixie leaned forward and gave Julia's hand a squeeze. "Have you any idea how long it took me to forgive Howard for taking away my best friend?"

Tears welled in Julia's eyes, and for a moment both women sat quietly, savoring the endurance of their friendship. But after they had finished their food, Trixie became uneasy, asking questions without listening to the replies.

"How's Will?" she asked, and then a moment later she asked again.

"As I said, he's a wonderful boy," replied Julia. Once again she asked about Wayne, but Trixie ignored the question a second time. Then she folded her napkin and rested it on the table.

"Let's go for a walk," said Trixie.

"In this weather?" asked Julia, but Trixie was already headed toward the door.

Outside the tap room, a fierce November gale rattled the traffic signs while trees thrashed wildly on Witherspoon Street. It was a hell of a time for a leisurely stroll. But Trixie walked, and Julia shadowed her, knowing her friend had some ulterior purpose. But after they returned to the same spot, it seemed as if Trixie were employing the elements to avoid the subject, like Ariel, the chief of spirits, who whips up a storm in *The Tempest*.

"Trixie, what made you finally call me?" asked Julia.

As Trixie took a deep breath, the wind tossed her hair into disarray, and her color vanished.

"Wayne, Julia. Wayne died a month ago."

"My God, Trixie, what happened?"

"Suicide."

Trixie bit her lip, and embraced Julia.

"Why? Whatever was wrong?"

Trixie shook her head, unable to speak.

"Oh, Trixie, you poor dear," Julia cried.

"Oh God, Julia, how I miss him!" Trixie sobbed. Then, as if she could permit herself only a small quota of self-pity, she wearily gathered herself up, tidied her hair, and checked her makeup.

They crossed the street to the campus, and silently ambled through the quadrangles. It seemed to Julia that Trixie desired the company of a kindred spirit more than she wanted consolation.

They exchanged numbers before Trixie climbed back in her car, but as dearly as they loved each other, it was a relationship of limited province. Julia knew that it would be another lifetime before Trixie called again.

On the drive home, Julia remembered Trixie's conviction that Wayne needed to know the facts of his adoption from the first day he could understand it. And while she couldn't imagine what had driven Wayne to suicide, she feared for her own son's peace of mind, and renewed her vow never to tell Will the facts of his birth.

CAREY BRISTOL WAS AT a realtors' convention in Atlantic City when Julia closed a deal on an expensive town house in Princeton. Since it was a tradition in Roper to celebrate every sale, Brautigan offered to buy Julia a drink after work. The nearest bar was part of Joey's Bowl-a-Rama, a bowling alley three miles down Route 99. They could hardly hear themselves over the crash of ninepins.

"So what are you gonna do with your commission?" asked Brautigan.

"Oh, pay back the credit card company and Roper Realty, and the rest will cover the mortgage for a while. And perhaps there will be enough to pay for a new stove and fridge." Julia explained that when the refrigerator stopped working, Howard's solution was to place bags of ice in the freezer. The cool air would drift down and keep the milk and eggs fresh for a day or two.

"Jesus," muttered Brautigan. "He sounds crazy!"

"Howard doesn't want to go further into debt."

"Then why doesn't *Howard* go out and earn some money of his own?"

Julia flinched.

"Sorry," said Brautigan. "I had no right to say that. Forgive me. I guess there's some insanity in every marriage."

Brautigan drove Julia home. As his Delta 88 pulled into the Laments' gravel driveway, he peered up at the gray-clapboard house: a heap of debris for a porch, peeling paint, and cracked windowpanes.

"Renovations sure are tough," he said with obvious tact.

Brautigan's glance turned to Julia. Trixie was right—he was still handsome. If he had been less smitten with her, Julia might have liked him more.

"See you tomorrow, Mike," she said.

Brautigan reversed out of the drive, and Julia noticed Will standing on the porch, his glance following the car.

"Will," Julia said, "I sold a house today!"

Will, now more than a head taller than his mother, gave her a congratulatory hug and they entered the house together.

"Let's tell Dad the news," said Julia.

"He's been sleeping all day," Will explained anxiously. "Mum? What are we going to do about him?"

Julia was touched that Will used the word "we," and that he worried about Howard's condition when the twins obviously considered their father a hopeless case.

"Will," she replied, "I think your father suffers from a lack of pride."

"Pride?" replied Will.

"At the beginning of his career your father had so many ideas— ambitious and brilliant ideas." Julia paused. "Of course he still does, but he's faced obstacles that would break anyone. What's that line from *Henry VIII*? 'My high-blown pride at length broke under me and now has left me, weary and old with service . . .'"

Will noticed his mother hesitate and turn from him to wipe her cheek.

"Well, he's not that old, is he?" she added. "He'll be fine."

Will put his hand on Julia's shoulder. "Isn't there something we can do for him?"

Strangers in the House

In spite of the many years that had passed since Julia had written to Rose, the letter she sent was easy to compose, for it was motivated not by obligation but by concern for Howard. Her mother had always adored Howard, and Julia felt sure that a visit from Rose would do wonders for him. She waited anxiously for the reply:

Thank you for your letter, Julia. After so many years, I was beginning to think you had given up writing completely! What a shame that would have been after the expense invested in Abbey Gate School.

The children sound well. No doubt Marcus's infirmity will strengthen his character. As for all the fuss over this Watergate affair, when will Americans realize that politicians are scoundrels by nature and saints in the exception?

Though you didn't mention Howard in any detail, I must assume that he is doing wonderfully well. Such an inventive and brilliant man.

While I appreciate your invitation to visit for Christmas, I really can't imagine such a journey at my age.

Julia had felt sure that Rose would seize the opportunity to visit, if only to see America and give it the full blast of her criticism. As for the excuse about her age, Rose was only sixty-four. With disappointment, she wondered how else to interrupt Howard's withdrawal from the world.

AT THE THURSDAY MEETING, Frieda Grecco showed up with her daughter, Minna.

"I'm leaving," she explained. "I've been offered a job at a new restaurant in Tatumville, and Stevie doesn't know about it. Minna's coming with me. We just need to find a place to stay while I save for a rental deposit."

"There's plenty of room in our house," offered Julia.

"Oh, Julia," said Frieda, "that's so kind of you, but what about Howard? Shouldn't you check with him first?"

"No need," Julia replied. "I know *exactly* what he'll say."

"*GUESTS? WHAT DO YOU MEAN, GUESTS?*"

In a matter of hours, Julia had cleared the toys, books, and clothing stored in the upstairs study. Howard stood behind her in protest, his fists clenched in his khaki pants.

"I don't want strangers in the house," he said.

"Howard, I've known Frieda for years. She's a friend and she needs my help. Besides, she's a fabulous cook."

"You're forgetting about the kitchen; it's hardly equipped for seven people!" said Howard.

"Darling, you'll come up with a solution."

Julia watched her husband's expression change as his territorial hostility was replaced by the appeal of a practical challenge.

Under Howard's supervision, a plumber repaired the bathroom faucets while Julia offered silent thanks to Frieda. A new fridge and stove were purchased in preparation for the houseguests. The boys examined the two spotless appliances with bewilderment and suspicion;

the former because their parents had settled a war simply because visitors were coming, and the latter because the visitors appeared to wield more influence than the heirs to the Lament name.

ON THE WINDY SATURDAY when Frieda arrived with her daughter, the driveway to the Laments' gray Georgian was carpeted with red maple leaves; the autumn sun bathed the weary house in a soft light that forgave its peeling paint and warped clapboard.

Will and the twins peered out with barely concealed resentment as two outsiders stepped from an old Gremlin. The little woman with wire rims, an aquiline nose, and a face framed in ringlets handed her daughter a bag to carry. Minna's hair was short and covered by a woolen cap, but her eyes were enormous; they overpowered her delicate features and gave her the appearance of a hatchling. Sensing the boys' scrutiny, she looked up at the window, but they ducked together, like troops in a foxhole.

"Welcome!" cried Julia, giving Frieda a hug.

"Where's Howard?" asked Frieda nervously.

"Oh, God knows," said Julia. "Don't worry about him."

Minna pulled her suitcase out of the car, knocking a box of books to the ground. Julia bent down to help pick them up.

"Minna is a reader," murmured Frieda.

"Excellent!" said Julia. "I'm sure Will can help you carry them inside. . . ."

But Minna started alone toward the house, dragging her belongings behind her.

From the second story, the boys observed the trench left in the gravel by Minna's load of books. "Is that a girl? She's got no boobs and no hair!" exclaimed Julius, whose libido had come a long way since he'd stashed the saucy magazine beneath his mattress. He now possessed an extensive collection of *Playboy*s, *Penthouse*s, and *National Geographic*s to augment his fantasies. Cursed with unpredictable erections, Julius walked in a permanent slouch and kept his fists balled in his coat pockets to cover his crotch. In his dreams he debauched all the

glass, "for their generous hospitality. I just hope we don't drive you all crazy!"

Julius cast an eye at his father and murmured, "Too late for that."

All this time, Will observed that Minna said nothing. When she rose to collect the plates, he took them from her.

"I'll finish up," he said.

"No. It's my pleasure," said Minna, her tone suggesting it was no pleasure at all.

"But it's my job," insisted Will. Minna sat back down at the table, but Will now found himself watching his family through Minna's eyes: his parents seemed impossibly isolated from each other, while the twins pawed the pasta bowl like urchins in a Dickens workhouse.

After a dessert of biscotti and ice cream, when it was obvious that everyone loved the meal, Frieda burst into tears. "I promise we'll be out of your way soon," she said. "I'm determined to get back on my feet!"

"There's no hurry," Julia assured her.

"But you have to make dinner tomorrow," demanded Julius.

Frieda hugged Julia, while Minna stood against the wall, mortified by her mother's emotional outburst. Will imagined that she was counting the minutes before she could slip away.

MINNA ATE BREAKFAST—white bread with peanut butter—on the porch by herself. In the afternoons, she did her homework in the room she shared with her mother, and she emerged only to help at dinner. In the rare moments when she passed through the common part of the house, there was always a book propped in front of her face. When Will found a soaked copy of *The Nick Adams Stories* beside the bathtub one evening, he read it cover to cover, hoping to discover something about her, and then knocked on her door to return it.

"Oh, thanks." She frowned, snatching the book as if it were a lost item of underwear.

"I like the way he describes a cup of coffee," said Will. "Makes you want one even if you hate the stuff."

"Hemingway was in Paris," Minna replied, as if this were significant. When Will failed to reply, she added, "Just like Fitzgerald, Stein, Joyce, Eliot. All the great artists were wanderers."

"They must have been miserable," concluded Will, and Minna appeared troubled by this reply. "By the way," he added, "you might want to stuff something in that hole over the sink, the one by Norfolk on the map. It goes through into my brother's room."

Beneath her cap, the tips of Minna's ears glowed red.

"Now you tell me," she said, and slammed her door.

ONE EVENING WHEN WILL RETURNED from his job at Dutch Oil, Minna was in the kitchen huddled beneath the fluorescent glow of the range hood. She was finishing *The Autobiography of Alice B. Toklas.* Will poured himself a bowl of cereal and sat down.

"Have you made friends at school?" he asked.

Peering over the top of her book, she shook her head. Minna attended most of Will's classes, and she spoke very little. Will guessed that she was shy by nature, as he was, and this interested him.

"Look," he offered, "I hardly have any friends, but I'd introduce you around, if you want."

He observed skepticism in her eyes, which were a pretty walnut brown—not as pretty as Dawn's icy blue eyes, but pretty enough.

She lowered her book. "I don't need to be introduced to Calvin, if *that's* what you mean."

"I don't consider him one of my friends," Will replied.

"Dawn Snedecker says he's your friend."

"Dawn was talking about *me*?" replied Will, suddenly full of hope.

Minna qualified her reply with a shrug. "I wouldn't want to be talked about *that* way."

Summertime

In the last days of school, Queenstown was thrown into a sweltering haze. Timbers in the old house groaned, their joints expanding from the humidity so that doors stopped closing properly and windows jammed in their grooves.

Minna's hair grew quickly; by June she had given up her cap to reveal a head of silky brown hair. She was quite striking, and Julia made the mistake of pointing this out to Will.

"She's beautiful, don't you think?" she remarked. "Those eyes, and her mother's cheekbones, and she has such a very nice figure! But she seems so lonely. I wish there was something more I could—"

"Oh, Mum, please," Will replied, scowling. "Haven't you learned *anything*?"

"Whatever do you mean?"

"Remember Scabby? Curing his pinkeye didn't help our friendship. So *please* don't try any of that with Minna."

WILL WORKED EXTRA HOURS at Dutch Oil. In July he replaced his bicycle, and was thinking about saving for a secondhand car.

"Absolutely not!" cried Julia. "You may not have a car! Half a dozen of your schoolmates die on these roads every year."

"But they drive drunk; they're idiots. I wouldn't let that happen!" argued Will.

"You're safer without the car, Will. I want to see you graduate. After that is your own business!"

Julius grew three inches that summer, leaving Marcus behind. At thirteen, their faces burst with fiery pustules, and their profiles took on adult proportions. Julius became the spitting image of Howard: his nose lengthened to echo his father's waxen droop, his shoulders broadened, and somewhere along the way he had picked up his mother's opinionated manner. Marcus had a slighter frame, and hair that hung in a black sweep. His features were more delicate, his manner gentle and introspective. When he raved about reading *Macbeth* in school, Julia gave him a copy of Shakespeare's collected works she'd found in a used-book store. Except for those rare moments when Julius enticed Marcus to swim with him at the quarry pool—a secret spot where, unobserved by prying eyes, Marcus could swim without his prosthesis—the boy passed his entire summer chain-smoking in the company of Juliet, Miranda, Ophelia, and Viola.

Howard disliked the summer because his solitude was interrupted. In spite of his resolution never to do repairs, he spent August fixing the insulation in the attic because nobody would bother him up there. When it became necessary to replace shingles on the roof, he was obliged to hire Julius as his assistant, and immediately regretted it. For most of the month, passersby could hear father and son bickering above the eaves.

"What should I *do* about them?" Julia asked Will one evening.

"At least they're talking to each other," replied Will. "It'll be the first job Dad's completed in years. I'd say leave them alone."

Julia followed this advice, realizing that she trusted no one more than Will when it came to matters of family harmony. No longer a boy, Will at eighteen was nearly but not quite a man.

The twins were growing up quickly, too. Julius was gregarious, an extrovert, but when he brought girls home it was Marcus they fell for. Often, a girl would come home with him just to meet Marcus, who (if he was in the mood) would start to read Shakespeare's soliloquies out loud, then abruptly vanish into his bedroom. Julius would then show the girl his dirty-magazine collection, which, of course, would send her flying out the door, leaving Julius to jump into the shower to console himself in the usual way.

ONE THURSDAY EVENING, Will arrived home from work to find his mother pacing and worried. Howard had been away for many hours. Will set out with a flashlight and eventually found his father in a cul-de-sac half a mile from their house, struggling with the pieces of a tarnished brass bedstead he had found on a curb. Though the bed must have weighed three hundred pounds, Howard refused to leave unless Will helped him carry it home.

"People don't realize," panted Howard, "that this bed is a wonder of design."

"You're crazy, Dad," Will gasped.

"You know, it's easy to say that," he muttered. "Anybody who feels strongly about *anything* is called crazy in this society."

"Perhaps the crazies," countered his son, "are the ones who feel passionately about *things* instead of *people*!"

Howard paused to shift the weight of the bedspring and the footboard. "Things?" he echoed.

"Yes, like beds! What about the *people* who care about you? Mum was worried sick when you didn't come home."

Will agreed to carry the headboard, and they staggered along with their load beneath the streetlights—scavengers, with only the rattle of the cicadas singing in the trees.

"I'm not crazy," said his father after a while.

"You're not yourself," replied Will, before the sting of what he had said brought tears to his own eyes. "Why can't you be yourself, Dad? Why?"

Howard gave his son a faint smile. "Don't worry, Will. I'll be all right."

Nothing more was said until they had stashed the bedstead in the basement with Howard's other rescued objects. As Will gazed at the odd assortment, he noted that his father had made a mission of defending unappreciated items, the discarded, the obsolete, and the out-of-style. No wonder the man felt comfortable down here.

Julia met them at the door, looking immensely relieved. "Everything all right?" she asked.

"He found a bed," explained Will.

"And I'm *not* out of my mind!" said Howard, staring angrily at Julia before stamping off to bed.

MINNA FOUND WILL SITTING at the kitchen table, a look of anguish on his face.

"Find your father?"

He nodded.

"I know what's wrong with my family," he said.

"What's that?" Minna replied.

"My mother is driven by a sense of purpose. But my father is lost. He spends all his time with things that have no purpose anymore." Will fell silent for a moment. "What a mess."

Minna listened as Will poured out his frustrations. Finally, she offered a solution.

"It's simple," she said. "You should go to Paris."

"Paris? Why?" replied Will.

"Because Gertrude Stein said, 'America is my country and Paris is my home town.'"

"What does that mean?"

"It just means that you don't belong *here*," Minna replied.

Minna and Dawn

The first days of school are always sweet with surprise; Julius looked around his new class at all the girls with their recently developed figures, scooped blouses, and carefully applied lipstick and eye shadow, and pronounced himself in heaven. Meanwhile, the girls observed Marcus's delicate features, his dark hair down to his shoulders, the prosthesis hidden like some gothic sorrow, and declared themselves heartsick.

Will's senior English class was taught by a small, bustling woman from Brooklyn named Mrs. Burbell. Calvin mocked her Canarsie accent, and the teacher demonstrated her amusement by sending him to the vice principal's office four times in the first week. In spite of the verbal abuse she received, Mrs. Burbell was a caring soul who believed that her students needed to look further into their future than graduation. She demanded an oral presentation of every student; the subject: Who will you be when you are thirty?

"Miss Grecco? Why don't you begin?" said Mrs. Burbell.

"When I am thirty I shall be running a coffeehouse on the Left Bank in Paris," began Minna. "I will welcome novelists and artists from all over Europe. My coffeehouse will be a refuge for travelers, a haven for thinkers and dreamers. All poets will be welcome there. Desperate writers will have a place to read their work. Musicians will come to find lyricists; lyricists will come to find composers. I don't plan to be rich, but I want my life filled with art, and ideas, and beauty."

Minna's odd remarks about Paris began to make sense to Will. He started to clap, and Minna smiled. But her smile faded as it became apparent that he was the only one applauding.

Dawn Snedecker replaced Minna at the podium. "When I'm thirty, I plan to be a shivil rightsh activisht. I will help people sheek their legal rightsh and I will sholishit shignaturesh to elect honesht politishians!"

A chorus of sniggering from the back row interrupted Dawn. She blanched, her eyes narrow with fury. Will looked back and saw Calvin, clutching his sides. Dawn pursed her lips, refused to continue, and stalked back to her seat.

Mrs. Burbell picked off four students, including Calvin, and ordered them to the vice principal's office. Still, Dawn couldn't be coaxed to finish her paper.

Minna watched Will squirm in sympathy.

AT LUNCH, WILL APPROACHED DAWN as she nursed a spoonful of yogurt. She raised her eyebrows skeptically. "Dawn," he began, "I just wanted to say that I admired your essay."

The sun caught her hair in motes of silver and gold. When her cheeks turned red, Will smiled, not recognizing the flush of anger. The pin on her collar said FIGHT OPPRESSION.

"Why would a rashisht admire my eshay?"

"I'm not a racist."

"Your friends are rashists."

Will felt a torrent of indignation. "All my life I've had to get along with people who think differently. Shouldn't what I *think* matter to you more than who I talk to?"

"It'sh what you *do* that mattersh," sniffed Dawn. "Not what you shay!"

She rose and stuffed her yogurt into a trash bin, wiping her fingertips on a napkin, which she twisted into a knot.

"Listen, Dawn . . ."

As she walked off, Will felt his misery observed. He turned and saw Minna quickly hide behind her copy of Henry James's *The American*.

"WHERE'S GODDAMN CALVIN?" said Eddie.

"He told me he was sick," answered Will.

Because Julius had borrowed his bike, Will walked the two miles to Dutch Oil that evening, following the sun as it dissipated into a pool of gold between the poplars on Pye Hollow Road.

"What the hell is wrong with him? *Hmmmm?*" asked Eddie.

Calvin mentioned a headache, which probably meant he had been drinking. The previous Friday he had stolen another quart of ethyl alcohol from one of the labs. An entire weekend of Dixie cup cocktails.

When Will left work that night, the darkness beyond the lot seemed as impenetrable as the depths of the quarry pool where the twins swam. Will held his breath for a few moments as he ventured past the floodlights and let his eyes adjust to the engulfing night. Soon a horizon appeared, and a sky full of stars, and he heard the applause of crickets like some vast, unseen stadium audience, while bats flew overhead in their jerky loops and spirals.

Will followed Pye Hollow Road toward home. After a quarter of a mile, he felt the grooves of the train tracks in the asphalt and saw the outlines of the crossing signs against the sky. He began to enjoy hearing his own footsteps, and became anxious when a car passed—the lights were disorienting, and the whine of its engine shattered the calm of the night as the vehicle swept past.

Minna frowned when he entered the kitchen. "What took you so long?"

"I walked home," he replied.

Without a word, she snapped her book shut and padded off to her room. Though she would never have admitted such a thing, Minna looked forward to Will's return, and sometimes even shadowed him between classes. She was fascinated by the odd drawings in his notebooks and his intense frown as he drew. To Minna, Will personified the brilliance and isolation of the artists she read about.

WHEN CALVIN'S HEADACHE kept him home for a third day, Eddie could bear it no longer.

"Will, who do you know who needs a job?"

The following night Will brought Roy Biddle. Hadn't Dawn told him that actions spoke louder than words? This would surely set her straight.

Will showed Roy how to clean the bathrooms, and found himself promoted to Calvin's job.

"But what about when Calvin comes back?" asked Will.

"Calvin's outta here," snapped Eddie. "I don't care what excuse he has. Place looks cleaner already!"

WILL HEARD HER FOOTSTEPS behind him on the way home from school. He turned, momentarily halted by those walnut eyes. "Going home?" he asked.

"*Oui,*" she replied.

They walked in silence for a minute.

"Seriously, are you going to Paris?"

"Of course I am."

"So what you said in class was true?"

She seemed offended. "Of *course* it was true. I'm going to get a job in a café, and eventually have my own. Perhaps I'll have a bookstore, like Sylvia Beach, and hold soirées and accept paintings as payment from penniless artists—and in a few years they'll all be priceless."

"Why Paris?" asked Will.

"My father was from Paris."

"Your father? Steve Grecco?"

"No"—Minna shivered—"*Steve* is the guy my mother married ten years ago. My father was a Frenchman; he died before he could marry my mother. I have his eyes," explained Minna. "Nobody else in my mother's family has my eyes."

This touched Will. "Nobody has my eyes, either," he said.

Minna studied his features. "Did anyone ever tell you that you look French?" she asked. "You have those sad French eyes, like Yves Montand. Perhaps you're adopted. You should come visit me, and sell your pictures in Montmartre, where the artists live. Who knows, maybe you'd find your real parents."

They passed the wrought-iron fence of the graveyard.

Unsettled by Minna's words, Will changed the subject by explaining his theory that the Daughters of the American Revolution were really ghosts.

"Oh, I don't believe in ghosts." Minna laughed.

"But what about the flowers that never die?" said Will.

"Show me a flower that doesn't die," she said.

Will led her along the paths of the graveyard, pointing out the eroded stones of the heroes with their perfect flower arrangements. Though Minna scoffed at his theory, she slipped her hand into his and drew him farther into the cemetery, where the stones were brown and flaking and a giant cedar swayed in the wind. When they reached the brick wall at the back of the cemetery, they stopped and leaned against it. A cloud darkened the gravestones, and raindrops began falling.

"We'd better go," he said.

But Minna didn't move.

Will wiped a raindrop off her cheek and she turned slightly, closing her eyes. He kissed her, and she returned the kiss, biting his lip with that suggested lustful impatience. She reached down to his crotch and felt for the bulge in his pants and began kneading it. He felt for her breasts, but she steered his hand down to her waist, and tucked his fingers in the tight space between her jeans and her underwear. Suddenly her waist button snapped off.

"Sorry," he murmured, but she bit his lip gently, as if to silence him, and continued steering his hand down until he could feel the cleft between her legs through her panties. And she groaned.

THEY WERE WALKING OUT of the cemetery when he asked, "Did I do something wrong?"

"Of course not," she said with a hungry smile. "I just think we'd have more fun where we're going, in a real bed."

"Where?"

"Your basement," she said. "Remember that old brass bed your father has stashed there?" Will slowed down, and Minna noted his hesitation, so she smiled reassuringly. "Look, it's *my* first time, too."

"It's not that," he said.

Her smile faded. "What is it, then?"

He paused. They stood at the hatchway to the cellar, Minna's fingers entwined in his.

"I wasn't thinking of her before, but now I am, and I feel terrible."

"Who? *Who!*"

"Dawn."

Minna wound up and slapped him on the cheek.

"Ow!" he cried. "That hurt! What was that for?"

But Minna had already stamped into the house.

ON FRIDAY, CALVIN SHOWED UP. He had a long excuse about having the flu and throwing up fifteen times. Said it was probably the chemicals he had to breathe at Dutch Oil that made him sick and mentioned that his father had talked about a lawsuit against the company. Eddie suddenly changed his mind about firing Calvin and assigned him to the other side of the complex, known as Building B. There was a whole different pecking order in Building B; the maintenance workers were mostly women from Guyana.

"Building B?" Calvin balked. "I'm not working with niggers!"

"You'll work where I tell you to work, Calvin! Tell that to your lawyer, *hmm*!" snorted Eddie.

As Calvin followed Eddie, he leveled a glance at Will. "Hey, Rhodesia, don't expect a ride home from me today or ever. You almost cost me my job, bringing in Roy."

Will and Roy walked home together. Roy hated the darkness, and insisted on walking along the road, in the path of traffic, rather than up on the embankment, as Will suggested.

"Probably goddamn bear traps up there, English!" he said.

Will assured him that bear traps had been outlawed at least half a century ago. Still, Roy refused to leave the road, even when Calvin's Mustang swept past, horn wailing, spraying them with gravel.

MINNA DIDN'T SPEAK TO WILL for three days. Meanwhile, Will gave Dawn a birthday present, a paperback entitled *Steal This Book*, by Abbie Hoffman. It was a radical's guerrilla handbook, chock-full of advice on how to avoid being disabled by tear gas at a street protest, disrupt a city's phone system, and mix Molotov cocktails. Will thought she'd be flattered.

Dawn sent him a note on Day-Glo-pink heart-shaped paper.

Will,

Thank you for your present, but I cannot condone any of the actions suggested in that book. I am donating it to the Presbyterian fall rummage sale, so that less fortunate people can benefit from your generosity. It was very just of you to help Roy get a job.

Peace on Earth,
Dawn

November brought more rain, and with it a flooded cellar. The hot-water heater lost its flame, and all seven occupants of the Lament household were treated to cold showers one Saturday morning. Howard enlisted Julius to help him remove the water and dig a hole for a sump pump.

The two of them worked side by side for hours, arguing the entire time. Howard took issue with Julius's habit of overfilling the buckets, then spilling half the contents as he staggered up the stairs.

"We'd get much more done if you filled the buckets halfway," remarked Howard.

"We'd get more done if you stopped talking," shot back Julius.

To their credit, they cleared the cellar floor and built a small concrete tub for the pump. But a piercing moment came as they were rearranging the furniture. Julius found an item covered with sawdust, about the size of a large Idaho potato.

"What's this?"

"Put that down," commanded Howard.

Julius ignored his father and blew off the dust to reveal a translucent white device with smooth contours and a ribbon of steel around its equator.

"What is it?"

"Didn't you hear me? Put it down!"

"C'mon, Dad. What's it supposed to be?"

"It's a heart. Something I designed when I worked at Fay/Bernhardt, in the months while I was waiting . . ."

Julius giggled. "You're kidding. A heart? *You* designed a heart?" For Howard, the disbelief on his son's face was the final indignity.

"Give me that and go!" shouted Howard, his hand outstretched. Julius returned the item and sauntered out of the basement. Howard waited for the cellar door to shut before sitting on the brass bed. Then a sob burst from his chest, and he bent over, clutching the item in his hands.

"WHERE'S YOUR FATHER?" asked Julia when she found Julius, freshly showered, watching TV with his toes pressed against the screen.

He shrugged. "Probably in the cellar."

"How long ago did you finish?"

Hearing that it had been several hours ago, Julia ventured down to the basement, but there was no sign of Howard, just the rearranged items from his trash rescues and the pungent odor of freshly dug clay. Then she heard the uneasy rattle of the car in the driveway as she rushed back up the cellar stairs.

Emerging from the hatch, she saw the Buick idling in the driveway, blue smoke billowing from its exhaust, its single occupant illuminated by the faint dashboard lights.

"What's wrong?" asked Will, who had heard her anxious footsteps.

Julia peered at the car, her features rigid and pale. "It's your father, Will. He's been missing for hours, and I just had the most awful feeling . . ."

"I'll bring him in," Will offered, venturing toward the car.

But Julia replied sharply. "No, Will!" And she insisted that he go into the house. "I'll get him," she said.

THE CAR HAD AN UNEASY RHYTHM, as if one piston weren't firing properly—like an irregular heartbeat. It reminded Howard of his weak-spirited father and the stroke that had killed him in his armchair. He turned the artificial heart in his hand as he sat nestled behind the wheel of the Buick, shaded from the moonlight by a curtain of thick pines. Perhaps he had meant to repair his own feeble heart with his invention, rather than cure his father's disease. If so, then the device was a dud. He had lost his resolve, his pluck, and his passion. When he heard footsteps coming across the gravel, he stuffed the disappointing relic into his jacket pocket.

JULIA GENTLY OPENED THE DOOR. Her husband opened his eyes without looking at her.

"Come, darling," she said. "We need to talk."

"I don't want to talk."

"Howard, please. Aren't you cold out here?"

"I'm fine."

"You're shivering. Why don't you have a warmer coat on?"

"Because I was going to kill myself."

She paused.

"Freezing to death like Scott of the Antarctic? Was that the idea?"

"Possibly."

Julia held her breath as she considered the awful logic of her husband's admission. Of course he had settled on this solution. The signs were all there, and she had ignored them. But indignation seemed to unravel in her throat for letting it come to this. And almost immediately, it found vent.

"Howard, I will *not* let you do this! Get out of the car right now!"

"I'm going to drive into a tree."

"You are not!"

"I'm not a child." He frowned at the injustice of her tone. "I'm a grown man! Stop telling me what to do. Just because you have a job doesn't give you the right to boss me around!"

Julia held her reply for a moment, remembering Howard once declaring her ignorant because she did not have an occupation, and realized, now, that he feared that very judgment himself.

"Howard, of *course* you're a grown man," she replied. "You have three children and a wife. But you can't walk away from us."

"I'm a failure. Nothing I do comes to anything. I give up."

"You can't give up. What sort of a man deserts his family?"

"I'm not deserting my family. I'm ending my life."

"You're deserting *me*, Howard," cried Julia. "How *dare* you desert me!"

Howard considered his wife's trembling lower lip and fierce gaze, all this from a person almost half his size, and yet so defiant, her hands placed on her hips, hair tossed by the night's breeze. How *could* he desert such a woman? She had followed him across three continents. And yet her resolve was the very thing that had stood in his way these last few years. Now she looked afraid of losing him, and Howard couldn't help but marvel at her devotion.

"Howard, it's twenty-five degrees out here, and I'm asking you to come inside the house, or we'll both die of pneumonia!"

Howard swallowed and shook his head. "I've been ridiculed by Julius. He has no respect for me."

"Good heavens, darling, the boy helped you dig out the cellar! Show some appreciation, some affection, some generosity of spirit! The boys don't know how to have *fun* with you anymore!"

Howard sighed. "In other words, I *deserve* their contempt?"

"In other words, dote on them a bit and they might possibly dote on you. Now, can we please go inside? I have a letter for you to see; it's rather important."

Julia strode back to the house before he could reply. He saw her pause at the door, her breath billowing under the porch light. Howard stubbornly remained in the car. Then, as if to concur with his wife, the Buick's engine shuddered and died.

The Letter

Julia made tea, and Howard cradled his mug until the feeling returned to his fingertips. The envelope waiting for him on the table had red and blue airmail slashes, and instructions along the edges written in Afrikaans. He recognized Rose's curly scrawl.

"It's open, Howard. Just read it," said Julia, now shivering beneath an afghan shawl.

> *I'm writing to tell you of my intention to visit. I realize that this may seem sudden, but, as I am not getting any younger, it seems time for me to see America. The boys will be men soon; as you have denied me the pleasure of seeing them grow up, I feel entitled to a look at them before they go out into the world and succumb to all the idiocies and conceits of a society that has gone completely mad.*

A visit? Howard reread the words. Yes, Rose was actually intending a visit, and she planned to stay with them.

By the way, I made the acquaintance, when I was last in Florence,
of a Mrs. Pritchard, who, by some remarkable coincidence, was
the nurse during Will's birth. What she told me was shocking.

I shall be arriving on December 1 at Philadelphia Airport.
Perhaps you can arrange to have a room ready for me at the
house, as I expect to be exhausted by the trip and will require a
great deal of sleep to recover.

The Laments stirred into action like Britons preparing for a
Roman assault; instead of sharpening saplings and digging pits, they
cleared out Howard's office for an extra bedroom to accommodate
Rose. It was a small room with wooden shutters and a white marble
fireplace; it had charm, something Julia feared would be in short supply once her mother appeared.

Then Frieda announced that she had found an apartment several
blocks down on Oak Street, above the barbershop, and would be leaving the very weekend that Rose arrived.

"Frieda, do stay another month. I cannot face this woman alone!"
pleaded Julia.

"You have Howard," said Frieda. "And to be honest, Julia, I don't
know if it has helped your marriage for us to be here for so long."

"Frieda," Julia confessed, "we were in trouble before you came,
and I hoped your presence might help bring Howard out of his depression."

"Depression?"

"Yes. He used to be a much happier man."

Frieda was not persuaded to stay, but she insisted on cooking a welcome dinner for Rose. She and Minna would move out the following
day.

IT WAS AMAZING what could be accomplished under pressure. Howard
patched the gaping hole in the living room ceiling—the hole that had
been there for two years. Marcus and Julius helped Howard clear the

remaining debris from the collapsed porch and constructed a sturdy ramp to the front door. Howard tried to talk to the boys evenly; the twins made a similar attempt (they had been spoken to by Julia), but it required considerable effort on both sides.

"What's this for, Dad?" asked Julius. "We never use the front door."

"We don't want Granny to think we live in a shabby house."

"Then maybe we should hire a carpenter," quipped Julius.

Marcus shot his brother a warning glance.

"Sorry, Dad," Julius said. "I didn't mean that."

Howard gave his son a faint smile.

"Of course you did, Julius. I can't blame you."

After the task was finished, the twins stamped on the ramp a few times and Julius offered his father praise on his handiwork. It was a rare moment, and Howard felt his affection rekindled.

"You know, if we have a deep snow this winter, there's a terrific sled run along Pye Hollow Road. I'll take you there."

The twins accepted this offer with enthusiasm. Perhaps Julia was right, thought Howard. Perhaps if he showed the twins some generosity, they would treat him with more respect.

AT DAWN ON THE DAY of Rose's arrival, a cold front came from the north, whistling down Route 99 and bringing with it a frigid blast that glazed the tombstones at the cemetery and turned those withered boughs over Oak Street into a glittering tangle of ice.

Inside the Lament house, the weather was no less tumultuous. Minna woke that morning with a stomachache; she was pining over Will, and sad to be moving. That morning the boys carried the Greccos' belongings over to their new apartment. Will noticed a copy of *Steal This Book* in Julius's jacket pocket.

"Where'd you get that?" asked Will.

"From the rummage sale at the church," said Julius. "You can have it when I'm done."

Howard planned to fetch Rose from the airport with the Buick, which had run out of gas in the driveway a week before. But on this morning, it simply refused to start. Perhaps it was the sleet, or the cold, or, as Julia suggested, Rose's very presence on American soil. Howard phoned the local garage and a mechanic came by to give him a jump, advising him to replace the battery and have the alternator checked.

IT WAS AROUND FOUR O'CLOCK when Will saw the car reappear in the driveway. Howard emerged and, with extraordinary vigor, raced around the car to open the passenger door. Will was surprised at how handsome his grandmother was—all he remembered was the blue vein on the side of her face from the time when she had presented him with the paper and fountain pen. Though she seemed pale, her cheek-bones were strong, her eyes a brilliant blue, her posture straight. Her linen skirt and blouse were utterly inappropriate for an American winter but a reminder that she had flown here from an African summer. She removed a straw hat to reveal a mane of perfectly white hair.

Julia, a few steps out of the door, was also awed by her mother's appearance. How marvelous it would be to age so gracefully, and to have such presence in twenty-five years. But as she crossed the driveway she felt herself shrinking to schoolgirl proportions. She reminded herself to keep her arms from swinging like oars (as her mother used to tell her) by clutching the sides of a skirt she hadn't worn in ten years and keeping her gaze level, not too eager, or too reticent.

"Mummy, you look *wonderful,*" she said.

"Thank you, darling." Rose gave her daughter a sharp scan. "You're eating *well,* I see."

Julia felt herself shrink again as she received a crisp hug and the faintest breath of a kiss.

"Good flight, Mummy?" Julia persevered.

"Perfectly awful."

Julia turned for support. "Boys! Come here! *Meet Granny!*"

"Plenty of time for that," said Rose. "First someone must see to my bags."

"Got the bags," puffed Howard, staggering under the weight of three canvas suitcases from the back of the car. Julia assessed their size. This would not be a brief stay.

FOR ROSE'S WELCOME, Frieda had prepared a simple dinner—an antipasto of olives, slivers of mozzarella, and artichoke hearts, then a subtle marinara sauce made from fresh plum tomatoes, a little seasoning, no garlic, no onion. The pasta was fresh and full of flavor. It was a homey, comforting dish.

"Isn't Frieda a wonderful cook?" said Julia.

Rose nodded. "My compliments," she said. When no one spoke, Rose steered the conversation into new territory. "It must be all the warm weather in Italy that fostered the Italian cooking tradition. Italians have nothing better to do than cook and drink."

"Excuse me?" said Frieda.

"Hedonists," Rose said. "It's part of the Italian character. Don't you think?"

Julia was preparing an apology when Frieda replied:

"I disagree. What about Leonardo, Galileo, Columbus?"

"There are exceptions to every rule," Rose said.

"Certainly," agreed Frieda softly. "Exceptions who changed the face of Western civilization."

Julia allowed herself a brief smile.

Rose smiled, too. She took another drink from her wine and reappraised Frieda, as if taking the measure not of Frieda's convictions but of her capacity to take a little ribbing.

"My dear," replied Rose, "you must admit, you yourself are a fine example of a classic Italian. Clearly, you belong in the kitchen!"

Without flinching, Frieda laughed. "Actually, my mother was Jewish. As for my Italian father, he couldn't boil an egg to save his life."

"Nevertheless, it's obviously in your blood," said Rose.

"My mother loves these generalizations," Julia apologized. "You'll never talk her out of them."

"Yes," agreed Rose. "I've been all over Europe, and there are unmistakable national traits."

As Julia cringed, Frieda took these comments in stride. She guessed that over the years Rose had kept herself in the spotlight with these provocative remarks. "Rose," she asked, "what are the national traits of South Africans?"

"I can answer that one," said Julia. "Obliviousness to misery, bloody-mindedness, and resistance to change!"

There was a fearful silence as everyone watched for Rose's reaction.

But Rose merely smiled. "We seem to be lurching into politics, Julia, and I make it a rule never to spoil a good meal that way."

AFTER DINNER, ROSE OBSERVED that everybody looked tired, which Julia took as a sign that her mother was exhausted. She led her up to her room, which Rose pronounced "pleasant," to Julia's immense relief.

"Poor Howard," Rose sighed. "We chatted quite a bit on the way back from the airport; he sounds quite disillusioned, Julia. I think it's America that's wearing him down."

"You think so?" Julia replied.

"Yes," said Rose. "You need to build up his ego. That's a wife's first responsibility. . . ."

"Good idea, Mummy. When I'm finished making a living and taking care of the children, I'll see what I can do about his ego."

"It's the moving, I suspect." Rose frowned. "He needs stability."

"Stability? Mummy, Howard would give *anything* if we'd just pack and move to New Zealand, or Australia, or Canada. Howard is a wanderer. He can't settle. He's incredibly unhappy. *You* can't expect to solve his problems after one *chat* in the car."

Rose folded her arms, adjusting her sights. "You've tried, I imagine."

Julia shrugged. "Tried and failed. Now I'm doing my best to keep the boys fed and clothed."

"They seem very healthy; though the boy with one hand . . ."

"You mean Marcus."

"He's a little unfriendly. In fact, he looks at me with suspicion. Then again, I suppose he's never been encouraged to get to know his own grandmother."

"I've invited you to visit."

"Once."

Julia drew in a breath. "Marcus is a very sweet boy. You'll like him— he's passionate about Shakespeare and he likes to perform, and as for Julius . . ."

"He argues with Howard, I noticed," said Rose.

"He's full of opinions—*like you*, Mummy," Julia continued. "He has lots of energy, loves television, and happens to be crazy about girls."

Now Rose appeared dismayed. "It saddens me that I know so little about these boys. Why couldn't you have told me about them before?"

For the first time that evening, Julia felt genuine sympathy for her mother.

"Forgive me," she said. "But I'm so glad you're here now."

Her mother's eyebrows rose dubiously.

Julia noted with astonishment that this expression, which had landed her in so much trouble with Mrs. Urquhart, was a gift from her mother.

"If it hadn't been for Will's letters to me I wouldn't have had a clue whether you were alive or dead. Was it your intention to isolate me? What have I ever done to deserve such treatment?"

"Your letters to us have been assaults, Mummy. *How* could I live in this country? . . . *Am* I taking care of Howard properly? . . . *Why* don't I write more often? A litany of criticism!"

Bewildered by this force of emotion, Rose blinked.

"Questions, darling. Was it wrong to ask questions?"

Julia gasped. "Questions are fine, Mummy, but did it ever occur to you to offer a compliment, to say something kind?"

Her mother paused. "I've always said you picked a wonderful husband."

. . .

IN THE MORNING, the children cleared out quickly for school, leaving mother and daughter to face each other over toast and tea. Howard slept late enough to avoid seeing everybody hurrying off with something to do.

"What's our plan for today?" Rose asked Julia.

"Well, I have to show some houses to a client," said Julia, "but Howard could take you into Manhattan for the day. It's not more than ninety minutes by car."

"Nonsense. I couldn't impose on Howard."

"Impose? Why? He's got nothing planned. And as I said, I have to show some houses. . . ."

"Houses, yes," murmured Rose. "What would they say at Abbey Gate School if they knew what you were doing now?" She sighed.

"I like selling houses," replied Julia. "I enjoy helping people start new lives. I understand their concerns, Mummy, because my life has been spent moving from one unfamiliar place to the next. Finding the right house is no easy task. . . . And besides that, I happen to like closing a deal."

Rose seemed amused. "Yes, Americans talk about profit as if it were a biblical virtue."

Julia decided to be blunt.

"Mummy, we're finally out of debt. Because of *my* job, there's food on the table."

"Yes, but at what cost to your husband's pride? Howard is vexed by your career, Julia. You may have fed your family, but what have you done for him? . . . I *always* supported my husbands."

"What?" cried Julia. "You dropped them left and right like ballast from a balloon!"

Rose's long, tapered fingers floated skittishly over her teacup. "Perhaps you'd like me to leave," she said quietly.

"Oh, Mummy! I meant exactly what I said last night. You really are welcome for as long as you wish to be with us! If I seem to have a short fuse, it's only because I have so much to do."

"Very well," said Rose quietly. "I shall stay, but only as long as I feel welcome." There was something frail about this ultimatum, as if Rose weren't sure how convincing it would sound. This surprised Julia, because in the past her mother had thought nothing of making grand demands.

Rose passed her second day recovering from jet lag. Howard slipped out of the house to do some shopping, and produced an abomination for dinner (an overcooked chicken that still had its giblets inside in a paper packet). Julia ordered a pizza, after which the boys disappeared into their rooms to do homework while Julia spent the evening balancing the checkbook in Rose's company.

When Julia inquired about her mother's day, Rose seemed disappointed.

"It was uneventful," said Rose. "Everyone seems very busy—even Howard, who has nothing to do."

Julia promised to take her mother sightseeing soon.

That evening, Rose slept fitfully. She had not expected to find her daughter's life so complicated—an aggressive career, a struggling marriage, and a husband in such pathetic condition. She had always pictured her daughter's life as placid, because even though Will's letters pointed out tragedy and mishap, the Laments traveled with undeterred frequency, across continents and cultures. Nothing seemed to stop them from moving. Rose, on the other hand, tired of foreign customs after a week or two.

Rose desperately needed a kindred spirit, someone in whom she could confide a most personal matter. Years of sharp criticism for friends and lovers had left her friendless and alone. The Laments were her last hope. In fact, she had counted on Howard to be her confidant, but during the drive back from the airport she was shocked by his self-involvement. As for Julia, there was too much unfinished business between them. When the early light of the morning peeked into her room, she felt most terribly alone.

The Dance

"That Dawn is a nice girl," said Roy.

"You've said that twice," replied Will.

It was a cloudy night. No moon. No stars. Only a whisper of traffic in the distance. They had been walking home together from Dutch Oil for the last six weeks. Though Roy could afford a bike, he was saving his money for something special, he told Will. Will didn't mind walking with Roy; he was easy to talk with, and their conversations often became intimate in the darkness.

"What I mean is, English, I think I love her," said Roy.

"What?" Will laughed, but his voice was uneasy.

"She invited me over her house last weekend. Just to talk. So I went. Sat on the porch. We talked a *lot*, English."

The low whine of a car interrupted their footsteps, and its distant headlights illuminated them. Roy glanced anxiously at Will.

"I know you like her, too, English. You upset?"

"Have you been back to see her?" asked Will.

"A couple times, English."

As the car got closer, Will clambered onto the embankment. He urged Roy to join him, but Roy stubbornly remained on the edge of the road.

"Goddamn bear traps, man!"

The jagged whine became louder. Realizing whose car it was, Will leaped down, seizing Roy by the arm, and hauled him out of the path of the car, which sprayed them with crumbled asphalt and swerved back onto the road.

"Goddamn Calvin!" shouted Roy.

"*That's* why you gotta keep off the road," said Will, releasing Roy, who promptly clambered back down to the shoulder.

Perhaps it was gratitude that compelled Roy to come clean. "You know, English, Dawn asked me to take her to the Christmas dance."

The worst news is often the least surprising. Will heard himself congratulate Roy while his heart hammered a hole in his chest.

WHEN JULIUS AND MARCUS BROUGHT the girl home, they hadn't a clue what a fuss it would cause. Sweet Cleo Pappas. Almond-shaped eyes, the lips of Buddha, and breasts that danced beneath her Peter Frampton T-shirt when Julius made her laugh. She was a godsend for the twins.

Julia invited her to stay for dinner. Cleo sat quietly, hands wedged between her thighs. When Julius spoke, she giggled. When Marcus spoke, she sighed.

The trouble started when Rose asked her name.

"Well, my friends call me Cleo, but I was christened Nancy. Nancy Pappas."

Rose's brow furrowed. "Pappas? That's Greek, isn't it?"

Cleo nodded. "Yes, my father's Greek, but my mother's Turkish."

"Quite a conundrum," remarked Rose. "After what the Turks did to Greece, it's a wonder you came into this world!"

"Pardon?" said Cleo.

"Surely you know what the Turks did?"

"I like their hats," Julius interrupted, prompting another giggle from Cleo.

"Am I ignorant of the facts?" said Rose. She was fanning herself in the heat of Julia's reproachful glance. "The Turks *did* destroy the Parthenon, did they not?"

"Oh God, Mummy, so what?" cried Julia.

The twins and Cleo left to watch television in Julius's room. When Marcus turned in after *The Six Million Dollar Man*, Julius showed Cleo one of his *National Geographic*s. When he got to a page depicting a naked Kreen Akrore tribeswoman, he asked her whether her breasts were similarly shaped. Cleo giggled, and asked whether Julius's penis was the size of the tree on the opposite page.

"I don't know—you'd have to compare them," said Julius.

With astonishing timing, Cleo's mother telephoned at that precise moment to summon her daughter home.

Julius, convinced he might have lost his virginity if Cleo had stayed a few more minutes, consoled himself with a long shower. When he reached ecstasy, Rose heard him from the kitchen.

"My, what an exceptional vibrato Julius has!" she remarked.

THE CHEERY CHRISTMAS LIGHTS that were strung up along Oak Street by the Queenstown Chamber of Commerce gave Officer Martin Tibbs, who was an undiagnosed epileptic, a petit-mal seizure while driving his patrol car. This caused him to plow into the wrought-iron cemetery fence, shattering the gravestones of the six patriots of Queenstown. Though Officer Tibbs, father of Calvin, was unharmed, he threatened the township with a suit. Mindful of his son Otis's successful suit against the railroad, the town fathers gave Officer Tibbs early retirement with full benefits. Meanwhile, the blinking lights made it impossible for Will Lament to ignore the season, or to forget that Roy would be dancing with the love of his life on December 23.

For the Laments it was a season of unrequited desire. Howard yearned for something to awaken his life; Julia wished for her husband's recovery; and the twins were both lusting after a girl whose mother had an uncanny sense of when to summon her daughter home.

Will, suffering over Roy's claim on Dawn, wished for a stone heart. As for Rose, she yearned for a confidant.

ONE MORNING ON THE WAY TO SCHOOL, Minna caught up with Will. In the weeks since she had left his house, her greetings had been sullen at best. But Minna didn't look heartbroken this morning.

"I have a present for you, Will," she said, matching his step, smiling giddily.

"You don't have to give me anything," he replied as she pressed a white envelope into his hand, his name written in script on the outside.

"Open it," she urged as he tried to slip it into his pocket.

Will tore open the envelope and shook out the contents. Two tickets to the Christmas concert at the Capitol Theatre in Passaic. Frank Zappa would be performing with the Mothers of Invention.

"It's for December twenty-third," said Minna, "the same date as the dance."

"Minna, I can't accept—"

"You don't like Frank Zappa?"

"I think he's incredibly cool," admitted Will, "but I can't accept this."

"Yes you can," Minna insisted. "How about this: you invite Dawn, and if she doesn't accept, you take me."

Will paused, struck by the perversity of this deal.

"But she *has* plans that night," he replied.

"I know," said Minna. "The big dance. What a thrill," she added contemptuously. "If she turns you down this time, she's a hopeless case. And if she's the sweet thing you *think* she is, you'll take her to the show and fuck her brains out on the train home."

"Funny," said Will.

"So where's my thank-you?" she asked before he could reject the proposal.

Will was about to reply when Minna dug her fingers into the waistband of his jeans, pulling him closer until her hips bumped against his. As their tongues met, she uttered a sigh that weakened his knees and sent a whiplash of desire down to the hardening knot between his legs.

When he sought out Dawn Snedecker at lunch, Will felt charged by Minna's dare. He wasn't afraid of rejection anymore; he was delivering an ultimatum.

"Dawn, would you like to go to a concert with me?" he asked in the busy school corridor.

She looked at the tickets, clearly impressed.

"Oh, I'd love to but I'd have to break my date with Roy for the Chrishmash Dansh, and I jusht couldn't do that."

"Roy would get over it," said Will.

She looked at Will, then at the tickets, as if weighing two different aspects of her dilemma.

"No, I'm shorry, Will. It wouldn't be right."

"That's true," Will agreed. "It wouldn't be right. Roy's counting on you."

"Then why did you ashk me?" she replied.

"To test you, I guess," Will answered. "You've called me a racist for years when I know I'm not one. I suppose I wanted to know if you were just full of opinions and righteous attitudes, or if you had any personal decency."

"Well?"

"Well what?" he replied.

"What did you deshide?"

"I decided that it didn't matter," said Will, tucking the tickets into his pocket. "I'm over you, Dawn." And, with that, he walked away.

Composure

The Roper Realty Christmas tree had been decorated by Mike Brautigan with all the delicacy of a hurricane. Angels hung upside down; half of the Christmas lights twinkled, while the other half were dead. The tree had been strung with popcorn, mostly nibbled to the threads by Emil DeVaux during one solitary afternoon in the office. Carey Bristol had dangled bells made of rainbow-colored crepe from the ceiling, and spray-painted snow on the windowsills.

"You might say the place needs a woman's touch," confessed Carey as he showed Rose around the office, "but Julia is too busy selling houses! Two, this week alone! And who buys a house in December? She's amazing! And now I can see where she gets her good looks!"

Julia winced at Carey's flattery, and hurried her mother out before Rose could criticize the worn carpeting, overflowing ashtrays, and shabby furniture of the place. Once they were back in the car, Rose remarked that Carey Bristol needed a new pair of shoes, and a gray suit that would match his eyes.

They drove up Route 99, then west, past miles of faded fields lined with gray-limbed trees. Julia pointed out the properties she had sold, and the ones she was showing. There were Cape Cod houses with cedar shingles nestled in the woods, and row upon row of identical split-levels. The occasional classic white farmhouse in the distance turned into a wreck of shattered glass and peeling timbers as they drove by. There were square plots of trees, with Roper Realty signs and not so much as a driveway to mark a home.

What vexed Rose was Julia's tendency to talk about the land in terms of what it *could* be, rather than what it *was*.

"I rather like the fields the way they are," Rose finally said. "Why can't they just be fields?"

Julia tried to explain that the area was poor, and that development would raise the tax base, but after a moment she realized that Rose was looking at her uncomprehendingly. They came to a small town that lay between the Delaware River and a tow-barge canal—a slick, polluted ribbon of water as black and shiny as a crow's cowl. The Tatumville restaurant resembled the other white Georgians overlooking the canal, save for a cheerful shingle that promised HOT SOUP. They decided to stop for lunch.

The conversation drifted as slowly as the black water beyond the window. Julia tried to get her mother to explain her plans, but Rose was oblique and changed the subject.

"How are you going to get Howard back to work?"

"He's depressed, Mummy, and he won't see a doctor."

Rose sniffed. "A doctor? Hardly a solution."

"I mean a psychiatrist. Somebody who deals with depression. Americans are more comfortable with psychiatrists," Julia explained.

"Clearly, then, Howard's not as much of an American as *you've* become."

Julia flinched. "What do you mean?"

"Real estate. Development. Turning perfectly nice countryside into commodities. It all seems frightfully American to me."

This time it was Julia who changed the subject.

"Were any of your husbands ever depressed, Mummy?"

"Never," snapped Rose. "All of them drank, of course, but that was nothing unusual. Oh, yes, one had an addiction to morphine, but that was entirely the doctor's fault."

"And Papa?" asked Julia.

Adam Clare hadn't been mentioned in many years, and Rose looked slightly wounded on hearing his name. "I remember your father always being a sad man," she replied. "But it wasn't the sort of thing you saw a doctor about in those days."

Julia gave her mother a searching glance.

"Perhaps seeing a doctor might have helped him. . . ."

"Well, it's too late now," said Rose. "We'd been divorced for years by the time he died."

Julia looked at her mother. "Why wasn't I told about the divorce, Mummy?"

Rose shifted in her seat. "I'm sure I was trying to protect you, darling."

"Oh God, Mummy, how *could* you keep it from me? I was just a child. I didn't know whom to trust after that, whom to believe. . . ."

Rose was relieved when the waitress appeared with a lemon tart and two spoons.

"Figured you'd want to share," said the waitress with a smile.

On her first taste, Julia felt her eyes well up; she wasn't sure if it was the sourness of the tart, or the residual sting of the conversation that had preceded it. But the subject was dropped. Rose insisted on paying the bill, but Julia noticed that she had shortchanged the waitress. Julia added several quarters once Rose reached the door.

On the drive back, Rose turned to the future.

"Isn't Will going to university next year, Julia? I haven't heard a word about his plans."

"He may want a year off before applying," said Julia. "He's not quite ready to go off yet."

"What's wrong with him?" replied Rose. "Most young men his age want to be off in the world, exploring their prospects."

Julia chose her words with brittle clarity. "There's nothing wrong with him."

"A boy so obsessed with keeping the family together that he can't think about his own future?" said Rose. "I think that's rather ironic, considering the facts of his birth."

It struck Julia that her mother had been digging around for a vulnerable spot, and she had finally found one as sensitive as the suicide of Julia's father. Ever since Rose's mention of Mrs. Pritchard in her letter, Julia had feared this discussion.

"He doesn't know," said Julia.

"In other words," Rose observed, "you are trying to *protect* him, just as I was trying to protect you. . . ."

"Mummy, the most stable thing in Will's life is his place in this family," replied Julia. "How can I tell him he's not really my son?"

"I faced the same dilemma," replied Rose. "I spared you the news of our divorce because I wanted you to have some stability, darling."

"It's not the same thing!"

"It's a secret, Julia."

"Your secret devastated me!" cried Julia.

For a long while, they drove past the huddled Capes, split-levels, and colonials without uttering a word. *Your secret devastated me.* Julia's words echoed in her head. For the first time, she imagined having just such a conversation with Will in twenty years.

Finally, Rose spoke her mind. "I regret not telling you about the divorce. I was young, I wasn't equipped to cope with my feelings, let alone yours. I should have told you, Julia. . . . And I know you'll make the right decision about Will."

Julia steered the car into the familiar gravel drive and took a moment to search the contents of her bag. While Rose walked to the house, Julia paused to wipe her cheeks dry with a tissue.

Miss Liberty

Howard hated driving into the city. He despised its traffic jams, the mobs of sightseers, and the expense of everything. So Julia had planned to take Rose to see the Statue of Liberty. But Brautigan fell ill the next weekend, and she had to cover for him in the office. As the boys piled into the car, Howard was still trying to talk everyone out of the trip.

"The car might not start," he warned.

"Mum replaced the battery," countered Will.

The Buick started in spite of Howard's complaints about a flashing alternator light. As they coasted along the turnpike, the twins seized the opportunity to interest Rose in all the sights they had yearned to see since coming to America.

"You *must* see a baseball game, Granny!"

"At Yankee Stadium," added Marcus. "It's a landmark."

"And the Cyclone at Coney Island!" said Julius.

The ferry to Liberty Island puttered through churning, metallic-toned water. Gulls sang overhead and dipped for dropped morsels as the twins took copious advantage of Rose's generosity at the hot dog counter. At the granite entrance, Howard refused to take the winding stairs up through the statue's interior.

"I don't like confined spaces," he told the boys as they pleaded with him.

So Marcus and Julius tore up the winding stair, leaving Will to escort Rose at a slower pace. By the time they reached the top, the twins were dashing back down.

Rose seemed to relax in Will's company; she was excited, curious, and she absorbed the view from Miss Liberty's head with barely contained awe.

"America is such a crass, ugly place," said Rose as she peered through a window stuffed with gum wrappers and soda cups. "I suppose one must accept its marvels with its vulgarity. It's all part of the human soup, you know." She breathed in, as if this spirit were somehow lingering in the air over New York Harbor; then she glanced curiously at Will.

"Are you happy here in America, Will?"

Will shrugged. "I miss England. I miss all the places I can remember. . . . And some of the people I left behind."

"Really?"

Will nodded. "I dream about them all the time."

"I dream about people, too," admitted Rose. "Even the happiest person has regrets. You can't rejoice in a sunny day if all you've ever known are sunny days, any more than you can grieve the loss of someone you've never met. Happiness and sadness go together."

"I think I know more about sadness than happiness," said Will.

"I'm sure this will change," Rose replied.

They were walking down now, around and around the circular stairs, their footsteps echoing through the statue's green metal viscera. They could hear the twins, far below, taunting each other. Will stopped for a moment, and looked up at his grandmother.

"Do I look French, to you?"

"French?" Rose looked puzzled. "Why?"

Will shrugged. "Someone told me I looked French. I certainly don't look like anyone in the family, do I?"

Rose frowned. "Why—why would that matter?"

"I'll tell you a secret," said Will. "Sometimes I imagine I'm an orphan. I imagine that there's no one in the world like me, no parents, no brothers, no family, no one expecting anything of me, no one to worry about. And for a few minutes, I like the feeling." He shrugged. "And then it suddenly seems the very worst thing to wish for. And I'm glad to be who I am."

"Yes," Rose said. "I can see that."

From below, the twins began shouting for Will to hurry up. He offered his hand to Rose, and, together, they continued walking down the stairs.

"I have a secret, too," admitted Rose after a few minutes.

"What's that?" Will replied.

"I came to America to see my family, of course, but I also came because I have nowhere else to go. I've spent my money, Will. All of it."

"Good," he replied. "Then you'll stay with us forever."

"I don't know how your parents would feel about that," confessed Rose.

"Actually, Mum and Dad need someone to watch over them. I can't do it forever," he replied.

Concert Night

The sky darkened like an inkblot as Will and Roy crossed paths on the trestle bridge after school. They waved, but didn't stop to talk. Roy was in a hurry to pick up Dawn's corsage from the florist before he began his shift at Dutch Oil; he would then sprint to Dawn's house at eight-thirty and walk her to the dance.

Will had made peace with all this. While everyone at school was talking about the dance that night, he and Minna acknowledged their plans in secret: her fingers trailed his palm as they passed in the hallway. As he turned along Oak Street, past the cemetery, falling snow began cresting the gravestones, gathering on the wrought-iron fence, and forming delicate spires on its filigree.

Where Pye Hollow Road continued past Oak Street, it dodged pasture and woodland for about three miles, crossed the railroad tracks and passed Dutch Oil, then, after another two miles, ran alongside the Pye Hollow Country Club. After a good snow, the golf course became the terrific sled run Howard had told the twins about just before Rose's arrival.

When Howard heard reports of a blizzard on the radio, he remembered his promise to take the twins sledding, and brought the matter up with Marcus.

Will and Julia went over to Frieda's apartment together; Will was picking up Minna for the concert, and Julia was attending her Thursday meeting, which was being held on this Friday—tonight—because Avé had had to take her sons to choir practice on Thursday. As they walked along the icy street, Julia broke her own vow not to talk about Minna. She was bursting with curiosity.

"You know, I always hoped you two would get along. You were such a romantic little boy. Do you remember Ruth and Sally?"

Will answered slyly. "You know I never remember any girl once the next one comes along."

"You know that's not true," Julia said, buttoning his army coat at the neck. "Please do be careful tonight—the roads look awful."

Will promised.

THERE WAS A FULL-SCALE BLIZZARD by sunset. When Julius phoned Cleo Pappas to invite her over after dinner, she said, "I'll never get through the snow!"

But Julius was insistent. "We could watch TV, or look at magazines."

Cleo giggled; she knew what that meant. "Will your brother be there?"

"Of course," said Julius. When he put the phone down, Marcus appeared, carrying the two rusty sleds from the cellar.

"Dad's taking us sledding at Pye Hollow Country Club."

"But Cleo's coming over tonight!"

Marcus argued that they couldn't let Howard down. They agreed to spend two hours sledding, which would give them time to meet Cleo back at the house at nine.

"Want to come sledding, Granny?" asked Julius as they bundled up.

"You'll catch your death." She shuddered, and went to make herself some tea.

. . .

AS HOWARD DROVE OUT with the boys, Will and Minna were boarding a bus for the train station. All the while, the falling snow kept changing—from a sprinkle of powder, to an open sky, to a cascade of thick flakes. The roads were becoming slushy and treacherous. The train bound for North Jersey wailed over marshland and through suburbs, smothered by the advancing drifts.

Minna wore a black leather jacket, a burgundy velvet skirt, black tights, and low boots. Her cheeks were rouged, perhaps just a little too much, but she wanted Will's eyes fixed on her for the evening. And they were.

"What is it?" she asked when he kept glancing over at her in the train.

"You're somebody else." He smiled. "Do I know you?"

She looked at him first with anxiety; then an appreciative smile played on her lips.

Will wore his olive army greatcoat over a faded sweatshirt and jeans that fell short of his battered red Converse sneakers by more than an inch. His blond hair hung to his shoulders. To a stranger, Will was a boy on the cusp of manhood. He towered awkwardly over Minna, long-limbed and gaunt; but his downturned eyes became full and expectant when Minna spoke to him, and his large hands meshed in hers. Though his nose was prominent and his jaw too long, these features struck Minna as poetic. His casual sorrow was arousing, and evocative of her own discomfort in the world.

The train took on more passengers at Princeton Junction, and Minna anxiously studied her printed schedule. She admitted to Will that she'd never been north of New Brunswick, because her mother disliked trains and was fearful of the city.

"Then what makes you want to travel?" he asked.

"I just want to go to Paris," she replied. "I want to walk on streets a thousand years old, and see all the things I've read about. And find my father, of course."

It occurred to Will that although he disliked travel, it might not be so bad with Minna for company.

They were surprised when they found themselves at their destination, a windy station on the North Jersey corridor. The snow had tapered off to a powdery flurry. On the horizon, a gas refinery twinkled with thousands of lights—the disingenuous beauty of the industrial rim.

Will and Minna hurried along the platform, following the other shadows that alighted from the train. About ten blocks away, the neon lights of the concert hall beckoned.

"YOU'RE WORKING BUILDING A TONIGHT," ordered Eddie as Calvin brushed the snow from his shoulders in the foyer of Building B.

"How come?" said Calvin.

"People are out. I'm switching things around. You'll do the toilets, *hmm*?"

Calvin bristled. "Hell no! Roy does the toilets!"

Eddie shook his head. "Roy's promoted. He's doing floors. *You're* doing toilets."

"Shit, Eddie, I've been working here two years. I got seniority!"

Eddie was in no mood for arguments. The Guyanese ladies lived fifteen miles away in Trenton and he had to let them off early because of the weather.

"Attitude is what you got, *hmm*? And toilets!" barked Eddie.

Calvin spun around, buttoned his jacket, and kicked the door open, trudging off in search of Building A.

NOW THAT NIGHT HAD FALLEN, the golf course was cast in pink by the few lampposts on its rolling slopes. In some areas the snow had blown away to reveal a hilltop of solid ice; the speed, on a sled, would be breathtaking.

Howard parked the car at the edge of the road and clambered up the slopes with the twins, joking about who was entitled to take the first run.

"We go first, because we're the kids," argued Julius.

"No—age before innocence." Howard laughed.

"C'mon, Dad, we haven't been sledding once this year."

Howard paused at the top of the course, catching his breath, feeling the sting of the cold air in his lungs.

"Well, I've never been sledding before," he reminded them. Marcus then insisted that Howard take his sled for the first ride. So Julius and Howard went down the slope, side by side.

Riding on his belly, with his knees bent, Howard was terrified. Ice beneath the runners vibrated in his chest as the sled picked up speed. Air rushed past, cold and bracing. The smell of pine and wet wool stung his nostrils. Ahead, Julius gave a yell as he hit a bump that sent him flying. When Howard struck the bump, he gasped, arms flailing in panic. Julius glanced back anxiously, but Howard waved, then lost his breath again as the sled landed and tore up an embankment before lurching down a quarter-mile run with frightening velocity. His cheeks were burning, his heart pounding, and then, suddenly, it was over. Howard lay in a drift, on his back, taking stock of his vital functions.

Julius peered over at his father.

"All right, Dad?"

"Fabulous," whispered Howard.

"C'mon, then. Let's do it again!"

But as Howard rose, he winced. "Wait a moment!"

Julius turned to see his father limping forward.

"I've hurt my leg. It's probably that old injury from Ajax. I have to warm up at home, but you two can stay."

"C'mon, Dad," insisted Julius. "You'll feel better in a minute."

Howard, though gratified by this invitation, ventured only a few steps before grimacing. He urged Julius to join his brother.

"Can you pick us up in two hours?" asked Julius.

Howard nodded. Julius waved, and jogged up the slope dragging the two sleds.

Howard reconsidered going back to the house when he thought of being alone with Rose. So he doubled back through town, past the houses on Oak Street—snow-blanketed and solemn—over the trestle bridge toward Route 99. He turned right, noticing that most of the businesses along the highway had closed early. Raymond Biddle was tying up his Christmas trees for the night. A mile ahead, an enormous yellow snowplow blinked its headlights, urging Howard off the treacherous road.

WILL AND MINNA WERE SEATED way in the back of the concert hall, but it didn't matter. Two overweight, gray-haired former pop stars warmed up the crowd with a slide show of their brief rise to fame in the sixties, when they were young, slim, and innocent. Then they sang a few perfect renditions of their old hits mixed with a lot of self-deprecating jokes.

All the while, Minna leaned against Will in the darkness, letting her lips caress his ear as she whispered to him. As the lights darkened for the main attraction, she slipped her hand between his legs and could practically feel his pulse.

"This is nice," he murmured in a clumsy effort to tell her what she already knew.

ROY HAD FINISHED HIS WORK and was wheeling the floor polisher back to the third-floor elevator when he saw Calvin nursing a cigarette outside the ladies' bathroom.

"Hey, Roy," said Calvin, "will you help me out with this bathroom? I'm running late."

"Sorry, man," said Roy, hurrying past. "I don't wanna smell like no toilet. I'm picking up a girl after work!"

As Roy disappeared into the elevator, Calvin stared after him, a muscle throbbing in his cheek. It took him another half hour to finish up. When he finally sauntered down to the lobby, Eddie was waiting for him, holding out a pay envelope.

Calvin scanned the empty foyer. "Where's everybody else?"

"Sent 'em home early. If you'd kicked ass, you'd have been out of here by now, too. *Four* smoking breaks. *Hmm?* Jesus!"

Calvin's jaw went slack. "Is that what Roy said? That nigger's a liar!"

"Roy is not your problem, Calvin. *You* are your problem. Here's your check. Merry Christmas."

Calvin stuffed the check in his pocket, his eyes fixed on Eddie; then he zipped up his parka and spat out his farewell: "Fuck you, Eddie, fuck your mother, and fuck this job!"

MARCUS FELT AS IF HE AND JULIUS were back in the young and invincible years before his accident. They took breathless risks on the icy course and landed unscathed. But the snow kept coming and the wind on their cheeks felt like a jagged razor. After the first hour, Julius lost the feeling in his toes, and Marcus's prosthesis was so caked with ice that the pincers wouldn't open or close. They debated what to do.

"Julius, let's walk home."

"It's five miles back."

"Well, it's better than sitting here for another hour," Marcus replied.

"If we jog it, we can surprise Dad before he comes looking for us. Straight along Pye Hollow."

ALL HOWARD WANTED was a cup of coffee that he could hold to warm himself up until it was time to pick up the twins. The Roundabout Inn had an oval bar serving one patron. There was a rim of dust on the ceiling fan, a tangle of flashing Christmas lights draped along the sconces, and a jukebox with a big crack in the glass where some patron had vented his unhappiness at Bobby Darin or Tony Bennett.

Howard took a seat at the bar. The other customer, a gray-haired guy with a gut and aviator glasses, raised his bourbon to Howard, who avoided his glance.

"Drink, sir?" the bartender asked Howard.

"No, just a coffee," said Howard. He looked for his wallet in his jacket pocket and found instead the prototype heart he had stuffed in there a week before. He had meant to throw it out. Now its smooth white plastic shell reflected the Christmas lights around the bar. How-ard set a five-dollar bill down before the bartender.

Waiting for his coffee, Howard turned the invention over in his hands. He twisted it open at the steel seam so that the chambers were revealed.

"What the hell is that?" said the man in the glasses. He had taken a seat beside Howard and was peering at the device. "If you don't mind my asking."

"Nothing," Howard replied, looking the fellow over once more.

"Unless I'm mistaken," said his neighbor, "that looks like a me-chanical heart."

Howard couldn't conceal his surprise.

The man offered his hand. "Bill Ferris."

Howard introduced himself. "Are you a doctor, then?"

"God, no." Ferris laughed. "Venture capital. We get funding for drug companies and medical research. . . . We funded a heart, too, but it didn't look as beautiful as this."

SNOW BEGAN FALLING AGAIN as Roy hiked along Pye Hollow. He still had another mile to walk to Dawn Snedecker's house and his pants were as stiff as cardboard from the knees down. He cursed the weather, because the minute he entered Dawn's cozy home the ice would melt and his pants would drip into a puddle on her floor. He imagined the reaction of her mother and father—they'd probably put him out on the step to wait, like a stray dog. But then he thought of Dawn, that golden hair and the peachy blush of her skin, and he kept walking while he imagined her wearing his corsage, posing with him for the photograph, and dancing with him under a mirror ball, cheek to cheek.

IN A DISTANT CORNER of the Dutch Oil parking lot, Calvin was prepar-ing a laboratory-grade cocktail in his car when Eddie Calhoun's black Coronet rolled alongside.

"What the hell are you doing?" shouted Eddie.

Calvin guessed Eddie couldn't see the tin liter of alcohol he'd stolen from Building A. So he mouthed a coarse reply and rolled the jaundiced Mustang forward, snow crunching below his tires, out past the guard's booth at the entrance to the complex.

Only when Calvin's taillights turned onto Pye Hollow Road did Eddie heave a sigh of relief; the last thing he needed was some violent final gesture from this kid.

Less than a quarter mile down Pye Hollow, Calvin slowed to a crawl and took a good slug of his orange cocktail. Ahead, the snow fell in straight lines, as if determined to bury the landscape. A broad grin suddenly spread across Calvin's face; he felt as if his cocktail had flipped a switch marked "Happy" in the back of his head.

THE TWINS HAD BEEN JOGGING for twenty minutes, and the numbness in their legs had given way to shin splints. "How long is a fucking mile, anyway?" complained Julius, kicking his sled ahead of him. They slowed to a limping walk, and Marcus, who had developed a hoarse rattle in his chest, fought to speak.

"I think we're two miles away."

"You know," huffed Julius as he peered through the blizzard, "this is dangerous! A car might not even see us until it's too late!"

Marcus nodded. "I can hardly tell where the road is." He glanced at the four-foot embankment on their right.

"Maybe we're better off running up there!"

"No way," panted Julius. "Bushes, trees . . . it's faster on the road."

Marcus, however, clambered up onto the embankment, dragging his sled behind him. His raspy chest was hurting. He wanted to be home, in bed. The snow was stinging his eyes. He closed them as he scrambled along the embankment, trusting the ridge to guide him.

Julius limped along the shoulder of the road, kicking his sled every few yards. With all his heart he wished for the headlights of a car to appear. Then they could be home and warmed up in time for Cleo. He picked up his pace, driven by the image of Cleo's dancing breasts.

. . .

CALVIN'S BUZZ HAD TAKEN A TURN. His cheeks began to burn and a fissure in his skull had opened with what sounded to him like a rip of brain tissue. He felt a flash of lightheadedness, and hoped it was the crest of his high, but he was wrong. It was only the vacant millisecond before the plunge. Now a new sensation rose between his temples, a black mare with blazing red eyes screaming out between the separated hemispheres of his brain, her white-hot hooves pounding one-two, one-two, like Thor's hammer on an oil barrel. His eyeballs began to take up the drumbeat. Then, with a hellish whinny, the mare lurched into a thunderous gallop. Tears rolled down Calvin's cheeks, and his foot pressed harder on the accelerator. Why had he quit? And why had he drunk that shit? What the hell had he been thinking?

It was all Roy's fault. Goddamn Roy.

He turned on the radio to stop the pounding. It was a live concert, broadcast from the Capitol Theatre in Passaic. A devilish voice spoke to Calvin from the back of his skull.

I'M MOVING TO MONTANA SOON.

The crowd knew this silly song and joined in at the chorus. But all Will heard was Minna's whisper at his ear.

"Let's go," she said.

The thumping bass notes of the next song followed them outside the theater and evaporated in the blizzard. Will and Minna looked for a place to be alone. No cars were to be seen, just rounded lumps sleeping beneath a vast white counterpane. In a bus shelter at the edge of the lot, he spread his army coat over the bench and they huddled together. Overhead, Will noticed a momentary patch of sky appear, like an awful black hole; then more clouds swept in, the snow continued, and the city resumed its deep slumber.

"Hold me, Will," said Minna. "Tighter."

As an errant snowflake lingered on Minna's cheek, he drew her closer. Without thinking, Will leaned forward and licked the snowflake away. When another landed on her lips, Will leaned toward it and she opened her mouth.

A boom echoed in the distance—the crash of a Dumpster lid, perhaps; then a siren wailed, reminding them of the little time they had before the crowd emerged.

Will grabbed at the unsullied drift around his ankles and threw a fistful of snow into the air. Crystals rained on Minna's face and hair; the flakes that alighted on her skin melted quickly, forming a silvery pool at the dip of her sternum. He licked at the pool and heard her gasp softly. Then her fingers reached for his belt and unfastened his pants.

He slid his shorts down as Minna, in one graceful movement, raised her skirt and eased herself gently onto his lap. Will thought she was scared, but then she pressed forward and he felt a surge of heat as her body closed around him. They swayed, ever so slowly, and then Minna groaned, and they began to ride together. The storm spun around them, and they cried out. The next moment Minna felt a spasm of pleasure, and her body turned liquid. Will heard a roar in his ears, but it was her sigh as he came, and they fell against each other in a state of spent ecstasy.

Stunned survivors of their own desire, Will and Minna clung together. Will found himself marveling that he could be so happy in such a barren place. With Minna's soft breath on his neck, and her arms clasped around him, he vowed to remember this moment, to keep it somewhere close, where it could be summoned the next time he felt lonely or heartbroken.

THE MORE BILL FERRIS TALKED, the more Howard liked him.

"Where have you been, Howard?" asked Bill. "This is a remarkable little contraption you put together. You should see the thing we sell; it's about as attractive as a goddamn distributor cap. Where the heck have you been?" he repeated.

"Well," replied Howard, "I worked for Chapman Fay."

"Chapman Fay? The fella who wanted to colonize Mars?"

Howard paused, fearing ridicule, perhaps. "That's him, yes."

Bill thrust out his hand. "Shake my hand again, Howard. Fay was a genius. A goddamn genius! And I bet Howard Lament has a touch of genius, too, eh?"

Suddenly, all the isolation and misery of these last years seemed to engulf Howard. He excused himself and went into the men's room, waited for his chest to stop heaving and the sobs to work their way out of his throat. Then he threw up. It was a while before he could compose himself enough to come out.

"You okay?" asked Bill when he finally emerged.

"Fine, fine," said Howard faintly, but in earnest.

"Better now? Good," said his new friend, smiling. "So, tell me, what are you doing with yourself now that Fay's gone—what a loss to humanity. . . . Tell me, what's life like after Chapman Fay?"

Cautiously, Howard admitted the sad details of the past few years. Bill listened, and gently placed the prototype on the counter.

"What a goddamn world it is," he said, finally.

On the jukebox, Sinatra sang "In the Wee Small Hours of the Morning" as their drinks were refilled. Bill gulped down his shot and gave Howard a guilty smile.

"Look, Howard, I have a confession to make. I was laid off myself fifteen months ago."

He raised his palms in anticipation of Howard's reassessment.

"Forgive me," he said. "But if you tell strangers you're out of a job in a bar, you look like God's loser. But I'm not, Howard, I'm not a loser any more than you are. We're gonna get through this, buddy. Everybody gets a second shot. This is *America*, goddammit. The land of opportunity. Right? Howard, between you and me, I think we could *make* something of this device."

"Really?" said Howard, his tone shifting slightly.

But Bill Ferris didn't notice. He just kept talking. And Howard was reminded of the man who had recruited him for Dutch Oil, or perhaps the one from the mines in Albo. Men with plans. Men who feed off the dreams of the idealist. He silently cursed himself for believing, for a second, that his redemption lay in a dusty, run-down bar.

Suddenly, Howard rose and threw on his coat.

"You're leaving?"

"I'm afraid so," Howard replied. "I'm late to pick up my sons." This wasn't exactly true. He had forty-five minutes, but he knew he'd be happier with his sons than listening to Bill Ferris weave a fantasy.

The snow was up to Howard's knees as he plodded to the Buick. Ferris called from across the parking lot.

"Howard! You left *this*, buddy!"

Howard turned to see the familiar object made of dull white plastic. A narrow band of steel caught the light.

"Oh, it's yours—keep it," he called, impatient to get back on the road. He slammed his door and put the key in the ignition, but the motor turned over once and the Buick fell silent.

CALVIN THOUGHT HE RECOGNIZED the figure walking by the side of Pye Hollow Road. It was waving at him. *Goddamn Roy*. His red-eyed mare replicated into a stampede of wretched creatures, their fiery hooves smashing against the walls of his skull, crying for vengeance, and Calvin swerved toward his victim.

Reaching down to pick up a sled, the figure paused, taking stock of the merciless speed of the vehicle, and issued an open-mouthed cry. The impact itself seemed almost gentle as he slowly tumbled over the hood and struck the windshield, shattering the glass and rolling away into the darkness.

Now the mares shrieked into Calvin's ears, urging escape, and he complied. All he wanted was to get these awful beasts out of his head. What had they made him do? He jammed his foot on the accelerator, and the car did a fishtail in the snow as it picked up speed, until the event seemed blessedly far behind him.

Suddenly a second figure appeared between Calvin's headlights,

this one shielding his eyes from the oncoming light with a hand glint-
ing in the moonlight, imploring him to stop. Calvin closed his eyes.
There was a soft thump as this obstacle fell. The road curved, but
Calvin preferred not to see. The car spun into a ditch on its side. He
finally opened his eyes when he felt the flames creeping up his legs.

Rose's Moment

Rose would later remark on the odd way that tragedy seemed to strike those around her—Adam Clare's suicide, the lost Lament baby, and now the twins.

"A dark angel seems forever perched on my shoulder," she confessed to Julia. "I don't enjoy being the survivor of so much suffering, but perhaps it's God's way of getting me to finally make myself useful."

That was certainly how she conducted herself that evening, for when Cleo appeared at the door, her face aglow, Rose invited her in, fixed her a mug of hot chocolate, and entertained her with stories of poor hotel service in Athens. When the telephone rang, Rose spoke briefly and tactfully, and replaced the receiver.

"Cleo dear, I think you should go home."

Cleo groaned. "Was that my mom already?" But then she noticed Rose's fingers shaking uncontrollably, and she picked up her coat—afraid of asking the question on her mind.

HOWARD HAD HITCHED A RIDE with a snowplow, and he arrived on the scene as three ambulances illuminated the countryside with their flashing lights. Pye Hollow residents walked through the drifts in their slippers to see what all the fuss was about.

Howard called Rose from Central Methodist Hospital. "We've lost both of the twins," he sobbed. "If only I had been here sooner!"

Julia arrived home from Frieda's house a few minutes later. Rose greeted her at the door, but Julia, clutching her temples, almost walked right past her.

"Darling——" began Rose.

"I must go to bed, Mummy," said Julia. "I've got an awful head-ache——"

"There has been a terrible accident, my love," said Rose.

WILL AND MINNA'S TRAIN was delayed because of the snow. He walked Minna to her house at about five in the morning, then hurried home to find Howard, Julia, and Rose seated in the kitchen. Will had never seen them in such repose around one another, and imagined, at first, that there had been some long overdue discussion between his parents and Rose, in which barriers had been torn down and a kind of peace had finally been established. In a way, that was exactly what had happened.

IN SUBSEQUENT DAYS, Rose was the first up and the last to go to bed. When no one spoke, she asked questions. When Julia lost the will to work, Rose gave her a push. When Howard lost the will to rise in the morning, Rose woke him and made breakfast. And when Will stared blankly out the window, Rose encouraged him to draw.

"I can't," said Will.

"Draw Minna," suggested Rose.

Will found this almost impossible to do; he was used to drawing imaginary things—the odd, the fantastic, and the grotesque. Not surprisingly, Minna looked strange and unhappy in those first sketches, reflecting Will's obvious misery.

"Talk about something—Paris, for example," he suggested. So Minna described the city she had never seen, and the people in it whom she had been reading about for years. Will drew the amusement in her eyes as she described Gertrude Stein's baggy dresses; he mastered the angles of her eyebrows as she explained the bread famine, and he figured out the curve of her lips as she listed the Métro stops from the Louvre to the Arc de Triomphe, and her passion began to appear on the paper—or perhaps it was simply Will's passion for Minna, because over those many hours they spent together, he began to fall deeply in love with her.

IT WASN'T AS EASY for Julia and Howard. There were so many things to regret.

Julia blamed her own distraction. She shouldn't have gone out on such a terrible night. It was like the barbecue: if only she hadn't turned away for that critical moment.

Howard also blamed himself. He woke Julia to explain all the mistakes he had made that fateful evening. Taking the boys out in dangerous weather; deserting them; and, worst of all, being seduced by the praise of a stranger in a bar.

"But you couldn't have known that they would come home early," said Julia.

"I should never have left them," cried Howard.

"For godsakes, Howard, it's not your fault," she repeated again and again, until Howard took her hand and their grief merged.

The Funeral

When Will's brothers were buried, the eulogy was drowned out by the jeering of crows in a large cedar tree, their blue-black heads preened and oiled like the hair of swells at a prize-fight. The Presbyterian minister was a short man with a high voice, who had caught the twins draping some of the cemetery stones in toilet paper a few Halloweens ago. Their punishment was to attend three of his sermons; Julia thought community service would have been far more appropriate, but she deferred to his judgment and concluded, after attending with the boys, that the man had more passion for the sound of his own voice than for God. Still, she chose him to speak at their burial.

"Better the minister you know than the minister you don't," she explained to Rose.

Because of the crows, Will ignored the eulogy and silently recalled his brothers' mischievous lives: their revenge on Ajax; their near descent into the *inky black* from aboard the *Windsor Castle;* the trails they cut through the barley near a Roman ruin; Marcus, wearing Rillcock's shiner. He remembered the suddenness with which they shed their British accents in America; Marcus's fateful flight over the Finches' barbecue; and Julius's cries of ecstasy from the bathroom.

The twins might have been a colossal burden to Will, but they had also been a critical ingredient in the formation of his character; they ignited his rage, provoked his sympathy, and stirred his courage. Though they were unmerciful to Buck Quinn's Ridgeback and tormented the Avon Heath cat population and kicked the fight out of Howard in his depression, Will saw how their opposing natures complemented a vital alliance. The twins had inspired Will to seek companionship with Sally, Marina, Dawn, and, of course, Minna. Marcus's gentle spirit and vulnerable condition reminded Will that life was a fragile thing, while Julius's unquenchable lust reminded him of its limitless delights.

His reverie was broken by the sound of the crows taking off with shrieks, leaving just two on a branch to observe the burial. They shifted weight, first shaking one foot, then the other, in idle comment at the length of the proceedings.

Julia's hair was tied loosely behind in a single black ribbon; tamed by age, a few gray strands caught the breeze. She wore a slate-colored cloak, giving her a tragic nobility discordant, in Will's opinion, with the energetic woman who was constantly clattering about at home and never stood still for a moment. When she wept, Howard clasped her hand. He wore one of his old suits, and there was a solemn grace in his manner—he appeared more composed today, perhaps because there was no uncertainty in a funeral. Howard had always hated uncertainty. Beside him stood Rose, her face gaunt in the winter light; Frieda held her arm for support.

Cleo Pappas wept, flanked by a small cadre of teens with mullets and wispy facial hair. Carey Bristol and Emil DeVaux were there, as well as Mike Brautigan, whose handsome features and silvery hair prompted a few mourners to mistakenly compliment him on the eulogy.

When the crowd started to leave, Will noticed, the two crows in the cedar tree erupted with what sounded like laughter before taking off into the ashen sky.

Good-bye, Marcus. Good-bye, Julius, he thought. Then he felt Minna's hand in his, and rested his head against hers, and cried.

Dawn and Roy approached together; Dawn expressed her sympathy to Julia, while Roy rocked nervously on his heels. There were many things Will *wanted* to say to Roy—that Roy had unwittingly brought Calvin's wrath down upon his family, that he really *was* a Midnight Chinaman, a specter who had brought death and destruction. But he never would.

What was the point?

He might just as well blame himself for bringing Roy to work at Dutch Oil. He might just as well blame Howard for taking the twins sledding. He might just as well thank Roy for diverting Dawn and allowing Minna into his life.

After the burial, Will, Rose, Julia, and Howard walked through Queenstown beneath the gaunt and cheerless oaks.

"Oh God," said Julia finally. "What now?"

Nobody had an answer to this question. And it was taken with some relief that the sun continued its daily arc, forcing the Laments to, at least, assume a ritual of normality.

CALVIN SURVIVED, but the lower half of his body had caught fire, thanks to the can of alcohol at his feet. He would find walking and pissing extremely uncomfortable for the rest of his life (and masturbation more trouble than it was worth). His father sued the township for not having effective barriers on the sides of the road. The settlement of a few hundred thousand dollars went toward his son's hospital bills. Officer Tibbs noted a fact with which he was already familiar—that if Calvin had lost his testicles, they could have extracted a million dollars more.

The Weight

The blizzard over Christmas had stolen winter's traditional punch. January was wet, dark, and grim. The relentless patter of rain kept the Laments indoors. In these dim and confining weeks, Will began to feel his mother's hand present on his shoulder at odd moments. A gentle pressure, though it resonated more deeply on his conscience.

Remember your importance to me, it said. *Don't leave me. Stand by me. Only son. All I have. My one and only.*

This didn't comfort him. Many years before, he might have felt gratified by it, but he was eighteen now, and he no longer desired her attention the way he had as a little boy. Nevertheless, the pressure was constant, and when they spoke, Will often sensed its presence under the surface.

He tried to discuss it with Rose.

"I don't know what I can do for her," he explained. "But the look on her face is expectant, as though I'll do something, or explain something she needed to know."

"Perhaps it's something she wants to tell you," said Rose.

"What?" replied Will.

Rose offered no answer, but her guilty expression reinforced Will's suspicion that the matter, whatever it was, would upset him.

WILL GOT HIS LEARNER'S PERMIT in February, and Minna, who had passed her driver's exam a few months before, took him for a few spins in Frieda's old Gremlin to improve his parallel parking. The Queenstown Jumbo Market lot was the ideal place for this, and it lay across the road from Roper Realty.

From the office windows, Julia observed Minna's hand on the nape of Will's neck as he drove.

"What's so interesting out there?" asked Brautigan.

"My son is growing up and I still have so much to tell him," Julia replied.

Julia deeply feared the impact of such revelations, and so she let the weeks pass until the sun returned, inspiring Howard to finish rebuilding the porch. He raised a new roof, and pillars, and he shingled the structure without mistake or mishap. The other Laments were astonished. After work each day, Julia looked forward to seeing his progress. She sensed that Howard was rebuilding himself—proving, in this reconstruction, that he was no less capable of reform than 33 Oak Street was. His last task was the hanging of a porch swing.

"For the two of us," he explained.

"How sentimental," replied Julia skeptically.

"C'mon, darling," he coaxed. "Sit with me!"

Julia took her place beside Howard, and they rocked on the porch until the sun went down. Howard insisted they do this every evening, as long as the weather was mild.

"It's so silly," remarked Julia.

"Yes, we haven't been this silly in a long time," said Howard. "Do us bloody good to be silly for a change."

Even Rose was impressed with Howard's handiwork, and when she paid him a compliment, Howard looked visibly stunned. She took advantage of this goodwill to speak to him about the matter that seemed to have become everybody's burden these days.

"Why won't you tell Will the truth about his birth?"

"Well, that's up to Julia," Howard replied.

"Don't you feel some responsibility, too?"

"Yes, but she feels most strongly . . ."

"Well, she's confused," declared Rose. "You owe it to your son to send him into the world knowing the truth. Good heavens—he graduates in three months! What will you do when he leaves home? Send him a telegram? You may never have this chance again. And he may never forgive you if you don't do it now."

HOWARD WAS SURPRISED when Julia agreed that it was time to tell Will.

"I've been thinking about it a great deal," she said. "I just don't know how."

"Do you want me to tell him?" he offered.

"No, it was my decision to keep it a secret; I should be the one," Julia replied.

But she lacked the resolve, and more weeks passed.

One day late in March, the winter sun filled the house with a cool, unfamiliar brightness. When Julia saw Marcus's room lit up, she peered inside, expecting a light to be on. Howard had tidied things up; the clothes had been sent to the thrift store, the comics thrown away. But the poster of Ganesh remained; Howard refused to throw it out, because Ganesh was the remover of obstacles, and the Laments had faced enough obstacles as it was. Julia studied the potbellied god, with his broken tusk, raised trunk, and wise and forgiving eyes.

She considered her own obstacles, and found only one—the truth she owed her son.

Below the poster was Marcus's bedside table. His copy of the collected works of Shakespeare lay open. She noticed that several lines had been underscored. As she flipped through the pages, she found many passages that had been marked. Most of them were monologues that Marcus had spoken aloud for girls: Hamlet's soliloquy, Mark Antony's speech after the death of Caesar, Richard III's introduction. But then, in *Henry IV,* Julia noticed a small passage in the first scene that took her breath away.

When Will returned from work that evening, he immediately noticed his mother's anxious expression and the book facing her. "That was Marcus's, wasn't it?" he said.

"Yes," replied Julia. "I wanted to show you something he found." She tried to smile as she turned the book around for him to see. A small passage was underlined with a red pen.

"It's from *Henry IV,*" said Julia. "He's disappointed in his son because he spends all his time in taverns, and Henry wishes his heir were Hotspur, Lord Northumberland's son, who is a terrific warrior. So he imagines the babies being switched at birth."

Will read the passage. "'O that it could be proved/That some night-tripping fairy had exchanged/In cradle-clothes our children where they lay . . .'" Will looked at her. "Funny, Marcus used to imagine he was adopted. I suppose we all did."

Julia's eyes brimmed with tears. "Why would any of you think that? What have we done to make you think that?"

"Nothing," Will assured her, "but one wonders. Well, I wondered. I don't *look* like anybody else. I never have, have I?"

Julia shook her head. "No, you never have," she admitted. Their eyes met, and her expression struck Will as strangely apologetic. All at once, he guessed its full meaning.

"Darling," she said, "I never wanted you to feel different, or separate, or . . ."

"I understand, Mum," Will replied.

But of course he didn't know about his true mother's rejection and abandonment, and Julia felt determined to protect her son, even now, from the damage these facts might wreak. "The truth is," she continued, "that your parents died in a car accident shortly after you were born, and so we took you as our own. Our baby had died in an accident." Then, wiping her eyes, she added, "As far as we were concerned, you were our son for good."

Will nodded, then suddenly embraced Julia tightly, as if to seal the matter. "For good," he echoed. Later, Will admitted to Minna that he felt a perverse sense of gratitude for his mother's explanation. Though Julia had only confirmed what he had suspected for years, it was a tremendous relief to know that his feelings weren't the fantasies of an ungrateful son.

Moments later, Howard appeared and joined the embrace, and for a brief time they felt a whisper of the early days when they were bound together as a threesome.

A Lament

Will had shown no interest in going to college yet, which troubled Julia and Howard enormously. When they brought it up, Will didn't dismiss the idea; he simply replied that he wasn't ready.

Then, in May, travel brochures started appearing on the kitchen table. The first time she noticed them, Julia put them in a pile under the Yellow Pages. That evening they reappeared, strewn across the table again: pictures of the Eiffel Tower, the cafés of the Left Bank, and the Seine rippling beneath the bridges of the Ile de la Cité. All visions of enticement as far as Julia was concerned.

"They're not mine," said Howard.

When Minna came to dinner that evening, Julia confronted her.

"I believe these are yours," she remarked, a slight edge in her voice.

But Minna regarded the brochures and shrugged. "I wish they were mine."

Julia turned to Rose.

"I *know* my way around Paris; why would I need these silly things?" snorted her mother.

"They're mine," confessed Will. "It's where I'm going with Minna."

Julia looked at Minna, provoking the girl to defend herself once again.

"But I'm not going *anywhere*!" Minna protested.

Now it was Will who looked betrayed.

"Didn't you tell me that you were going to Paris after graduation?" he asked. "What about all those books? The café? The speech you gave?"

"Yes, but that was all a fantasy. I don't have the money."

This seemed to restore Julia's voice. "Well"—she smiled—"we all have our fantasies. I can understand that. I had a few of my own when I was your age."

She sat down, as if the matter were settled. But then Will spoke. "So we'll both go."

"What?" Julia was hoping the rumble of a passing truck had distorted Will's words.

"I was going to buy my own ticket," explained Will, "but I'll get two. I have the money saved up from work. We'll go together, eh, Minna? The two of us in Paris."

"Why Paris, of all places?" asked Julia.

"I want to *see* it," he said. "I want to see the paintings of Daumier, Ingres, Degas, and Matisse; I want to walk the same streets that Hemingway and Joyce and Fitzgerald walked." He glanced at Minna with a giddy smile. "I want to hear jazz, and walk in the rain at night, and lose my way in the streets of Montmartre and the Ile St.-Louis and draw the faces I see."

"But why now?" implored his mother. "Why must you go *now*?"

Will blinked. "Because I'll be done with school in a month."

"But Paris will be around for a long time," argued Julia.

Will looked at his mother. "But I want to do it *now*, Mum. I may never have the money again. What's wrong with going now?"

Julia had no answer to this; she just knew that she didn't want Will to go.

. . .

SHE WAITED UP FOR HIM after work, drove him to school on rainy days, walked with him to school some mornings. And she would talk about all things—all but Paris.

"Your father wants to build a sundeck. He was wondering if you'd help him build it over the summer."

"Please, Mum, you know that I'll be in France."

"Nonsense," she replied. "You don't even speak French."

Will was patient with his mother. He understood that Julia had measured the Laments' travels by their losses. Without admitting it, she was slowly preparing herself for another one.

"I'll send you my sketches; I'll write, too," he promised.

"The Left Bank has enough penniless artists. You'll starve," she replied.

"There are worse places to starve than Paris," he said.

ONE EVENING JULIA JOINED HOWARD on the porch swing after work. She had important news.

"I was offered a job today," she said.

"Darling, that's wonderful," Howard replied. He had come to accept Julia's role as the breadwinner, and even looked forward to hearing about her victories and defeats.

"It's in Roper's Tatumville office, twenty-five miles from here," she explained to Howard. "There's a lot of business over there, so Carey asked me to run things."

"When do you start?" inquired Howard.

"Start? Oh, I turned it down," said Julia. "I need to stay close to home. Close to Will."

"But, Julia," said Howard carefully, "Will is *leaving*."

"No, he's *not*," said Julia.

"Darling," Howard gently replied, "he *must*."

Compelled to accept Will's departure, Julia still had worries. It came down to her conviction that in telling Will about his adoption she had deprived him of his identity—as a Lament. All of his child-hood had been spent seeking some vital place in his adoptive family—ever since she had embraced him as a waif with a paper-thin heart.

ON THE NIGHT BEFORE HIS FLIGHT, Will spent most of the evening packing his things. When his bags were zipped and everything was tidy, he heard a familiar clatter in the kitchen.

"It's only me," said Julia when he appeared.

"I thought so." He smiled.

"All packed, then?"

"Yes." He sat down beside her.

"You can still change your mind," she said.

"Mum," he replied in mock dismay, "I followed your advice: mem-orized dozens of phrases—if I don't catch the next plane, they'll slip out of my head for good."

"You promised to write," Julia reminded him.

"Of course I will," he said.

"Remember all the frightful things you wrote to Granny?"

That made both of them laugh for a moment.

"I'll tell you everything, too," he promised.

She seemed touched by this. "I don't need to know *everything*, dar-ling, just that you're safe, and happy, and whether you need anything."

This, Will realized, was Julia's farewell blessing.

"I'll miss you, Mum." Will struggled to clear his throat, as if the red dust of Africa still hung in the air they breathed.

There was a faint wail outside, a cat perhaps, that suddenly re-minded Julia of Bahrain, the dusty pink sunsets, and the mullah's cry. And she imagined for a moment what lay ahead for her son. All she could picture were those brief moments in her own life when the fu-ture seemed a marvelous, vast, and unfathomable thing: the soaring mist of the Victoria Falls from her train compartment, the engulfing swell of the *inky black* from the railings of the *Windsor Castle*, the bustling damp of that rainy Southampton pier, and the buoyant sway of a Buick speeding down a six-lane highway. And she couldn't help but imagine the inevitable mishaps ahead, and she feared for him.

"*Why* are you doing this, Will?" she asked.

Will looked up at his mother, caught off guard by this question. But then the reason presented itself. It was simple and irrefutable: the bane of his childhood and the rule of the family.

"I'm still a Lament, Mum. Laments travel."

Acknowledgments

I would like to thank my wife, Terri Seligman, my first and most loyal reader; David and Elizabeth Hagen for their inspirational contribution; Marisa Silver and Peter Blauner for their sound advice and support; and Kerry Madden-Lunsford, whose comment launched this novel. Many thanks are due to the fine people at Random House, including Claire Tisne, Nicole Bond, Veronica Windholz, and Robin Rolewicz, for their labors on behalf of this book. I am indebted to a remarkable editor, Ileene Smith, for her embrace of the Laments; and, finally, to Henry Dunow, who found a good home for *The Laments* and has guided me through this experience with wisdom and humor.

The
Laments

George Hagen

Questions for Discussion

1. "No one could doubt that this baby, in spite of his lack of a name, was destined for a happy life." How does the Lament family's vision of happiness change as they wander from country to country?

2. As a baby, Will has an intense investment in the unity of his parents, linking his mother's dress and his father's belt loop with his finger. How does this investment play itself out to the novel's end? What is the significance of his comment to Rose at the Statue of Liberty when he says, "I can't do it forever?"

3. What is the significance of roses in the novel? For instance, when the Midnight Chinaman first appears, he has roses embroidered on his silk pajamas. What does his presence portend?

4. What causes Howard's depression? Is his ambition at fault? Is Julia responsible? Or is his wanderlust the problem?

5. Will reaches out to many girls in the novel. Are Ruth, Sally, Marina, and Dawn more like sisters than crushes? What about Minna?

6. What is the significance, if any, of Howard's attempt to design an artificial heart?

7. On their ocean trip to England, Howard worries that Will needs to be tougher to adapt to England. Does Howard also need to be tougher in order to adapt?

8. Julia finds the moves from country to country more and more difficult. How do her rationalizations for moving change? Do they reflect a fundamental shift in the terms of her marriage with Howard?

9. Will is seduced by British pop culture as he witnesses it in Sally's bedroom, with pop stars plastered all over the walls and door. Who in the Lament family is seduced by American culture, and how?

10. Britain is depicted as a nation that cannot "get over" its role in World War II. Are the Americans that the Laments encounter reconciled with their past?

11. Trixie Howitzer's marriage to Chip is rather a cynical arrangement, yet Julia is fascinated by Trixie, while Howard is repelled. Why is this? What, if anything, does Julia have in common with Trixie?

12. When the Laments arrive in America, they are directed by several characters to make friends with the Himmels, who are German immigrants. How does the Himmel family's integration into American culture compare to the Laments'?

13. Roy Biddle remarks to Will that "everyone is a racist." How is racism depicted in the different cultures the Laments encounter? Is Will a racist? Why, or why not? Is that important to the novel?

14. The Laments place tremendous faith in what the future will bring. But Hagen describes a number of characters who revere the past: Mrs. Pritchard, for example, and Dr. Underberg, who prefers the "thousands of years of experience" that Africans have in producing happy babies to modern child rearing. How is the past pitted against the future in this novel?

15. What might have happened if the Laments' natural-born son had lived? Would they have traveled? What of Howard's ambition and Julia's frustration with her domesticity? Would they have been destined for a happy life?

16. Would you consider the Laments to be driven to travel by their political principles? Why do they leave Africa? Is there a contrast between the America they anticipate and the one they find as revealed by the attitudes of their American neighbors?

GEORGE HAGEN had lived on three continents by the time he was twelve. *The Laments* is his first novel. He lives in Brooklyn with his wife and three children.

ABOUT THE TYPE

This book was set in a digital version of Monotype Walbaum. The original typeface was created by Justus Erich Walbaum (1768–1839) in 1810. Before becoming a punch cutter with his own type foundries in Goslar and Weimar, he was apprenticed to a confectioner where he is said to have taught himself engraving, making his own cookie molds using tools made from sword blades. The letterforms were modeled on the "modern" cuts being made at the time by Giambattista Bodoni and the Didot family.